So Are You to My Thoughts

By Connie Kronlokken

The author believes that all quotations in this book have been used under the "commentary and criticism" fair use of copyrighted materials.

Published by

**Lightly
Held
Books**

DEDICATION

To Don

"So are you to my thoughts as food to life,
Or as sweet season'd showers are to the ground."

[Shakespeare, Sonnet 75]

So Are You to My Thoughts

By the time Marty began hanging sheets on the line in Boulder Creek, the morning fog was lifting, the clouds thinning to let in the sunshine. The sheets smelled of soap, but the sun and air would freshen them. Nearby, Zoe, who was eleven, threw a few of her father's shirts over the line in a careless manner. She had been detailed to help Marty, but she was doing it as badly as possible. Marty had shown her how to pin a shirt to a clothesline, but she resisted going to help Zoe now.

Soon Zoe became absorbed by the black cat wandering across the lawn. The sun played up the gold in her light brown hair. She was just starting to have breasts and loved dressing up, as her mother Mackenzie had. But in July, when no one was going anywhere, Zoe just dressed in shorts and a t-shirt like her brothers and sister.

Marty didn't try to hang out the many cotton shirts and shorts the kids wore. They just got thrown in the dryer. But Doug, her partner, liked his shirts dried outdoors. And they both loved to sleep in sun-dried sheets.

Having lived with Doug and his four children for almost a year now, Marty was reminded of how much she loved family life. She was proud to be Doug's wife, and have a place of her own at his side. Though not technically married, they had made their vows to each other in private. Marty loved this family full of lively people, each contributing their passions to the mix. It was a complex household, the opposite of Marty's simple life on Russian Hill in San Francisco. Even after a year, Marty wasn't sure she had gotten to the bottom of it. But she was cautious, moving slowly, steadily into its heart.

Her clothes hung out, Marty knelt down beside Zoe, who had taken the cat into her lap. "How're you doing, Mrs. Blackie?" she asked. Marty was dressed in worn black jeans, a white t-shirt, and a salmon-colored cotton hoodie. She no longer liked her legs in shorts, old bruises and veins showing. Her hair was graying a little too. It worried her. She

1

rinsed it in henna occasionally, but she did not want to dye it. Doug told her not to worry about it. "You're still a total fox," he told Marty, alluding to her slim figure. He was graying around the temples himself.

Zoe looked a little guilty, having sat down on her job. But she was outwardly defiant, silently challenging Marty. The two of them had reached a truce. Marty didn't chide her and Zoe didn't whine. They both loved Doug, Zoe's father, deeply.

"I'm thinking about lunch," said Marty. It was Saturday, slow to start, though not for Marty. She had already been to the tasting room to see that everything was clean and in order for the day. It was only a ten-minute walk away. Unlike the Henderson house, the tasting room was generally orderly and spotless. Two young women ran it, pouring wines for people who came by to taste and taking their orders for Boulder Creek Vineyards wines.

"Come on," said Marty, standing up. "Let's go find out how the bunk beds are doing."

Doug and the three other kids were sawing, bolting and screwing lumber together in the boys' room. Doug got the twins, Nic and Natasha to do all the calculations for the pieces they cut. "Shows them the use of fractions," he said. Jason found the whole thing interesting and hung around, watching as they sawed 2x4s and 4x4 posts, using a power drill to screw them to the studs in the wall.

The room smelled of new wood. Jason jumped up and down. "It's so good!" he said, climbing like a monkey to the upper bunk.

"Are you going to sleep up there?" Marty asked. She was worried 7-year-old Jason might roll out of the narrow bed. She looked at Doug, who beamed at her.

"We'll put a railing on it," said Doug. He gripped a post, which seemed to be solid as a rock. "Has to withstand the two-grade-schooler test," he said. He wore ragged blue jeans, tevas and a clean t-shirt. He had cut off his long hair and beard for the sake of his divorce case. But they were growing out now, his hair shaggy again.

Marty smiled back at him. The sweetness of their relationship underlay the family they were building, still thickening like spun honey. All the sweetness time allowed.

"See where the book nook is going to be?" asked Natasha. She showed Marty and Zoe the place where the person who was reading that night's bedtime chapter could sit. "It isn't very big, but it's another way to climb up." She pointed to the large sheet of drawings, which were covered with math and calculations. The nook was a little wooden platform in the corner half way between the bunks.

Nic stood up proudly from where he was holding a 2x4 in place. "Dad's going to put a light over it," he said.

Marty clapped her hands. "Oh, I'm so glad you are making that!" she said. She had turned out to be the reader because everyone liked her voice. They were currently reading *The Three Musketeers*, gathering in the boys' room, and then shepherding Zoe and Natasha into their room when the chapter was finished each evening.

Even before moving in with them, Marty understood the pattern of the kids' relationships. Nic and Natasha were as thick as thieves. They were curious and pleasant to be around at ten, but they didn't need anyone else. Zoe, a year older, felt above this special bond, the leader of the pack. But little Jason was always trying to be part of it, a hopeless endeavor. Marty and Zoe tried to shore up Jason's anxious little ego, but he had become a performer, the family clown when he was allowed to be. Marty knew, as perhaps even the older kids did, that he was darker, different, not Doug's child. But no one was allowed to let this fact divide the family. "I'll tell him," said Doug. "When the time is right. Secrets never work out well."

It had been Doug's first order of business after Mackenzie moved out to get Natasha into Zoe's room. Mackenzie's clothes had taken up most of it! By this time, however, Zoe and Natasha had carefully divided the room into shares. Natasha still gravitated to the boys' room and loved being with Nic, but Doug felt she was too old to sleep there.

Bedrooms did define a family, Marty thought. The dark Persian carpet Marty brought with her had been put into Doug and Marty's large, peaceful bedroom. She loved sleeping beside him on the California king futon, spread on a wooden mattress platform he had built. He said his toes stuck out over the end when he slept in anything smaller. He told Marty that Mackenzie often slept in Zoe's room when she came home late. He himself sometimes slept on a cot at the winery during crush, as Marty had discovered during last fall's intense months.

For Marty, the kitchen was another complicated place. Essentially she shared it with Ana Maria, the wife of Javier, the ranch manager. They lived in a small house of their own at the back of the garden. Ana Maria was probably not much older than Marty though she had grandkids. She did not want to give up her job of cooking and cleaning for the family. She made dinner every night except Sunday: Mexican stews, tamales, hearty soups full of meat and potatoes, with beans, rice and salad. She had been the one who made school lunches for the kids, though Zoe prodded them onto the school bus with Doug's occasional help.

Marty did not want to encroach on Ana Maria's place in the household. She looked for things Ana Maria didn't want to do, such as the shopping and clothes washing. Marty took over breakfast and lunches, and cooked Sunday night dinner. She had grown tired of beans and often ate only a bit of rice and vegetables in the evening, with a glass of wine. But Ana Maria's cooking did give Marty time to help with homework and have a moment with Doug before dinner if he was home.

Doug professed himself very happy with Marty's management. They discussed everything down to the details, a covert undercurrent to the family which sheltered and nourished the kids. "I've wanted this forever," Doug told Marty. Marty's arrival had made their lives easier. Zoe could relax, be a kid; Ana Maria could slow down and just do the things she wanted; and Alice, Doug's mother in Santa Cruz, no longer braced herself for the arrival of four kids on the weekends.

It was summertime now. And lunchtime. Marty peeled and sliced avocados while Natasha and Jason set the table, a cloth napkin in its individuated holder by each place. Jason was always anxious to eat. "I'm going to be a cooker when I grow up," he told Marty. At Grandma Alice's house, where there was television, cooking shows were the order of the day. Television cooks apparently were competitive, dramatic and often male, Marty understood. And they certainly got to eat!

"Please get us some lettuce and tomatoes from the garden," Marty begged Natasha. Doug grilled bacon on a gas burner outside as she sliced vegetables. Kids did eat a lot. Marty placed mounds of food in the middle of the table and arranged slices of bread on a cookie sheet so they could toast all at once to make bacon sandwiches. It was one of their favorite meals. Marty thought civilization was reflected in the number of times a family sat down together around a table.

The kids buzzed around, excited by the presence of their Dad, who was so often out in the vineyards, sourcing grapes in far away counties or helping to sell the Boulder Creek Vineyards brand. Nic carried in the platter of bacon. Doug sat down at the head of the table as Zoe filled the water glasses. The younger kids drank milk, but Zoe felt she had graduated to being a grownup.

"More fun than building with Legos?" Doug asked Nic, of their building project. Over the winter Nic had been the Lego king, covering the floor of the boys' room with bridges and buildings and vehicles. It was one thing Natasha didn't join him in. She spent more time outdoors.

"Oh yeah," said Nic. "Power tools are the best!"

"So, we'll finish the bunk beds this afternoon," said Doug. "You guys can sleep on them tonight. And then tomorrow, we'll all sleep in tents!" He was expecting a large harvest that year, but before it began, he had managed to carve out a week for camping. Backpacks and tents stood against the walls in the family room as equipment was sorted and re-sorted. Doug was in charge of adventure.

Marty looked around at the sun-kissed faces, shining with excitement. And at Doug. She too felt that when Doug was home, everything was fine.

"Can we have a fire?" asked Nic.

"Yep," said Doug. "They have fire rings. We'll take some of our wood." They would leave in the morning and stay out for a few days over July 4th at Manresa Uplands, a nearby walk-in campground.

Jason got up to get more milk, but then came back and sat down. "Knock, knock," he said, bubbling with his joke.

"Who's there," said Natasha, somewhat resignedly.

"Lettuce," said Jason.

"Lettuce, who?" asked Natasha.

"Lettuce in and you'll find out!" chortled Jason.

"Why were the apple and the orange all alone?" asked Doug.

Zoe looked at him, rolling her eyes. "Daaaad," she said expressively. "Don't encourage him!"

"Why not?" said Doug smiling. "So, why were the apple and the orange alone?"

"No one knows," said Zoe. "Or cares."

"I do! I do!" said Jason, wiggling in his seat. "Why?"

"Because the banana split!" said Doug, laughing at their chagrin. "Orange you glad I asked?"

"No!" said Zoe.

"There's more where that came from!" said Doug. "Fruit is funny!"

"Punny," said Nic. "Punny and funny. I've gone one."

"Okay," said Doug. "Let's hear it!"

"What happens when you sit on a grape?" asked Nic, looking around. When no one seemed to know, he continued. "It gives a little whine!"

"Good one," said Doug. "I like that." He stood up and stretched. "Well, back to the salt mine, boys. Lets go finish that drilling and screwing."

Nic, Natasha and Jason were quick to follow Doug away from the table, but each took their plates and put them next to the sink. Zoe helped Marty finish clearing, but then faded back into the woodwork. Marty whisked the dishes together, organizing as she went. She looked forward to being outdoors on the camping trip. She was worried about the food. Doug insisted they would pack in good vegetables, meats and fruits, just like they ate at home. "No retreat, no surrender," he said.

Marty had planned the food. But would there be enough? What if they ran out? She worried about all kinds of things, often felt overwhelmed. Somehow things worked out with Doug's help. They agreed on the basics, good food, good water and sleep. The rest was gravy, lots of gravy.

Marty felt that Doug was uniquely able to take a moment and wring the best out of it, infusing it with all one could expect. He delighted in variety, details and living in the real world. Lunch had been ordinary, everyday. But it felt as if it were the last food they would ever need, the best, the quintessential meal. And this feeling of wholeness, of complete attention to the moment at hand happened again and again.

Marty had never seen anything like it. By focusing completely on the present, Doug demanded all of its possibilities. Marty would be done, ready to move on, but Doug would have thought of another spice to add, another way to do something. Marty herself always wanted to treat daily life as if it were sacred, with the capability to transform. Their twin aspirations made domestic life brim with richness. Beside Marty, Doug had woken up to how he wanted to live. Marty had too.

Manresa Uplands was on a bluff, with wooden steps going down to a wide beach on the Pacific. Doug had nabbed the campsite as soon as reservations were open, knowing he wasn't the only one with the idea. It wasn't far away; just down the mountain and a bit south of Santa Cruz.

They arrived early. If they were lucky, there might be a bit of sun in the middle of the day, but in July, the fog was so thick there might not be any. Doug unpacked the van and helped the kids shoulder their backpacks. "Look for number 38!" he told them. Marty had a backpack too, plus she carried a bag of groceries in one hand and one packed with her precious tea things in another. Doug shouldered the biggest backpack and dragged a cooler on wheels.

As she followed the trail of kids through the paths of the crowded campground, Marty noticed that many of the sites were on bare ground, unprotected by a single tree. Theirs, luckily, was set back among low manzanita and scrub, with eucalyptus in the background. More private and homelike, thought Marty.

Marty unpacked while Doug and the kids went back for another load. She spread the blue and white oilcloth over the rough wooden picnic table. She could hear the ocean down below, the regular pulsing of the waves and the convection wind in the trees.

The kids were anxious to go down to the beach, but Doug considered tents and organizing the first order of business. Nic had gone camping with the Boy Scouts, and he and Jason sometimes slept in their tent on the lawn, but for Zoe and Natasha, it was all new. They helped put up the tents, snapping the light aluminum poles into position and hooking the colorful nylon tents over them.

"Pin those babies down," Doug told them. "The wind could blow them right up the beach!" He handed Zoe the mallet to pound in the tent pegs. There were three tents, one for the boys, one for the girls and one for Doug and Marty. Doug showed Marty how to spread out the Thermarest mattresses so they could take in air. He laid the thick cotton sleeping bags he liked over them. They were not mummy bags, but big flat coverlets that could zip together so Doug and Marty could keep each other warm.

It was cozy in the tent out of the wind. Marty put towels into a pillowcase for Doug to sleep on. She didn't like having a pillow herself. Tent camping was new to her as well. Her own family had spent their vacations at the cabin on Lake Michigami in Minnesota. She had done some car camping with her first husband Erik. With no mosquitoes and pleasant dry heat, California was perfect for being outdoors. The coastal climate was said to be like that around the Mediterranean, which had fostered the first great human civilizations.

Doug hung sash cord in the trees so the towels and wet things could dry. He filled a water bladder which hung in the trees and a net bag in which clean dishes could dry. He and Jason rigged an old branch against the picnic table to hold a lantern. Marty unpacked her tea things into the wooden larder. They were not things raccoons would want. The kids set up the woodpile near the fire ring. The place took on the look of a little home.

Carrying sandwiches and raw veggies, everyone trekked down to the beach and spread out on a Mexican blanket. The sun came and went behind wispy clouds. After eating, Marty and Doug lay like beached whales, taking in the warmth of the thin sun while the kids played chicken at the edge of the water. They ran into the surf, screaming as the waves washed up around their bare feet. Marty remembered how she had first discovered the patterns in the surf in Hawaii while taking a tab of acid. How it broke down as it rolled in into foamy poufs, regular as lace. Doug had never done drugs. "I was on the opposite commute," he said. "I was a dreamy kid, just trying to get straight."

Doug got up to join the kids, but Marty lay, keeping their spot, letting the warm sun soak into her muscles. She could see from under her straw hat the rushing, sun-lit forms of Doug and the kids as they walked along the beach, bending to inspect something, picking up sand dollars and bits of sea-polished glass, bright pebbles and shells. "The important thing," Doug had told her, "is to get them out of the rectangles they live in, to be outdoors under the sky in the evening and in the early morning. Opens us up to nature."

Marty thought of Paul, her brother, at Lake Michigami with Marie his wife, who was wasting away with cancer. And of Line, her closest sister, who now had her daughter Fern's first child at home in Santa Cruz, a tiny, month-old girl named Sofia. Marty's own parents were gone by now, bright spirits, unforgettable. How blessed she had been, Marty thought. And now this new and extraordinary family.

Later, at the campsite, Doug laid out the Scrabble board on the picnic table. Four people could play, while a fifth chopped kindling for the evening fire and Marty strung a big pile of fresh green beans. Leaning over Jason's shoulder, she coached him, pointing out where he could make a word that would get better points. Jason insisted on taking a turn chopping as well. Doug stood over him, showing him how to use the axe. Nic and Natasha were already pros, often chopping wood for their fireplace at home.

When Doug took his Scrabble turn, he was slow, considering all the possibilities. "Move!" said Zoe, harrying him. "While we're still young and you're still alive!" Everyone giggled.

Above them, the manzanita and eucalyptus bent in the evening convection wind. Being outdoors was a celebration of the uneven, thought Marty. The rich variations of color and the textures of multiple layers of dry leaves and stones. A yellow leaf drifted down into her pile of beans. Seagulls wheeled and called nearby. A piece of wood leapt musically off the chopping block. Wood was certainly a celebration of the irregular, the knotty. Chiaroscuro light surrounded them. Perhaps there were few Taoists in the world, who enjoyed nature just as it was, but Marty felt lucky to be one of them, and to have found Doug, a natural born Taoist, if ever there was one.

The shadows of the trees grew long as the kids built a fire and grilled hamburgers and chicken apple sausages. Doug cooked the green beans with garlic and toasted the buns over the fire. Everything tasted especially delicious since they were hungry and eating in the cool open air.

Zoe brought the bars of chocolate Doug had told her to pick out for tasting. She only liked milk chocolate, but she had found bars from four different manufacturers. Divine, Guittard, Ghirardelli and an orange-infused bar from Newman's Own. They were all delicious spread out in their silver and gold papers. Marty thought it was a little late in the day for her to be eating chocolate, but she decided it didn't matter if she didn't sleep. She let the lovely pieces melt on her tongue.

"I like the Divine," said Zoe. "It tastes like chocolate should."

"Yes," said Doug. "But the Newman's is nice too." He had met Nell Newman and admired her work promoting organic and sustainable agriculture.

Marty smiled to herself. She could not choose between them. Chocolate was heavenly. She was worried about the dishes, but it was growing darker. The fog rolled up around them like a puffy quilt.

"We'll do the dishes in the morning," said Doug firmly. He collected all the food bags, coolers and baskets and hung them from a block and tackle he had swung into a tree top. Every California campground had its raccoons.

"But we have to go down to the beach!" said Zoe. "There might be a sunset!"

Indeed there was. A line of clear horizon beneath the fog showed that the sun would slip down between the ocean and the clouds. "Wait for it," said Zoe. The tide was coming in, so the beach was narrower. Zoe began making letters on the sand, trodding them deep, the other kids following. "WAIT," she spelled out in giant letters. "I want to see if they will be there in the morning," she called loudly over the noise of the waves.

The sand was denser and wet where the surf curled higher. Marty started a slow set as close to the surf as she could without getting too wet. She grasped sparrow's tail, pushed, turned and blocked in the single whip position, her bare feet scrunching into the dry sand beneath the wet crust. Doug fell in behind, sinking, turning, copying her motions. It was not ideal. Like driving, no one should teach their partner tai chi. But there was no one else to do it. Marty did her best. Doug had promised that they would go to camp in September, where he could learn from others.

As they moved, the sun slipped below the fog, piercing the sky and flooding the ocean with light. Zoe marshaled all of the kids, jumping and whooping at the edge of the surf. Marty and Doug kept moving slowly, waving hands like clouds and doing four corners, smiling as the kids leapt around them. As the sun sank, the clouds above pinked and flamed, lending opalescent colors to the water below, the foamy tops of the waves full of color as they rolled steadily in.

At last the clouds turned dark mauve and it grew too dark to see. The beach was empty except for a dog and its owner loping north. The waves boomed in, breaking off shore.

Doug led the way back up the wooden steps to the campground, Marty bringing up the rear behind the springy little Jason. Everyone rolled into their sleeping bags and Marty pulled out *The Three Musketeers*. She sat on the ground between the kids' two tents and Doug held the flashlight as she read of the infamous Milady, the brave young D'Artagnan and the sage and baleful Athos.

"Good night," they called at the end of the chapter, but only Nic answered. The wind in the trees and the breathing of the ocean below were loud. Marty heard the three clear notes of an owl.

As they crawled into their own tent, Marty put the book away in a pocket at the edge. "It's a rectangle," she teased Doug softly as they slid into their own warm sleeping bags. "Of the most harmless kind."

Doug didn't say anything, but wrapped his big, powerful arms around Marty.

2

When the first cold nights in September came, Paul and Marie left the cabin on Lake Michigami and went back to St. Paul, to stay in the small apartment beneath Ellie's spacious house. They were uncertain about what to do that winter. Marie wanted to go back to Oaxaca, where they had had a lovely winter the previous year. But Paul did not think he could handle the stress of the long drive, plus his increasing care for Marie. She was too weak to stand in lines, for instance. Or walk very far.

It took Ellie, Paul's older sister, to get Paul to see reason. Paul and Marie, along with Archie, a black and tan mix of border collie and shepherd, sat in front of the gas fire, having a cup of cocoa late in the evening. Paul noodled on the guitar, not too surprised that he was playing a Mexican song.

Ellie breezed down the steps. "I'm getting you two plane tickets," she said. "It'll be easy. You can find a wheelchair at the airport, and push Marie around when you change planes or go through customs."

Marie looked up gratefully. Ellie stood in the doorway, arms folded across her chest, her blonde hair turning ash grey, the picture of middle-aged competence. Ellie's generosity had eased the way for them many times.

Paul nodded too. "That makes complete sense when I think about it," he said. "I don't really need a car in Oaxaca, because we don't do anything but wander around, listen to music and eat. We can take a taxi if we need one."

"Janice could find us an apartment!" said Marie hopefully. "Oh, can we go before Dias de Muertos? We missed it last year and I'd really like to be there."

"I can get the plane tickets," said Paul to Ellie. He and Marie had sold their house in Ely that summer, because who were they kidding? They could not pay the mortgage unless Paul was working, and he was taking care of Marie full time. They needed the money to live on. Paul also hoped to put a little of the house profits away for Marie's grandkids' college funds.

"Oh come on, Paul," said Ellie. "It isn't such a big deal. We'd really like to help. It can be an early Christmas present!"

Ellie's offer changed everything. Now Paul knew what to do. He began planning what must be done before they left, and what they would need to take. Archie would go back to stay with Marie's daughter's family in Bemidji. Paul wanted Marie to go to the doctor to assess her condition. Except for being very weak, she did not seem that different. Just a much paler copy of herself, moving from chair to sofa to bed and back.

Two mornings later, however, Paul woke to find that Archie was stretched out stiff on the kitchen floor, dead. Paul was shocked. Had he not been paying attention? Archie was at least twelve years old, and had been slowing down a little, maybe breathing a little harder. But not that much. Paul felt along his chest, where his great heart no longer pulsed. He went in to tell Marie.

"Oh, Paul!" she said. She got up and followed him into the kitchen. "Poor Archie," she said. She let Paul move her hand down Archie's chest to feel the lack of movement. "He looks as if he's sleeping."

"I'm going to wrap him in a sheet," Paul said. "I don't want to bury him in the city. I'd really like to take him up to Lake Michigami and find him a happy hunting ground." He was thinking of a place he often sat in the cabin's back forty, near the little nameless lake with the beaver lodge on it.

"That sounds like a good idea," said Marie. "Look at him. So peaceful. I really hope it's that easy to die."

Paul stiffened, but he went and found a sheet in the linen closet. He wrapped up Archie and awkwardly carried the rigid body out to the car. Three hours to the lake, and three hours back. He wondered if he could leave Marie that day. Ellie would already have gone to school, and Bruce to his office.

"So," said Paul to Marie, who sat on the sofa with a cup of tea nearby. "I'll make you a salad, and there's that great hummus I made last night. Do you think you'll be okay if I leave today?" Paul had been making inspired bean dips full of garlic, lemon juice, tahini and olive oil. This one had a bit of cumin and parsley.

"Yes," said Marie. "You should go. I'll be fine." She looked thin and vulnerable, her curly black hair standing out from her face. She was wrapped in one of the heavy old Hudson blankets with a maple leaf woven into it that the Mikkelsons had had forever.

"I'll fill the teakettle," said Paul, knowing Marie couldn't lift it easily. "Can you think of anything else? I'll be gone all day," he said.

"I know," said Marie. "I will think of blessings for Archie. And you, my wonderful husband. I'm really fine."

Paul made the lunches, held Marie's frail body tightly as he said goodbye and left a note for Ellie to check on Marie when she got home.

It was a warm, golden day, the kind of day Paul loved when his heart wasn't so heavy. The trees in the neighborhood were colorful patches of orange, green-gold and burnt umber, the sky bright blue behind them. The air smelled of the drying sun-burnt leaves. But here he was, driving his loyal companion north to bury him. It seemed the last stroke, a heavy blow and a rehearsal for the day, which could not be put off forever, when he would lose Marie.

Alone, Paul gave in to the deep exhaustion and pain he felt. He banged on the steering wheel, would have hit his head on it if he could. Everything he had tried, all of his efforts, he thought, had failed. His attempts to establish a stable home first in Alaska and then in northern Minnesota, his attempts to do any kind of science with his own observations, his attempts at companionship and a family were all going down the drain. He had tried to build a solid life, but it had shattered, all of the pieces rolling off into the corners. He and Marie lived in the present, with no sense of future.

Paul knew it was just a feeling, partly due to how stressed he was. He at last understood why the safety instructions on airplanes required that you put your own oxygen mask on first before assisting others. It had always seemed so crass. But if you didn't take care of yourself, you certainly couldn't take care of anyone else.

After admitting his failures to himself, Paul actually felt better. By the time he arrived at the lake, he was ready to take up the plow again. He felt he should have known how old Archie was getting. Things were bad and he did not know what he could do about it, but he was in the middle of a lot of richness too. His family, music, the natural world. The present was a good place, the only place to be, in truth.

Paul parked by the cabin and got a wheelbarrow and a spade out of the basement. He loaded the wrapped Archie into the wheelbarrow, and trundled him up the lane and across the gravel road out into the Paul Bunyan State Forest which was empty for miles. "I'm going to put you somewhere the deer will stop to say hello, squirrels, raccoons, beaver, hawks," he said silently to Archie. He thought of his parents, buried in a meadow on the other side of the lake. Their cemetery wasn't a wild place, but it was under the open sky with a few great trees in attendance.

Up the remains of a logging road and near the tiny lake, Paul found the spot he had been thinking of. Three large pines marked it. He found a place not too close to the trees and began to dig. The ground was alternately sand and clay. Luckily, not yet frozen. Archie was stiff in a dog-shape, so Paul dug places for his feet and his head, as deep as he could. Struggling, Paul worked up a sweat, but then he carefully put Archie in the hole and covered him up.

Settling himself in the pine duff under the trees, Paul sat for a while beside the little mound he had made, watching a hawk with the light shining through its spread wing and tail feathers. So beautiful. A red-tailed hawk probably. He had seen a bald eagle that summer. Because populations of bald eagles had increased, their endangered status in Minnesota had recently changed from "threatened" to "of special concern." DDT, which had been responsible for the loss in many bird populations, had been banned across the United States since 1972.

Now that was great observational science, thought Paul. But Rachel Carson's book was also a pioneering effort in making people think about their environment. Up until that time, people had been happy to "live better through chemistry," accepting the "advances" corporations and advertising had foisted upon them. It was still going on, of course. Parts of the world felt covered in plastic. But by this time a lively alternative medical culture and a questioning of cultural norms countered mass advertising. Paul had noticed that the Internet was helping.

Paul had long wondered what environmental effects caused cancer in people, but this question was so complex he did not think it could be answered. In Marie's case, he could point to many emotional and physical agents. He did not try to second guess it. Dad had had liver cancer, perhaps because of living near farms. But Mother's death had been a result of heart disease. Even now, while he and Marie were careful about what they ate and tried to keep Marie from stress, she was simply declining. All of us, thought Paul. Dogs too. No one escaped in the end.

Archie had probably died of age. Paul did not think he would get another dog. It was beyond his ability to imagine getting involved with any other being at the moment. Archie had shared much of Paul's northern Minnesota life. Paul saw him romping through the woods, barking up trees, sniffing out dead animals. A dog after my own heart, he said to himself, always ready for adventure if it meant going out in the woods. Rest in peace, Archie, my faithful friend, he said as he left. It was a beautiful spot.

Paul walked back to the cabin, aware of the fall light. The cabin was somewhat north of the Twin Cities, a slight change in latitude. Trees were losing their leaves, getting ready for winter. Paul put up the tools, looked around to see how the weather was treating the place, got in his car and left. As always, his thoughts with Marie, he wanted to get home quickly.

But, driving back, Paul was happy to be alone for a moment, to think thoughts he didn't dare around Marie. Darkness, loss, death. And eventual acceptance. But not just yet, he thought. Marie still had life in her.

A lot was going on that fall. A presidential election was being fought out between Vice President Al Gore and George Bush, the son of former President Bush. Paul didn't have much heart for the race, but he made an effort to meet Line's son Christy, who was on the hot campaign trail that summer. Christy worked for the Democratic Farm-Labor Party in Minnesota. He told Paul that Gore had progressive ideas about the environment, but had to keep them under wraps in the campaign. Many people in the country, surprisingly to Paul and Christy, would not admit to global warming, though the evidence was clear.

Paul was also learning to program in HTML, a language which allowed people to make their own web pages. It was essentially just a way of marking up text, graphics and links to other pages so they could be read by any browser on any computer. It was a powerful concept, and Paul had found he could make a little money helping people with their web pages. Every business needed one. Paul worked on the Ely Canoe Country website, as well as others. The hourly rate for web page designers was more than Paul had ever made before, but he made sure his clients got their money's worth.

Paul could see that newer, simpler ways of making web pages were coming in. He had heard of a product called Blogger which allowed people to format their own pages, and he was sure others would follow. He had also been hearing about a company formed purely to search and point to keywords on web pages, something advertisers were desperate to do. The web was exploding with ideas and ways of making money off them.

But the thing that excited Paul the most was the chance, once again, to sing in a great choir. Whenever they stayed in St. Paul, Paul and Marie went to Ellie's church, which had also been Mother's church. Gloria Dei Lutheran not only had a choir, they had choirs! Including children's choirs and a handbell choir. The church had an excellent musical director who had graduated from St. Olaf College, Brad Engstrom. Paul loved him. For the weeks that they stayed in the city, Paul and Marie were welcomed into the chancel choir.

When Paul got home, Marie was fine, but there was an Archie-sized hole which cut through Paul. He put away Archie's bed, his left-over food and chewing toys. Paul found there was also an Archie-sized hole in the day, just after supper, the time the two of them usually went for a walk. Paul made himself go anyway. Marie herself needed a little space and he felt better if he processed the day by himself. He made the waxing moon, which came up crisp in the fall air, his companion that week. But also Sirius, the dog star! Archie's reflection, thought Paul, smiling down on him. It was the brightest star in the sky, and though it was hard to see stars in the city, Paul could usually find Sirius.

On Wednesday night, Paul and Marie went to choir practice. Paul parked as close as possible to the red-brick church entrance and helped Marie up the steps. Down in the front pews, the choir rustled and fluttered, organizing itself to rehearse. Paul and Marie processed slowly down the long burgundy-carpeted aisle past the white-painted pews, people covertly watching them. Paul had let Brad Engstrom know they were coming. Marie had been hoarding her energy all week for this practice. Everyone could see the effort it cost her.

With a little cry of welcome, one of the sopranos recognized Marie and made a place for her. Paul was grateful. He did not think he had ever felt so thin-skinned, every glance, word, image around him full of meaning. He found himself a seat among the tenors.

Engstrom welcomed them. Marie had been an occasional choir member ever since Mother had begun going to Gloria Dei, Marie's thrilling voice beloved. It was not much more than a whisper nowadays, but her spirit was there.

They began with a hymn intended for All Saints, at the end of October. "I must confess that I chose this arrangement for the organ," Brad admitted. "We come in with an Alleluia." He bid the choir watch their music and cued the organist who at once opened with a towering blast of martial fervor. The choir began in unison, without harmony. It was extraordinary, the metaphors all about fighting, the music straightforward, marching along. "An English Victorian hymn," Brad told them.

Against the organ, the choir stood up and sang loudly, Paul with them, letting the song fill his body. Saints were warriors in the hymn, their Lord the captain in their well-fought fight. They sang many verses. Tears came to Paul's eyes as he sang: "The golden evening brightens in the west; Soon, soon to faithful warriors comes their rest; Sweet is the calm of paradise the blessed. Alleluia, Alleluia." Had he been singing these words all his life and never felt them so intensely?

"Okay," said Brad, giving them all a break. "That all sounds good. So now we're going to change it up." The accompanist moved to the piano and began a light, syncopated rhythm. Paul instantly wanted to move his body. "Lord, I know I've been changed. Lord, I know I've been changed. Angels in heaven gon' sign my name." He looked down at his wife in the pew below. Yes, she was standing up, moving with the rhythm. Poor girl; no one could help it.

The words were simple. They sang them over and over. "Angels in heaven gon' sign my name." It was astonishing. A song for Marie. "I went to the river and the water was cold, Angels in heaven gon' sign my name; it chilled my body but not my soul. Angels in heaven gon' sign my name." A key change took the melody up a notch as Engstrom's arms moved purposely above them.

What great songs, thought Paul. He thought of the years in Bemidji when his choir had been inspirited by the Hungarian Janos Szabo. Paul had sung in many church choirs, but it took a great director to find songs and ideas in them, to move with taste and courage between the staunch German and English hymns and the gospel rhythm of an old spiritual describing redemption. It made for a good choir too. Paul felt the voices around him. Everyone gave it everything they had.

16

With the customary discretion and reticence of their Scandinavian Lutheran heritage, no one asked Marie how she was as the practice broke up. It was perfectly clear. She sat dumbly, her face full of emotion. Paul knew she was looking at her two favorite angels, golden figures with their wings pointed straight up, holding up candlesticks on the altar.

Paul stood beside her, waiting for people to take their leave. He thanked Brad, the director. "I've often wondered how gospel singers know how to move together," he said. "It's kind of obvious!"

"Someone gets it started," said Brad. "And the others fall in, moving left or right. It's very free, too, I've noticed. It doesn't matter if someone moves a little differently. They all give each other space."

Marie leaned on Paul a bit as they walked past the darkened windows up the aisle. At the end, Marie sat down in the last pew to catch her breath. Brad had walked slowly with them. "You folks come whenever you can," he said. "It's so good to see you!"

Tears ran down Marie's face as she said goodbye. "It doesn't matter whether I sing or not," she said. "I'm singing inside. So happy."

Brad put an arm around her and hugged her. "We've missed you," he said. "See you on Sunday!" The choir usually processed up to the front to sing. "We'll have a little chair for you, Marie," he said. He hurried away, quickening his pace.

That week, Marie agreed to go to the doctor. Paul had given up on the stiff COBRA payments which would have kept their health insurance in place. The few times they went to the doctor, he just paid the bill. But Marie did have a doctor. She had had a double mastectomy at the university hospital a year and a half ago, refusing the subsequent treatments. Now she agreed to go back to the university hospital for a check. Paul knew they would want a CAT scan. It would be expensive, but Paul buckled down to the idea. He wanted to know too.

They spent the day at the hospital, Paul pushing Marie around the pale corridors in a wheelchair. The next day they went back for diagnosis. In his office, the doctor showed Paul and Marie the scans on a computer monitor. "Tumors in the liver and lungs," he said, pointing. "No surprise to you, I am sure. These can be some of the less painful places to have tumors. But you can't expect them not to multiply."

That was the risk, that tumors would appear in places that caused pain or prevented digestion or movement. "We want to go to Mexico," said Marie. "We were there last year, and it was so warm and lovely."

"I can't predict your outcomes," said the doctor. "Growth has been slow. Probably you are taking care of yourself. But we also can see you're very weak."

"Yes," said Marie.

"We could get you on oxygen," said the doctor. "Help you breathe."

Paul blanched. Oxygen tubes!

But Marie refused. "If I can't breathe, I can't breathe," she said. "I just have to take it slow." She breathed deeply, as if to remind them that she could.

"Well, lungs aren't going to regenerate much," said the doctor. "But they are surprisingly big!" He stood up. "Millions of little air sacks in there!"

Paul had no questions. He had seen Dad die of liver cancer and knew that Marie's cancer would metastasize one way or another. Hopefully they had some time. Paul had come to agree with how Marie wanted to treat herself and her life, without poisons or radiation. Neither of them looked back. Paul did wonder whether he could get his hands on painkillers, should they need them in Mexico.

Once again, Ellie came to the rescue. She had a small arsenal of prescription-worthy painkillers. "When we were in Chile, we couldn't depend on anyone but ourselves," she said. "So I always have a few put by. Don't buy any drugs in Mexico," she told Paul firmly. "Take this with you." She handed him a plastic bottle half full of Vicodin. Paul thought it was plenty. If things got tough, they would have to come home anyway. These would tide them over. Paul put baking soda into the bottle to protect the pills and hid them deep in his luggage.

Finally the day came. In the middle of October, Ellie took Paul and Marie and their small luggage to the airport. Marie had bravely worn her white Mexican blouse, embroidered with colorful birds and flowers, but over it she had a down coat! Paul too wore his winter coat against the chill. "You'll be warm soon," said Ellie. "Have a wonderful time." She stopped her car briefly at the departures platform, waiting while Paul found a wheelchair.

Traveling was a bit of an ordeal, but they would be in Oaxaca that night. Paul hadn't flown that often in his life. He looked hard as they took off, his head pressed against the small oval plastic window as he sat beside Marie. It was raining in the Twin Cities, but the fall colors stood out in the grey drizzle as the big plane lifted off. The Mississippi and the city's large lakes, Harriet and Calhoun, shone in the light. As they flew over the orderly fields, laid out green and gold below them, Paul could not resist a feeling of pride. Home. Minnesota.

Paul sat back, relaxed as they flew above fluffy clouds for several hours. When they began to prepare for landing, Paul again pressed his face to the window. Mexico City was hugely spread out on a vast dry-looking plain. Prepared for the worst at the airport, Paul found it wasn't as bad as he thought. The airport staff were as friendly as could be. He and Marie did not have passports; just their drivers' licenses. They had little luggage.

Airplane country was the same the world over. Paul didn't mind that there was little time between flights. Just as Ellie had said, he was able to push Marie up the long corridors in a wheelchair. It did feel foreign, however. Paul was glad for the tiny bit of Spanish he had picked up the year before.

In the air again, Paul began to get excited. They were in a smaller plane for the short flight, hopping over the mountains into Oaxaca. Beneath them were some green quilts of stitched together farms, but also what appeared to be dense areas of housing. Paul remembered the long drive from the previous year. As the plane glided to a stop, he looked at Marie. "It's magical to be flying over that space it took us so long to drive last year," he said.

Marie looked a little wan, but excited. "Yes. It's wonderful."

Airport people rolled a stairway right to the door of the plane. Oh-oh, thought Paul. "Stairs," he said aloud. "Do you think you'll be okay?" he asked Marie. "I'll be right beside you."

"Yes," said Marie. "I'll be okay."

When they stepped out into the evening light, the warm air whooshed toward them. It felt like summer. "In the 80's," said Paul. "I'm sure of it." It was why they had come!

"Una silla de ruedas, por favor," said Paul to an attendant. The baggage was spread out all around them. Paul stubbornly waited with Marie, supporting her until someone brought a wheelchair. Paul picked up their luggage and piled it around Marie. They rolled across the tarmac toward the taxi rank, Marie riding in state. They had a place to go. Janice had managed to reserve them a small apartment in the same building they had stayed in the previous year. It was all working out.

The sun had gone down, an orange streak across the sky, which was purple and grey in the twilight, but it was very warm. "The air feels like a miracle," whispered Paul to Marie as they held each other in the back of the taxi.

"I'm so happy we got here!" said Marie.

Paul felt relieved. Marie was weak, but she was upright. It was astounding. They passed a cathedral. There would be angels in the morning, Paul foresaw. Warm air, angels, music. They could already hear the mariachi bands in the street.

3

Line held out a towel as Ivy, her youngest daughter, handed her five-month-old Sofia, fresh from her bath. The little girl liked the water, happily splashing in the tub, but she was fussy when no one was holding her. She wanted her mother, Fern, Line's second daughter.

Line rubbed the little girl down, talking to her. "Now, doesn't that feel nice?" she said. "Warm and dry, Sofia. We'll get you all warm and then we'll go sit in front of the fire!" It was November, and the house wasn't very warm.

Ivy, who had been in the tub, rubbed herself down as well. "Oh, that sounds nice," she said. "A crackling fire, Sofia. You will like it!"

Line and Ivy were taking care of Sofia while Fern was at an archaeological conference. Fern had been at home for almost a year, having her baby. But she was restless. She was taking any history courses she could at the university and sending out resumes and correspondence to people in her field. "She's like your father," Line told Ivy. "She needs to work!" By next summer, when Sofia was a year old, Fern hoped to have a job and to take Sofia with her.

In the mean time, Line's household all enjoyed tiny Sofia. She wasn't crawling yet, but she did roll around, and she was fascinated by her own hands, reaching for things and clapping her hands together.

Line brought Sofia out into the living room, where Poppa, Line's father-in-law, was mixing a drink for himself. It was the sociable hour, when the light had left the sky and people gathered before dinner. Poppa had a fire going, which snapped and danced. Line plopped Sofia on the couch and sat down beside her, holding a soft red ball for her.

Poppa brought his drink over. He took the red ball from Line and put it behind his back. "Where'd it go, Sofia?" he asked. "Where'd it go?"

Line watched as Sofia's big eyes looked all around. It must be good for a little girl to be surrounded by love and attention, even if her mother wasn't there.

Poppa took a sip of his Scotch and then sneaked the ball into view. "Oh, there it is Sofia! Want it?" He handed the ball to Sofia, who promptly tried to put it in her mouth. She was beginning to teethe. "Smart little girl," said Poppa. "You know where it went, don't you."

"So," said Line, "Do we have a president yet?" she asked Poppa, who kept an eye on the news.

"Nope," said Poppa. "The Florida Supreme Court has extended the deadline for the count. Who knows when it will all be over." The presidential election between Al Gore and George Bush that month had resulted in such a close call that Florida was recounting its ballots in many counties. Gore had 268 electoral votes and Bush had 246. Whichever of them won the 25 Florida votes would become president; Bush very narrowly.

Line sighed. It was disconcerting. Al Gore had won the popular vote by half a million, and the Florida vote was also close.

"Some chicanery going on there in Florida," said Poppa. "They're fighting about off-shore votes, deadlines. The Florida congress is in on it. Jeb Bush, the brother, is governor. I doubt if Gore can win it."

Line could hardly bear to think about it. The Republicans had such depressing fiscal ideas: they were friends of big business, against regulation, against funding for health care and education. No one in the Cohen household, or among their friends, was a fan of George Bush. In fact, in California Gore was assured the state's 54 electoral votes. Because of this, Line was pretty sure Stephen had voted for Ralph Nader.

Ivy brought Sofia's bottle and Line checked to see whether she wanted it. "I'm glad Fern's coming tonight," said Ivy, sleepily. They had put Sofia's crib in Ivy's room, but Sofia wasn't sleeping well without her mother.

Sofia put her little hands around the bottle and drank while Line held her. "Yes," said Line. "As adversity goes, not having her mother around for a couple of days isn't a bad thing. But a couple of days is enough." Stephen was picking up Fern at the airport at that very moment. Fern had read a paper on her archaeological ceramics work on Menorca, one of the Balearic Islands off Spain.

"You are a lucky little girl," said Poppa, "With a Bush for president or no Bush. Four generations in one house. That's pretty special." Poppa

21

was eighty, and slowing down a little. These days he came back from his morning rounds and took a nap after lunch.

"But what's her life going to be like?" asked Ivy. "Since we are polluting our oceans, population is surging and the earth is warming?!"

Line was a little surprised at Ivy. She heard this rhetoric from Ivy's friends often enough: You've messed everything up. You've squandered any inheritance we might have had, they said. Line preferred to be optimistic. "You'll solve these problems," she said to Ivy. "Your generation has lots of ideas. And so will yours," she said smiling down on the little Sofia. "It's such an odd inversion of my childhood," said Line. "This little girl has five adults to look after her; while we were six kids, isolated with our parents in a small North Dakota town." She remembered how lost they had felt when Mother and Dad left for a day. Never more than that.

"Even for me," said Ivy, "there were more kids around than grownups."

"Times change," said Poppa, repeating: "She's a lucky little girl." Poppa wasn't worried about the future. His four-story brownstone house in Brooklyn currently funded his life, plus his generosity to the rest of the Cohens. Poppa had not squandered anything.

Sofia's big intelligent eyes followed the bright spots in the room as she drank her milk.

"Are we supposed to wait for Stephen and Fern for dinner?" asked Poppa, rattling the ice in his scotch.

"No, I don't think so," said Line. "Traffic is surely terrible at this hour. Let's start and they will probably come soon." Having the big house full of family and expected family made Line feel rich and contented. It was certainly not assured, with her grown kids, but she was enjoying it as long as it lasted. Christy, Line's eldest, was in Minnesota, most likely spending his time in front of a television, armchair-quarterbacking the election. And Heather, Line's eldest daughter, was married and living in Chile. There were rumors she was pregnant.

Line left little Sofia on a blanket spread on the floor with Poppa to keep an eye on her while she made pasta to accompany the sauce she had made that afternoon. Ivy put together a salad. As they sat down to eat, in came Stephen and Fern.

"Oh my goodness!" said Fern, hugging everyone in turn and picking up her daughter. "It's so nice to be home!" Sofia began to cry a little, showing the anxiety she had felt at Fern's leaving.

"Oh, you," said Ivy, coming over to stroke the little girl's cheek. "We took good care of you. Yes we did. But she didn't sleep so well," Ivy told Fern. "And neither did I!"

"I've missed you too," said Fern, snuggling her daughter. "Ugh, I hate breast pumps," she said. "Painful! I need you to help me."

Line looked back and forth between her two lovely girls. They both had Stephen's figure, thin, with small hips and long legs. Heather was the one who had inherited Line's pear-shape, with its big hips. Fern's hair and coloring were a little darker than Ivy's. Fern was bent on external success. Line wasn't so sure about Ivy.

Line poured Stephen a glass of wine as he dished himself some food. "How are you, my handsome husband?" she asked.

Stephen cocked his head from side to side noncommittally. "I'm glad to be home too!" he said. His classes were well under way and he was getting to know the new students associated with his college, Oakes. Every student and teacher at UC Santa Cruz had an affiliation with one of the ten colleges on campus. Stephen was well over the intense student politics which seemed to him to repeat ad infinitem. But he was resigned to it. He generally had a few great students, and he was also free to write and research the books he published.

That year the university faculty had finally voted to give students letter grades, from A to F, but narrative evaluations also had to be given for each student's work. Teaching, for Stephen, was intense.

Dinner conversation was lively. Fern told them about Austin, Texas. Poppa talked about the film club he was still running. He had discovered films coming out of China and Hong Kong, such as that year's wonderful Wong Kar-Wai film *In the Mood for Love*. Line and Stephen had loved its quiet, languorous love story too.

Ivy talked about the costumes she was helping to make for the university production of *Hair* scheduled for the spring. "One hundred actors!" she said. "And some of them have more than one costume!"

At 24, Ivy was still not sure she would take a degree. She took classes she liked and had only lived on campus, at Kresge college, her first year. Since then she, like her Dad, bicycled to campus for classes. She loved the costume shop in the theater arts department and had a sewing machine at home too. It might not make a career for her, but no one seemed very worried about it.

All of us, thought Line, have benefited from Poppa's largesse. Line had sometimes been bothered that Stephen deferred to his father in decision-making, but by this time, when the kids were grown up, Poppa's place in their family just made everything easier. Each of them was able to pursue their own best abilities without worrying about money too much. Line herself was still working for the hospice foundation, visiting two or three terminal patients each day in their homes.

After dinner was cleared up, everyone retired early. Line made sure the fire was out, the lights were off and the doors locked before she too went to bed. She was very grateful for the spacious house where she had lived, except for a couple of years in Edinburgh, for more than ten years. Six of us, she thought, live comfortably together here. She fell asleep thinking of how sweet it was to hold a little granddaughter, just five months old.

On Sunday, Line put on a fleece and swept off the decks. The crisp air smelled of burnt leaves and the mountains were blue in the distance. The roofs, which had been wet, let off steam in the sun. Line was rigorous about the leaves on the deck. Wet leaves could lead to wood rot. She swept off the top deck first, then went down a level and swept off the deck outside Poppa's room and den where the curtains were still drawn. Poppa had never wanted his own apartment, with kitchen. He wanted to eat with the family.

The house fell down the hill in a series of decks and garden terraces. At this level there were redwood planters where Line kept flowers and a few vegetables. Below was another terraced garden, and below that a steep wild place of trees and grasses.

Line put up her broom and went down the steps to have a look at the gardens. The fruit on her favorite Fuyu persimmon, among the trees at the bottom of the garden, was ripening. Orange globes stood out on the branches which had only a few brown and dried leaves left on them. The tree was so shapely, Line thought, and at the height of its powers. She never pruned it, just let it go to see what happened.

Line put persimmons in a basket and climbed back up the wooden steps. She had a few green beans left, winter squash, herbs and potatoes. There would also be a box from what Line thought of as the 'homeless gardens,' tended in town by transient people and sent out to those who subscribed. Plenty of produce for the Thanksgiving feast they would share with Marty and Doug's family up at Boulder Creek. Doug wanted to rotisserie some chickens over an outdoor fire. Line and her girls would bring salads, savories and side dishes.

Line wondered about Paul and Marie, deep in Mexico. How was Marie holding up? Perhaps she would speak to Paul on the phone at Christmas. She thought of Hanna, her youngest sister, living on a farm in upstate New York, and her two sisters in Minnesota, Ellie and Kristen. All of us made our choices, Line thought. Extending our families, stretching them across the country.

And now the world, thought Line, thinking of Heather. It would be spring in Chile. All Saints was the most important day in November. How odd it would be to have inverted seasons: Easter in the fall and Christmas in the middle of summer.

On Thanksgiving the Cohens took two cars up the winding mountain roads to Boulder Creek. Poppa drove Fern and little Sofia, while Stephen, Line and Ivy brought the food. The mist was thick and milky in the trees, illuminated by shafts of sun. Colorful shrubs and trees shone in among the trunks of the tall pines.

Line liked going up to the sprawling winery. In front was a small, rustic building which had long been the tasting room. The house itself was a simple ranch style, but gardens were set out behind it. A road past sheds and buildings led to the winery, where hoppers, tanks and warehouses looked orderly and business-like. Some of the vineyards were visible, but they were also apparently tucked into the hills on the mountain.

Years ago, when Heather began to get involved with the Hendersons, she had shown Line and Stephen around. The winery complex felt home-like to Line, though she couldn't quite understand how her intellectual younger sister, Marty, had found her way there!

Doug welcomed them in a well-worn sweater that smelled of smoke. He wore thick leather gloves with which he reached right into the fire to move burning logs. His kids were exuberant, excited by the outdoor fire. Nic and Natasha turned the rotisserie off which fat from the chickens dripped, snapping and popping. Little Jason hopped from one group to another, telling jokes. Alice, Doug's mother, arranged the food on cloth-covered tables. Everyone wore sweaters and fleeces, though the air wasn't exactly cold and the afternoon sun still made long shadows.

Marty went from group to group, snapping candid photographs. "I know it's annoying," she said to Line. "I'll quit in a few moments. I'm just taking advantage of the light." She had often told Line that she couldn't take nature photos. You had to be out in nature to appreciate it. "But family, that's what I love. Photographs of us capture the fleeting moment."

"What about Ana Maria and Javier?" asked Line. "Are they here today?" Marty had told her about the complicated relationship she had with Ana Maria in the garden and kitchen.

"They are celebrating with their kids and grandkids," said Marty. "In San Jose."

Down the road from the winery came Jeremy, Doug's partner, wearing a jaunty scarf around his neck and bearing as many bottles of wine as he could. "There's more where these came from!" he said triumphantly. He set them up on a table ranged with wineglasses, bottled water and juice for the kids. "Aperitif, anyone?" He was thin with weathered skin, and looked like a European, reflecting the many years he had spent in France.

Stephen followed Line to the drinks table. "This is last year's Pinot Noir," said Jeremy, pouring them each a glass. "I've been wanting to try it." He swirled his glass and sniffed, expertly. "Not bad," he decided.

Fern worried about Sofia. "Do you think it is warm enough for her?" she asked Line.

"She is sleeping," said Line. "Babies have higher temperatures than we do. Do you have enough blankets on her? If she's uncomfortable, I'm sure she'll wake up."

Zoe reached her arms in toward Sofia, but Fern stopped her. "There'll be plenty of time for that!" she said. "Let's not wake her."

Marty too appeared to look with longing at the tiny girl in her soft crib/basket. "How was your conference, Fern?" she asked.

"Great," said Fern. "I met so many people. And got a lot of interest in my paper. I'm hoping that my specialty in ceramics translates into a job in America."

"In the Southwest, maybe?" asked Marty.

"Southeast too," said Fern. "In Georgia and Florida they have found interesting sites."

Line sipped her wine, enjoying the warmth as it slid down her throat and the warmth of the big gathering. She could hear Stephen quizzing Jeremy about the harvest. "What do people do when there's no tank space left for their grapes? I hear my friends with vineyards complaining that the harvest is really big."

Jeremy looked at him darkly. "The Gallos or people like Fred Franzia come in and offer rock bottom prices! And people have to take them. That's where that Two Buck Chuck is coming from that's all over Trader Joe's. Some people drink the stuff!"

Line smiled. Poppa had brought home some of the Charles Shaw wine once, when all of his friends were talking about it. Line had occasionally drunk really fine wines and knew what Jeremy meant by his insinuations.

Line restricted her liquids to water, tea and wine. There were hundreds of other tantalizing options lately, flavored waters, fruit juice coolers and special tea drinks. But it complicated your life to be attached to all of these flavors. Line was not a fan of the ubiquitous smoothie habits people were growing either. She wanted to get fluid and fiber from actual fruits and vegetables. I'm old fashioned, I suppose, she thought. But she stayed out of the middle of the grocery store, where the advertising and flavor industries held sway with their processed items. Line was certain that some of this processing industry was contributing to the health problems she saw in older people.

Thanksgiving, thought Line. It was a time when most people actually cooked! The stores had been filled with all of the typical foods people associated with Thanksgiving: pumpkin, pecans, Brussels sprouts, sweet potatoes, apples, cranberries, stuffing mixes and, of course, turkeys! Long lines at the checkout counters indicated people were filling their larders. How lucky we are, thought Line.

When the chickens were cooked and everyone assembled at the long table in the twilight, Doug sat at its head, pleased as punch, Line could tell. There were fourteen people, if you counted little Sofia, five kids and nine grownups. Doug toasted them all.

"Thank you all for coming!" he said. "It makes me so happy! This is my favorite holiday and I'm so glad to share it with you." He invited others to toast.

"L'Chaim!" said Poppa decisively. "And to great-grandchildren!"

"To one more year!" said Jeremy. "One more harvest. It's a miracle," he said.

Line knew he was alluding to the fact that the winery existed on a shoestring. Jeremy, Doug and their wild marketing partner Victor had met almost twenty years ago at the University of California, Davis. None of them had money, but the three of them had somehow managed to leverage the winery and its vineyards ever since. The place did seem to be doing well. Jeremy was a master at making whatever grapes he was given into fine

European-style wines, according to Doug, and Victor a public relations genius. The three of them were a viable combination.

Line found herself sitting between Poppa and Jeremy, Poppa plying Jeremy with questions over her head.

"So where do you live?" asked Poppa.

"Over the mountain and a little east," said Jeremy. "In Saratoga. Takes me about forty minutes to get here. It's not bad at all. I like the feel of the place. Closer to civilization than we are here up on the mountain. There's an arts center with great concerts and theater."

"Yes," said Poppa. "No shortage of things to do around here."

"But I think you lived in New York," said Jeremy. "I came out of Chicago, and got caught up in the *vendange* in France one summer. Never looked back."

"I grew up in Brooklyn," said Poppa. "My Dad got us started in immigration law. Interesting times."

Line knew a lot of Poppa's stories. She didn't tire of them, but she was terribly pleased to be in this company and delighted in the young people. She kept watching Zoe, the twins and Jason, Marty's stepkids. In the growing darkness, Zoe ran around lighting votive candles and putting them out on the long table. Line remembered that Marty had been more likely to take care of their younger sisters than she was. Yet I'm the one who had all the kids, she thought.

Dinner was long and slow. Line heard crickets begin their night-time sounds. The kids disappeared into the house and Fern took Sofia inside too. Line helped Marty and Alice clear dirty plates and dishes into the kitchen.

"We made so many pies!" said Marty. "I wonder if Doug wants to have them inside or outside."

"Doug calls Marty the 'Queen of Tarts,'" said Alice, smiling. "She'll whip up a tart on the least notice. I loved the blackberry tart you brought me," she said to Marty.

"It's so easy," said Marty. "I have this tart pan with a removable bottom and I can make a crust right in the pan almost. But we made the traditional pies today: pumpkin, Doug's favorite pecan, apple and Zoe made a chocolate banana pie. She's shy about it, but I am sure it will get eaten!"

"Zoe," said Alice as Zoe entered the kitchen. "Where's your pie? I want to see it."

"We're going to have whipped cream, right?" asked Zoe. "I need to cover it with whipped cream. It's pretty ugly."

Line agreed that the pie was ugly, covered with banana slugs she thought, though she didn't say so.

It was still warm enough and Doug put more wood on the fire so they could have pie and coffee outdoors. There was no moon and stars were more visible, Line thought, than they were in town. Line took a piece of pumpkin pie and topped it with whipped cream. She pulled a chair up to the fire near Marty, determined to ask her how she felt about living in the country. Marty had been in Boulder Creek over a year now.

"I really think I'm a country girl," replied Marty. "I'm mesmerized by the trees up here, by the sky, by the slow unfolding of the seasons. The rain is as wonderful as the sun. I don't even want to leave home, don't want to miss anything!"

"Well I know you minded the concrete up on Russian Hill," said Line. "And those ficus trees that wouldn't drop their leaves!"

"Yes. I never could get as comfortable up there as I am here in the woods. I miss tai chi class, and certain friends. But Doug is a natural born Taoist, and we're such farmers up here. All we talk about is the weather! It's kind of poetic."

"What about your precious books?" asked Line.

"I can get them here," said Marty. "The branch library's beautiful, and they will order books for me. And," she leaned forward and her voice broke into a whisper, "there's Amazon!" Amazon was an online book retailer where, it was reputed, you could get almost any book you wanted.

"I don't buy many books any more," said Line. "I seem to have the ones I need."

Doug had come to stand behind Marty, listening to the conversation. He reached down and put his hands on her shoulders. Marty laughed and kissed his fingers. Line changed the subject. "So do you think you have any little winemakers in that bunch?" she asked, indicating Zoe and the twins, who were piling whipped cream on pieces of pie.

"Nah," said Doug. "Not if they're as smart as I think they are." He laughed. "But you never know." He picked up seven-year-old Jason and put him on his knee as he sat down beside them. "Now this one!" he said. A wide smile spread across Jason's face. "This one's going to be a fireman," he teased. "An astronaut? A clown?" Jason shook his head. "Oh yeah, I know," said Doug. "You're going to be a cooker!"

"So I can eat hamburgers all the time," said Jason to Line.

"Hamburgers are good," said Line. "Did you have some pie?"

Jason nodded.

Zoe came over to the fire gingerly carrying the tiny Sofia over her shoulder, closely followed by Ivy. "See Dad," said Zoe. "I got to hold her."

"I do see," said Doug. "She's like a little corncob. Like in *Totoro!*" Sofia was tightly wrapped in a blanket, her little hands reaching for people, a smile on her face.

"Bigger than that," said Zoe. Ivy stood protectively behind her, ready to take the baby when Zoe had had her chance. The glow of the coals in the fire pit illuminated their faces.

Line stood up and turned her back to the fire to warm it. "Getting cold," she said. Marty too stood up. They began to clear the coffee cups and pie plates.

"Just leave the tables and chairs," said Doug, helping. "We'll get them in the morning. There'll be more light!"

Line looked at Marty conspiratorially. I get it, she thought. I see what the deal is between them.

4

"Could we stop and light a candle for chère Maman?" Grace asked Marty, as they packed baskets full of clean clothes into the back of Paul's mini-van at the laundromat in the resort town of Walker, near the Mikkelson family cabin on Lake Michigami. It was July and the weather was warm, slightly humid to Marty's desert sensibilities.

"Of course," said Marty, who was driving. "Tell me where to go." Next stop was the grocery store, but there was certainly time to light a candle for Marie, Grace's mother, who was out at the cabin, living like a shadow in the background.

"It's St. Agnes, on this side of town," said Grace. "Just go up this block. See?" Walker was not a very large town. It had one main street strung along the huge Leech Lake and a few streets backing off it.

St. Agnes looked to be a rather new church with a large cross in glass under its eaves. They parked and Grace, very familiar with it, jumped out of the car and went in a side door, Marty following. In front of a painted statue of the Virgin Mary, Grace put some change in the collection box, lit a candle and said a prayer for Marie. Very simple and natural, thought Marty.

Grace seemed relieved when she got back in the car. Marty had enjoyed getting to know Grace. She was reliably humble and sweet, asking little for herself except time to do her rosary. Marty and Grace were the resident moms, each with four kids to worry about at the cabin. Grace's oldest, Dory, was now 16 and had a job for the summer in Bemidji. She had stayed home with her Dad.

"I've noticed that our Zoe really enjoys your son Joe," said Marty. "I think they're writing a play together."

"Yes," said Grace in her slightly French-inflected English. "Little Joe is the well-rounded one. He is a good athlete but he likes music and he was in a musical this spring. He loved it." Though he was 13, tall and attractive, Joe was still sometimes called "Little" out of ancient habit.

"I'm impressed at how little you worry about them," Marty said.

Grace smiled. "They come up every summer. It's like home to them. But I do miss your Mother. She was a gracious presence."

"It seems like just yesterday we were all up here together for her 70th birthday," said Marty. "I remember making a video of her shucking corn down at the dock! And I think it was the first time I met you, too." Marty had been single at the time.

Grace pointed, "There's that farm stand! Let's see if they have sweet corn."

Marty turned abruptly off the main road. The farm stand had positioned itself just at the turnoff to the grocery store. They did have early sweet corn, green beans, cucumbers, tomatoes, summer squash, all of which Marty bought. But then she and Grace went to the grocery store too. There was never enough breakfast cereal, milk or meat for their hungry brood. After filling up the van, they took the highway, and then the sandy gravel roads back to the cabin.

Early that morning, two canoes had set out across the lake, to see how far they could get up the channel and into the lakes that fed into Leech. Doug was the leader of this expedition, which he called the "Copper Man" trip, to distinguish it from the earlier legendary "Iron Man" trips on which the brothers-in-law got all the way into Leech Lake and were met in Walker by the rest of the family for a beer fest.

Doug was the only grownup on this trip, which involved sandwiches, fishing poles, life jackets, water and sunscreen. Paul reminded Doug to take money for ice cream, should they get to the Benedict Store. Paul could hardly be induced to leave the cabin, where Marie spent most of her time either in bed or in the big recliner in the living room. Paul noodled on the guitar or helped Marie move about or eat, coaxing as if she were a child.

Doug had been thrilled with the cabin and declared it a "media-free" zone, except for books, of which there were many. He also ruled that the kids should not go to town. For two blissful weeks, he hoped, his kids would not be reminded of popular culture and could live in the natural world. The cabin was stuffed with things to do, and eight kids kept each other busy! Doug did not think they could get in too much trouble, though the kids could not go in swimming without a grownup on the dock.

Grace's kids, Little Joe, Andre, Jeanne and Benjy were both older and younger than Doug's kids. The Hickman kids made their headquarters in the beach house, where Joe and Andre slept.

Equally interesting to them all was the derelict craft barn. The barn had never been finished or had its floor put in. Generations of raccoons had grown up in the cracks and crevices, leaving quite a stink. But the kids loved exploring the archery equipment their grandfather had once assembled, the collections of art supplies, rocks and other odd bits, as well as years worth of moldering *National Geographics*. Paul said everything in the barn was trashed and he intended to clean it all up. It wouldn't happen this year, though.

Marty and Grace had little to worry about except shopping, cooking and laundry. Grace made delicious bread every other morning, pouring whole wheat flour into an oatmeal mash. The bread got eaten up very quickly for toast and lunchtime sandwiches. Paul and Grace drank coffee in the morning, but Marty had brought her smoky lapsang souchong tea. In the evenings there was a big family meal.

That afternoon, Marty shooed Paul out. "Go on a ramble," she said. "Grace and I will be here. I'm sure you need it." Paul helped Marty carry a comfy rocking chair out on the little deck which jutted out from the east side of the cabin and get Marie situated so she could get some air and sun. Marty sat with her. She would have liked to know more about Marie, but she did not want to pressure Marie to talk. She sat close to her, just looking out at the birches and the lake beyond, thinking about Mother, and how much Mother would have known about the birds.

"Are you happy with your new family?" Marie asked, her voice barely above a whisper. Her face was pale and the once vibrant black curls around her face were graying and lank. Her eyes burned with spirit, however.

Marty smiled. "Oh yes! It still feels odd. Here in northern Minnesota I remember my old, lonely little self. But I'm kind of proud of that stubborn self and what it became. And now I've found a mirror for it, in Doug." It had been two years since Marty had moved to Boulder Creek to live with Doug and his family.

"Instant family," said Marie, smiling.

"It happens," said Marty. "Probably more often in California than it does here." She wished she knew what to ask Marie. Marty knew her story, but not the details. Prattling on probably helped Marie, though. Diverted her.

Marie's face registered some pain. "I have a history in California myself. But things have been better for me since I met your brother. And I never expected Grace to have such a big family." She licked her lips. It seemed that she was having trouble keeping her mouth moist.

Marty brought the nearby water glass to Marie's lips. "Don't talk unless you want to," said Marty. "It's lovely just to sit here." The water at the lake tasted like iron. Marty liked the taste which she remembered, but Doug wasn't so sure.

Marie made an effort to drink, but then sank back. "Thank you, Marty," she said quietly. Her eyes closed, as if she was napping.

Marty tried to remember how often she had heard Marie sing, her face full of life and color. The light was going out now, or perhaps, thought Marty, it was going into Marie's grandchildren.

Marty sat listening to all the sounds around her, mostly the breeze soughing in the trees, a few birds nattering and twittering. Below, the ever-changing lake reflected the grey-blue sky. It wasn't a windy, rough day, but there was a breeze. Marty hoped the canoe trip was going well.

Marty thought about how her mind had been shaped by Chinese poets, countering the deep Scandinavian Lutheran culture with the poets' sense of being in the physical present. It had led to studying tai chi and Marty's determination not to compromise in her thinking. She had thought of herself as a lonely little Taoist laughing in the hills, even gone deep into China to visit Tu Fu's farm in Chengdu. But then she met Doug. I suppose it's a consistent life, she thought.

When Paul got back, they took Marie indoors. Marty brought her book on *The Celts* and a pair of binoculars down to the dock. The breeze was beginning to settle down and long shadows lay across the wooden seating area Dad had long ago built around an upper platform, with steps down to a long dock going out across the water. The weathered platform was littered with towels, abandoned flippers and goggles, a few seating pads.

The sounds of the water beating up on the rocks and the wind in the branches of the pines above blended together. A few mosquitoes were left, but the breeze tended to disperse them. A chipmunk churrred nearby and Marty saw it run under the platform. Marty arranged herself at the far right end in the commencement pose for a tai chi slow set. She had done the set in the past down at the platform. She began, moving slowly, sinking, letting her turning waist bring her hands up. She only had concentration enough for the first section of the set, but it felt good.

Marty flipped up the binoculars she wore around her neck, pressing them to her glasses. She scanned the lake horizon for the shapes of canoes. It wasn't that she was worried about Doug and his fellow adventurers. It was just that there was a hole in the company until they returned. Marty was struck by the way her own little family didn't need to talk much when they were all up here sharing the same experiences. They knew each other, trusted each other and just went along, enjoying everything.

After two years, Marty had spent the time with her family needed to calibrate hearts and minds to each other. Marty and the kids had endured long days when Doug did not come home. They kept to their habits, school, meals. Doug had shown Marty how habit-driven she was in daily life. She had not even realized how she cut the days up into appropriate times. But sometimes she and the kids gave up and plugged themselves into nature videos or the few approved movies they had. Doug was the meat in the sandwich, the pole around which their little universe turned.

When Marty finally discerned the small, dark shapes of canoes on the far horizon, she ran up the hill to the cabin to tell Grace and Zoe. They were frosting graham crackers as an afternoon snack. Paul had made a jug of lemonade. The two smallest kids, Jeanne and Benjy, who had been playing a card game at Marie's feet, followed Marty down to the dock.

Far over the water, Marty could hear someone say, "Is there a reception committee?"

"Yes! I see them!" said Jason, who was surely tuckered out by canoeing all day. "There IS a reception committee." Zoe and Grace came down the path with a cake pan full of frosted crackers.

"We are the Copper Men! We are the Copper Men!" sang the kids as the canoes got closer.

Doug pulled his canoe alongside the dock and Marty held it against the side, as its passengers, Nic and Jason climbed out.

Marty shared a look with Doug. He was a little sun-burned and worn, but also as pleased as he could be. "I'll father anyone I can get my hands on," he had told Marty. He had gotten a chance that day! Grace's kids had a good strong father of their own, but Doug, who had lost his at 16, was deeply aware of how important fathers were.

"Did you get to paddle?" Marty asked Jason.

"Yes!" said Jason, holding up his paddle. "Dad said I was good at it!" Nic was in the forefront of the canoe for the hard mile-long slog across the lake, but Jason had probably paddled on some of the easier parts.

"Paul said it might rain tonight," said Marty. "He suggested that we pull the canoes up and turn them over."

"Good idea," said Doug. He paddled over to the V Dad had once made of old rubber tires to protect the fiberglass canoes on the rocky shore, stepped out of the canoe and pulled it up. Little Joe, who had piloted the other canoe, followed him, expertly helping pull up the canoes and turning them over on the bank.

Andre held up the three striped perch they had caught on a stringer. "We got these in the channel," he said. They would only be about four bites each, but they would certainly get eaten.

"The channel was sandy on the bottom!" said Natasha, who had become great friends with Andre. "So clear and nice to wade in! We could see to the bottom. We ate our lunch there." She and Andre had been in Joe's canoe.

Joe, tanned and handsome, took a frosted cracker from Zoe, who was in awe of him. Not enough to want to go on the canoe trip, however. Zoe, a year younger, had spent the day on her own private dreaming Marty guessed. She was solicitous of Marie, however. Marty was often impressed with Zoe's altruism, though Zoe was also quite taken with herself. Marty thought she might make a good leader in the end.

"Who's going to clean these fish?" asked Doug.

"I'll do it," said Andre. "I know how." Natasha, Nic and Jason crowded around as Andre helped them all take turns scraping off the scales, cutting off the heads and emptying the organ cavities. Jason was thrilled that for once, he wasn't the youngest kid. Jeanne and Benjy were a couple of years younger than he was.

Marty went up to the cabin to see about the evening meal. The cabin was like a museum of her past. The cutting board was one she remembered from childhood. Dad's handiwork was everywhere. The photographs on the bulletin board had not been changed since Mother put them up years ago. She had rigged the curtains at the beach house. Everyone also laughed at the fact that they still called a cupboard full of craft items the "green cupboard," when it had not been green since who knows when.

That night Marty couldn't sleep. She and Doug's family occupied the log cabin which belonged to the Bakken cousins right next to the Mikkelson cabin. The four kids slept in the loft. Marty got up and went and sat on the screened-in porch. Water plopping off the trees was so thick and steady she was sure it must be rain. The space between the trees grew lighter and lighter. Marty imagined herself a monk meditating, surrendering to lack of sleep, just sitting, aware.

Being at Lake Michigami reminded Marty of Russian novels, which often described families living together deep in an isolated, woodsy setting. Or the Tarkovsky movie *The Mirror*, set near Moscow in a woods much like their own. In the movie, a family waited in a log cabin for their father to return from the war. The trees were birches, poplars and pines. The air was probably mild and wet, as it always was deep in the middle of a continent. So different from their own dry air on the west coast.

Marty went in and lay down beside Doug. He was reading a 1959 Boy Scout manual he had found on the shelves at the cabin. "This manual meant so much to me as a kid," he said. "I wasn't able to be a Boy Scout, but I used it to imagine a life of honor and challenge for myself." Doug's family had never been well-off. He had done his share of field-work, picked fruit and harvested artichokes as a kid, eaten the welfare cheese when his father died. But he was always hopeful, with aspirations that thrilled Marty.

Marty was a little surprised that Doug was content to lie in bed in the morning reading, not too anxious to join the breakfast fray. Doug was shy with new people. Marty found it hard to believe, but the Mikkelsons were not his family. He kept in touch by phone with his partners in California, but July was a quiet time just before the grape harvest. It was the best time for him to get away.

Marty lay beside him admiring the Bakken cabin. It grew more beautiful every year, she thought. She watched the soft light as the sun stole out from behind the thin overcast. She could remember when this cabin was built, slightly after their own, from a set of carefully milled logs, uniform in shape. Perhaps its main beauty was from this unity. The logs were probably pine, but the entire cabin, including window and door frames, and the beautiful hardwood floors were made from the same wood.

Marty looked at the rafters holding up the sleeping loft. One wall was dominated by a large stone fireplace and there were stone tiles in the kitchen. The plan was simple, organic. It was furnished with hand-me downs, but here they were leather chairs, lovely wooden rockers. The place was all of a piece.

Their own rackety cabin was chock-a-block with furniture, pieces from Aunt Rose and Marty's parents which had never been totally absorbed. Paul had shown her the place where the cement block foundation was buckling and cracking. The Mikkelson cabin was over forty years old. It had been built cheaply and all the expectations for it had been shelved when Dad died. It needed money and attention, but none of the siblings who used it most had either one to give.

It was a great place for a family reunion, however, and perfect for kids. That week the kids spent lots of time on their play. With Paul and Marty's help they pulled out all kinds of clothes to wear as costumes. Paul opened the cedar chest which had been Mother's hope chest before she was married. It still was used to preserve the woolen Hudson blankets in the summer, and held ancient family keepsakes, such as the handmade doll Aunt Mabel had sent from Alaska dressed in fur skins and beautiful little mukluks. The skin on its hood was breaking down, but otherwise it looked just as Marty remembered it.

The play required that the kids dress in rags. They rubbed their faces with charcoal briquettes to make themselves look poor, dirty and hungry. Adults had decreed the play could not be put on in the barn because it smelled too bad, so it would be staged in the Bakken cabin. The kids rehearsed every day.

Marty was thrilled by this spontaneous effort. She loved watching what kids came up with. Little Joe and Zoe wrote it. Marty recognized the name of the play, "Synonym Toast," as something Zoe had made up. Zoe liked words, as did her father.

Sunday morning Gerald, Grace's husband arrived from Bemidji, with Dory, who had a summer job at a movie theater. She was lovely, with shiny highlights in her dark hair, her skin quite dark when she stood next to golden Zoe. Dory was clearly happy to be making money. All of the Hickmans went to mass that morning. They brought Kentucky fried chicken home to have with the corn on the cob Marty boiled up for Sunday dinner.

And then it was time for the play! Everyone gathered at the Bakken cabin. The audience sat near the fireplace looking up at the open loft with its ladder. Even Marie had made her way across the path to the Bakken cabin on Paul's arm and sat in the best seat, a cushioned rocker.

The kids stayed "off-stage" in the bedroom while Joe came out and introduced the play and its setting. Natasha played the villain of the piece in an elegant gown, the landlord who threw the family out of their home, making them into hobos. Their belongings were done up in bundles and handkerchiefs tied to sticks as they traveled. Part of the time they lived in a boxcar and made food for themselves around a pretend fire.

"I wish I had some synonym toast," wailed Jason as they sat around the campfire. He, among the younger kids, liked performing the best. Small Jeanne and Benjy looked appropriately sad and hungry in their rags and charcoaled faces. Andre had opted out altogether and was the stage manager, moving props back and forth.

"Someday," said Zoe, the mother. "Some day we'll have a proper tea, with proper cinnamon toast." In the end, the family made it to California, where there was work for Joe, the father, and all the kids picked fruit!

In the end, everyone lined up across the stage and sang together, "Oh we ain't got a barrel of money, maybe we're ragged and funny, but we travel along, singing our song, side by side." Marty was impressed! They seemed to know all the words!

After their bows, Marty and Grace stepped up to play their part, serving lemonade and the chocolate chip cookies Marty had made.

"We've got one more act," cried Joe. "The most impressive guitar player in our midst, my grandpa! Once a member of The Dots, and then of the folk duo Marie and Paul Mikkelson. I could go on, but I won't," said Joe, releasing the stage to Paul.

Paul stepped out in front, bringing a stool on which to rest his weaker leg. He looked, as he always did these days, a bit long-haired, bearded and scruffy. Not like a high school teacher! "I had plenty of time in Oaxaca last winter," he said. "So I worked on learning a little Spanish guitar, with encouragement from my partner." He nodded to Marie as he strummed a bit of what sounded definitely Spanish. "This is a song everyone recognizes," he said. "Malagueña."

Paul played the notes, picking with his right hand instead of strumming, interspersing it with percussive techniques. All with his right hand. Marty tried to see what he was doing, but couldn't tell exactly why it sounded so Spanish. The minor chords, she thought. A bit of a Mexican flavor had not hurt Paul one bit. He seemed more intense, lit from within. Perhaps Marie's light was going into him as well.

"I don't know what this is called," said Paul as he played another. "I learned it from a guy in a park. Helped my Spanish a little, but not much. He kept telling me to take it slow at first."

It made Marty think of tai chi. She had had to start so slowly, doing unfamiliar moves before they became normal. Paul was as self-deprecating as any of them were, thought Marty. His guitar sounded very credible. She shared a complicit smile with Doug, who insisted that the Mikkelsons kept their lights under bushels. But that was the Scandinavian way. No tree should be taller than any other tree, it was said.

The kids were respectfully quiet, but after the second song, Benjy got up and wandered off and Jeanne followed him. Paul bowed and thanked everyone for their attention. He was followed on stage by Joe and Zoe, who introduced the actors of the play who were still left. They looked so comfortable together, Marty thought they didn't want to leave!

"A swim might clean up that charcoal," said Doug. "Anyone want to come?" Most everyone did. "Come on Marty," said Doug. "You too!"

Marty looked over at Grace. Marty was lazy about swimming, but it was fun to be in the lake now and then and the late afternoon was the best time. Grace nodded at her. "Go ahead Marty!" said Grace. "I can manage!" Gerald stood behind her, nodding in agreement. After chicken dinner, leftovers would do for the evening meal. No need to worry.

Marty changed into her bathing suit with Doug and wrapped a towel around her middle. The light was yellow-green down at the lake. "Jump in!" said Doug as he dived into the deeper water at the end of the dock.

But that was more than Marty could do. She left her sunglasses on her towel and brought a pair of goggles out with her. She slipped down into the chilly water at the end of the dock. The water all over felt wonderful as she began paddling to warm herself up. She had never really learned to swim, partly because of this lake! It was so shallow that even quite far out, a swimmer could just stand up. She put on the goggles and swam down into the water, holding her breath. She swam around Doug's legs, teasing him. She surfaced, wrapping her arms around Doug who had Benjy on his shoulders.

"A fishy creature is after us!" said Doug. He went swimming away with Benjy yelling excitedly. Doug was an excellent swimmer. "It's all about trust," he had told Marty. But it didn't help. She had never learned to breathe. She dived down, swimming along the bottom in the yellow-green light, looking at the seaweed, the ridges of sand, holding her breath. All around her kids were playing, shouting and splashing. "Happy as clams," thought Marty. And there was the bivalve shell of a clam. She grabbed it and surfaced.

5

It was Tuesday. Line sat down companionably beside Poppa, who was reading the *New York Times* with his cup of coffee. When the phone rang, Line picked it up.

"You might want to turn on the television," said Stephen's diffident voice. He was already at the university on a chilly September morning. "Planes have flown into the World Trade Towers in New York. Seems to be a terrorist act."

Line looked at Poppa, repeating what Stephen had said. "Thank you, Stephen," said Line. "We'll go have a look."

Poppa, with Line right behind him, went down to his den and turned on the tv. Smoke billowed out of the large square frame of one of the twin towers of the World Trade Center. "Where's the other one?" asked Poppa, puzzled. It was hard to take in what was happening. In front of their eyes, the second tower imploded, collapsing in clouds of dust. "Oh my God," said Poppa.

Newscasters tried to report, but no one knew anything. Panic crept into the voice of one of them and he was cut off by the CNN anchorman. Rounding up the news, they reported that a plane had crashed into the Pentagon and that another fatal crash had happened in Pennsylvania. It began to appear that the events had been coordinated. The Federal Aviation Authority had ordered all civilian planes out of the sky and was turning back any flights from other countries.

"So many people in those buildings," said Poppa. "I could see them from the top floor of my building in Brooklyn!"

Line felt sick. The news began to replay what had happened earlier, planes flying into the upper floors of the twin towers, footage of people jumping to their deaths from windows backed by flames. No one seemed to have any real information about what had happened, but everyone agreed it was devastating. Who knew how many thousands of people had been killed. And was it over, or was it just beginning?

Leaving Poppa to watch, Line went back to the kitchen. She heard noises from the direction of Ivy's room and went in to tell her daughter.

Ivy, dressed in jeans and a hooded sweatshirt, her golden hair pulled tight into a ponytail, was packing a backpack to take to the university where she worked with the costuming department in the theater arts building.

"I wonder if you should go to school today," Line mused. "Let's call your Dad to see what he thinks."

When they called, Stephen seemed to think everything was outwardly fine. "But no one is getting anything done," he said. "Just listening and watching. You could just as well stay home."

Ivy felt strongly about the dance performance she was designing costumes for, however. "I'm going," she said. "I'm sure it's fine." She went out to the garage to get her bike. Line watched her cruise down the hill.

It was a very surreal day. Line too had work to do, hospice patients she needed to see. But everywhere she went, people were having a hard time concentrating, their ears pressed to a radio or television.

One of Line's patients required only routine care. The other, a woman in her 50's named Sheila lay in a hospital bed in her parents' house. Her breathing was full of mucous, shallow and sporadic.

"She spoke to me yesterday," said her distraught mother. "But today I can't understand what she is saying. She is talking though. To someone."

Line administered a bit of morphine, gently rubbing it on Sheila's gums to ease her breathing. Sheila was full of cancer and reminded Line of her sister-in-law Marie. They were close in age and Line knew that Marie too was not far from her end. Marie and Paul were in St. Paul, in the apartment beneath Ellie's house. Line planned a trip to see them, to help if she could, but now what? All planes had been grounded.

As Line bathed Sheila, she felt Sheila's heart suddenly quit. Her breathing too, the room filling with quiet. Line comforted Sheila's mother and her father, who had been watching television in another room. Sheila's death, long anticipated, was accomplished. Her father's face looked long and somber. Line did not ask him about what was happening in New York.

Sheila was a retiring office worker, who lived with her cat, long since given away. She had no children. Line called the coroner. He sent over an officer with forms to fill out and Line stayed to help smooth the process. She was somewhat used to it, but Sheila's aging parents seemed flustered, unprepared. Line helped them call an undertaker. Two men in black coats came with a gurney, zipped Sheila's body into a black bag and took it away. It was a fitting metaphor for the day.

That night, when Line and Stephen, Poppa and Ivy convened for dinner, everyone told what they had heard. Bush was in Florida, reading to elementary school children at the time. Dick Cheney had retreated to the presidential bunker. Opinions and fears flowed freely. It was assumed that Osama bin Laden, leader of al-Qaeda which had carried out other bombings, was behind the attacks. A great deal of coordinated commitment would have been required.

Poppa was anguished. "New York is my town!" he said. "I feel like I should be there." He flew once a year to meet with the property manager of his Brooklyn building and any of the old friends he could find. Admittedly, they were dying off.

Stephen looked at Line. "I don't think that's a good idea," he said.

"I feel like I want to sit shiva for New York," said Poppa, referring to a Jewish tradition of mourning.

"You can do that," said Line. "We can all do that."

Stephen was angry. "That jerk Cheney," he said. "He wants a war. That's how Republicans make money! I wouldn't be surprised if they were in on it somehow." The Bush family was known to have Saudi connections. Bin Laden was from a very wealthy Saudi family.

But all of this was jumping to conclusions. What was really uncertain was whether more terrorist acts would follow. "It's surprising how our life goes on," said Line. "All of our resources intact." She told them about Sheila's death, how the coroner and the undertakers had been available as usual.

"The terrorists are trying to get us to become fearful," said Ivy, repeating what her friends at school were saying. "If we become fearful, if we change our lives to suit them, they have won."

"That's exactly it, Ivy," said Poppa. "Nail on the head there."

The world did seem different, however, in the days to come. The National Guard was called out to surround highly visible targets, such as the Golden Gate Bridge. American flags flew half staff in front of many buildings and houses, and Line noticed that one of their favorite small restaurants, run by an Iranian and his Italian wife, had hung a huge American flag as a banner, trying to claim their patriotism. Clearly tensions and fears were running high.

In New York and at the Pentagon rescue workers braved horrible, noxious fumes and crumbling structures to look for survivors. Many police and firemen had died trying to rescue others. There were no survivors of United Flight 93, which went down in a field in Pennsylvania. Passengers had called relatives on their cell phones. They had stormed the cockpit and forced the plane, which was headed for Washington, D.C., down.

All four planes were flying toward California (presumably chosen for their heavy fuel loads), but Line did not know anyone who had lost a family member. On television, stories of victims and heroism prevailed, but Line did not watch. It seemed shameful to wallow in the tragedies of people she didn't know.

The Cohens all went about their daily lives as they normally did. There were no more obviously connected terrorist acts. As she watered her garden in the evening, Line's thoughts were with her children, all of them safe but farther away than Line liked.

Line's heart ached particularly for Heather, whom she saw the least of. She and Stephen had left Heather at home in college when they went to Scotland. When they got back, Heather went to Chile on an internship, and then, quite quickly, married and moved to Chile. She had just had her first baby. Line felt she had missed too much of Heather's young adulthood.

They did speak to Heather by phone, who was more worried about them than they were about her. "Everything is fine here," she said. "The baby is fine. We are all talking about New York." Line and Stephen reassured her, but Line was miserable. A phone call was short and Heather was so far away.

"If things settle down by Christmas," Stephen promised, "perhaps we could go see them." Line only nodded.

Fern had moved to Phoenix with little Sofia. She worked for the Arizona Museum of Natural History just outside of Phoenix, which had programs in archaeology: digging, preserving, curating and educating. Fern worked in the ceramics lab and had found a wealth of dedicated, interesting people there. She was happy. "And so is Sofia," she said. "She's the darling of the museum. It feels very safe here. We're just working on ancient history. No one cares about us!" said Fern. Line hoped this was true.

Christy worked with Hmong communities in St. Paul, at Minnesota senator Paul Wellstone's request. The Hmong refugees came from all over southeast Asia and had aided the United States in Vietnam and Laos. There were more than 60,000 of them and Paul Wellstone wanted to get them integrated politically. The Hmong, though cohesive and resident for more than twenty years, had high rates of poverty and low education levels. Christy too was happy, though the work was frustrating. "I'm learning to just hang out and listen," he said. "That's how I get in. Gangs are a response to being ignored."

After the phone call with Christy, Stephen huffed that Christy had always been great at "just hanging out." But Line reminded him that that was how grass roots organizing was done. Had he forgotten? Line had realized, to her great surprise, that the slight sourness between her husband and son was a result of jealousy. Over her! Christy had had Line to himself his first two years, before Line and Stephen reunited. The rift had never entirely healed.

With the equinox upon them, darkness grew more obvious in the mornings and the evenings. Line felt the poignancy of the seasonal in-drawing of the warmth and light. Vegetation was drying up, leaves on the trees burnt by the heat and the sun.

About terrorism, there was really nothing to be done. It was hard on Line. It was not her style. She liked to get in there, arms akimbo. "The mills of God grind slowly, but they grind exceeding small," Line thought to herself. Retribution would come. It was not up to them. Working in her garden was the best revenge. But the days continued, surreal, with a dual consciousness. Line was always thinking of people on the other side of the world while she lived her own life.

At night, family meals were festive with relief. Here they were, as if in wartime, enjoying peace and plenty in their own corner, while destruction surrounded them. Ivy lit candles against the growing twilight.

Stephen reported that one of his colleagues wanted to "nuke Afghanistan," where Osama bin Laden was reported to be living. The Afghanis refused to turn him over. "We took the guy on, but I imagine that's a possibility Cheney will consider."

The identities of the pilots who hijacked the planes all pointed to al-Qaeda backgrounds. The FBI and CIA moved in and rounded up people both suspicious and not. The assets of anyone remotely associated with al-Qaeda in the U.S. had been frozen. Security was being re-evaluated.

"One of my better friends lamented that the dedication and commitment of the terrorists had gone toward destruction, when it could have done so much good," said Poppa. "I respect him for this. But what's done is done."

"Intellectuals in New York are saying that public officials are hiding behind sanctimonious, reality-concealing rhetoric about patriotism and America's strength," said Stephen. "That we should realize that the attacks on us are a result of our own self-proclaimed superpower and aggression in the Middle East."

"Absolutely," said Poppa. "But others are beginning to talk about a 'war on terror.' In wars, the government pulls together. There's no chance that America is going to admit its mistakes right now."

"I told you they wanted a war," said Stephen. bitterly.

"This sounds like a hidden war," said Line. "Right in our own country." But it had always been so. "People just mouth what they've heard in the media. Lots of fears and opinions." No one knew what direction things would take. Line was not fearful but she did not like the pall that hung over everything. She tended to keep quiet and tried to stay present. Only time would tell what would happen out in the big world.

One evening, Ivy took Line into her room to show her the work she was doing for the student dance performance. "It has a California theme," said Ivy. "With music from Calexico, the Red Hot Chili Peppers, and Los Lobos. We're still doing that, but it's become more important," said Ivy. "Like a protest, like our own defiance of history and destiny," she said. "There's an atmosphere of 'seize the day' about it."

Ivy sat down at her drafting table and took out her sketchbook. "It's all about movement," she said. "With dance you want the costumes to flow with the emotions the dancers are showing. Color, lighting help you."

Line was impressed. Ivy's drawings were sketches, filled in with colored pencils, just suggestions. Tacked on the wall behind her were favorite photos from magazines.

"This is Calexico," said Ivy, hitting the buttons on her CD player. "I've been listening to it."

Strains of mordant guitar filled the room, backed by drums. "It sounds kind of Mexican," said Line. The strings split into a weird harmony. Line liked it.

"Like a street in the desert, yes," said Ivy. She pointed to sketches she was doing. "A hot night in LA. I don't really know what I'm doing. We all do it together. Sometimes the dancers come in wearing what they think would be the right thing, and we just modify it. They're making up the dances as they go along."

"Someone must coordinate what you're doing," said Line. "The director?"

"Yes. There's a director. She thinks the design of the whole thing, the dances, the costumes are important! The materials! Sometimes you want material to waft lightly around a dancer, and sometimes it needs to be heavy and swing out." Ivy showed Line the dance magazines full of photographs she had collected. "You never know how a costume is going to act. All you can do is try. That's the fun of it! We're using some denim, soft, old denim in these dances. And floaty, cheap-looking dresses for the girls. Southern California, you know."

"Who's that?" Line pointed to a photo on the wall of a rather scruffy-looking guy with an impish grin and a beard.

"He's the master," said Ivy. "Santo Loquasto. He designs for Twyla Tharp, Baryshnikov, the movies." She sighed. "Shows me how far I could go. In New York," she said. "Once. I hope they're okay." Ivy looked a little doubtful. If a pall lay over the west coast, it could only be a thousand times worse as you got closer to lower Manhattan where the horrible events had occurred.

The theater world was one Line didn't know. "When's the production?" she asked.

"In November," said Ivy. "But it isn't the only one. I'm working on other productions too. So much going on."

Line kissed Ivy's forehead. "I'm glad, my darling daughter," she said. "Takes your mind off things." She looked around the room. Ivy had never needed to be in front. She liked being in the background, subdued, contributing but not flashy. Her own clothes were simple, jeans and knit tops.

"Your aunt Hanna would be proud of you," said Line as she left, thinking about her youngest sister far away in upstate New York on a farm.

On Saturday, Line and Stephen joined Paul Lee and other old friends for a picnic. Under a mammoth old oak tree whose craggy limbs reached down all around them, they spread the food they had brought on a picnic table. Line had made a quiche, with bacon, eggs, cheese and cream in a pie shell. Plus she brought wine and a baguette. Other people spread out their offerings of deviled eggs, many salads, plates of ham, cookies.

It was a warm and windless day. Gold and deep auburn leaves added a visual warmth. Paul Lee had found the tree at the edge of Schwan Lake, a little southeast of Santa Cruz. He was working on what he called a "circle path" around the greenbelt of Santa Cruz.

Schwan Lake had been made when a highway was built between a lagoon and the ocean. It was in the process of losing its salinity. Beyond tall reeds Line noted it was full of a marsh pennywort. There was probably a lot more lake than it looked like.

Paul Lee called the group that had gathered "old timers," those who had been in on the experimental early phase of the university. Two of their number had died in the intervening years: Paul's great friend Page Smith had been the first provost of Cowell College and Stephen's mentor as a history professor and writer. Alan Chadwick had started the organic movement in California with his French intensive and biodynamic gardening methods. Chadwick left after three years when the university refused to make him the head of its agro-ecology programs. Both men were revered.

"I thought it would cheer us up to come out here by this lovely little lake under this oak," said Paul to his remaining friends, speaking gruffly through his white beard. He was a bear of a man, always trying to create or make something happen. He and Page Smith had been behind the homeless programs in Santa Cruz, and he was now in the process of getting his "circle walk" designated and mapped. "Nature can absorb a great deal," he said.

Line agreed. "It's such a lovely time of year too," she said. The sky seemed more intense to her and so did the colors. "It's like we've had our heads buried in the sand."

"Looks pretty normal on the outside, doesn't it," said Stephen. There were eight of them, drinking wine around a picnic table, all older by most standards. Stephen and Line were the youngest. They had come out when the university was just getting started, when, according to Paul Lee, there had been so much possibility for experiment and change.

"So does the university!" said Paul Lee. "Just what Ken Thimann wanted it to become. A research institution. But I can't help thinking what it might have been. I'm determined to keep Chadwick's memory alive. I'm trying to get an archive started. I've got boxes of letters and memorabilia stuffed away. For my money, Chadwick started the organic movement in California. I want that understood!"

"Get that stuff on line," said Ed, one of Paul's friends. "That's where it will be accessible to people."

"You're absolutely right," said Paul. "I've got someone working on that. Chadwick's interns are all over the place and they are making a difference. But I'd like to get them interviewed, get them to tell how it was to work with him."

"Remember when your colleague told you that Alan's garden was the single worst thing that had happened to the university!" Ed slapped his knee. "Because he was growing things without pesticides or chemical fertilizers! That's a great story!"

"The place already had a reputation as a bunch of hippies, basket weavers and such," said Paul Lee. "Chadwick didn't help. He couldn't even mention that he came out of the Rudolph Steiner school of thought! And he didn't. He just worked like the devil."

Line remembered that Alan could always be found, rain or shine, on the steep slope of the hill at the entrance to the university. He had brought a shovel and begun his garden. It was still there, but a pale copy of the old one. A sort of memorial. Line had worked with him a little, but she had had babies to worry about at the time.

"When you look at the university and what it has become," said Stephen, "which is a viable member of our powerful military industrial complex, you can see that alternatives might have been useful." Stephen had chosen history over activism, for the sake of his family. The historians' mantra was that, if you didn't study history you would be condemned to repeat it.

"Exactly what I've been saying," said Paul Lee. "The physicalist/vitalist conflict." The "old-timers" knew Paul's theories well. Self-selected, they pretty much agreed with him. In Paul's view, vitalist botany had lost out to the onslaught of exact mathematical physics over what counted for knowledge. "Earth Day helped," said Paul. "Got the toe of ecology in the door. But there is a long way to go."

"It all comes down to money," said Ed. "Botany doesn't command money. The military industrial complex runs on investment, and so does the university. Make people fearful and they will pay. That's what's going on right now."

"Al Gore had some good arguments for putting money into ecology," said Ann, looking down into her glass of chilled wine. "Drumming up the fear of climate change."

"From bin Laden's point of view," said Stephen, "we are morally corrupt. And we have exported our culture throughout the world."

"Makes us question," said Ed. "That's for certain."

Line was proud of Stephen. He had acquired the necessary impartiality of a historian.

But there had always been hidden wars, either at the university or in the world. According to Paul Lee, the military industrial complex had killed cock robin, to the great detriment of the earth. He saw Alan Chadwick as the exponent of the vitalist philosophy, an exponent of Rudolf Steiner and Goethe; whereas Ken Thimann, also a botanist but Alan's nemesis, came from the exact sciences, from Newton, and had built the university's reputation on the making of synthetic science.

Line saw the conflict through her nursing. She felt that putting her hands on patients was necessary, healing. That herbs and acupuncture were often less invasive medicine. These things couldn't be measured. But Line didn't discount western medicine, its surgery, painkillers, diagnostics, chemotherapy and radiation. The two kinds of medicine worked better together, rather than in conflict.

The blue of the lake beckoned Line away from all the talk. She stood up, leaving her wineglass on the table. Betsy, Ed's wife, followed her.

"Men," said Betsy. "Think they can solve the problems of the world." She laughed. "Women just go about doing it!"

But that wasn't it either, thought Line. We're humans, she thought. Humanity had never been peaceful, necessarily. "They do have their soapboxes," said Line. There were eucalyptus trees along the lake, she was happy to see. She walked over to a place beside the reeds where she could get at the pennywort. A white egret stood out against the green at the edge, its pliant neck folded against itself.

Line leaned down and picked a bit out of the lake. "I think this pennywort might be the same thing as the Asian herb gotu kola," she said. She chewed a bit of it, experimentally. The fan-shaped little green leaves didn't have much of a taste.

"What's it for?" asked Betsy.

"It's used for arthritis," said Line. "Swelling and joint pain." She pulled some more out of the lake. "People make a tea out of it," she said. "It's anti-bacterial and anti-inflammatory, used for wound healing, I think. I'm not sure this is the same as the Asian variety, though." She resolved to go home and look it up.

"I live near here," said Betsy. "Bill Simpkins who runs the swimming pool complex over there wants to clean it up so the lake can be used for recreation. He's been working on it for a while. He says this is an invasive marsh plant that'll take over the whole lake!"

Line nodded. "It's probably helped de-salinize the lake," she said. "Once the ocean was pushed out." People thought one thing, nature did another. Stephen was right, thought Line. Only time would tell. She did feel refreshed however, by the birds singing, the reeds at the edge of the lake, the lovely fall colors. For her, the pall was lifting a little.

6

By December, Marie could not get out of bed. Once again, Paul and Marie were living in the apartment beneath Ellie's house. Paul called in hospice workers and a hospital bed was set up in the main room. Nurses came in daily. Line flew out to help them settle into the routine.

Marie's breathing was ragged and uncertain, but she did not want an oxygen tube. Paul could also see in her eyes that she was sometimes in pain. "Headache," she told him. But she was resigned and patient with everything that was happening to her.

"Let them give her morphine," Line told Paul. "As much as she needs. It helps with that uncomfortable breathing and pain." She thought the cancer was metastasizing to Marie's brain.

Paul made chicken soup, and brought trays in so he and Line could sit around Marie's bed while they ate. Flat lozenges of low-angled noon sunlight crept in to the warm room and lay on the bed, the center of their little universe. Marie took a few spoonfuls of soup from Line's hand. Line made it all seem normal.

"Marie's sister Gilberte came last month," Paul told Line while Marie rested. "Down from Quebec. It was good to get news of Marie's family." He sat in the rocker Mother had once used to ease her back. "But the most wonderful thing was Cheryl. Cheryl's family rescued Marie when she lived in Los Angeles and got her back on her feet when she was very ill. We keep in touch with them, of course. And Marie talked to Cheryl on the telephone. I was so glad she called in the fall when they could still have a good talk."

After a week, Christy, Line's son, collected Line to take her to the airport. Paul hadn't seen him in a while. "How are you doing?" he asked Christy.

"Could be better," said Christy, who stood, thin and attractive, his clothes hanging off him. "We've been bombing the hell out of Afghanistan," he said bitterly. The U.S. had convinced NATO to help with the effort to smoke the Taliban out of the country. They would not give up Osama bin Laden.

"Sounds like it has been effective," said Paul, mildly.

"The Afghans will never quit fighting," said Christy. "It's their life. They've just retreated to the hills. We're being our usual belligerent selves and we don't care about the civilian casualties."

"Come on, Christy," said Line, as she zipped the bag she had brought. "I can't be late for my flight." To Paul she said, "Security takes forever now. You have to be there a couple of hours early!" More softly she said, "Take care of your lovely girl. Our thoughts are with you." Line's eyes betrayed what she and Paul both knew. Marie would not live much longer.

Paul hugged Line and Christy as they went out into the cold air. "Chess game one of these days?" asked Christy.

"Sure," said Paul noncommittally. He had very little concentration for such a thing, but he could try.

In the next weeks, Paul could hear Ellie bustling about upstairs, making Christmas preparations. Paul did not have much heart for it. It was all he could do to keep groceries in the house and cook.

At night Paul lit the four candles the flames of which powered tinkling gilt angels around in a circle, bars below them hitting the bells. He read from the Psalms for Marie, the most comforting ones he could find. "The Lord is my shepherd. He maketh me to lie down in green pastures, he leadeth me beside the still waters, he restoreth my soul," he read from the thin pages of an old King James Bible. Afterwards, he climbed into the hospital bed with Marie for a bit and held her thin body close, their upper bodies against the raised mattress, the plastic beneath them crackling.

"Mon cher mari," whispered Marie after a coughing fit. "I've tried to take care of you, and now you have to take care of me."

"It's my honor," said Paul softly, stroking her face. Time felt very strange. He did not know what day it was, or what time. Twilight came early and the nights were long, Paul supposed, but he wasn't sure. How to make the most of the moments, he wondered. During the day he played his guitar and sang the songs he and Marie had sung together. Paul felt happy when they were alone. His and Marie's two conscious minds blended in the room's stillness.

On Christmas Eve, the sounds of footsteps resounded over their heads as people gathered for dinner and the Scandinavian festivities Ellie never failed to prepare.

Paul put cushions in the wheelchair and lifted Marie into it. He wrapped two blankets around her. He did not dare carry Marie upstairs because he was awkward on stairs even without a burden, his good and bad legs uneven. Instead he wheeled Marie out the front door, intending to go up the walk to the main door of Ellie's house.

"Stop, stop!" said Marie in the most intense whisper she could muster as the cold air hit her face.

Paul knew what she was feeling. It was snowing a little and the air was so fresh. Snowflakes fell on Marie's hair and blankets. But Paul didn't want Marie to sit out in the cold. He turned toward the house and pushed the wheelchair up the long curved sidewalk.

The rooftop edge of Ellie's house dripped with tiny Christmas lights, there was a large wreath on the door and in the window they could see the many-colored lights on the Christmas tree. Paul pushed Marie's chair into Ellie's living room where a gas fire burned and Christmas carols streamed out over the stereo speakers. Welcoming faces greeted them. Under the Christmas tree, which reached to the ceiling, were piles of presents. After their quiet, austere existence, it felt strange to burst into these warm colors and a cacophony of people.

The people were all family: Christy, Paul's nephew; Ellie's daughters Brenda and Rhonda; Rhonda's husband and two small children; as well as Bruce and Ellie. The adults were deferential to Marie's thin candle of spirit. The little girl and boy were full of excitement, just old enough for Christmas to mean something to them. Marie's face shone as she greeted them, but Paul, watchful, did not leave her side.

While the others ate, Paul and Marie sat in a corner of the living room sharing a plate of turkey and mashed potatoes with gravy and Brussels sprouts. The music was from an album performed by Placido Domingo and French and Mexican soloists, backed by the Vienna Symphony. Lush music of all kinds, classical and pop Christmas songs filled the room with the wash of strings behind them. Paul could tell Marie liked it, but also that she was growing tired.

"We're going back," said Paul to the assembled company who were eating in the dining room.

"Oh, Paul," said Ellie, rising. "Don't you want some pie? We have pumpkin pie, and almond bark and cookies!" She went into the kitchen with Paul, who filled up a plate with pie and cookies.

"Thank you all! And merry Christmas!" he said, as he left. "God be with and bless you all."

"Can you hold this?" he asked Marie, putting the plate in her lap. He wheeled her out the front door and down the walk as slowly as he dared. Night had settled in. Snowflakes could still be seen drifting down under the porch lights.

"Are you okay?" asked Paul as he shifted Marie into the bed.

"Yes," said Marie in a weak voice. "Such wonderful music. I loved it." She coughed and the phlegm in her throat made her breathing raw.

Paul could still hear music alongside the talk and clatter of people on the floor above. "Nothing beats a symphony sometimes," he said. He covered Marie up and let her rest.

That week Grace and her family came for a visit. It was a three-hour drive from Bemidji, which Paul appreciated. When they were expected to arrive, Paul gave Marie a morphine tablet and swabbed her gums with morphine, as the hospice nurse had shown him. He was trying to find the fine line where Marie would not be in pain, but also not too sleepy.

All five kids stood around Marie's bed to wish her a merry Christmas. Grace asked them to tell Marie their Christmas pieces, what they had each done in the church Christmas pageant. Gerald and Paul lifted Jeanne and little Benjamin up, as the hospital bed was so high. They sang together: "Away in a manger, no crib for a bed."

But Marie's face was damp and Paul could see it was an effort for Marie to respond. She reached her thin arms out to them, trying to hug and kiss her grandchildren.

Gerald gently drew them away. "You kids have too much energy!" he said. "Let your Mother be with Grandma a little." Paul took them upstairs to say hello to Ellie and Bruce and see the Christmas tree, and then sent them out for a walk around the neighborhood.

Grace sat with Marie. Paul hung out nearby in case they needed anything. Marie was barely awake; her eyelids kept falling shut as Grace whispered to her.

The weather was clear enough, but Gerald didn't want to stay long. As a pilot of small planes, weather was his life. He gathered up his family, for the long drive home.

Paul was grateful. "Glad to see you!" he said. "But Marie's pretty sleepy these days."

"Had to come," said Gerald, standing beside his tearful wife.

"Bonne année!" said Grace and the kids all chimed in: "Happy new year!"

"Headache?" asked Paul when he saw the hurt in Marie's eyes after they left. Her graying curls stuck to her face. She nodded and he gave her another tab of morphine. "Just rest," he told her.

On New Year's eve, the big house was utterly silent. Ellie and Bruce had gone out to a party. Paul put classical music on, Beethoven's "Ninth Symphony," with only German words in it. Marie seemed to like it, her body moving slightly to the music. Paul felt it inside of him, a message of power and joy. But Marie was not very conscious. The hospice nurse had told Paul it would not be long now. Marie spent most of the day in a half sleep.

A few days later, Paul woke in the dark. Something seemed wrong. The room was entirely silent. He went over to the hospital bed. Marie was not breathing and her heart was not beating. Paul breathed a long breath out himself. Without effort, Marie had simply slipped away. The long vigil was over.

Paul called the hospice office, which sent someone over to confirm as well as help him make other necessary calls. By afternoon, Marie's body was gone, the hospital equipment was gone. Paul was alone. He sat with his guitar, playing. "But you see those people running through the station? I told you, I told you, I told you, I was one of those," he sang in the words of Leonard Cohen. Marie had predicted it. She was one of those.

The memorial service at Gloria Dei Lutheran church was attended by most of the members of the choir and Paul's nearby relatives. Grace and her kids didn't come. It was too blustery a day for the long drive. Paul himself was unable to speak, but Ellie and Christy each stood up to say something about Marie's value to the family. Such a bright spirit she had been.

Afterward, Paul was really alone. Ellie and Bruce went to work every day and Paul lay in bed, listening to the January wind howling around the house, which creaked and groaned. It wasn't a very snowy year, actually quite a mild winter. Paul didn't really know. Everything had gone into taking care of Marie for so long that he didn't know what to do with himself.

Paul gave himself up to mourning. At last he had no one to scare, no one to shore up. No one cared what he did. He could go as low as he wanted. He put his arms around a pillow to represent the non-existent Marie and bawled as long and as often as he needed to. He ignored the phone, waiting until he was good and ready to talk to people. Pent up emotions surged through him and he let them take over. Paul had tried to prepare himself for this time that he knew would come. But it was not like anything he expected. Time felt vastly empty without Marie to talk to and to share it.

After a week, Paul began to feel less hollow. He knew that the well of himself would fill over time. He was grateful that he had plenty of time to think, however. All that winter, he'd been wondering about time. Perhaps we aren't able to perceive time well enough, he thought. He knew time was a human creation, made up of people's records of the seasons, the planets and stars above them. But perhaps there was more to it. Perhaps Marie did exist in some other time that Paul couldn't perceive.

It did not make sense that the hard-won spirits and intelligence that people developed over their lifetimes should just disappear. In physics, Paul had taught the law of the conservation of energy which stated that energy could be neither created nor destroyed. It could only be transformed. He knew this law had been modified by Einstein's general theory of relativity and quantum mechanics, which he did not really understand. But surely nature must do something with the extraordinary spirits people developed over their lives.

No one had ever come back from the dead, however. Paul received a metal box with Marie's ashes in it after her cremation. It was heavy, but that was because the metal was heavy. Paul did not open it. Marie herself could not have made many ashes. In the spring he would take the box to the lake and dust the ashes into the woods where Marie and he had spent so many fine summers.

Paul tried to establish stricter habits for himself: making his bed, straightening the house, cooking, going out. One evening Ellie invited him upstairs for pizza with Bruce.

Paul was astonished by the smells of the tomato sauce and spiced sausage on the pizza. He had been so sunken into himself that he hardly registered the outside world.

"Have a glass of wine," said Bruce, pouring Paul a goblet of a dark red from a seductive bottle. "Do you good."

They sat on stools next to a high kitchen counter in the bright light of the kitchen, digging pizza out of a box like a bunch of teenagers. Ellie and Bruce chattered about their work, about their bridge club, about the church. Paul listened, knowing they were trying to get him back to the real world. "The choir director has been asking about you," Ellie told him.

Paul blinked and nodded. "Thank you," he said. "I'll go to rehearsal this week." The warmth of the wine settled into his body, making him feel fuzzy and relaxed.

"You should come to my gym," said Bruce. "I can't get through the winter without it. And it's great in the summer too."

"Singing makes me feel really good. It's almost like exercise," said Paul. "And I really like walking, even now in the winter. I'll get out more," he promised them, and himself.

"Life is for the living," said Bruce, nodding sagely.

Paul felt like he had been knocked sideways. Perhaps it was true. Bruce had risen into the executive branch of 3M Corporation, a businessman who had lived in Italy and Chile without changing one whit. He was smart about money, liked jazz and was an upstanding member of his church, but Paul did not have much in common with Bruce. Still, as Bruce tried to drag him back to the community, Paul was grateful.

"More pizza? Salad?" asked Ellie, bustling about. When she sat down again she said, "Mother liked the widow and widower's group at church."

Paul smiled. He should have known it was coming. "Thank you, Ellie," he said. "I'll think about it."

"What are your plans?" asked Ellie.

Paul thought rapidly. He did have plans and Ellie and Bruce had a right to know them. "You guys have been so great," he said. Ellie and Bruce had not charged him and Marie rent all this time. "I'd like to go stay at the cabin again this summer, give myself time to think about things. But I can't go just yet. I can pay some rent if I stay another couple of months," he said. The cabin was large and the walls thin, uninsulated. It would not be possible to heat it enough to live there until April or May.

"We're not worried about that," said Ellie. "We're just wondering what you plan to do. I know you have some website contracts. Are they enough?"

"Enough for now," said Paul. "I'd like to get a handle on the cabin this summer. See what can be done with it. Get rid of some of the stuff that's in too poor shape to be used. And maybe next winter I'll get an apartment in Bemidji, or something." Yep, those were his plans, Paul thought to himself. As good as any other. He was homeless, once again.

Ellie sighed. "Oh," she said, as if it were a problem. "The cabin." She looked at Bruce. Obviously, they shared the sentiment.

The winter continued, alternating freezing sunshine with grey days of snow. Paul hung out on web design forums, trying to keep up with the rapidly expanding tools. Website design was something he was able to charge a reasonable price for, while working at home. Search engine optimization was the current buzz phrase. Paul's HTML was getting better. His websites looked good, but what was the use of a website if no one could find it. He studied the different methods of moving a website up into the algorithms of search engines. A new one called Google had captured people's imagination.

At choir, Paul handed out his card which pointed to his website as a demonstration. One of the choir members had a small side business making wooden furniture. He asked Paul to get him a domain and find him a server, as well as design a website. When Paul did that, his name was passed to the other participants in a craft club. All of a sudden Paul had as much work as he wanted.

In the afternoons, Paul walked all over St. Paul. He was feeling the loss of Archie, too, but he did not want to get another dog until he felt more certain of himself. What was he up to? Who was he? What should he be doing?

January was a study in solid water. Everywhere steam poured out of heating vents and factories; different kinds of ice made walking hazardous; frost crystals gathered in windows and on plants; and there were enough kinds of snow that Paul understood why the native Alaskans had so many names for it. Paul helped shovel snow, but Bruce preferred his snow blower, getting out after a snowstorm and making a huge racket.

The Mississippi curled in an odd way around St. Paul, flowing south, then east and even north around the small city. It was too large to freeze, of course. St. Paul had begun as a fort at the confluence of the Minnesota and the Mississippi rivers. It predated its great twin, Minneapolis, though it was smaller. Both cities were thriving, full of parks and trees, lakes and rivers. The sky was interesting in January also. Often leaden grey, but the cloud cover sometimes broke up, letting in light and color.

Paul went out to Minnehaha Falls park, where a creek entered the big Mississippi. He walked behind the falls, its wall of bluegreen ice gorgeous in the sun. Where the creek fell over rocks was a beautiful series of icicles. The park had been engineered, of course, as had most of the rivers in the cities. Data processing might pay the bills, Paul thought, but he was more interested in the outside world, the geography which resulted from the receding of glaciers, the particular botany and biology of the area, species, weather. No one really has to worry about me, he thought. He was in the real world. It was just that he had backed out of the social world for the time being.

One afternoon, Paul called Marty back. She had been trying to reach him for weeks.

"Oh Paul," said Marty's voice. "I've been thinking so much about you. Remembering the years that I was alone. And now, I'm surrounded, happy; and you're by yourself."

"I've been remembering how you talked about your tai chi practice," said Paul. He was nested into a big comfy chair with a woolen blanket keeping his legs warm after a cold walk. "How it shored up the rest of your life."

"Yes," said Marty. "It still does, though I don't do as much tai chi as I used to. But I think about it, my posture, the way I move. I'm still trying to be impeccable, as far as I can. That's a practice, believe me, in this big family."

"I've gotten so empty," said Paul. "I'm being careful. What I let into my life now, will fill it. So I'm being careful. Thinking about time a lot. How we perceive time."

"That's a big subject!" said Marty. "I hardly have any! Nothing to think about!"

"Oh, I'm making the most of it," said Paul. "All I can do."

"Come out when you have a chance, Paul," said Marty. "We would all love to see you. California is wonderful, any time of year."

"Yes," said Paul. "I'll think about it." He didn't want to make any promises.

Christy called, asking again for a game of chess. Paul was certain Line had sent him to spy on him. But that was okay. Paul did not mind a little supervision from his sisters.

Christy brought beer and chicken wings. It made Paul smile. The two of them sat in the kitchen, hunkered over a table, the smell of the spicy chicken wings unctuous and comforting. "This reminds me of when you came to live with us in Ely," said Paul. He did not say it made him wish that Marie would walk through the door, coming from some errand.

"Yes," said Christy. "You didn't know then that I'd make a Minnesotan, did you!"

"Nope," said Paul. "But I guess stranger things have happened." He got out the chess pieces and set them up, king, queen, knights, bishops, rooks. They were comforting too, had been around for thousands of years.

"I'm getting to the point where I get pressure to settle down," said Christy. He picked up Paul's guitar and strummed on it experimentally. "Still in tune," he said. He put it down. "Girlfriends, and stuff."

"We liked that girl Emily," said Paul. Christy had brought Emily to the lake one summer.

"I'm not much of a prospect," said Christy. "And when it comes down to it, it scares the be-Jesus out of me." He shook his head.

"I wouldn't worry about it," said Paul. "How old are you?"

"Thirty-three," said Christy.

"When a relationship takes over your life, you'll know," Paul said. "I don't do anything until something really insists." He had met Marie in his 20's, he thought. Twenty-six years they had had. Paul remembered that Christy liked to play white, and Paul certainly felt black enough these days. "White?" he asked, turning the board around.

"Sure," said Christy. "And how are you doing?" He moved a pawn out into the mid-space.

"Don't know yet," said Paul. "When I do, I'll tell you." He smiled at Christy. He didn't like to let his conscious mind control him. He was digging deeper to find out how he really felt. Chess was a good thing to occupy his puny little rational mind. "Thanks for coming over," Paul said. "I appreciate the diversion. You're still working for Wellstone, right?"

"Yup," said Christy. "Saw a bit of him when he was home for the holidays. Great family. His work is so important now with Cheney running the country!" Christy looked contemptuous.

Paul paused and moved a black knight. He had known Christy would have political opinions. Paul himself did not think along those lines. He was pleased to see Christy though. Aside from the hollowness at his center, Christy reminded him that he was still an uncle, a brother, a grandfather.

7

Marty hovered in the kitchen, watching as Doug directed the morning concert. He was frying pancakes on a gas grill just outside the kitchen door. Marty had helped Zoe make the batter for the famous Mikkelson pancakes, showing her how to measure the dry ingredients first, then pour in the melted butter, beaten eggs and buttermilk, mixing them, but not enough to kill the rising action of the baking powder. Pancakes were a celebration, made on days when the family could eat breakfast together.

Zoe stirred the maple syrup on the stove while Marty and Nic cut up bananas and strawberries. "It's boiling up!" said Zoe as bubbles threatened to rise out of the little pan and the sweet smell of burnt caramel rose in the air.

"Take if off the burner!" said Marty. The teakettle was also starting to erupt. Marty poured hot water into two teapots and put the teakettle back on the burner. She poured the water out of the pots and put loose lapsang souchong tea in one of them. Boiling water poured over it released the smoky scent of Marty's favorite black tea. She let it steep a little, but not enough to make the tea bitter.

"I need a butter person," called Doug. Natasha and Jason ran out to help him, but Natasha got there first. She slathered butter between cooked pancakes as Doug took them off the griddle. He put a tall stainless steel bowl over them, to keep them warm. No one could eat until all the pancakes had been cooked and everyone sat down at the table.

The air was chilly and damp around the edges in April. It was a Saturday, spring break, and everyone was excited. The plan was to drive down to southern California and hand off the kids to Mackenzie and her boyfriend, who had gotten tickets to Disneyland for the coming week. Marty and Doug had the week to themselves.

Marty poured two blue and white Chinese teacups of the fragrant tea and took one out to Doug.

"Okay, Jason," said Doug. "Last pancake. Shall we make a tai chi pancake?" He held Jason up and helped him drizzle the last batter into the shape of a figure doing a single whip posture.

"I see it, I see it!" said Jason. "He's doing this!" He scrambled down and imitated the posture he had seen Marty and Doug trying to perfect.

Doug turned the last pancake over and when it was done, turned off the gas. He triumphantly bore in the tall plate of pancakes and everyone sat down. He smiled at Marty, who sat at the end of the table. She was excited too. Breakfast was celebratory.

"I told you we should have made three recipes," said Doug, playfully, when all the pancakes had been decked in fruit and maple syrup and scarfed up.

Marty shook her head, smiling. "We will eat again, someday," she said. "I promise." Two recipes seemed like a lot to her. But Doug was always ready to have more of everything. Marty didn't want to have leftovers.

"So, everybody packed?" asked Doug.

"Yup," said Natasha. "We packed last night."

"I could hardly sleep!" said Jason. "I can't wait to try all the rides!"

The kids had heard about Disneyland from their friends. Doug had visited, when he was a little kid. But Marty never had and didn't want to. She was glad Mackenzie was doing the honors, though both she and Doug were a little nervous about it.

"What could happen?" asked Doug, when they discussed the invitation. Mackenzie did not often request to have the kids, but Doug and Marty did not know this new boyfriend, Clay Burns, a music producer. It was hard to say no, nevertheless. "If they live in Santa Monica, he can't be that much of a loser," Doug told Marty. Disneyland was reportedly very good at working with crowds and had thick security.

"It's a long drive," Doug cautioned the kids. "But it's cool. A good day for it." After dropping the kids, Marty and Doug would take their time driving back along the coast, visiting a couple of wineries.

It was a long day. Doug drove the quickest way, down the interstate highway #5, stopping for burritos at a small Mexican restaurant. Marty was encouraged by the desert plants growing along the road. The air grew warmer and drier. She remembered driving down by herself to visit Nathan years ago. "Grapevine?" she asked Doug, when they abruptly came off the flat valley to a stretch of steep road.

"Yep," said Doug. "We're going to wind up through the Tehachapis and then down."

Marty was always thrilled by the names of places that appeared in songs and movies. "You should tell the kids," she said. "It's their California heritage after all."

Doug stopped the car at a pass near the top and everyone got out to look around at the vast hills stretching in every direction. They were mostly brown, but had a flush of spring green, as well as the sage colored pines and grey-green chaparral.

"California's really big," said Jason. He had been sleeping and his eyes were heavy, his skin wrinkled.

They arrived in the evening at a narrow frame house sandwiched between other houses on the crowded streets of Santa Monica. Old and new white-painted houses were right next to each other, with a few old trees here and there and a palm tree up the street. The town felt claustrophobic to Marty, compared to their own spacious ranch. The kids were a bit subdued as they collected their things from the back of the van.

Clay, who looked like a well-off golfer in a pink knit shirt with a little crocodile on it, was affable, hand outstretched. Mackenzie fluttered and cooed over the kids. "Zoe, you're so pretty!" she said. "And you've all grown so much!"

"Come in for a drink?" Clay asked Doug and Marty.

"No thanks," said Doug, a bit grimly. "Take care of each other," he said as he hugged each of the kids. Marty hugged them too. She did not know about all the freight that Mackenzie carried for Doug.

"The ocean's only a few blocks away," Mackenzie said, shepherding the kids into the house. "We'll go down after dinner."

"I wonder how long that'll last," Doug said sardonically, as he and Marty walked back to the car. He wanted to have as little to do with Mackenzie as possible.

"I'm sure they'll have a great time," said Marty. "It's all new to them. And Clay looks a good sort." She was hoping that Mackenzie would settle, not keep racketing around as she used to. After all, her daughter Zoe was now in her teens.

"Well, it is what it is," said Doug. "I thank you Marty," he said, holding and kissing her before she got into the car. "I couldn't do any of this without you."

"I wanted it," said Marty. "I wanted it all!" But she was secretly glad to have Doug to herself for a few days.

As they drove away, Marty thought about the kids. Her relationships to them weren't turning out as she had initially thought. Though Zoe was still capable of acting like a princess and trying to manipulate Doug, Marty respected her care for the other kids. Nic and

Natasha, on the other hand, had turned out to be the most feral of the kids, careless of others and a little wild, with mostly their own interests at heart. Jason, hapless and hopeful, had captured Marty's heart. Marty used her own parents' techniques of treating all of them as equals, and Doug treated them that way too.

"I just plain like Zoe," Marty said to Doug.

"I was just thinking it's easier to have four kids than to have one," said Doug. "One kid has to tough out the changes in cultures around him, but four carry their family culture with them!"

"Well, you have Mackenzie to thank for that," said Marty. Mackenzie had had kids without trouble and was still in her mid-thirties.

"Yes," said Doug. "But it's up to you and me to bring them up right."

"And civilize them!" Marty said.

"You're good at that," said Doug. "This week is for us, though," he smiled over at Marty and put a hand on her thigh.

That night they stayed at a bed and breakfast Marty had found, run by a French woman, Dominique. Marty was impressed especially with the linens, thick towels, and soft, old coverlets. Perhaps Dominique collected them. They certainly were more luxurious than what you could buy now, if a trifle frayed. Everything was very clean and Marty and Doug made good use of the bed!

In the morning they drove into the hills above Ojai, which Jeremy spoke of so often. The orange groves that lined the sides of the road were in the last of their fruiting season. Brilliant little globes lay smashed and buzzing with insects under the trees. The sweet dry air was aromatic, intoxicating.

They found the Krishnamurti library, the public information spot at the home Krishnamurti had built for the sake of his brother, who had tuberculosis. Jeremy had felt his life changed when he heard Krishnamurti in Switzerland. Marty had never read Krishnamurti's work, but she bought a biography of him.

For lunch, they stopped at The Ranch House. It was a lovely, airy place built in a garden with wooden walls and masses of windows. The garden was lush, full of herbs which were used by the chefs. You could eat back among the terraces surrounded by ferns and bamboo, with a water fountain trickling down beside you. But at lunch, Doug and Marty sat near the deck which edged out into the garden.

Alan Hooker, a devotee of Krishnamurti, had started The Ranch House. Marty was astounded to find that he had written the green cookbook, *Vegetarian Gourmet Cookery*, a staple in her early San Francisco household. The Ranch House had been inspirational in founding what people called California cuisine, lighter fare using herbs and vegetables lightly cooked. Jeremy had come to Ojai because of Krishnamurti also, and worked as a sommelier at the restaurant.

When Doug said Jeremy was his partner, the current owner, David Skaggs, welcomed them. Skaggs had started as a busboy and become manager. "Remember me to old Jeremy, will you?!"

"I will," said Doug. "He directed us here."

David suggested the scallops, seared on a grill and served over curried corn. Doug readily agreed. When their server came by, Doug asked, "Have you got any wine from Edna Valley?" For Doug, every choice was an opportunity. "A Sauvignon Blanc?"

"Victor sees Central Coast wines as our competition," said Doug. "I'm going to do a white this year because Jeremy doesn't want to." White wines were more difficult than red ones, requiring more attention. "We're going to buy another stainless steel tank for it."

"That will be fun for you," said Marty. "Not from our vineyards, right?" Boulder Creek estate vineyards were mostly planted to reds, with a bit of chardonnay tucked in to their 70 acres.

"No, a vineyard I've been looking at that's a bit south of us," said Doug. He tipped back his goblet of cool, silvery Sauvignon Blanc. "Pretty good."

"Grapefruit?" asked Marty.

"Yeah," said Doug. "A little sweet for my taste. They're putting in these tropical fruits, I think. Mine's going to be pretty dry." He looked across at Marty. "I love seeing you here, my intellectual wife," he said. "I worry about you stuck up on our mountain with just me and the kids."

Marty liked being thought of as Doug's wife, but they weren't married yet and she hesitated to call Doug her husband. "I love being stuck up on the mountain with you and the kids," said Marty. "And we have that lovely little library. I can get anything I want there!" The Boulder Creek library was a beautiful little building that tapped into a county system which included other public libraries and even some colleges. Marty always had a pile of books in her reading corner.

"Anyway," said Doug, "I like looking at you across a table in beautiful surroundings like these."

Marty acknowledged his compliment with a grateful smile. "This bread is so lovely!" she said. It had been baked on the premises. "And the butter!" The cool butter slab was topped with a blue borage flower.

"California uber alles," said Doug, playfully raising his wineglass. He referred to a favorite song, in which the Dead Kennedys mocked the new age culture of California. "It's the suede and denim secret police. They're about to come for your uncool niece!"

But Marty could not help but be thrilled. "It's so amazing," said Marty, "the confluence of Jeremy, Krishnamurti and then finding that Alan Hooker wrote that little green book we used to cook out of! I remember the cover, with the scallions on it. This puts so many things together for me! And the oranges! I love it here." It was as if each of these things had its own weight and together they thickened the air.

Doug waggled his head back and forth. "Don't worry," he said. "I'm totally Californian," he mocked. He was almost a generation younger than Marty and shunned what he called the "wu-wu" culture. Jeremy was right between them in age. "And I have my enthusiasms. I can't wait to see Sanford Winery this afternoon!"

"Oh yes," said Marty. "Tell me the story again." Marty found that she liked wine well enough, but what she really loved were the stories that went with it. Heroic tales of people coming to winemaking from philosophical and artistic backgrounds, making something out of nothing, and competing with European wines. The stakes were always high, because vineyards took so much investment.

"Well, Sanford was in the Navy, as I understand it," said Doug. "Came back from Vietnam disillusioned and began studying temperatures in the hills above Santa Barbara. He compared them to 100 years of temperatures in Burgundy, where the grapes are mostly Pinot. He used to drive around with a thermometer stuck out the window of his car! So he buys a bean field, and with a partner begins growing Pinot in the Santa Rita Hills where they had never been grown before."

"We haven't tried his wines, have we?" asked Marty.

"Oh yes," said Doug. "I've tried some with Jeremy and Victor." Doug kept voluminous records of every wine he had tried, every vineyard, every vintage. But he also had an excellent memory. "So now," he continued, "Sanford has built this winery. He's spent ten years on it with some pretty interesting ideas. It opened last year. Just got his appellation carved out, too, Santa Rita Hills AVA."

"I look forward to it," said Marty. She spent hours and hours in the tasting room in Boulder Creek, listening to people's feelings about the wines they were tasting. Many people just passed through and weren't very interesting. But often enough, wild people happened by with wild stories.

The scallops were extraordinary. They sat like little mounds of white flesh, beautifully browned on top. "These are diver scallops," their server told them. "That means divers go down and pick only the mature ones, rather than some trawler scraping everything off the sea floor."

"Wow," said Doug. "I'm impressed."

The whole meal was lovely. Marty savored everything, especially Doug's presence. But he was a moving-on kind of guy. It was a couple of hours to Sanford Winery. They didn't linger over lunch.

At Sanford, the new adobe building was laid out in a valley surrounded by vineyards. "Cost more than twice what it was supposed to," Doug whispered to Marty. Thick adobe bricks had been made on the premises, the floors were cool stone, and the wood had been reclaimed from a Washington state sawmill, including the mill! What thrilled Doug though were the huge elevators which allowed the wine to be gravity-drained instead of pumped. "It was all built for Pinot," they were told by a long-haired pourer named Chris in the tasting room. "Bruises easily, you know."

Marty and Doug tried the Pinot, which was smooth and silky, tasting a little like blackberry. "Goes down like the Baby Jesus in velvet trousers," said Marty, quoting the phrase Jeremy had once brought back from France.

"So it's these Transverse Ranges that create the weather pattern?" asked Doug.

"Yes," said Chris. "You got the north-south alignment of the coastal mountains, intercepted by these east-west ranges. The cool ocean air and fog flow up into the valleys and get trapped."

"Yeah," said Doug. "I get it. And the vines are all organic? Sustainable?"

"Yep," said Chris. "Amazing isn't it. But costly. Quality doesn't come cheap."

"Yeah," said Doug. He sighed. "Anyone care if we walk the vineyard?"

"Hmmmmm," said Chris. "Let me check." He picked up the phone.

The vineyards were messy. Late rain had grown the vetch with its purple flowers and other weeds and grasses between the rows. They would be mowed and disked under to provide organic compost, just as they were getting ready to do in the Boulder Creek vineyards. Wild grasses could not be allowed to take up water the vines needed.

Doug put his hands in the dirt and tasted the soil. "Minerals," he said. "Salt." The leaves were out and clusters were starting to form on the chardonnay vines. "Interesting," said Doug. He pulled out a notebook and jotted a few notes.

That afternoon they drove slowly up El Camino Real, the king's highway. Rusty bells on curved shepherd's crooks marked the historic highway which had wound from one mission to another in the early days, each mission a day's ride from the previous one.

"Victor is suggesting I write articles for the web about what happens in the tasting room," said Marty pensively, as they drove.

"He's trying to find a way to use your talents," said Doug.

Marty shook her head. "I can't write sales pitches," she said. "Romance sells wine and I'm really about realism."

"You don't have to do anything you don't want to do," said Doug. "You're already doing so much."

Marty didn't feel she was doing too much. Once she had gotten organized, she had found plenty of place for herself on their mountain. She managed the tasting room, arranging for its cleanliness, hiring the young people who poured for the tourists on weekends and spending time herself with buyers and brokers who came on weekdays. She tried to be home by the time the school bus arrived so as to provide the kids with a parent in the house and she worked with Ana Maria on shopping, cooking and cleaning.

In fact, Marty felt she had a bit of mental space left over. She photographed the family and wrote in her journals, just to keep herself company and remind herself of what she had been thinking about. She'd been working with her brother Paul a bit too. Paul had just lost his wife, but he was working on a website where he made natural history observations. He sent each short article to Marty for her comments and edits.

All of the Mikkelsons were good at writing, with a strong command of English grammar and vocabulary. It had come down through the Bakken family line, though Dad was no slouch at story telling either. You had to have something to say. And Paul did have something to say. Marty wasn't so sure about herself.

"I am interested in brand building," said Marty. "But I don't want to do it myself. Victor and Jeremy are the ones. They're really good at it!"

"They're working on it," said Doug. "But they're not as good as Derek Benham!" The Benham brothers had just sold their Blackstone Merlot brand, which Derek had built up over a ten-year-period. Their Merlot was so popular it was thought young people might turn to wine drinking instead of beer! Quite a coup. "Of course he has Dennis Hill in his corner." Dennis, a perfectionist winemaker, was known as the magic behind Blackstone wines.

"I love wine," said Marty. "I love the warmth it gives to gatherings of people and the lore of it. But I'm not much of a product or sales person." Outside the window, golden hills, orchards and vineyards sped by.

"I know that," said Doug, looking over at Marty. "I wanted a wife and partner when I asked you to come live with us." He looked back toward the highway. "Haven't gotten any desperate calls from Disneyland," he said, picking up his mobile phone. "Must be doing okay."

Marty watched Doug's masterful hand on the wheel. Her California boy. But it was hard to separate him from his family. Did she want to? Probably not. She felt deep gratitude for Doug, for his finding her, for his steadfastness. She reached up a hand and stroked the back of Doug's neck. Doug stretched into Marty's hand. "You're the most sensual guy on the planet," she said. "And I've got you right here."

Marty did want to take advantage of their brief time together. She knew she could tell Doug anything, her fears, her wants, even the things that she couldn't yet verbalize. "I love California," she said as they watched the fields and hills slide by. "You know when we are out traveling the experience itself becomes mine. I don't really need to possess things. Even you." Borrowed landscapes, Marty was thinking, had always sustained her.

"A good thing too," said Doug. "You can own me all you want, but as you know, I'm not worth much," he laughed. "The ranch doesn't belong to any of us! The bank owns everything."

"They let you make your own decisions, though," said Marty.

"So far," said Doug darkly. He was something of a pessimist. "It's why I work like a maniac all the time. It would be nice to take more time, but everything is work for me right now." He turned off the freeway toward Arroyo Grande in the twilight. "And the kids, and you," he said.

"At least it's seasonal," said Marty. She had come to understand that, even though Doug always had the vineyards on his mind, there were times when not much could be done. Marty was sure that Doug had just stated his priorities. Work, the kids, Marty. But it was fine. It was partly that he thought of her as a partner, as himself. He expected of her what he expected of himself.

When Marty and Doug had gotten together, he had been worried about so many things. Marty had been surprised to find that, even though they were together all the time, it was not like when she lived in the city and they had been friends. Though he loved Marty, Doug did not have a lot of mental time for it. Marty had had to learn quickly to invert her self, to stop thinking of herself as 'a skin-encapsulated ego,' as Alan Watts said, and see the world around her as her self. She had to leave her little self behind and grow into the bigger one. The bigger the world around you, the bigger the self. Marty suspected Krishnamurti might have had something to say about this also. Doug's family and ranch were a pretty big world!

They drove down into Arroyo Grande where they stayed the night. In the morning they had time to walk out on the beach at the edge of the ocean, before stopping at Laetitia Vineyards. All of it was beautiful, Marty thought. Doug's was a life of hard work, but it was spent in beauty. Marty was pleased by all of it.

Late in the evening a few days later, Mackenzie and Clay arrived at the ranch with a bunch of tousled, sleepy kids. Brusquely collecting the kids and their stuff, Doug did not encourage the grownups to stay. Zoe seemed to be the most self-possessed.

"Did you have a wonderful time?" asked Marty. "What did you like best?"

"Roller coasters!" said Nic and Natasha together. "Clay took us. Mackenzie wouldn't." Nic wore a red bandana around his head and an earring! Natasha was wearing pirate boots.

"It was fun to talk to Ariel," said Zoe. "She had this rich, full red wig she had to wear and a big princess dress. Everything was really clean. And I liked the teacup ride."

"Mickey Mouse ben-ys," said Jason.

"Ben-ys?" asked Doug as he and Marty got the kids off to bed.

"He means beignets," said Zoe. "They are little Mickey Mouse-faced doughnuts with powdered sugar on top. Really good!"

"True to form," said Doug. Jason still wanted to be a cook.

They each had a trove of souvenirs: mouse ear hats, Disney pins, mugs, and Zoe had a pair of twinkly shoes. Doug looked at them dourly, but said little. If that was what Mackenzie wanted them to remember her by, it was fine with him, he told Marty later.

"I'm happy everyone is home safe," said Marty, when the kids had been tucked up. A bunch of little Californians, she thought.

8

Line and Poppa found a bench in the sun for him to sit on in the civic center park stretched out in front of San Francisco city hall while Stephen parked the car. Ivy and a girlfriend, Rosemary, followed.

"I'm afraid you're going to be cold," said Line, putting down a blanket for Poppa to sit on. She looked around. It was February. The trees had been pollarded; their stubby limbs stuck up in the air. In front, people were setting up a podium and speakers under a big banner which said, "Not In Our Name." The Cohens had driven up to the city to swell the numbers of an anti-war march just ahead of the Iraq conflict President Bush had been stumping for, for months.

"Oh, don't worry," said Poppa, tucking his muffler around his thin neck. "The sun is going to come through this haze in a minute and I'll be warm as toast." He was 83 and couldn't walk too far. But no one could keep him home.

"So you'll stay right here until we get here?" asked Line.

"I'll be right here when you get back," Poppa said, waving the little rainbow banner he had brought with him. "Keeps the ladies at bay," he chuckled.

"And what about the gentlemen?!" asked cheeky Ivy. "This is San Francisco, you know."

Poppa threw up his hands. "What can you do?" he asked.

When Stephen arrived, the four marchers went underground to take the train to the Ferry building where the opening rally would be held. Ivy and Stephen carried homemade signs attached to sticks that said: "The Whole World Is Watching." And "Their Children for Our SUVs!" All of them were dressed in down coats, hats and scarves.

Underground, hundreds of people streamed toward the end of Market Street on trains and trolleys. Emerging up the steep escalators, Line heard bagpipes. In front of the swirling mass of people a line of policemen on motorcycles lined up, revving their motors, ready to clear out any remaining traffic and lead the march. The rally appeared to be over, but there would be another one when they reached the civic center.

It wasn't very organized. Line, Stephen, Ivy and Rosemary stuck together, walking up the wide street along with hundreds of people. Some people chanted: "What do we want?" "Peace," came the answer. "When do we want it?" "Now!" A forest of signs reached up. "Regime change begins at home," read Line. A woman in a wheelchair carried a sign which said "Walk and roll for Peace."

Huge paper mache heads were carried high above the crowd. "Impeach me now," said a sign painted with a cartoon President Bush. Bush and his cronies had convinced themselves that they should invade Iraq because it had "weapons of mass destruction," that it was a "rogue state" and harbored terrorists. They had not been able to convince the UN, but Britain was going along with it. Congress had passed a resolution the previous year allowing President Bush to "use any means necessary" against Iraq. Many people in the U.S. were still mortally afraid of terrorists.

Looking at the buildings and trees along the street, Line thought back to the first time she had arrived in San Francisco, so many years ago. Marty had picked her up at the train and brought her to the city. Market Street at the time was covered with cautionary yellow tape and lined with huge timbers. The underground train under construction made everything confusing. But there, behind them, where the street met the water, the clock tower of the Ferry building still stood. It was even more beautiful now, as the freeway ramp which obscured it, made derelict by the 1989 earthquake, had finally been taken down. "My city," thought Line. Even though she had barely lived there two years. She had lived longer in Chicago, but since leaving, she had never been back.

The march seemed like not much trouble, though Line knew it was almost two miles to the civic center. She felt warm and happy, her arm in the crook of Stephen's elbow. "Wake up and smell the Fascism," said a sign near her.

Ivy and Rosemary walked along the edges of the crowd. "Join us!" they said to the few shoppers and gawkers. "Join us." They passed a silver metal fountain and walked down a wide avenue lined with a homeless encampment beside one of the federal court buildings. A few bundled people lay about on the concrete, but many had joined the march. The homeless population hadn't changed since Line had lived in the city, though it was probably larger.

When they arrived at the civic center, Line looked for Poppa, and there he was, his blanket tucked up around his legs, his rainbow pennant floating above his head. The plaza was full of people.

Speakers began. Many of them were taking the opportunity to complain about Israel's occupation of Palestine. "It is not anti-Semitic to be on the side of Palestine," said one. The Cohen family had a complicated relationship to Israel. Poppa, in his work as an immigration lawyer, had helped many immigrants to America and to Israel. But he thought that fairness demanded a "two-state solution," some land for Israel, and some for Palestine. The current prime minister, Ehud Barak, had gotten Israel out of Lebanon, but he had called an election, and Poppa was afraid the hard-liners, all military men, would be back.

Line found that anti-war speeches hadn't changed much in all the years she had been going to marches. What was there to say, in any case? There was little justification for Bush's imperialistic war, which seemed to be a legacy from his father's Gulf War more than ten years before. Line wished some of the tremendous energy generated toward war could be directed towards Africa, where the huge loss of population from AIDS was affecting the endemic famines. There would be famine again this year, she had read. No one seemed to know what to do about it.

Milling people hung toward the back of the rally. When Poppa seemed to be tired, Line collected her family and they went to an Italian restaurant and had a wonderful lunch. Of course we should enjoy ourselves, thought Line. But it always seemed to be at the expense of others.

In the coming weeks, Line could hardly go out of the house without hearing war talk. She was surprised to discover some of her colleagues at work did not feel safe. They wanted an all-out war on terrorism. "Let's just nuke all those towel-heads," said the black janitor at the clinic. Line found that the nurses who hadn't traveled outside the country were quite likely to believe that the US was in danger. They could not imagine that the people on the other side of the world were just people like themselves who wanted peace as much as they did.

Even with Marty, Line had a political conversation on the phone: Marty said that she had learned to be an 'internal émigré' from all the Russian literature she had read. "Like Pasternak," she said. "My favorite. He stayed in the country, though he was reviled and his work couldn't be published. I refuse to give this war my attention."

"But our children!" said Line. "We must fight this sense of imperialism the United States has."

"Yeah," said Marty. "I often think of England. Since they got over being imperialist, they've become a wonderful country."

"Pretty much," said Line. "The Scottish people still don't feel quite equal though." She changed tactics. "And how are your kids doing?"

"Oh," said Marty. "We're just cherishing this last year we all get to be together. There's no high school up here, you know. So Zoe will go to high school in Santa Cruz. She'll be living with Grandma Alice during the week. Maybe stopping with you guys once in a while, if that's okay."

"We look forward to it," said Line. "Somehow I can't get enough young people under my roof!"

At the March equinox, the United States, Britain and Australian troops began the invasion of Iraq, while Polish and Australian Navies secured the oil fields and ports. Heavily armored infantry moved toward Baghdad. At the home of one of Line's hospice patients, the television was on during the day and everyone watched the war. Line knew that it seemed frivolous to do anything else, to do anything that wasn't a dire necessity. But how sad to spend one's last weeks or days in this way.

The beginning days of the invasion were quite surreal. The world seemed to go on pause. Everyone expected that the Iraqis would not be able to stand up to the "shock and awe" tactics of the West, that the conflict would be settled quickly. Protests went on all over the world. 1,300 people were arrested in San Francisco on the second day of the war.

At home there wasn't much respite either. Stephen and Poppa railed against Bush and the war hawks, Dick Cheney and Donald Rumsfeld, whose companies, such as Halliburton, stood to make money provisioning the war. "Classic imperialism," said Stephen.

"The French are calling Tony Blair Bush's poodle," said Poppa. "Just falls right in."

Stephen played Phil Ochs' songs. "Every word is even more true than when he wrote them in the 1960's," he said. "Is there anybody here who'd like to wrap a flag around an early grave," sang Ochs. "Is there anybody here who thinks that following the orders takes away the blame."

"Come for a walk with me," Line begged Ivy after dinner. They walked out and down the hill. The air was crisp and cold. Line laughed at Ivy's bare feet. "Just like a California girl," she said, "in your tevas and down coat!" The stars were very bright, the moon not up. The moon, almost full, had been very strong the past few nights since the air was so clear.

"I can smell the acacias," said Ivy. Yellow acacia blossoms were the first thing to come out. "Not my favorite," she said.

"Nor mine," said Line. Acacia had a sickly sweet smell. But by this time, the hillsides were very green with new grass and all the deciduous trees were beginning to burst out in clouds of little leaves. "Sap too. I can smell the little leaves getting ready to come out." They walked through residential streets where houses were set back in phalanxes of trees. Their hill was a somewhat new settlement. "People are watching the war as if it were a video game," said Line. "I remember thinking this during the Gulf War. You were much younger then," she said.

"I remember," said Ivy. "I was 14, I think."

"A war is not entertainment," said Line.

"I keep imagining the lives of those people," said Ivy. "Their lives are a matter of survival, the effort to get food and ignore the weapons and explosives which surround them. The effort to keep in contact with their loved ones, all of which we take for granted."

Line hugged Ivy. "My lovely, strong, good girl," she said.

"Those people are in trauma and danger," said Ivy. "They capture our imaginations. So we put our own lives on pause."

"Such an effort for you young kids," said Line. She sniffed the cold, aromatic air.

"We're not too young," said Ivy. "We're strong and we need to know what's going on."

Line thought of her own mother. Mother had taken care of her own emotional and intellectual needs so as not to burden her kids with them, though after Dad died, she had become somewhat dependent on Hanna, Line remembered. Much as she was on Ivy. She hoped she wasn't burdening Ivy.

Line remembered Mother taking up hobbies, weaving especially. Line was doing the same that winter, following Ivy to a drawing and watercolor class. Ivy intended to improve her drawing skills, but dropped out when it became apparent the class was a bunch of bored middle class women copying other pictures. Line stuck it out, however. She wasn't a housewife looking for a hobby, but she did want to revive the side of herself which had been so involved in looking and seeing as a young person.

With Mother in mind, Line went happily to her class that week. The teacher, Julian, was a sweet young hippie with longish hair, ragged jeans and a dark t-shirt. The women all loved him. Julian tried to get them to learn the age-old techniques of drawing from the right side of the brain and then become familiar with what watercolor could do.

"Okay," he said. "Take out your watercolor block. Today we're going to try some wash techniques, just to get used to them. First, tape down a piece of that watercolor paper and rule six squares on it." He began to do the same. "Don't let the squares touch each other for this exercise."

With lots of chittering, everyone grouped at tables in a U-shape around Julian began to take out their supplies. Ivy had proudly given Line an old portfolio to carry her things, which included large sketch pads, a block of watercolor paper, brushes of different kinds, paints and little plastic dishes to mix colors in. Line took out a sheet of paper and taped it to the light board which rested at an angle in front of her. Using a fine pen she ruled the boxes with a slightly wavering hand.

"First box," said Julian. "This is going to be a flat wash. Take your ¾" flat brush and paint in the first square with clear water. Just paint right to the corners. Not too thick!"

The paper bubbled up a little as Line painted. She dabbed it with a tissue.

"Then take one of your pre-mixed colors, a bright one, and just lay it in on that wash. Go in one direction only, rather fast," said Julian. People came up behind Julian to watch him and then went back to their seats to try the same thing themselves.

Line didn't say a word. She laid in a rose madder color from her precious tubes of paint, trying to get the color to lay flat. It felt so good to have something sensual to concentrate on, to watch as it happened, the water infusing the paper with color right in front of her.

"Second box," said Julian. "We'll do a gradient wash. I like to use my Payne's grey for this one. A sky color. Perfect for Santa Cruz fog," he said. "Just lay in the plain water first. Then put down a line of darker color at the top and then flat lines with less pigment in the brush as you go down the square. You can tip the paper a little, watch the color as it moves down the page. All we're doing is trying different ways to work with pigment and water. That's all this is."

Line looked across at her neighbor's paper. The boxes had been made with a ruler, as Julian's had. Hands, she thought to herself. She knew how powerful hands were, and how each was different. She and her neighbor were both using Payne's grey, but the washes down their squares were completely different.

"I can't really teach this stuff," said Julian, echoing Line's thought. "You have to feel out how your own hand works, how your eyes respond to what you're doing. But I can show you how to experiment." He went on to explain other wash combinations, how to work with wet into wet color, wet on dry paper and dual colors. He then showed them how to take one of their earlier pen sketches and wash it with color.

As Line packed up her things at the end of the class, her eyes felt relaxed and mild. She had washed in some color on a drawing of flowers which she liked. She hadn't thought about anything but her picture for an hour and a half!

At home, the garden gave Line some relief from the pervasive heaviness in the air, but it did not stop her from thinking. She had done all the pruning and planting she wanted to. The roses were budding out by this time and seed casings blew off the trees. The wind in the spring did its part to knock down old leaves and weak branches. Line spent her time picking off and sweeping up dead things, making sure there were no dried brown colors left to mar the glorious green growth about to come.

On the other side of the world, women like her would have the hardest time. Line thought about women's tasks which never quit: about provisioning her household, nurturing her kids. It had once been necessary for her to work to help the family economy, but this was no longer true. Line now worked at the hospice clinic because she could, because she was good at healing and interested in the many ways life and death played out in people's lives.

Responsibilities for her kids were tapering off, Line knew. She clung to them in her mind, but she did not want to do anything to prevent them from having successful lives of their own. Mother had been good at pushing her kids out of the nest. Line had indeed felt pushed out because the younger kids still needed help.

And though she and Marty had had to insist on their own values, both of them rejecting their Lutheran religion, Mother and Dad had not done more than pray about it and talk among themselves. They never outwardly rejected their young rebels, but always welcomed them home. Mother and Dad seemed to feel that things would come right in the end, that God would not let them go.

Emerging from that strong Scandinavian Lutheran background had been hard at the time, but it was not a problem for Line's kids. What was their generation's problem, Line wondered. Perhaps things were too easy for them. In the early years, their family had not been very well off, living on Stephen's small salary, so they weren't too spoiled. And Line and Stephen had tried hard to give their kids a wide enough view of the world.

The kids did seem to feel that resources were being used up. The world's population had more than doubled since Line was born. Land had filled up and there were dire predictions about the extinction of animals and plants, the pollution of the oceans, the warming of the planet and holes in the ozone layer. There was no lack of problems to solve.

What she wanted for her kids was passion and independence, thought Line. It was what gave you a basis for growing. She did not care about whether they had degrees, or went to excellent schools. Stephen and his father showed a bit of that elitism, but Line rebuffed it with her own solid belief that people educated themselves.

The kids are each becoming the flower they were meant to be, thought Line as she swept up refuse and put it into her compost bin. Life was profligate, as well as careless and grim at times. We will all turn brown and blow away, becoming compost, Line thought. But not yet!

Of Line's kids, Christy was at the top of her consciousness this year. Christy had been miserable since the death of Paul Wellstone, along with his wife and daughter Marcia in a plane crash the previous October. Christy had become close to all of the Wellstones when he traveled with the family during the summer Wellstone researched a presidential run a few years before. Christy and Marcia, who had brought her three-year-old son, had taken notes and recordings while Wellstone talked to people.

Christy was having trouble shaking what had happened. "It could have been me, Mom," Christy told Line. Three of Wellstone's campaign aides had also died, along with the pilots. "They went up to Eveleth for a funeral, and a debate that night," said Christy. "We were all jamming to get Wellstone re-elected to the Senate in November. I stayed in the Twin Cities to work the fund-raiser Mondale and Ted Kennedy came for. Just devastating. Unbelievable."

Line had insisted he come home for Christmas, but now he was back in Minnesota, working again for the Democratic Farm-Labor party. It wasn't lucrative work, but Christy was good at organizing and keeping databases, communicating with the members of the DFL party as his father had once done for SDS. Without a family, Christy didn't have to make a substantial living, but it did worry Line. She had always noted that being able to keep yourself in food and rent was a way to have an independent mind as well. Line knew a few trust fund kids who were not sure what to do with themselves. Christy was passionate about what he was doing and had a mind of his own, but Poppa was probably still subsidizing him.

Line hoped Christy and her brother Paul were getting together. She knew they occasionally played a game of chess. Paul's wife Marie had died just over a year ago. Paul had spent the summer at the lake and the winter in Bemidji nearby. He seemed to be doing all right, making a life for himself, Line hoped.

Of her girls, Line was delighted Ivy still wanted to live at home, but she did worry about how Ivy was going to support herself. Heather was pregnant with her second child. Little Matteo was now almost two and her family vineyards in Chile were thriving. Fern's Sofia was apparently precocious, living around so many adults at Fern's museum in Arizona. Line was as thrilled as Poppa to see this new generation being born. She only wished they lived closer to home.

That night, as Stephen mixed the drinks, he suggested to Line, who was making salad dressing, "Let's call Christy. I want to ask him about that project I've been thinking about."

Stephen's book on the British politician John Smith was in the final stages of publication by a university press and Stephen had been mulling a biography of Paul Wellstone. Line was proud of the books Stephen had written. He always tried to take on the significance of the people whose biographies he wrote. He read his work in manuscript to Line, who sometimes made suggestions, though she did not feel she was any sort of editor.

Line considered. It was two hours later in Minnesota. Christy had a Blackberry now, and was responsive to it. "Okay," said Line. She knew Stephen wanted her to set up the call.

After establishing that Christy was fine, and a few disparaging comments about Bush and Dick Cheney, Stephen told Christy about the project he was considering.

"Ironic," said Christy. "You'd be sorting through the notes your very own son took down!"

"Notes and intimate comments, I hope," said Stephen. "You really got me thinking over Christmas. I think I might be the right person for this job."

"You are, Dad," said Christy. "It's perfect. And I'll help you however I can."

"The question Wellstone was asking, about whether the U.S. could handle a progressive presidency, really grabs me," said Stephen. Christy had spent a lot of the Christmas holiday de-constructing his relationship to Wellstone in Stephen and Line's presence. Wellstone had been known as "the conscience of the Senate," by fellow progressives. "And God knows I need something to think about besides the current bunch of idiots in Washington," said Stephen.

"Did you know they finally diagnosed Wellstone's physical problems as multiple sclerosis?" asked Christy. "That's why he had to give up his presidential run."

"No," said Stephen. "I don't think I knew that."

"I don't know anyone in politics who was better," said Christy. "Or more interesting."

"It sounds like a great project," said Poppa, who was listening on the other phone. "Though I think we are pretty far from a progressive era. I don't see any Teddy Roosevelts out there. Or any really great journalists taking Bush on." They had been aware of Paul Wellstone mostly through Christy's work.

Line did not dare say how wonderful it would be if Stephen and Christy worked together. She did not want to jinx the idea before it got started.

Not yet, thought Line. Not yet are we ready to blow away. In defiance of wars and the men who started them, they must all work to make the world better.

9

In a small forest of arms and legs moving in unison, Marty, with Doug a few rows behind, did a tai chi slow set on the wooden stage at the La Honda camp. It was the last week in August and the sun was hot at mid-morning, shining down into the woods. Marty tried to focus on moving with the group, sinking on legs which felt springy and lithe after a week of using them hard. Her rounded arms reached out from her body, her hands making circles. Energy came up from the soles of the feet, was directed by the waist and expressed in the hands.

But Marty was having trouble concentrating. Almost as much as Doug, she thought. He was preoccupied with the grape harvest. He had already sneaked out one night to go look at his vineyard, which was not that far away. Perhaps that was the problem. They were only an hour away, on winding mountain roads, from home.

Doug had promised Marty that, since there was no tai chi class nearby, they would go to the week-long La Honda camp each year. But it wasn't that easy to take a week out of their lives. The kids were staying at Grandma Alice's house in Santa Cruz and the brix on Doug's vineyard wasn't quite up to the mark when they left. But it was close. Doug worried. They would leave for home late that afternoon.

Marty knew that the kids were having fun. Alice would take them to the swimming pool during the day, and probably to the mall to buy school clothes and supplies. But what would Zoe be doing? Would she find friends? And how was Jason making out among his rowdy siblings? Marty turned her whole body, lifting one leg and stretching up in the rooster pose. She was among the short people in front, near tiny, perfect Ricka. A fly buzzed near her, the sun melted down on her toes. It hadn't quite reached the middle of her body, but Marty could feel the sweat trickling down her back.

Doug was in a row of six-foot guys at the back. That was the good thing about camp. He got to be with people his own size, people who had studied for years and could show him what tai chi was really about. Marty and Doug had come one other year. Each time, Doug made a lot of progress over the week, learning the martial applications, and thus strengthening his set.

After slow set, Master Liu called for family sets, one after the other. These were both fast, and then slow, very beautiful, Marty's favorite. A hundred feet stamped down at once, shaking the wooden floor, a hundred hands flashed through the air. "One more time," called Master Liu. "Begin," he said. And then, "Continue." Again feet and hands flashed, moving together.

No problem with concentration during family set! Marty had to stay out of other people's way. And then class was over. After the salute, everyone wandered off toward the cafeteria.

"I noticed you were packing up your tent," said Ricka.

"Yes," said Marty. "We're leaving tonight."

"Oh! You'll miss the bonfire!" said Ricka. The last night was given over to music and dancing. People played bongo drums and guitars, sang and told jokes.

"We have to get home," said Marty. "Doug's worried about the harvest. And we've got four kids stashed at their grandmother's. I'm sure she's had enough!"

"That's amazing," said Ricka. "Quite a reversal for you!"

For most of the time she had been studying, Marty was single. In fact most of the people in tai chi were either single, didn't have kids, or their kids were grown. Tai chi was all-encompassing for many of those practicing. Ricka and her partner were teachers in Modesto. They had gathered up students from miles around and taught 17 classes a week.

Marty and Doug brought their lunch trays over to a table where the Colorado guys were hanging out with Ernesto and Stan from the San Francisco class. It was wonderful to see Sachiko and others Marty had known, a gathering of the clan. But Marty didn't presume to be in the core group around Master Liu. She was happy on the margins. The core group were all teachers. Marty did tai chi for the health of her body and mind. It had been the best thing she had found for wholeness. She wanted to share it with Doug.

Lunch was sandwiches, brown bread with bacon, and choices of cheese, avocado, tomato and lettuce. Delicious food to be eating in a large old place built as the cafeteria for a logging camp in the 1920's.

Ernesto had moved up to the country, to a tiny A-frame in a forest above Point Reyes. "It was a tree farm once," said Ernesto. "Trees planted in straight rows, now grown up. There are wild peacocks who hang around when I do tai chi. The noisiest creatures! Noisier than turkeys."

"We have wild turkeys," said Marty. Their guttural cries sounded exactly like the traditional "gobble, gobble" they were represented to say. "They're so funny, following each other as they waddle through the woods looking for acorns. Noisy too."

"Chinese meal tomorrow night," said Stan. "Yuet Lee's seafood. You'll be missing it," he told Doug. All of these students planned to do more sessions in San Francisco once they left camp, as long as Master Liu would have them. Many were from Europe, but Marty's friend Sabrina had not come.

Doug shook his head. He loved seafood. "Too worried about harvest," he said. "My Sauvignon Blanc grapes are just about ready."

"More power to you!" said Ernesto. "Hope you have a great crop!"

"We don't usually do Sauvignon Blanc," said Doug. "But I convinced them to try it this year and bought grapes from a neighbor. Lots on the line there."

Marty looked at Doug admiringly. She was so proud of him. The stakes were high, but he didn't shy away from them.

The talk was mostly about tai chi and tai chi gossip, however. The San Francisco building they had done tai chi in for many years, 50 Oak Street, had been sold. It would be reconstructed as a music conservatory. Ernesto was teaching qigong in Santa Rosa and Stan had taken over his San Francisco classes, teaching in the park on Saturdays and at a new studio he had found. "I have fewer students," he said.

"Things are fragmenting," said Ernesto. "There are so many teachers now, and so many forms. This group will always hang together, though. Around Master Liu. People are so grateful for his deep teaching."

In the afternoon, people went out to the stage to practice individually and in small groups. It was shady and cool by this time, the big trees laying their shadows across everything. Marty did partner knife with Ricka. Doug worked with Stan to finish learning san shou, a choreographed two-person set. Later Stan watched as Doug did it with Marty. "Soft with your upper arms and shoulders," he told Doug. "It's an opportunity to work with someone small. Makes you work harder, get lower. And she's feisty!" Marty had a reputation for loving two-person work and pushing people around!

With Doug Marty didn't quite feel the physical triggers she was used to when doing san shou with Sachiko, but she did her best. She had longed for the day when she could do san shou with Doug, had hardly dared expect it. And here it was! Marty thought he might be even better than she was, technically.

When people began to head to the cafeteria for the evening meal, Marty and Doug packed up. Saying goodbye to Master Liu, Ernesto, Stan and Sachiko, they slipped away.

"I'm so happy!" said Marty. "We've become a tai chi couple!"

"Yeah," said Doug. "Amazing. They are wonderful people." He considered as he put the mini-van into gear and pulled onto the highway. "Might as well take the coast road to Santa Cruz," said Doug. "Probably faster than going through the mountains." They stopped at the general store in San Gregorio for a bottle of wine and snacks.

As they sat out at a flimsy table in front of the store, there was enough wireless signal for Doug to check his Blackberry. For almost a week, there had been no connection to the outside world. As Marty watched, a tattered orange Monarch settled on the purple blossoms of a buddleia, the butterfly bush. It sat there, opening and shutting its huge wings. Part of one of them was torn.

The late afternoon drive along the coast was gorgeous. Marty could hear the surf rolling up the beach, though often the road was on cliffs high above it. The sun was about to go down as they pulled into town and the driveway of Alice's small house. The twins were playing a game of kickball out in the street with some friends, Jason running along the edges. They clamored up to the van. "Dad, Dad!" they said, proud of him. "Are we going home?"

"Yup," said Doug, getting out of the car and hugging each kid in turn. "Just as soon as we go in and say hello to Grandma. And thank her for taking care of you ruffians!"

Marty followed Doug and the kids into the house. It was on a crowded street, a vacation house built in the 1920's and painted in dark colors, as were others on its street. Alice's house was a dark forest green with deep rose shutters. Alice had lived in it since her husband died, along with Doug and his sister. Every once in a while, Doug and Marty ended up on the hide-a-bed in the living room, while the kids shared the other small bedrooms.

Marty found Zoe in one of the bedrooms. "Look at my new room!" Zoe said. Grandma Alice had bought a new coverlet and new curtains for the room Zoe would be staying in while she went to high school. "And see the little desk!" said Zoe. "It's for homework."

"Your very own room!" said Marty. It was very pretty with its white painted desk and white curtains.

"Yes," said Zoe. "I made Natasha wash her feet before she slept in the bed. Grandma says we'll have fun next year, like two peas in a pod, she says."

Grandma Alice was an energetic woman who still worked for a doctor's office in town, though she was in her early seventies.

"We'll come and get you though on Friday nights," said Marty. "We will miss you and want you to come home."

"I will," conceded Zoe. "I can't wait for school to start! We walked over to the high school. It's really close. And I talked to some girls playing soccer. I'm going to see if I can get on the soccer team."

"I'm so glad!" said Marty. "But that's the thing. We want to know about your adventures. So we will come and whisk you away on the weekends." Next year there would be three kids in school. Would Grandma Alice be able to handle that in her small house? Marty tried not to think about it. One day at a time, she told herself. We'll cross that bridge when we come to it.

Doug drove the van full of sleepy kids up the winding road to their home on the mountain, smiling in the dark over at Marty to show her how happy he was. Surrounded by his kids, he was always happy. Marty was lost in thought, knitting all of her family connections into the complex tapestry she kept in her mind.

It had been a remarkable summer. Doug, Marty and the kids had gone out to Minnesota for a couple of weeks in July. Besides the usual canoeing, swimming and hiking, Ellie had surprised the Mikkelson siblings with a proposal that they knock down the cabin and replace it with an all-year-round log home, built by the Bach company, as the beautiful Bakken cabin next door was. Ellie and Bruce wanted to make the upstairs comfortable enough for themselves, with the lower level available for everyone else. The log home would be owned by a Mikkelson family trust and inherited by their descendants.

Marty thought it the perfect solution to the cabin's ills. Its foundation was buckling, and there was no point in trying to shore up the cheaply built place. She and Line were Californians now, not apt to come very often. Hanna lived in New York state. Paul would live year round in the new log home, as a manager and caretaker. Ellie and Kristen's families, in which there were beginning to be grandchildren, would come more often.

Lake front property was no longer easy to come by in Minnesota. Sharing it this way would preserve Mother and Dad's legacy. Marty was impressed with Ellie and Bruce's generosity, but of course they would get what they wanted too. And Paul would find a home at the lake all year round. It was a win-win-win situation, Doug told her. Ellie sent around papers for each sibling to sign and notarize regarding the family trust and their agreements. According to the agreement, the cabin property could never be sold.

It gave the weeks at the lake an odd quality of both nostalgia and freedom. They did not have to keep the place clean! It would come down in the fall. Marty herself didn't like to hang onto the past. It was all there in her capacious mind, waiting for her to revisit it. She could see Mother and Dad, Aunt Rose, her grandmothers, uncles and aunts clearly in her mind's eye. Place did call them up, but the lake itself, the dock platform Dad had put in, the beach house would all remain.

Marty and Doug had taken the kids on California camping trips also, but the quick round of the summer was over. When they got home Doug touched all of his bases, organizing a crew and scheduling the harvest of the white grapes. It would be done at night, lighted tractors moving through the vineyards following the pickers. Besides the fact that the grapes would arrive cool and plump at the hoppers, the pickers would not suffer the high summer heat. Doug planned to be out in the fields with a razor-sharp knife himself, handpicking with the crew.

Harvest would go on for months. Doug's first batch of grapes were not on their own estate, but nearby. The crews would move on to the red grapes on their mountain, which might not be ready for weeks. It was stressful for Doug and Jeremy, who had to make the decisions.

Once the first harvest was scheduled, Doug relaxed. "Anyone up for ice cream and bouldering?" he asked at breakfast on the last day before the kids went to school. They had been trying to make ice cream all summer, but hadn't found a day to do it!

"Me, me!" yelled Nic and Natasha. The twins were always full of energy.

Marty looked at Doug. She thought he was biting off more than he could chew! As usual. He wasn't willing to split the family up, either. She and Zoe must go, whether they wanted to climb rock walls or not. Ice cream took some planning also. The freezer was full of milk cartons of ice, waiting for the day, but the ingredients must be purchased.

"We'll go down to the climbing gym this morning, and then after lunch, we'll freeze up some ice cream." All of a sudden the day was set.

"Could you make us some vanilla sugar before we go?" Doug suggested to Marty. Marty measured the sugar they would need for the ice cream and put a couple of vanilla beans in it to infuse.

No one needed anything special to go to the climbing gym. Ropes, chalk and harnesses were provided once you got there. The kids were ready to go immediately. Zoe seemed reluctant, but Doug encouraged her. "Come on," he said. "Our last day together. We want to celebrate before we take you down to Grandma's."

The climbing gym was in one of the buildings of a former cannery. Inside the big airy space, lit by skylights, were fifty-foot tall concrete walls studded with rocks, shells, and bits of flotsam. Steel rods embedded around the room at the top of the wall allowed the climber to wear a roped harness and climb with the help of a belayer who stood below. There were other rooms too, for fitness training and an area for bouldering without a rope. It was an amazing space, but Marty still thought it was a bit weird for kids to climb in such an artificial situation. It was safe, though, and climbing used a lot of muscles.

The gym was crowded, so they only got two spaces on the wall to work with. An innocent-looking young staffer helped them with harnesses.

Doug organized everyone, getting Zoe to belay Jason, separating the ropes into the guide rope and the brake. "Lift the brake rope, and pull with your guide," he told her. "It's just a matter of taking up the slack." He stood behind her protectively.

"Use your name and your partner's name," the staffer reminded them. "That way, your partner will know you're talking to them. Say 'Ready to lower, Zoe' when you're done climbing," he told Jason. He was helping Nic get the ropes right in his hands so he could belay Natasha.

"Thank you," said Doug. "Using the right language gets you ready, if you ever want to climb mountains."

Heaven forbid, thought Marty to herself. The first time they came, Doug had insisted Marty climb, so as to show everyone that anyone could do it. The kids had been a little scared. Marty's stomach felt hollow even today. She did not like heights. By this time, however, the kids were all used to climbing and bouldering.

It did seem to Marty that kids wanted more and more extreme adventures. Of course when she was growing up in North Dakota, there had not been any mountains to climb! California provided so many opportunities, for skiing, mountain climbing, bike riding, as well as all of the usual sports. There were many ways to take things to extremes. Nic and Natasha seemed especially prone to like wild adventures. Jason tried to be a clown, a performer, to keep people's eyes off his clumsiness. And Zoe was just above it all. The kids all wanted her approval and attention.

When it came to Marty's turn, she demurred. "You go," she said to Doug.

"Okay," said Doug. "You can belay me." He put on a harness, attaching himself to the climbing ropes with a grigri, a braking device. Another young staffer reminded Marty how to hold the ropes. Weight did not seem to be much of an issue with the grigri providing leverage.

"On belay, Marty?" asked Doug.

"Belay on, Doug," responded Marty hopefully. She held firmly, watching as Doug climbed. He seemed impossibly high, using the toeholds and rocks which stuck out of the concrete. Marty's neck hurt as she looked up. Beside her, Zoe and Jason watched, a little abashed.

At last Doug called "Ready to lower, Marty," and kicked confidently down the wall as Marty paid out the rope. Jason cheered as Doug came down. "I want to do that," he said. Doug gave Marty a kiss on the back of her neck. Nic and Natasha had gone over to boulder without ropes on a nearby wall, falling onto airbags when they were done.

They all watched as Jason climbed higher and higher and Doug belayed him. "Now just let go and let yourself swing down," said Doug. But Jason clung to the rocks, shambling down the wall.

Back at home, while the others made lunch, Jason came into his own. He loved cooking. With Marty's help he cooked egg yolks, the vanilla sugar and milk into a custard. During lunch, it cooled in the fridge, but then Jason softened bars of chocolate. The first time they had used the recipe that came with the ice cream maker, the chocolate had been very light. This time Doug bought three big bars of chocolate, and cream from a nearby organic farm. "Use all of it!" he told Jason. "All of it!"

When the custard was chilled enough, they added cream and the melted chocolate. Everyone took turns tasting it. "A little more vanilla," said Doug, testing the mixture with a finger.

"I think it's delicious," said Zoe. She loved chocolate.

The ice cream freezer was set up on the back porch. Nic and Natasha filled it with layers of ice and rock salt. The rock salt lowered the temperature on the ice, making it colder.

"My physics teacher once brought an ice cream freezer to school for an experiment," said Marty. "I'm not sure what he was trying to teach us!" She smiled at Doug. His main concern was that his kids not have a second hand life. That they know how things worked and where they came from. That they felt confident they could do things themselves.

Carefully, Doug poured the custard into the steel cylinder. He inserted the little steel churn into the cylinder and connected it to the crank in the wooden ice cream maker. Nic packed more ice and rock salt around and on top of it. He looked up, "Now all we have to do is turn the crank!" Nic said.

"All afternoon!" said Zoe dramatically. "Hey," she said to Jason, who was cleaning out the custard bowl with a spatula. "I'll take a bit of that."

They all took turns. The ice cream got stiffer and stiffer, the crank harder to turn. "I think it's done," said Natasha.

Marty watched as Doug took a few turns to see what he thought. He had the kind of leadership that collected people around his infectious enthusiasms. Her own father had had some of this too.

"Just a little more," said Doug. "Come on Nic," he said. "See what you can do."

At last the ice cream was pronounced done. Marty produced bowls and spoons and they sat around on the grass, eating ice cream.

"Luscious," said Marty. It tasted decadently rich with chocolate and creamy.

"Much better than last time," said Zoe.

"I agree," said Doug. "Couldn't we make some rose sugar?" he asked Marty.

Marty looked at him balefully. She did not quite understand Doug's fascination with rose flavor. "Yes," she said. "I can save some petals and put them in sugar." When did he think they were going to make ice cream again?

"Strawberry," said Natasha. "I want to try strawberry."

"Or cherry," said Marty. "But it isn't the season. We'll have to try it next summer, when the bing cherries are available."

"Chocolate cherry," said Zoe blissfully. "My two favorites."

"We've got it down," said Doug, putting a spoon in his bowl. "The sky's the limit now."

That evening, Zoe packed up and Doug drove her down to Santa Cruz, while Marty made sure the other kids got to bed.

"School tomorrow!" said Jason. He put out his school clothes, new sandals and his first three-ring binder, with the pencil case which fitted into it. It was required for fifth grade.

Marty read a chapter of the Harry Potter book, *The Prisoner of Azkaban*. Marty did not think the Harry Potter books were up to the level of *The Three Musketeers*, by any means. But it was a cultural thing. Kids were reading them all over the world. Nic and Natasha were way ahead in the series, having finished *The Order of the Phoenix* that came out that summer. But they seemed to like hearing the books again as evening reading, putting together and reminding each other of the characters. So much happened in the books it was hard to keep it all straight. But no ideas, thought Marty to herself.

When Doug got home and they went to bed, Doug went right to sleep. "Just put a cover on my parakeet cage and I go to sleep," he always told Marty. "The closed sign is up!"

Marty didn't have that much luck. She lay rehearsing in her head all that had happened that day, knitting family, friends and culture together into a vivid network. Too vivid! She could not shut off her mind. But she did have a secret weapon.

Soundlessly Marty got up and walked over the thick, plush of the Persian carpet she had brought with her to Boulder Creek. It had ended up in Doug and Marty's bedroom for safety. Marty found the familiar piece of wall against which she could sit comfortably. She pushed her tailbone as close to the wall as she could and sat up perfectly straight, crossing her legs and putting her hands, open, on her knees.

As she had learned from one of her Taoist books, Marty tried to move the energy, her chi, through her body along the microcosmic orbit. Beginning at the perineum, she tried to feel it moving up her back, slowly, feeling along her vertebrae. Up her neck and over the crown of the head, Marty felt the energy as lights going off. Around her eyes, especially, Marty felt all the tension and pain that she was usually suppressing. Slowly she let the energy move down her face, over the tongue and down. As it passed her heart, she felt a fountain of relaxation radiating down. Her body spasmed a bit as energy flowed down.

It took a few times, full inhalations and slow exhalations. Each time, Marty searched for the tension in her mind and let it slowly dissipate. Marty released the many connections she felt to people, the world, coming back to the feelings in her own body.

Marty had learned the method while living alone and reading so many books about Taoism as well as practicing a lot of tai chi. She'd been using it to shut herself up and take care of herself ever since. It was especially useful in Doug's large family, as Marty took up the responsibilities it required. It made her very happy to be needed, to be centered in Doug's heart and family, to have found her place. But she also needed this ability to release, to stand in her own grid, to be her own flowering plant.

When she had done a few more revolutions, Marty slipped quietly into bed. She could hear Doug's heavy sleep breathing. Her brain shut off in sweet sleep without her noticing.

10

When the old frame Mikkelson cabin on Lake Michigami was bulldozed in November, Paul was on hand with a camera. The cabin had been emptied of furniture and anything that could be used. What was left, windows, doors, shelving, came down like paper. Torqued on themselves in a sad heap, the walls looked pretty flimsy. Paul felt it in the pit of his stomach, as if he too was falling. What Paul thought of as Dad's dream came down in a day.

It hadn't snowed yet but it was cold. The idea was to clear the site before the snow came and be ready in the spring to lay new foundation. Paul took lots of photos of the demolition. His mind told him it was a good thing, but his heart felt sad. When Ellie first brought the idea to him, he was greatly relieved. The old cabin, with its buckling foundation and cheap construction, was not salvageable. And a coalition of siblings wasn't in the cards. Most lived too far away. Paul was very happy when Bruce and Ellie took the lead.

Bud, who ran the battered yellow backhoe, looked happy and warm, moving back and forth in layers of wool and an old fleece hat, pulling his levers. He selectively knocked down walls so that the roof wouldn't fall on him. Paul waved to him as the backhoe began to lift debris into a dump truck. The craft barn, which had never been finished, also had to go. Paul remembered working on the framing and flooring. When they were finished, there would simply be a level space where the buildings had been.

Scraps of an old dirty rag rug fluttered out of the loader, as Paul watched. Paul thought of Aunt Rose, who had put up her little gingham curtains so cheerfully when she first took over the cabin. None of these domestic details was left. It was all rubble. But neither were his parents, or Aunt Rose alive any longer to know. Paul thought Dad would have approved in any case. He didn't like waste, but he was always up for new projects. Paul snapped a few more photos. He was wearing gloves with the fingers cut off against the cold.

By this time, Paul had spent quite a bit of time with Bruce and Ellie on the idea of a new cabin, trying to make the plan workable for their far-flung siblings. The Morlands were thinking about retirement, about their grandchildren. But also about the family as a whole. Ellie thought Paul should live in the new log home full time, maintaining it for all of them. Given the peripatetic life he was living, Paul thought this a great idea. The new log building would become his year-round home.

As Dad had hoped to, Paul wanted to see the lake throughout the seasons, something no one had been able to do so far. He wanted to watch ice form on the lake and then break up in the spring. He wanted to keep records of temperatures, snowfall, animals and birds coming and going.

Ellie had gotten all the brochures she could from the Northwoods Log Homes Company. The Bach family who ran it was experienced and full of ideas. They had built their own home across the lake long ago. Paul, who was spending the winter in an apartment in Bemidji, visited this original home and took photos for Ellie. Building the equipment to strip logs and true them into uniformity, the family had been in business since the 1950's.

The late fall day was short. It was twilight when the big equipment quit for the day, leaving part of the craft barn to be collected the next. Paul went down to the lake to have a look. The waves were choppy and looked terribly cold. Grey clouds lay heavy over the lake, with a sliver of pink at the horizon where the sun had slipped away. Pieces of the dock had been piled up on the shore, the canoes tucked below the beach house. Deciduous trees had lost their leaves by this time; only the pines showing green.

Paul drove back to Bemidji, thirty miles north on a straight, empty blacktop, his headlights shining before him. He turned on the radio, a bit apprehensively. A year ago Paul had been blindsided by Linda Ronstadt singing "Willin'," a favorite song of Marie's. "I've been warped by the rain, driven by the snow, I'm drunk and dirty, don't you know." Paul had had to pull over to the side of the highway, convulsed with pain and sobs. "But if you give me weed, whites and wine," Linda sang from somewhere deep within her. "And you show me a sign, I'll be willin' ... to be movin'."

The hollow in Paul's body where Marie should have been was huge. But he had resolved not to shut off the pain, to experience it, though he was sometimes surprised by its intensity. It had been over a year, almost two since Marie died.

And Paul was also willin'. He didn't do weed, drugs or even much wine, but he was finding ways to survive. He was learning to make his own life. He did not want another woman. He could not even imagine someone taking Marie's place. In some unusual way, she was still there. He was considering getting another dog, however. When he was more settled. It would not be Archie, but it would be a companion.

Paul's apartment was empty. He went over to the computer and plugged in the camera to see what photos he had gotten. He would put them up on a website he was keeping so that his sisters, snug in their homes in California, New York and St. Paul, could see what progress was being made on the site. Everyone knew the cabin was coming down that day. They would be waiting for his post.

Notwithstanding the destruction, the photos were gorgeous spread across the screen, the green-painted cabin walls in splinters in the blue November light, as if a hurricane had hit. The heavy equipment looked powerful. Paul captioned each photo and uploaded them to his website. The deed had been done.

On Friday night, Paul took two large pizzas and a six-pack over to the Hickmans' house. He was trying to make a habit of it when he was in town. It was finally beginning to snow. Paul wrapped a blanket around the pizzas when he carried them into the house to keep them warm.

The kids greeted him with joy. "What did you bring?" Andre asked.

"Same ol' pizzas," said Paul. "This one's everything, with garlic. And this one's plain. Just tomatoes, cheese and sausage."

Pretty little Jeanne wrinkled her nose. "I don't like garlic," she said.

"How do you know?" asked Joe, who was 15. "Have you ever tasted it?"

"No," conceded Jeanne.

Grace laid plates around the table. Paul knew she was glad not to cook! Grace's life was full of church work and her kids, who were growing like weeds.

Dory, the oldest of the Hickman kids, poured out milk. She was ambitious and wanted to become a nurse, had started classes at the university. She was just 18, the same age as Marie had been when she became pregnant with Grace, Paul realized with a pang.

"Startin' to come down out there?" asked Gerald. Gerald worked at the town's small airport, flying, but also shipping and whatever else needed doing.

"Lightly," said Paul. "Beer?" he asked, handing Gerald a cold one.

"So the cabin got bulldozed?" Gerald asked.

"Yup," said Paul. "Flimsy as a house of cards. I put some pictures up. Want to see them?"

The computer was at a little desk in the kitchen. Gerald was suspicious of what the kids might do with it, and wanted to be able to monitor its use. Paul typed his website into a browser and the photos came up clearly on the screen. "Aaargh," said Paul ruefully, looking at the twisted scraps of green-painted wall. "That summer I spent painting it. Can't have been three years ago! What a waste."

Gerald chuckled. The kids crowded around. How many summers they had all spent at the lake!

"He looks like he's having fun. I'd like to drive a bulldozer," said Benjamin, the youngest, who was now quite tall at eight.

"I think it's a backhoe," said Gerald.

Grace put Paul at the end of the table and Gerald at the other. The two pizzas disappeared into the family with hardly a murmur.

"How's the team doing?" Paul asked Joe, who, like his Dad, was a basketball star, tall and rangy.

"Okay," said Joe. "We won last week." Andre, looked as if he was about to say something, but Joe put a lanky arm around his neck, squelching him. "No thanks to this little Indian," he said.

Grace beamed at her oldest son. Paul sensed a story. "What happened?"

"Hid my shoes. Almost didn't make it," said Joe, teasingly. Andre's smile was as wide as his face. "Jealous?"

"Naw," said Andre. He was much more interested in bugs and animals, a kid after Paul's own heart. Paul hoped he would be a scientist. Of all of the kids, Andre was taking most to the idea of Native American lore and history. All of the kids were enrolled members of the Leech Lake Band, with one quarter Ojibwe heritage. But, like their father, most of them just wanted to assimilate, to be ordinary, mongrel kids, to have the opportunities anyone did in Bemidji, Minnesota.

"I've got to get to one of the games," said Paul. He resolved to spend some time with Andre, to see what he was up to. Andre was eleven, stockier and shorter than his brother.

"You'll stay and watch *Joan of Arcadia* with us?" said Jeanne. "It's about a girl who talks to God."

"I remember," said Paul. "I saw it with you once before." Paul looked over at Grace, who appeared a little sheepish. Of course he would stay. Being in the bosom of this family was something Marie had given him. He was going to enjoy it to the fullest.

The kids put Paul in the middle of the sofa, right in front of the television, with Jeanne and Benjamin on either side, leaning on him. Paul relished the warmth and sweetness of their bodies. He was careful not to ask for it, but glad when it happened. Jeanne especially reminded him of Marie with her dark curls. She was nine now.

The television show was about an ordinary American family, whose daughter, just barely a teen, heard God talking to her through various people she met, telling her what to do. No one else in the family heard His voice, so they thought Joan's actions bizarre.

Paul filtered it through Grace as he watched, wondering what she thought of this. Grace was the most devout person he knew. She had loved the story of Bernadette of Lourdes. Perhaps she did not find the story of Joan of Arcadia, Maryland, blasphemous. All of us are more liberal now, Paul thought. He doubted if his own father would have approved. But then again, he wasn't sure. Dad could surprise you.

Paul was interested to see that even Gerald stuck around to watch the show and all of the kids were wrapped up in it. If you must watch television, Paul thought, it was certainly a good thing if the whole family watched it together. When the show was over, Paul hugged everyone good night.

"You'll be here for Thanksgiving, won't you?" asked Grace. The churches in Bemidji got together to host a huge Thanksgiving dinner every year. Paul always helped, but he was spending quite a bit of time in St. Paul as well.

"Wouldn't miss it," said Paul. "I'm looking forward to seeing your mother! Good night!" Gerald's mother Jane was a fixture at St. Phillips Catholic Church. She survived her sister, who had recently succumbed to diabetes. The two of them were full-blooded Ojibwe.

Paul drove home, the thickening snow lit up by his headlights. Heritage was so interesting, he thought. Jane was the only grandmother Grace's kids had now. Gerald's father had been a trucker, killed in a highway accident.

And Marie had been unable to enlighten Grace about her father. "It was all so shadowy," was all she could say. Marie had run away to Montreal at 17, to sing in clubs with various groups. She didn't even know the last name of the guy she had been with, though she thought he was English in background. The ensuing pain of her scandalous pregnancy and leaving Grace to be raised by her family in Quebec had been very tough.

In Paul's family, there was nothing shadowy at all. He had known three of his grandparents, all Norwegians born in America. Mother's Danish immigrant father had died when she was little. He had been an itinerant pastor, a much-respected man. Recently there had been a lot of talk about DNA tests, in police investigations and determining paternity, for instance.

E.O. Wilson contended that people carried emotional and intellectual traits on their genes, as well as physical ones. Paul was always going back mentally to Wilson's great book *On Human Nature*. He had read it long ago, but now was reading it again. It was a watershed statement, so well-written, about humans, their evolution and what could be expected of them. Wilson was still writing book after book. He was obsessed with closing the gap between science and the humanities, putting the latter on a stronger footing. Paul was in complete agreement.

Wilson also recognized the human need for religion, however. He said that human evolution was an epic, "the best myth we will ever have." But man needs the hot, emotional promise of transcendence in an often brutal life. Science was cold. It could not provide this. Wilson found hope in knowledge. "Man's destiny is to know," he said. Brain science was at the moment burgeoning and Paul was paying attention.

Paul was grateful for the freedom his web design work afforded him. He did not compartmentalize his mind, giving part to religion and part to science. He simply did the things he had always done: helped with the big Thanksgiving celebration of gratitude and good will in Bemidji, and sang in the choirs he loved. He listened to Christian sermons with a kind of historical interest and a mind attentive to the thoughts of the people he knew and loved. Paul often thought of his Uncle David's words, "The older I get, the bigger God becomes for me."

The Christian tradition was Paul's own, and Christ was his guide, as he had been Bonhoeffer's. But God was much more than humans could conceive of or understand. Similar to the way he left his mind open to pain, to all the winds that passed through it, Paul wanted to be empty of certainty. It seemed to him that truth could only be found in an environment of freedom.

At the beginning of December, Paul went back to St. Paul. He did not want to miss the Christmas choruses at Ellie's church, Gloria Dei Lutheran, led by Brad Engstrom. Once he had felt this way about the choir in Bemidji, but its great director Janos Szabo was long gone. And he and Ellie and Bruce were actively planning what the new cabin would be like.

When he rolled into the driveway in a light snowfall, Ellie was at the door to meet him!

"Come on, Paul," she said, giving him a hug as Paul blew into the warm house. "I want to show you the rough plans we've been making." Ellie with a project in front of her was unstoppable, Paul had found!

"Hang on," said Paul. "Hang on there. I'll just put my stuff away." He lifted the milk, hamburger and butter he had brought out of a grocery sack and into Mother's refrigerator.

"I didn't expect you," said Ellie. She was wearing jeans and a warm Norwegian sweater, her after school clothes. "But I have some lasagna left over. Do you want any? I'll just pop it in the microwave."

"Sure," said Paul.

Bruce was in the den, watching Monday night football when Paul went upstairs. "Hey," he said. "Now you're here, I'll turn this thing off. I just keep an eye on it so I can talk to people in the office," he said.

Ellie was spreading out the sketches on the table. "We can't change certain things," she said. "But we will surely make better use of space than the old cabin did."

"It was a mish-mash," said Paul. "This is an opportunity to do it right."

"The designers we talked to wanted to make it south-facing," said Bruce. "To use the southern solar advantage in the winter. But that's just not likely."

"Nope," said Paul. "The building faces the lake, with the big windows to the north. That's not really negotiable." He looked closely at the inky sketches made on paper with tiny blue squares. "I find that state law doesn't allow new buildings to be as close to the lake as the old cabin was either, so it will have to be set back a few feet. Plenty of space, though."

"We do like the idea of it being split level," said Bruce, "one side dug into the ground."

He pointed out how the two levels would work: The upper space would be designed to Bruce and Ellie's specifications, though any of the Mikkelsons could use it if the Morlands weren't there. There was a large living room, kitchen with dining area, a large bedroom and bath, with a smaller den.

"We'll put a screened-in porch on one end, for mosquitoy evenings," said Bruce, "and a big deck where people can sit outdoors. Maybe in the morning. The sun comes up here, doesn't it?" he pointed to the position not on the plans where the sun came up over the lake. Bruce hadn't spent as much time as the rest of them there.

Paul looked on, thrilled all of a sudden. "Yeah," he said. "It generally comes up there." The sun traveled quite a distance along the edge of the horizon over the course of the year. Paul usually saw it only during the summer, but now he would be able to track its movement!

"So, downstairs we'll have in-floor radiant heating," said Ellie. "There'll be a large living/dining room with a small kitchen at its edge, bathroom and two large bedrooms. You could take over one of those bedrooms for your own. It would probably be big enough for an office too."

"It's amazing," said Paul, "how much can be fitted in!" He was thinking of the crowded, moldy, rough space the old basement had been.

"Lots of systems needed to make a place livable all year," said Ellie. "But it would last forever if we kept it up. Well-treated and sealed logs are excellent insulation."

"Hot water powers the radiant heating, shared with the heating system for showers and sinks," said Bruce.

"It's a miracle," said Paul. "It is so great you guys want to do this! And use the best materials!" Paul was very grateful for Bruce's concepts. Bruce wanted to keep it basic, but use the best. Nothing extra or frivolous.

Bruce laughed. "It'll be good for all of us. Now," he said. "We're not going to put in a fireplace. We'll take the old Ben Franklin and put it upstairs in the living room. It's more efficient than a fireplace anyway. You lose less heat."

"We thought about a loft room," said Ellie. "But we think it would be too expensive."

"The main thing is to be there, in the woods, beside the lake in all that relative wilderness," said Paul. The Paul Bunyan State Forest was mostly set aside. "Have we been coming to this lake for fifty years?" he asked Ellie.

"More than that," said Ellie. "Those early years at the Lande cabin." Pastor Lande was the first Lutheran pastor on the lake, convincing others to join him.

"Yeah," said Paul. "It's still standing, but it looks pretty shabby."

"Do you want some ice cream, Paul," asked Ellie, going over to the refrigerator.

"Why not!" said Paul. "It's a celebration!"

Ellie brought out a square cardboard box full of ice cream and cut slabs off it. "Chocolate?" she asked. A plastic bottle of Hershey's syrup appeared.

Paul sighed and squeezed chocolate on his ice cream.

"We'll change the trust to reflect the inheritances," Bruce said. "Each sibling is a member, with inheritance going down through their children."

"Does that include Grace?" asked Paul. Grace was his step-daughter.

"If she's your heir," said Bruce.

"Definitely," said Paul. He wasn't used to thinking about inheritance.

"Have you stopped in at that Northern Lights casino up there in Walker?" asked Bruce, as he rinsed his bowl and put it in the dishwasher. "I'm curious."

"I did peek in," said Paul. "But it is such an unnatural environment, and so loud! I didn't do more than look." The building had opened that year, a hotel, restaurants, and a gaming location, all run by the Leech Lake Band of Ojibwe.

"Looks like a nice establishment from the newspapers," said Ellie. "The restaurants might be good."

"More people are moving up there year round," said Paul. "Since we started talking about this, I've been going to the little Laporte Lutheran church. Remember? It's the community space for the Lutheran pastors who live on the lake. And I find that more and more people are retiring up there! It's good timing for me!"

"Probably a result of better technology," said Bruce. "They know how to build up there now."

"There are trade-offs, one guy told me," said Paul. "If he has a heart attack or a stroke, he might not make it to the hospital in time. But he'd rather end his life up there, he said, than anywhere else."

"It makes some sense," said Ellie. "We're not going anywhere. St. Paul is where we want to be, but we do like the idea of spending more time at the lake. It's so restful up there. And the grandkids are just the right age for it." Rhonda now had two children.

Paul went downstairs to his own bed late in the evening. The apartment would always be Mother's somehow. Paul could see her sitting in her chair by the gas fireplace on a winter's evening. Marie too, wrapped in a shawl and lying on the sofa. It wasn't a bad thing, Paul thought, to live with his loved ones. Time was a rather permeable membrane after all.

Before going to bed, Paul checked his emails to see whether he was missing anything. Work mostly came through emails now and he could not afford not to pay attention.

In the morning Paul was up early. He looked out on a white, cold landscape, though the sky was clear. The old trees at Ellie's were frosted lightly with snow.

The first item of business was a calisthenics program he had made for himself, just a short program for which he didn't need any equipment. He lifted his own body weight, the way they did in the military. Stress had made him put on weight over the years and he had been worried that his muscles were sagging. Also, Paul could not afford to let his poor, mismatched legs go. They needed tuning and use.

Starting each morning with a few minutes of stretching, pushups and other ways he was learning to lift his own weight was part of the life Paul was making for himself. He had found quite a lot of discussion of it on the web. It felt great for his upper body to be stronger, and his legs too.

Paul was at church early. He hadn't been to choir practice that week and he was hoping someone could tell him what songs would be sung.

"Paul!" Brad Engstrom hailed him as Paul put on his blue choir robe and hung the satin collar around his neck. "Are you going to be around for a few weeks? I've been thinking about doing some of the *Messiah* this Christmas, and your voice would certainly be a help!"

"Yes," said Paul. "I wanted to be here for the Christmas music, to tell you the truth."

"Ah, good!" said Engstrom. "I'm making plans. You'll be here for practice this week?"

Paul said that he would be. It was just as he hoped.

Gloria Dei was a more formal church than any Paul had grown up in. He processed into the church with the rest of the choir, following the pastors as the organ played, singing, "Praise to the Lord the Almighty, the King of Creation. Oh my soul praise Him for He is thy help and salvation." Sunshine streamed in through the richly-colored stained glass windows. At the front, on either side of the altar were the golden angels, each holding a candle, which Marie had loved so much.

Calisthentics was one thing, thought Paul, but singing from the bottom of his abdomen affected his whole body, heart, mind and soul. The powerful hymn rose up in him, both ancient and alive as he sang with the others.

Line hovered about while Ivy packed a few clothes, a few books and art supplies into the little Honda that Poppa had bought her, for her move to Los Angeles. Line's stomach was clenched in a knot, but there was nothing she could do. She had relied on Ivy for years to lighten her days, but Ivy deserved a life of her own. "Are you sure that's all you need?" Line asked. She could hardly see that Ivy's room had been disturbed.

"I don't think I need anything," said Ivy, tying up her long hair in an untidy knot on top of her head. "Marshall brought all of his kitchen stuff and some furniture. I think we'll be fine."

"It isn't as if you were leaving forever, I suppose," said Line. Ivy would be the closest of her kids. It was just that Los Angeles, to Line, conveyed an image of gang violence, drive-by shootings and crazy people.

"Of course not," said Ivy. She packed open bins full of clothes in the trunk, pillows and bedding in the back seat. She seemed anxious to get away!

Marshall, who Ivy had begun spending time with quite recently, had rented an apartment near the American Musical and Dramatic Academy smack in the middle of Hollywood. He would teach theater direction at the famous college, begun in New York, but now open in Los Angeles. He had gotten Ivy a job at AMDA in the costume shop. Ivy felt it was such a good opportunity, she wanted to leave at once.

The whole thing felt sudden to Line. Marshall had come to dinner a couple of times. He was ambitious, excitable, from a family which had left Yugoslavia when he was small. Dark and gypsy-like, with thick hair and facial hair as well, he made a contrast to the blonde Ivy. Ivy was careless about her appearance, though she was lovely. She always seemed to have deeper feelings going on, and perhaps, Line had to admit, she was also ambitious. Ivy loved the performing arts and the place she had found for herself.

"I do wish you could stay until Fern and Sofia get here," said Line, as she carried Ivy's carefully packed sketchpads and brushes to the car.

Ivy tossed her head. "I'd like to see them," she said. "But when did Fern ever change her plans for my sake?" she asked. Ivy and Fern had been terribly close as little kids, but when they lived in Edinburgh during high school, their paths diverged. Fern struck out into archaeology, spending years in Europe before finally coming home to have her baby. She and Ivy had been close during that lovely year. But Ivy was right. Fern never diverged from her own path for anyone.

Fern had gotten married, however, and was bringing her new husband, Todd Fleming, an archaeologist, for a visit. Line couldn't wait to meet him and see Sofia. The new family would arrive in a few weeks, in May, the month of Line's 60th birthday.

Poppa came out when Ivy announced that she was leaving. She had already said goodbye to Stephen, who was caught up in the frantic pace of the end of year at the university. Poppa hugged Ivy. "We'll be thinking about you," he said. His face looked a little quavery. Line thought it was from emotion.

"Oh!" said Ivy. "I'll miss you so much!" hugging him back. She turned to Line. "And you, Mama," she said.

Line held her youngest daughter's body to her, smelling her sweet smells. It really was goodbye. There had been many goodbyes, but this one felt powerful. "Take care of yourself," she said. "And please call us to let us know you arrived safely."

Ivy got into the little silver blue car. She shrugged ironically. "What could happen?" she said playfully. But they all knew that a lot could happen on the highway going south.

Line lifted her shoulders, lightening the moment. "Probably nothing," she said. "But please drive safely."

Line put an arm around Poppa as they watched the little vehicle move down the ridge. "That's our girl," said Poppa. "I guess it had to happen sometime."

Line shook her head. "I'm just not ready for it," she said. "Never would be, I suppose."

Poppa went back to his newspaper inside, but Line wandered around, looking at her plants. It was April, what Line thought of as the month of roses. The air was wet and thick, the vegetation green, fecund, rich. But, the sun was strong and it was thrilling to be out.

The pink Arizona rose in the front by the door was full of big, dinner-plate size blooms. Line went in the house to get her secateur and a basket to collect the blowzy ones. Then she went down to the second-level deck where several other rosebushes were fighting for sunshine with the taller pines around them. She deadheaded a few roses and clipped a few leaves.

Flowers were big everywhere, irises, California poppies, callas, bergamot, and the grasses were lush. April and May were the greenest months of the year. By June the hills would start to turn golden.

Ivy would already be far south, Line thought. And who was this Marshall who had whisked Ivy off without a backward glance? "AMDA is going to grow," he had told them. "We are lucky to get in on the ground floor!" And of course LA was full of performers, dancers, actors, musicians. Ivy would have many costumes to make.

We'll also have to get used to Fern's husband, thought Line. Welcome him into the family. Fern had gotten married in a very small civil ceremony. "No need to come," Fern had told Line. "It's just a formality." They had celebrated with their Arizona friends and colleagues. And now they would meet Line, Stephen and Poppa. And probably Marty's family as well, just up the mountain from Santa Cruz.

That evening, Ivy called while Line was cleaning up the kitchen after dinner. "No incidents," she said. "It's kind of slow driving on the coast. Like around Santa Barbara. The kind of driving I like."

"Good," said Line. It seemed to her that Ivy had rarely driven, that the whole thing must be new to her. "And you could find your way?" She motioned to Poppa and Stephen to get on the phone line.

"Generally," said Ivy. "I'm sure I messed up a few times, but I got here." She sounded pleased with herself. "I'm curled up here on the sofa," she said. "With a glass of wine! It's a beautiful apartment, with a jacaranda in the courtyard. There's a pool too. Marshall has really done most of the work."

Line pictured Ivy, her baby, secure and happy as a kitten. "Is the jacaranda in bloom?" she asked.

"Not yet," said Ivy. "June or something."

"A big apartment complex, then?" asked Poppa. "How many units?"

"I have no idea," said Ivy. "We're a little north of Hollywood. I'll send you an address. And some photographs." Ivy pleaded exhaustion and signed off, leaving her family to ponder her move.

"We'll go down and see a performance," said Stephen. "When she gets settled."

When Fern and her family arrived a couple of weeks later, Line found Fern's husband a complete contrast to the young and excitable Marshall. He was quiet and studious looking. But dark little Sofia hardly let

Line meet him. As soon as she got in the door, Sofia began looking around the house, Line following.

"What's downstairs?" asked Sofia, enunciating carefully. Four years old and precocious, she had clearly spent most of her time around adults. She was half way down the stairs already.

"This is Poppa's bedroom and den," said Line.

"Oh, a television!" said Sofia. She tried to open the glass doors to the deck, and Line helped her. Sofia went straight over to the redwood garden boxes which, on this level, were full of flowers, including the thorny roses. Sofia put her nose in one. Up above them, on the upper deck, they could hear Stephen serving drinks.

"The sun feels good here!" said Fern's voice. "I'm so used to heat by now, I quite miss it!"

"All year?" asked Poppa.

"Most of the year," said Todd. "In the winter we can get frost, but it's usually pretty mild then too. The sun has a big effect."

"Come on," said Line, taking Sofia's hand. "We'll explore more later, but let's go up and have a drink," she said.

Sofia followed Line up the wooden outdoor steps. "Do you have lemonade?" she asked. "We always have lemonade at home."

"Maybe," said Line. "Let's see." Around a teak table which sat outdoors all year, Fern, Todd, Poppa and Stephen were having tea and Walker's shortbread cookies. "We're going to make some lemonade," she announced, guiding Sofia into the kitchen. In April, there were usually lots of lemons. Line thought she could find some.

Sofia looked around at the large kitchen and dining room. She had lived in the house as a baby, but she did not remember. "Are there any other kids?" she asked.

Line sighed. "Not very close," she said. She was thinking of Marty's kids. All of them were quite a bit older than Sofia, though Zoe had enjoyed playing with her as a baby. Line squeezed some lemons in water, put in a little sugar and let Sofia taste it.

"More sugar," said Sofia.

Line laughed. "Maybe a little," she said. "Do you have lemonade at the museum?" she asked.

"Yes," said Sofa. "We have dinosaurs," she said solemnly.

103

"Dinosaurs?" asked Line.

"Bones," said Sofia. "Bones of old dinosaurs. They're connected together to look like dinosaurs."

"Hmmmm," said Line. They went out onto the deck and sat down among the others. Sofia quickly grabbed a cookie. Not unlike other kids, thought Line. Taking advantage of the sense of celebration. "Sofia tells me you have dinosaurs at the museum."

"Oh yes," said Todd. "Not my department, but we certainly have them. The desert preserves the bones. To my mind, the most astonishing are the birds, the pterosaurs. Huge wingspreads! Lots of work being done on them, right now. But Fern and I work with human artifacts. I'm working on the Hohokam's amazing irrigation systems, and I guess you know about Fern's ceramic work."

As the grownups talked, Line tried to imagine why her daughter Fern had chosen this affable, but slightly pedantic gentleman as a husband. He looked rugged, as if he spent a lot of time outdoors, wearing dusty lace-up boots even now. His blue eyes seemed lost in a brown face. But he was quiet, thoughtful. Like Stephen, thought Line. Sofia's father was powerful (as well as married!), had started an archaeological school on the island of Menorca to work with the abundant artifacts there. Was Todd a less imposing choice?

"What happened to the Hohokam," Line heard Stephen ask.

"That's a question!" said Todd. "The name itself means 'those who are gone,' but some remnants of the culture can be found in the Pima, who live in that area. In the end, it seems that flooding, which increased in the 14th Century, finally made the canals unusable and towns and villages were abandoned."

"The Hohokam were in a good position to trade with people to the north and the south," put in Fern. "Trading patterns show up in the ceramics and we date their culture back to our 1st Century AD. You have to come down to get some sense of the scope of the place! There's so much work to do there!"

"Some day," said Stephen. "Maybe soon."

"So how are my illustrious brother and Chilean sister doing?" asked Fern.

"Christy is doing great, as you can imagine in an election year," said Line. "He's desperate to get rid of Bush, as we all are."

"The 'evil empire'!" said Todd. Many people thought of the Bush regime in these terms. The Iraq war was nothing if not imperialist.

"I'm starting to work on a book about Christy's hero Paul Wellstone," said Stephen. "Gives me some insight into him too."

"But how can you get to be 36 and still not be married?" Poppa wondered.

Everyone laughed. "Heather's fine," said Line. "Her little boys, Paulo and Matteo, are well. I'll show you the photographs she sent."

"Captured by Catholics," said Poppa, dramatically. "I bet she'll have more kids."

Line saw Fern and Todd looking at each other significantly. Line doubted that there would be any more grandchildren coming from them. Todd already had two grown children.

"What's a Catholic?" asked Sofia, turning toward them. "Is it like pirates?" She stood at the rail, surveying the garden below. Once again everyone giggled, and Sofia looked mystified.

"It's a kind of religion," said Fern, gathering the little girl into her arms.

"So, how about that Obama?" asked Poppa. "Isn't he something? I'm reading his book," he said. "*Dreams from My Father*. The man's got quite a background!"

"Oh, come on!" said Stephen. "The guy's not even in the Senate yet, and people are predicting he'll be a political star!" Obama had won the Democratic primary for a Senate seat from Illinois, against a host of well-heeled opponents.

"There's more family news," said Line. "I don't know if you've been following Paul's website, or weblog, or whatever it is. But they're getting ready to lay the foundation on the new cabin. It wouldn't be a good idea to go this year, because of the construction. But by next year, you should take Sofia. It would be a completely different atmosphere for her. And so pleasant in the summer to be right on the lake."

"Good idea," said Fern. "We really should do that. I remember the summer of Grandma's 70th birthday, just before we went to Edinburgh." She turned to Todd. "We had so much fun swimming and canoeing."

"It would be nice if you came too," said Todd to Line.

"We might. It's going to be a beautiful place," said Line. "I'm so proud of all of them. It was Ellie's idea. And she and Bruce are funding most of it, but it will finally be a real family haven. Paul's going to live there all year and maintain it."

"Many beautiful places to live in this world," said Todd. "You might think it is too dry and hot where we are, but when you get used to the desert, it's amazing."

"The evenings and the mornings," said Fern. "There's so much sky. We're looking for a house."

"It's all built up down there, southern Arizona," said Todd. "Boeing's down there. You can imagine. But it's a fine place to live. The Mesa Grande site was privately held until almost 1990. So it hasn't been very disturbed. We're really lucky that way."

Yes, Line thought to herself, there were many wonderful places to live. She loved her own home, often could not believe she waked up in such a beautiful place. But it made her work harder. It wasn't fair that so many people had little, and she had so much. She still worked with the hospice organization, made home nursing visits several times a week. Her patients were usually well-enough off, but not always. She took another shortbread; such a lovely taste with tea.

Stephen, Fern and Todd took off on a discussion of history, how important it was, how much fun it was, the difficulties of getting funding for projects. Poppa leaned over and whispered to Sofia, and the two of them wandered off. Line didn't have a lot of playthings, she realized. She hoped that Fern had brought some for Sofia. She seemed to be a curious little girl, however. And Poppa might have something interesting stashed away. He had loved playing Chinese checkers at one time.

Line's eyes followed Poppa and the little girl with love. Poppa was slowing down a little, his body a little stooped and even thinner than usual. He never ate much. Nevertheless, he was still a peppery, lively presence in the house. He was set in his ways, of course, a bit autocratic, and increasingly querulous, but he was a blessing for the family. Line had grown to love him.

Poppa's complaints were mostly about the culture he saw around him. Every morning he read *The New York Times* avidly, but then told Line that he thought movies were growing more childish and child-centered. "*Spiderman, Lord of the Rings, Harry Potter,*" Poppa said. "It's all fantasy! Where are the adults?" He had given up his film club to a younger member, who seemed to be keeping it up, though Poppa didn't always go.

The current comedy also bothered Poppa. He could not understand how it had happened that comedy programs like Stephen

Colbert and Jon Stewart's were now trusted more than the actual news. "It's all sarcasm and satire," he told Line. "Nobody talks straight any more. Sarcasm is the last refuge of the weak."

Poppa was also starting to worry about his assets. He tried to get Stephen to become interested in the management of his property in Brooklyn, but Stephen resisted. "You're doing fine, Dad," he said. "You don't need me!" The two of them couldn't manage the property together. "It's either him or me," Stephen told Line. "He's got a lot more years in him. I'll figure it out when it becomes necessary."

Physically, Poppa seemed to be fine as long as he had his hearing aid and glasses. He walked less, as he said his legs pained him. But he still did exactly as he pleased. More power to him, thought Line. She could not imagine Poppa in a nursing home. Line hoped it would never happen. He was still most interested in his own progeny. In this, he and Line were completely united; they had all come through her!

On Friday afternoon, Line parked her Prius near the high school and stood outside it with little Sofia beside her, watching kids pour out of the building. "We're looking for Zoe," said Line. "She's got kind of poufy strawberry-blonde hair." It was really a light golden brown, but Line envied its thickness and curls. Her girls had long, straight hair, which fell around their shoulders. Norwegian hair. Except for Heather, whose curls had a bit more loft, were more like Stephen's.

"Oh, there she is!" said Line. She waved high in the air, hoping that Zoe saw her.

Zoe detached herself from a group of kids and came toward them. "Sofia!" she said. "You're so tall!" She smiled at Line. "Thank you for picking me up!"

Line hugged the bouncy girl. "School's almost out, isn't it?" she said.

"Another couple of weeks," said Zoe. California schools took a lot of time off during the year, didn't quit until mid-June.

"Do you need to go to Alice's house before going home?" asked Line. Line was driving Fern, Todd and Sofia up to Boulder Creek that afternoon and was delegated to stop and pick up Zoe. Stephen would come a little later, bringing Poppa if he felt like it.

"No," said Zoe. "She doesn't expect me."

"I want to sit by Zoe," said Sofia, holding onto Zoe's hand firmly. Todd obligingly got out of the car and let Zoe and Sofia take the back seat with Fern, while he got into the front beside Line.

The drive up the mountain was winding, lush and lovely, the light filtering down between the redwoods and pines. It took a while, because Line did not like to drive fast. The day was cool and windy, the mist long gone. A perfect May day. In the back seat, Zoe and Fern chatted with Sofia interrupting.

"My sister says her husband, Doug, is obsessed with paella at the moment," said Line. Doug and Marty had been quietly married somewhere that winter, not taking any time off for the wedding, and Marty still kept her own name. Doug didn't want the kids to obsess about it. They were planning a trip to Europe that summer, taking the kids. "I think he is going to make paella outdoors, the way the Spanish peasants do."

"Sounds great," said Todd. "Just so long as I get to taste some of those wines he is making."

"Oh, you will!" said Line. "He's not the main winemaker. That's Jeremy, his partner. But Doug has been making a few. And they all put in their ideas, I believe. Doug is really the viticulturalist. My daughter Heather, the one in Chile, studied viticulture because of knowing Doug's family. She interned at the winery, met a Chilean intern, and that was that!"

"Yes," said Todd. "Fern is proud of her siblings. Tells me lots of stories."

"And you?" asked Line. "Are you from Arizona?"

"You bet," said Todd. "Many of us studied at the University of Arizona. This major highway was going in, I-10 in the 1980's, and we all got on board to study the Hohokam villages in its path. Got captured by these amazing cultures. We've had to get geologists and climatologists together to study the ancient irrigation canals."

"I guess Fern landed in the right place!" said Line. She was liking Todd more all the time.

"For me, yes!" said Todd. "It's fun to get to know Fern's family."

"It's a far-flung family," said Line. "But I guess that's pretty common now."

When they got out to the ranch, there was much to explore. Doug took Todd out to the vineyards to discuss his drip irrigation. Marty showed Fern around. Sofia hung back with Fern, intimidated by the large, complicated place, though Zoe was ready to take her into the kids' quarters.

Cats and dogs wandered about. In the back of the house, it was evident that major food production of some kind was going on. Javier stoked fires and Ana Maria bustled about.

Line was happy to relax and let it all happen. I do live in a sort of austere house by this time, she thought. Quiet, intellectuals, no animals, with she herself the cook and gardener. I should come up here to draw and paint, she thought to herself, though the mountain road was formidable.

It still surprised Line that Marty lived in such a busy, thriving place. But she had seen the quiet place Marty kept for herself in the big, airy bedroom she shared with Doug. And Marty was no one to be trifled with. She was tiny, but she had a large mind. Doug and Marty had each told Line how happy they were with each other. It was no small thing to make a home for another person. Much had flowed from Line's partnership with Stephen. The kids were only the half of it.

The ranch was humming with the activities of scores of people: A couple of guys drove equipment back from disking under the weeds and wildflowers between the vine cordons which would provide bio-fertilizer. Bits of deep purple vetch and yellow mustard shown in the rows which had not been tilled yet. Cars were parked in front of the tasting room down the road. It was in full swing on a Friday evening. At the winery, Line could hear the clank and crash of the bottling line where Marty said Jeremy was bottling and labeling some of last year's reds.

Marty did not take them up to the winery. "They don't need us to get in the way," she said, darkly. "And don't ask me about whether corks or screw caps are better. It is all anyone talks about up here these days!"

"Why not?" asked Fern, immediately intrigued. "Are screw caps better?"

"We don't have the equipment for them yet," said Marty. "We've always worked with corks, but people do seem to like screw caps and they prevent some cork problems. Cork is expensive, but screw cap equipment is expensive and touchy. Whites are increasingly being given screw caps, though reds usually get corks."

Line laughed at her. "You've come a long way, Miss Marty," she said. "From being a teetotalling pastor's kid in North Dakota!"

Marty laughed too. "No wine in the house, but Mogen-David communion wine!" she said. "I remember coming back from England, where we drank wine with dinner every night. You and I plotted to buy a fondue pot for the family for Christmas, which of course required cheese and wine!"

"We've all come a long way," said Line. "You have no idea," she said to Fern. "Now it seems that we're all Italians. We eat and drink like Italians."

"Because it make sense in this climate," said Marty. "We live in a Mediterranean climate. It's not at all surprising."

No, thought Line. Privately she thought their California coastal town one of the best places to live in the world.

12

"You guys stay right here," said Doug to Marty and his kids, who stood with their bags against a wall of the huge, airy railway station in London. "I'll get the tickets."

Marty looked up at the windows high overhead, letting beams of light filter down on the bustling crowds below. Despite the numbers of people, it all felt rather peaceful. The kids stood still too, overwhelmed by the great space. High up against the wall, digital letters and lights proclaimed the train departures. Marty was surprised to see tiny kids with their little roller bags and backpacks, standing waiting for their parents. It seemed to be a safe space. Europe, Marty thought to herself. A civilized place.

When Doug came back, they counted and recounted their bags. They pushed them through the belts on the security system and went out the doors to the platform, each of the kids showing his precious passport at the gate. Their places on the Eurostar had been reserved and it was crowded, every available space taken up. They would arrive in Paris in two and a half hours.

On the train, Marty sat by Doug, while the kids collected around a small table. They were listening to Michel Thomas teaching French on little earbuds attached to a CD player. "I want to hear you order breakfast in French," Doug had told them. Zoe wrote down everything she noticed in the notebook which was to be a family record of the trip. The notebook was passed around among them.

Doug too was studying French. Freed from a need to do anything, Marty looked out the window. Fields bordered by hedgerows rolled past, then the long dark tunnel under the English channel. When they came out, they were in France, where the fields and roads rolling by were bordered by rows of straight, tall trees.

Doug thought of the trip as a geography lesson. "The world is just a place," he said. He wanted his kids to have realistic ideas about it. It wasn't about sightseeing. It was about seeing how people on the other side of the world lived. "You won't see many French people in Paris in August," Jeremy reminded them. But Doug didn't care. It was the time they had.

Doug also didn't seem to care about the money he was spending, Marty noticed. "I have no idea how much I have in assets," he always said. "So why not do what we want?" Marty knew he was in debt, but a wine business was usually in debt, cash coming and going with abandon. The trip was part of Doug's determined effort to raise civilized, educated kids, to give them more than he had gotten. Perhaps Jason was too young to appreciate it, but maybe not. He was 11.

Marty herself was pleased at the progress she was making. She felt she had resolved the two great problems of her childhood: According to Ken Wilber, "there are no others, technically speaking, to save," and "there is no self to sacrifice" in the larger sense. The self she had struggled so about was threaded into everyone she knew, everything she did or saw. There was no need to hold it tightly.

It was something age had given her, a wisdom that seemed ever more accessible. Every time she looked up and saw herself moving under trees, watching their branches change as she moved, she was reminded that she was a witness to the world, a character in it. The character wasn't her. She was really the greater world, free, with little to worry about. The world was full of beauty.

Mated to Doug and living in the crowd of Hendersons, Marty felt like the woman she wanted to be. Doug gave a content to her life. His major agenda was to make the most of real life, keeping it from disappearing in the media-soaked lives the kids were surrounded by. It was something Marty could do. Real life was sacred to her as well. She loved making order, attending to details. Doug told her she was habit-driven, which surprised her. But habits, daily rituals were a good thing, she thought. They grounded you. Filled with real food, real fabrics and real stories, their days were thick, rich and substantive.

Tai chi had also given Marty much. She was able to walk very straight and quietly. When she saw anxiety and pain around her, she breathed it in, trying to breathe out calm and peacefulness. She found herself wanting to act with great courtesy toward everyone. In all of this she could see her own mother, who had always had this dignity. Mother had told Line that she was actually anxious as a younger woman, but Marty had never known it. Mother's voice was always measured, quiet, powerful.

Mother tried to imitate Christ, and as far as Marty was concerned, she had succeeded.

Marty watched as the train rushed through the countryside. Prosperous farmsteads, lush fields, small towns oriented around the church, forests planted in rows. The sky was a watery blue, washed with indistinct clouds. Marty could see a long ways to the flat horizon. High structures holding electrical cables were arresting, but she purposely didn't see the industrial parts.

By the time they got to Paris, everyone was hungry. Doug wanted to drop their luggage at the hotel, at the top of a building on Rue des Ecoles. It was in the part of the city he knew best, the student quarter, near the Jardin des Plantes. They walked from the railway station, carrying their bags. Zoe, who had a sort of shepherding instinct, made sure everyone stuck together in the crowds.

"What a pretty room!" cried Zoe, when they had climbed the stairs to the top floor. The wallpaper was printed with romantic stenciled scenes in red. The beds were tucked into odd corners of the lovely old room, spread with flowery poufs.

The building felt very solid. Marty imagined with what difficulty these old houses had been modernized and plumbed. Ceiling beams were exposed, the rest painted white. From the windows looking out at the rooftops and chimneypots, Doug pointed out the steeples of Notre Dame, just across the Seine.

"Can we go eat now?" asked Jason. He looked particularly hang-dog.

"Keep your shirt on," said Doug. "I haven't been contacted by the World Health Organization regarding your emaciated body. We'll go look for some lunch in a moment."

Lunch was not hard to find. It was a little past the Parisians' normal lunch hour, so the Hendersons nipped into an almost empty restaurant and were able to sit at the windows wide open to the street. It was too late for steak or poulet frites, however, so some had an omelet Provencal and others a salad with oeufs and jambon. There was good bread and butter, and afterwards tarte tatin and an apricot tart. It was all delicious.

"It tastes like history," said Natasha. "Not like it's old, but like it has been done a thousand times, just this way. The tarts have been made on these same pans for centuries!" She pointed to the huge pans of tart laid out on a shelf.

Marty was impressed. It was an interesting perspective.

"Don't worry," Doug said. "We'll get to try lots of things. Paris is all about food."

"Good!" said Jason. "I want to be a chef and study here." It did not seem too far-fetched a dream to Marty.

It was a traveling day, so they were not very ambitious that afternoon, walking along the quay beside the Seine. Marks on the wall showed how high the water had been during flood years. Barges, tour boats and a few boats people lived on were parked along the quay.

The sun was hot on the right bank, where people sat along the wall, legs hanging over, some against the high walls, talking, eating, relaxing. "We're very near where the Musketeers lived," said Doug. "The Hotel de Ville." The monstrous building was stretched out across a great square, full of windows, mansard roofs, arched and sculpted gates. "All for one, and one for all!" It was the spirit in which the Hendersons traveled.

"It's beautiful," said Nic. "I wouldn't mind living there."

Doug pointed out that Robert Doisneau's famous photograph, "The Kiss" was taken in front of the department store, the BHV, with the Hotel de Ville in the background. "I had it on my wall as a student," he told Marty.

Doug took them to Berthillon Glace on the Île Saint-Louis. "The best ice cream in Paris, everyone tells me," he said. A long line stretched out from the small window in the shop. There were many exotic flavors, but Marty stuck to a deep chocolate.

They kept going towards Notre Dame, where they slowly walked through the church, past the many chapels in the deep colored light of the stained glass, hearing lots of foreign languages. Zoe lit a candle for someone. She did not tell Marty for whom.

On the street outside, a couple of crack skaters had put down orange cones and were slaloming wildly, inviting tourists to photograph them. Crossing bridges in the late afternoon, they walked past the Louvre, which had once been a palace. A modernist, light-filled pyramid graced the courtyard, which Marty knew had been designed by I.M. Pei, an architect her friend Meredith had worked for in New York. They didn't try to go in to the buildings. The Tuileries beyond was a carefully laid out garden of straight ordered rows of trees. "It's just interesting to get the feel of the place," said Doug.

They crossed the river on the Pont des Artes, a pedestrian bridge. Hundreds of people who looked like students had spread out their dinners on the bridge, sharing them. The Hendersons threaded their way between the picnickers. Big boats went up and down the Seine below them, one with a giant chess game on it. The air was warm and dry, the sky becoming overcast.

It couldn't have been true that all the Parisians were gone. Marty loved seeing a small boy with a school bag on his back, stuffed with two baguettes, his smaller brother, also with a school bag, and their mother, with a cello strapped to hers. They walked past the bookstalls along the Seine, and Zoe bought some postcards.

For dinner, Doug wanted to go a restaurant Jeremy had told him about, Le Petit Bistro on rue du Sabot. They headed up Boulevard Sainte Germain, had been walking for hours. The Boulevard was just as trash-strewn and construction-plagued as Market Street in San Francisco, Marty thought. She kept her eyes open for the famous cafes where writers drank coffee and argued the whole of the previous century.

The Bistro was impressive. It was small, but beautifully lit. The one waiter, who may have been the owner, was happy to practice his English on the kids. They ordered aubergine gratinée with chevre chaud, plates of steak with haricots verts with peppercorns and a white fish in a Beurre Nantois. Passing the plates around, everyone got to taste everything.

"I could make this," said Jason, cutting into the eggplant cooked with goat cheese.

They left nothing! "C'est magnifique!" said Doug.

"The best steak I ever ate," said Nic, the steak fiend.

When the dessert came, Natasha bit delicately into the apples coated with caramel. It was called Tatin de Pomme ala Canelle. "I think you should try to make this, Jason," she said.

"I could do it," said Jason. "I need a French recipe book."

Doug ordered his favorite Crème Brulée a L'Orange. Marty was interested to see, in the list of cheeses written on a small blackboard, the Ossau Iraty, a sheep cheese she loved and could buy in Santa Cruz.

The waiter was effusive in his thanks at the end of the meal, and so were the Hendersons. "That restaurant was worth finding," said Doug as they walked home up the Boulevard. "Jeremy was right!"

It took a while to get going in the morning, a happy time with the sounds of carts trundling over paving stones, the cries of children, the pealing of bells coming across the courtyard. Marty wrote things down in the communal notebook while she waited for everyone to finish washing up.

The family went down to the salon stuffed with furniture and an old tapestry on the wall, where breakfast was being served. They crowded around tiny tables. The food was exactly what Marty loved, flaky croissant, fresh rolls with butter and many kinds of confiture, as well as coffee or hot chocolate.

"Je voudrais du chocolat chaud, s'il vous plait," said Zoe carefully, mimicking the French she had been listening to. The waitress began rattling on in French! Zoe looked at Doug, who smiled at her as she struggled to answer.

The pastries were delicious. Marty had to still herself. More will not make you feel better, she told herself.

"When you think of a continental breakfast," said Doug, spreading butter and jam on a roll. "This is the continent."

That day was to be a museum day. Marty wanted to see as many Bonnard paintings as she could. It was all new to the kids. On the way, however, they were captured by a shop called Au Vieux Campeur. It was full of camping gear and equipment, especially, it seemed, mountain climbing equipment. Walls of carabiners, ropes, harnesses, belay and rappelling devices. As well as tents, sleeping bags, cooking stoves and pots. Nic and Natasha were mesmerized, and so was Doug!

Marty stood about, watching them all. Nic and Natasha were deep into bikes and biking gear at the moment. They were always making long treks along the mountain roads around their house. Doug encouraged them but Marty worried. Would the kids make it to adulthood, since they seemed so bent on adventure? The idea of mountain climbing made Marty's stomach churn. Hanging off a mountain was not her idea of fun.

The twins spent their money on very cool-looking, thin digital headlamps. And Doug bought a Swiss army knife. "We'll need this for a picnic later," he said.

The museum, the Pompidou, was a building which looked like a machine with its steel supports and infrastructure on the outside. It was designed by a team of architects, Renzo Piano being the only one Marty recognized. In the square in front of the building, many people sat about on the paving, watching performers. Others were packed into the square nearby, sitting on the Fountain of the Innocents: many exotic people, including black people speaking French. Les Halles, the huge produce market where Marty had, many years ago, spent a night with her friend Kate, had been leveled, moved to the suburbs, to make way for this space.

They took an escalator, a tube which ran up the outside of the building, to the top floor of the Pompidou. In the distance they could see Le Defense, which looked like a huge concrete window frame.

The great white rooms were sparsely populated. Marty quietly described what she knew of Bonnard to the kids. There were seven of his paintings in the museum: Marthe (Bonnard's wife) in a red blouse at a table spread with food, in the bath and at her mirror. Scenes from Bonnard's house at Le Cannet included a window with bright trees beyond and the almond tree in bloom, his last painting. The brightest paintings were done during the Second World War.

Marty moved close and then stood further back, experiencing the paintings with their flat patches of color differently. She had never seen a real one before. Doug seemed to like them too. The kids wandered about looking at everything, or sat on benches, watching people.

"This is how you travel with a lot of people," said Doug to Marty quietly. "First you follow one person's interests, then another. Everyone is happy and everyone learns."

"How did I find you?" Marty asked rhetorically. "Someone who thinks like I do!"

Shopping in many little stores in a way that drove the hungry kids wild, they bought a baguette of the wonderful bread, butter, a couple of cheeses, lettuce and radishes, slices of ham and apples. At the cheese shop, the proprietor was horrified when Marty tried to smell a cheese. No one was allowed to touch his cheeses! They also found loosely woven yellow, black and white plaid napkins, Marty's Paris souvenir.

They took all of these things to Jardin du Plantes. Under an allée of huge sycamores which had been cut on one side and let grow on the other to make a leafy arch, they settled on a stone bench. All of the purchases were unwrapped from their little paper packages. Marty passed out napkins and Doug cut the fruit and vegetables with his knife. It all made a wonderful lunch.

"I don't think fruits and vegetables are better here than in California," said Doug. "But people take more care over them."

"The cheeses are better," said Marty.

After lunch, Marty wrapped up the leftover food in their white paper wrappers. She shook out and folded up the napkins, putting them in a bag she was carrying.

"Souvenir," said Doug, rolling the word on his tongue. "That sounds like a French word. 'Venir,' to come?" He stopped a person who looked like he knew English.

"To remember, to come to mind," said the person. "It's an old French word."

"Ah!" said Doug. "To come to mind!"

Doug put his head in Marty's lap for a quick nap and the kids roamed the garden. The stone bench under the beautiful trees with people walking past felt like home to Marty. She did not want to go anywhere. The passing parade was like a movie, people and kids of all ages. Marty heard no English in the people's conversations, but it looked like an academic crowd. In the light beyond the allée were laid out flower and vegetable gardens in ordered rows.

Soon enough the kids came back. "We have to show you!" said Natasha, grabbing Doug's hand. "The pears are growing in bottles!"

"And apples wrapped in tissue paper in the trees!" said Nic. They dragged Doug and Marty over to an orchard. On a pear tree, glass bottles had been tied to the branches, so the pear could grow inside.

"For brandy, I think," said Marty, looking questioningly at Doug.

"Maybe," said Doug. "Or research purposes. This garden is a part of the university, after all."

After a few more days of exploring Paris, the Hendersons packed up and took the Eurostar back to London. They had flown into London, spent a few days and then gone to Paris. They would fly out of Heathrow. Doug had imagined the trip as a "tale of two cities," a book neither he nor Marty had read. Marty had visited both cities, but so long ago it was as if she had never been. Cities and people changed constantly.

On the crowded train, the voice coming over the intercom was British. The kids were delighted when he began using what they knew to be Cockney rhyming slang. "I'm sure you are all glad to be headed back to the greatest city in the world," he intoned. "Believe me," he said, in a conversational tone. "I'm not telling porky's! So settle down to that cup of Rosie Lee, take a nap and we'll wake you up when we get there." The smooth train was already speeding through the French countryside.

"He says we should have a cup of tea!" said Jason.

"And that he wouldn't tell us any lie!" said Nic. "Porky pies are lies, remember?"

"So, you are learning languages!" said Doug. "Even in England." He smiled at them. "Let's see if we can get back in one piece. No Barney Rubble, please!"

In London, they stayed in the tiny, crowded basement of a townhouse in Knightsbridge which Marty had found on the internet. Mary Potter and her daughter Imogene lived there. A narrow circular staircase took them downstairs, where there were just enough beds for everyone. Through the one window, they could see people coming and going at a party in an apartment so close they could almost touch it.

Marty felt claustrophobic. This was Europe too. Rooms in which furniture had collected for generations. Mary Potter castigated her 13-year-old daughter for mussing the pillows on a rickety-looking antique couch, but the next morning both of them were gone! They had left breakfast for the Hendersons, and gone to visit friends in Nice. Mary told Marty that when they left, a man would be arriving to stay for a few days. Mary had no idea who he was, but "He seemed nice," she said. She had left him a key in a pot of flowers by the door.

The Hendersons carefully drank tea from Mary's thin china cups, ate the cut up pineapple and heated the package of refrigerated croissants she had left for them. Marty was terrified her young people would be like bulls in a china shop. They got out of there as quickly as they could in the morning, walking south toward the Thames.

Knightsbridge was just below Hyde Park, which Marty knew had been one of Virginia Woolf's haunts. In one of Marty's favorite novels, *The Years*, the characters walk along the Serpentine and meet at the Round Pond. But Marty did not give more than a thought to Virginia that day. Their object was the London Eye, a giant ferris wheel just across the Thames from the Houses of Parliament. When the kids had put down what they wanted from the trip in the family notebook, everyone except Zoe wanted to ride on the famous London Eye. Jason wanted to "disturb the Buckingham palace guards!"

The trouble was that the Thames bent. They knew they would reach it by walking south, but they kept walking and walking and didn't get any closer. At last Doug realized they were too far west. They did hit the river, and followed it. By this time they could see the Battersea Power Station, which had been on a famous Pink Floyd album cover, a favorite of Doug's. The huge brick station, looming over the south bank of the river, had ceased spewing out coal smoke in the 1980's, and was now empty, though part of redevelopment schemes.

They had to walk a long ways by the river to get to Westminster Bridge and the London Eye. The sky was overcast, but as they walked, the sun began to come out.

It was all new for Marty. Beautiful trees hung over the Millbank Road along the river and then lovely gardens. They came upon a flock of older students in black and white uniforms, chattering to each other and playing on a swing set. "Maybe they are budding attorneys and parliamentarians," said Doug. They were about to reach the Houses of Parliament, with the Big Ben clock in its tower. The London Eye was just across the river.

Statues of statesmen and explorers beckoned from every direction. A memorial to the soldiers who won the Battle of Britain reminded them that London fought for its life in 1940, before Hitler gave up on invading.

"I'm hungry," said Jason, predictably. "And my feet hurt."

Walking was fascinating, views in every direction, but it was true that it was nearly lunch time. "We shouldn't have gone south at all!" said Doug, looking at a map. "We should have headed east in the beginning!"

Marty wasn't sorry. All of it added up to views of a fascinating city.

They found a pub over a packed, smoky and noisy ale house as Doug insisted on eating the food of the country they were in. They had steak and ale pie, and the kids liked the roast chicken with chips. Marty and the kids drank the delicious ginger beer, while Doug tried the local ale.

"The food's better in Paris," said Jason. Everyone laughed, but of course it was true.

"The bread!" said Zoe. "I miss it already." The smell of a Paris bakery was ethereal.

The pub served people who worked in the area, it appeared. An August Tuesday, just another working day for some.

"Our rooms must be very close to the Speakers' Corner," said Doug. It was a plaza just outside of Hyde Park where anyone could come, stand on a soap box and hope to gather an audience for his views. "That's real life democracy! We'll look for it on the way home."

After lunch, the Hendersons crossed the wide Westminster Bridge. Marty was impressed by the powerful statue of Boadicea in a chariot behind two charging horses at the edge of the bridge. She was a Celtic queen leading her people against the Romans.

"Shakespeare's Globe is on this side," said Doug as they arrived on the south bank. "The river once bounded the city, with circuses, theaters and beargardens over here. They've reconstructed the Globe. We'll go look for it after we've gone around." The London Eye took half an hour to make a turn.

Long lines led to the ticket window. "Only one of your party should stand in line," admonished a woman over the speaker.

"You guys go have a drink," said Doug. "I'll stand in line." He pointed to a building catering to tourists where it looked as though food was being served.

Marty and Zoe bought ginger beers while the kids found a table. Waiting for their turn would take longer than the ride itself, Marty guessed. She was thinking about Zoe, how good she was at keeping them all together. The other kids expected it and Marty was glad to find herself part of Zoe's flock!

Soon they were all collected into what Marty felt was quite a large, glass-enclosed capsule, floating into the sky. There was a seat in the middle of the capsule, but Doug and the Henderson kids hung out against the windows, looking, looking at the bird's eye view of the city spread out in the sunshine. Marty wasn't good at heights. She could feel it in her stomach. She stood close to Doug, holding his arm as they slowly rose into the air. "One for all," she thought to herself.

13

Ellie called Paul to let him know that the washing machine and dryer would be delivered on Tuesday.

"I'll be here," said Paul. "Don't worry." It was October and the new log home, though barely furnished, had become available for Paul to live in.

"They should be able to install it, shouldn't they?" asked Ellie.

"I'll call you on Tuesday evening, to let you know how it went," said Paul, standing by the wall phone. He had not turned on the furnace yet and the air on the lower floor was chilly, though the in-floor heat was on, making it livable. At night, Paul curled up in a sleeping bag on his bed. The crisp fall air, the golden low-angled sunlight coming in on the new wood and the glittering leaves of the birches and aspens made it a time he would not soon forget.

As he drank his coffee, Christy called. "Hey, Paul!" he said. "I heard you were in the new place. Is there anywhere for me to sleep? We've got a rally in Bemidji and I'd love to come and see your new digs!"

"There's a wide leather sofa down here," said Paul. "From Ellie's house. It's pretty comfortable. But you might want to bring a sleeping bag."

"No problem," said Christy. "I always carry one." Christy was still living a peripatetic life, based in the Twin Cities. It was barely three weeks until the presidential election and he had been criss-crossing the state, urging voters to the polls. There was little danger that the Democratic candidate John Kerry would lose Minnesota, but he was not doing well against Bush and Cheney. The Republican incumbents were not highly regarded either, but Kerry's distinguished Naval record was being challenged. It was anybody's guess how the election would go.

"I look forward to a chess game, if you've got the time," said Paul.

"Wouldn't miss it," said Christy. "See you soon."

Paul hung up. It had been quite a summer for him. Beginning with the digging of the septic system in the spring, through the construction of the cabin, the installation of plumbing, heating and electrical systems and finally the recent installation of a wi-fi system, Paul had been on hand for everything. It was fascinating. Systems for living deep in the woods had been developed so that there were virtually no sacrifices.

Thoreau would have been amazed, Paul thought. But Ellie and Bruce were dictating, and they were thoroughly modern, comfort-oriented. All of the problems of the previous cabin were being avoided. A de-humidifier and in-floor heating kept the lower floor of the cabin from developing mold. The hybrid furnace used propane and electricity alternately and would keep the pipes from freezing in the winter. Propane was delivered on a schedule kept by the gas company. Computers kept records of everything.

Paul had been on hand when soil samples were taken in the area designated a drain field for the septic system. The system was designed to support anaerobic organisms which processed the wastewater. The soil had to be permeable enough to allow percolation away from the field. Because he now could imagine this happening every day, Paul had become very aware of what went into the septic system. Chlorine could slow or stop microbial activity; detergents and fats might emulsify and gum up the system. Paul was reading labels carefully!

But Paul would not be able to stop Ellie. The septic tank might have to be pumped at various times. In general, the cabin's systems would not be overloaded most of the year. It was intended for family gatherings, which would happen in the summer and on holidays. Paul was glad he understood the systems which kept the cabin going.

That morning Paul split kindling in the bright, chill air. Squirrels and chipmunks scrambled in the trees around him. Lots of wood had collected from trees downed during construction. Paul had made an effort to get it into a woodpile which could be protected over the winter. A woodbox stood under the roof of the little porch at the front entrance. Split wood, ready for the Ben Franklin would be kept there.

Working with wood was very satisfying to Paul. It was something that never changed. Thoreau had not known a chainsaw or a log splitter, but he had certainly made kindling, listening to the musical noises of the wood as it split along its grain. Paul had been dependent on wood when he was in Alaska. Being out in the woods alone, watching a flicker hopping around and chopping kindling reminded Paul of those years. Here he was again, home for certain this time. No one, not even his own bright dreams could dislodge him now.

By this time Paul had had time to put up bird feeders. A number of evening grosbeaks had appeared on the big one the previous evening. They seemed to fly in flocks, demolish a lot of seeds and then disappear again. Paul had seen a coyote along the drive. The longer he was around, the more he would see, he thought.

When Christy arrived that afternoon, Paul showed him the new cabin. The upstairs, empty except for a pair of binoculars on the window sill and the black iron Ben Franklin on its stone hearth at the end of the room, felt palatial. Golden log walls had been thoroughly dried and sealed. One wall was a bank of windows looking toward the lake; the hardwood floors were smooth and silky. The building's footprint was not much larger than the old cabin had been, but that was so stuffed with things one could barely move.

"It's amazing," said Christy. "That pair of binoculars reminds me of Grandma. Wish she were here to see this." Outside the window the aspen leaves trembled in the breeze and the lake below looked green and cold.

"Ellie didn't want any of the old furniture, except a couple of things downstairs," said Paul. "We'll make a fire up here tonight. I'm trying not to turn on the furnace yet." He looked conspiratorially at Christy, trying to enroll him in his attempts to save money. The agreement was that Paul would pay for utilities, while Bruce and Ellie took care of the taxes.

Paul led Christy down the stairs. "This is where we hang out," he said. "When you take off your boots, you can feel the heat under your socks! Hot water piped under the tile! That's what I think is amazing."

The downstairs was still pretty empty too except for the sofa. Paul's guitar, which had sat unused since Marie's death, stood in a corner. A fairly new stove had been kept for the kitchen, and the ancient table, which had been made from a door and given wrought iron legs by one of Dad's parishioners in North Dakota, were the sole remaining pieces of furniture from the old cabin. The bulletin board Mother had once put together of old photographs hung on the wall next to the kitchen.

"This part feels more like I'm used to," said Christy. The lower level was one big room with a little kitchenette and two bedrooms off it, plus storage and utility closets. It too had big windows looking out on a cement patio which stretched out into what would become lawn once the mud and gravel of construction had had a season to recover.

"I'm using one room for my bedroom and office," said Paul. "It's going to make a great little bachelor pad," he said.

"I'm sorry," said Christy.

"Yeah," said Paul, ruefully. "Seems like just yesterday we were all together." He was thinking of the winter Christy had lived with him and Marie.

"She would have loved the place," said Christy. There was no need to even name her.

"Well," said Paul. "Let's warm this place up. See what happens. I've got some beans that would probably cook up pretty fast on a fire, and some hot dogs."

Christy stretched his long, thin form on the sofa. "This is the den, right? I see where the television's going to be," he said. "This is plenty comfortable. I'll sleep fine here."

"Yup," said Paul. "Wi-fi installed by Paul Bunyan cable company. The whole nine yards." He remembered when the cabin had been a media-free zone. No longer!

Paul and Christy loaded up on logs and kindling and brought them in to the Ben Franklin on the upper floor.

"Kind of a virgin place," said Christy. "I hate to muss it!"

"And Ellie wouldn't want you to!" said Paul. "But we'll clean it up. The place is for living in, after all. This is the first fire I've had, though."

Paul started the fire and soon the flames were licking around a larger log he put in. He brought up cushions to sit on, and Christy helped him bring up the low table which sat in front of the leather sofa downstairs. Shadows fell and light from the sky disappeared. Paul turned on the room lights. He brought up an iron skillet of beans with some hot dogs cut into them, a couple of beers and a chess set. Just amazing, he thought.

"So how's it going?" asked Paul. He wasn't sure if he really wanted to know. Christy would often give him a major political diatribe.

"Oh, it's going," said Christy. "We're fighting for every single seat lately. We're seen as a swing state these days!"

"Well, that means more attention, right?" asked Paul. He looked into the fire where flames curled about the logs, glowing over the red embers and chattering softly.

"I suppose," said Christy, gloomily. "Bush is leading in the polls right now in Minnesota. I think it's too close to call at this point."

"Well!" said Paul, standing up. "It feels pretty toasty in here! I might have to open a window!" It was astonishing. The logs insulated the building so well that no heat seemed to be lost! In fact, he did crack a window. "How about some chess?" he asked. "Take your mind off things."

"Right," said Christy. "I've looked forward to this. Not that I'm going to beat you, but I just might!"

The main difference between Paul and Christy on the chess board, Paul thought, was that he had more concentration. It was probably even worse now that Christy had a blackberry, which he put beside him on the low table. "How about leaving that thing downstairs?" said Paul.

"Are you crazy?!" said Christy. "Then half my brain would be downstairs wondering what was going on! I'm a nervous wreck already."

Paul laughed. He found it hard to imagine that for Christy the television news and data flowing over a cell phone were more important than the person or work in front of him.

The game went pretty much as Paul thought. Christy was really smart, but he played one move at a time. Paul wasn't a chess pro, but he did know a few tactical maneuvers. Christy just played from the hip. This evening Paul tried to maximize the use of his pawns, trying to see how much he could attack Christy's king with pawns alone. Interesting. It did not take long to defeat Christy.

"You've got me at a disadvantage!" said Christy. "My brains are somewhere else."

"No problem!" said Paul. He was wondering whether he wanted to put the word out, find more serious partners now that he was getting settled. He stirred the embers of the fire, separating the ash to cool it. The air in the room was warm and fragrant. "I'm impressed with the heat in here! It's a pretty big space, but these log walls are as tight as a tick!"

Christy was attending to his phone and didn't seem to hear.

Paul did not go to the rally with Christy the next day. He had many other things to worry about. For one thing, that morning there was a meeting of the Lake Michigami Association. The people who had cabins on the lake had been meeting as a group for as long as Paul could remember. Dad had been a member!

Paul got up early and drove to the tiny community of Laporte, where, in the town's only grocery, a woman named Stella sold flats of cinnamon rolls she had made at home. Paul bought an aluminum sheet of the rolls. He remembered to mention that he was looking for a dog. "A dog that enjoys the woods," said Paul.

"Oh!" said Stella from behind the counter. "I will let you know if I hear of one looking for a home." She got Paul's phone number.

With his tray of cinnamon rolls, Paul was very welcome at the meeting, which was held in the spacious living room of a home on Preacher's Point. The room smelled like coffee. "Hey, Paul!" said his hostess. "Those look amazing!" She put the frosted rolls out on plates. "I hear that you are going to be with us all winter this year!"

"Yup," said Paul. "I'm looking forward to it!"

"The more the merrier!" said another man, who clapped Paul on the back in greeting.

Paul looked around for his friend Peter, but didn't see him. Like Paul, Pete was the son of a pastor, close to Paul's age. He worked for a railroad and was gone for long periods of time on runs. He'd been living two cabins down the lake from Paul for many years.

The meeting wasn't like the major annual meeting held each August. By now there were only about fifteen people, those who lived all year around on the lake. It did not include everyone. Many spouses had not come. It was mostly men, the public faces of the households. By this time, Paul knew all of them. Most were at least ten years older than he was, had retired from pastoral or teaching work.

Paul had been surprised to find that a lot of activities in the lake community were separated by gender. It probably had to do with the ages of people and was a legacy of the immigrant communities. When he was growing up, there had always been a ladies' aid or Bible study group at church, and a Lutheran brotherhood. When his family went to the family reunions on the farms in their North Dakota or Iowa parishes, the women collected in the kitchen and the men sat on chairs in the living room or on the porch and groused. It was not typical of his own generation, but Paul ignored it. He was here to stay. Eventually people his age would also live year round at the lake.

When everyone had their coffee and sweets, they sat in the living room on sofas and deep chairs. The topics that came up had come up before.

"There's a red car that just tears down 37 every morning," said one older man. "Knocked me into my garbage can yesterday. One of these days that guy is going to kill someone!"

"The sheriff's deputy was here in August," said Gordon, who chaired the informal meeting.

"They're aware of it. Remember we were complaining that people weren't walking on the oncoming traffic side of the road? The sheriff's deputy didn't say a word."

"The driver is responsible," said one. "If I stop to watch an eagle or cross the road to get my mail, I might be on the wrong side of the road. But the driver should have that in mind. It's a gravel road, for Pete's sake!"

"What's their hurry?" said Arnie, one of the oldest men in the room and a founder of the organization. "We're already here!"

Another recurring theme regarded Lake Michigami's water quality. The lake was reputed to be among the clearest of Minnesota's 10,000 lakes. In August there had been complaints that people should not be bathing and washing their hair in the lake. "Phosphates get into the water! It's going to lead to the death of the lake!" Others brought this up again that morning, though no one, not even Paul, was swimming in the lake in October!

"Phosphates were outlawed years ago," said their hostess. "Everything's biodegradable now." She looked around and smiled at everyone, knowing she was talking to residents. "Some people don't want us to live up here. They're worried about our septic systems too, but I've heard our modern septic systems are better waste treatment than the million dollar systems in the cities!"

"This is not the Boundary Waters Canoe Area!" said one of the men. "We've all got a right to live here. Motor oil exhaust is a much bigger problem than shampoo in any case, and I don't see anyone trying to prevent boat motors."

"Let's get back to basics," said Gordon. "I think we can agree that our issues should be 1) the preservation of highway 37, the south shore road; 2) wetlands preservation, which means no development of back lots and forest roads; 3) the fair and even enforcement of building ordinances; and 4) reasonable and well-planned measures to preserve water quality. Have I got that right?"

"I'm for fish stocking!" piped up Arnie. "If the fish and wildlife thrive, we've got good water quality!"

"You still fishing, Arnie?" asked one of the older men. "Hope you don't keel over in the boat!"

"What a way to go, though," said Arnie. "Out among the loons where I belong!"

Paul appreciated the dry humor of these staunch older people. As the meeting broke up, people began to talk among themselves. "So Paul, what do you think?" asked Gordon, who had been the pastor of a large Lutheran church in Sauk Centre. "I'd like to start a men's book group. The women's group is going great guns. I think it would be fun to get up one of our own. Would you come?"

"Sure," said Paul. "What kinds of things do you want to read?" He already had a plan to read stacks of books over the winter.

"All kinds of things," said Gordon. "Some sociology, like there's that book *Bowling Alone*, which people are always referring to. Thomas Friedman. Maybe get into a Muslim book or two, politics, philosophy. I'm not so interested in fiction."

"Sounds good to me," said Paul. "Any science?"

"Sure," said Gordon. "You propose a few. I've got a couple of guys who want to do it. Just informal. Meet at each other's houses. Like the women."

"I'm all in," said Paul. "Keep me posted." He wondered whether this might be a good place to mention that he was looking for a dog. "You know," he began, "I'm looking for a dog, a dog that would be good in the woods."

"Puppy?" asked Gordon.

Paul sighed. He did not relish the thought of training a puppy, but it was probably the best idea. He wanted the dog to be accustomed to him, to be adventurous, but quiet. "Could be," he answered. "It would depend on the dog."

"I'll keep my ears open," said Gordon. "Send me an email with your ideas about books!"

Paul promised.

In the morning, Paul was up early, heading out with a thermos of coffee, binoculars around his neck. He tried to get out of the house for a couple of hours before turning on his computer and settling down to the work of the day. He generally went out to the beaver pond on the logging trails on the far side of the road, what Gordon called the 'back lots.' The pond had called to Paul since he was a boy collecting milkweed pods there for Mother to experiment with. He had buried Archie there.

Since there was little human traffic around the pond, Paul hoped to make it the site of the work he had been wanting to do for ages, the steady observation of the wholeness of one ecological community. He wanted to look not so much for particular things, but to observe the way things worked together, their symbiosis. He knew that the longer he looked at things in one place, the more he would see.

As he reached the end of their own, two rutted track, which even construction had not managed to smooth out, Paul noticed three women coming up the road, power walking in bright orange sweatshirts! Ah, he thought, hunting season. They were trying to avoid being mistaken for deer!

Paul had seen the women before. He stopped and waited by the mailbox for them to come up to him.

"Hello Paul!" sang out Jackie, one of his neighbors. "How are you this bright fine morning?" Her hot breath was visible against the chill air.

"Good! Good," said Paul.

"Off into the woods, are you?" she asked.

"Yup," said Paul. "I've got some turtles and beaver to check on."

"You're welcome to join us," said Sandy. They all seemed anxious to go. Jackie was actually running in place! "We do this every morning."

"You're a little too fast for me!" said Paul. "But I thought I'd let you know I've been looking for a dog."

"Ok," said Jackie, heading away. "We'll let you know!"

Paul plunged into the dry brush on the other side of the road. The sumac was now very red and most shrubs were dry and brown or golden.

Only the pines and evergreens maintained their deep northern greens. The sky was an intense blue. October blue, Paul had always thought of it. The earth's tilt made the season, and the color.

Paul realized that he was trying to find his human contacts before he settled down to really study. They grounded him. He was going to the little Lutheran church in Laporte, was a regular at these Lake Michigami meetings and he always stopped to talk to his neighbors. News could be important when you lived in the near wilderness.

A few days later, Stella from the grocery store in Laporte called Paul. "You know that little Forestedge Winery on the other side of Highway 64? They make those black current and rhubarb wines?" she asked.

A light passed over Paul's face. He had seen the sign for the winery, but had never checked it out. "Yes," he said. "I think so. I've never been over there."

"You should! They've got quite a nice little ranch down there. Arts and crafts gallery too," said Stella. "And I heard they may have some puppies! Born a few months ago. Lab and shepherd mix, I think."

"Wow," said Paul. "That sounds really good." He was wary. He knew that if he went and looked at the dogs, it would be all over. He would not be able to hold out against them, if one was really available. "Thank you so much! I'll probably go have a look. Who should I ask for?"

"They're open every day until Christmas, apparently," said Stella. "Just stop in at the winery and say I sent you."

"Thank you so much, Stella!" said Paul. "I'm excited!" A puppy. He was bowled over. But hadn't he been telling everyone he was looking for one? He could not back down now.

Paul slept on the idea, but the next morning he drove over to the Forestedge Winery. The driveway wasn't much bigger than their own, going off into the woods, designated by a small sign. But then the road opened into a large clearing with gardens, orchards and a wide patio laid out in front of the barn-red painted winery. The place looked ambitious and pleasant. Paul spoke to a woman named Sharon who was offering tastes of the wines.

"This is our cranberry from last year," said Sharon, handing Paul a glass. "You just missed our art show on the weekend. We have them frequently!"

The wine had a tart, rough taste which Paul liked. He nodded his appreciation. "Stella, over in Laporte, told me you might have some puppies," he said tentatively.

"Oh yes!" said Sharon. "She perked up when I talked about them the other day. Do you want to come and see them?"

There were two four-month-old puppies left, one a light caramel color with floppy Labrador ears, its coat short with interesting cowlicks on its chest. Its ears were slightly more golden. Paul knelt down and felt around the puppy's bones. It appeared to have been well-fed and seemed to relish his hands. The other was black with shepherd-like ears. Paul felt around this one's body as well, but the caramel-coated dog was his, he knew.

Paul looked up at Sharon. "Beautiful dogs," he said. "Can you really part with one of them?"

"We have to," said Sharon. "Their mother has been our mascot for a long time. She's all we can really handle. We didn't expect these guys, though we love them."

Paul arranged to pay $100 for the beautiful caramel-colored dog. "I'm not really ready for her," he told Sharon. "Could I wait a week to pick her up?"

"Sure," said Sharon. "Take a brochure for our wines. We'll expect you in a week."

Paul drove away. The image of the caramel-colored dog floated in front of him. It was the color of taffy, not too far off the golden and white colors of Foxy, a long-haired Sheltie, Paul's first dog. Paul thought of the book by E.O. Wilson he wanted to recommend to Gordon's book group. Wilson, he thought. Good name for a dog.

14

"Dr. Wolfe believes that most of the diseases associated with aging come about because our bodies become more acidic over the years," said Line to Stephen as they shared their morning coffee. It was January, and the kitchen was illuminated by a light hung over the table in the spacious room. Outdoors, the grey sky was full of light, the sun about to pop over the horizon.

"So what does that mean for us?" asked Stephen, a little apprehensively. The Sunday morning *New York Times* lay open in front of him on the table, but he was more relaxed than on any weekday, allowing Line to bubble on about her discoveries.

"We're pretty good," said Line. "But our plates should be 75% alkaline (vegetables and fruits) and 25% acid (meats and grains). I think we eat too much meat and carbs still. At least I do," she said ruefully. Line was a bit overweight, especially in her hips. She wasn't as big as Mother or Aunt Rose had been, but she carried a few more pounds than she wanted to. "Too much bread and pasta," she said.

"Whatever you think," said Stephen placidly. He was skinny as a rail at 62. He rode his bicycle every day it wasn't raining and just wasn't very interested in food. "You've kept us healthy all these years. I trust you, my Line."

"It's just amazing to me," said Line as she set the water boiling for a second pot of coffee. "I think doctors are finally having to face the fact that food affects disease. I mean, here we are, little chemical retorts. They don't want to admit it!"

"Yup," said Stephen. He pulled the paper toward him out of habit. "As in everything," he commented darkly, "you have to follow the money. If food kept you healthy, you might not need doctors! Or drug companies!"

"About longevity, the doctors I know say that love is important, heredity is second and food is a distant third," said Line. "But I trust Dr. Wolfe. He's Canadian. Money isn't as much of a factor in health care up there." She had been fascinated by a website for the Wolfe Clinic. In articles, Dr. Wolfe asserted that cancer was a fungus, feeding on older bodies overloaded with acids.

Sugar was a major acid. Line still loved cookies and ice cream. As a kid, she had eaten sugar all day every day! But in California she had managed to turn toward a more Mediterranean diet. Her kids ate much less sugar. Her girls had willowy bodies, except for Heather, whose body was more like Line's. Christy took after his father, did not seem to care very much what he ate.

"Anything I need to know?" asked Line, realizing Stephen had turned toward the newspaper. She was content to get her news from Stephen, who abridged it for her. The last year had been full of the sickening news that Americans were torturing prisoners in Iraq. The government of Iraq had been handed over to an interim coalition, but sectarian problems between Sunni and Shia Muslims had erupted. Americans could not leave.

"Not much," said Stephen sardonically. "President Bush will be inaugurated this week, remaining a heartbeat away from the presidency!" It was widely believed Vice President Dick Cheney ran the government. Cheney had privatized the war, making sure his corporate cronies made plenty of profit.

The room began to flood with low-angled light and Line stood up to organize the kitchen. "I'm hoping to do my pruning today," she said.

"Go for it," said Stephen, looking up. "I'll probably spend some time at the office." He was on a semester break, but he always had masses of work to do. Topmost in his mind at the moment, Line knew, was a biography of Paul Wellstone he was working on. "Do you want to spend a little time in Minnesota this year?" he asked. "I could use a few research days in St. Paul."

"Oh!" said Line. "I'd love that! A chance to see Christy and Paul. And the new cabin. Let's do it!"

"I don't know if I would get to the cabin," said Stephen. "But I'll try." Ironically enough, Stephen knew he would find in the Paul Wellstone papers, which were housed at the Minnesota Historical Society in St. Paul, notes taken by his own son Christy, who had accompanied Wellstone on an exploratory trip around the country, asking questions as Wellstone contemplated a run for the presidency. His aspirations were cut off when he, his wife and daughter were killed in an airplane crash. It had been very hard on Christy.

Line put on old clothes and found her oldest, most raggedy sheet in the linen closet. She spread the sheet out on a narrow strip of flagstones and began to prune the roses which bordered the front of the house. During the early fall rains, she ignored the garden, letting it become brown and scraggly. The roses, which did so well in their dry micro-climate were full of tiny branches anxious to come out. There were even a few rosebuds.

But in January, Line was vicious. She cut off the rosebuds and brought them into the house to put in vases. Then she cut every rosebush back to a few thicker canes, letting the thorny cuttings collect on the ragged sheet.

She was thinking about Dad. He had been an iconoclast, very independent, unwilling to take what came to him without a grain of salt. He would have liked Dr. Wolfe, who insisted people should take their health into their own hands. Wolfe told people to alkalize their bodies, using good water and the enzymes from fruits and vegetables. Healthy people should take responsibility, Line agreed, leaving health care resources to those with serious illness.

Dr. Wolfe felt the same way about the planet. It needed reclaiming from the toxic chemicals and industrial wastes lavished on it. "But the best weapon is an alkaline body," he wrote. He thought the body very smart with many lines of defense.

Line wasn't anxious to live to any great age. She accepted the natural limits to human life, but she did want to be healthy while she was alive. And she wanted her family to remain healthy. It was always wonderful to see feisty old people who took care of themselves. Poppa was a good example.

Line also knew a few great physicians, who worked with their patients to make the best decisions about the end of life. She herself worked with the physical side of life, though she was especially aware of unseen energies, the resonance which surged through living things. Humans were a wholeness, with physical, mental and emotional aspects deeply intertwined.

Line sighed, gathering up the edges of the sheet and carrying the thorny clippings out back to the trash bins. She did not want them in her compost. She moved on to the plants on the back decks, a few roses, but also her herb gardens and vegetable planters. In their temperate climate, Line had green vegetables all year round, though there wasn't much sun in the winter. In late January, she was thinking about the coming spring, about replacing plants and going out to the beach to get kelp to fertilize them. Kelp was full of the rich nutrients it filtered from the sea.

The holiday season had been particularly delightful. Ivy and Marshall had come up for a week, and Line now felt she knew Marshall better. Many festive meals had taken place, and all of them except Poppa had gone up to the city to help Doug and Marty with an idea of Doug's, a Christmas treasure hunt.

Doug thought his kids had too much stuff already and he did not like the way his ex-wife lavished them with presents to which they did not pay much attention. Instead of presents that Christmas, he prepared a treasure hunt which took place all over San Francisco. It had the added benefit of showing the kids the city which Marty and Line had both lived in and loved. Doug had not, but he wanted the kids to know it. He had written a series of punning clues which led from one place to another.

The clues led along the Embarcadero, from the ferry building, to Coit Tower to the historic ships on Fisherman's Wharf and the maritime museum. Ivy and Marshall had met the party at Coit Tower, where Doug palmed them a clue and they tucked it behind a colorful mural of people harvesting apricots and other fruit and vegetables, one of the many WPA projects from the 1930's.

Line and Stephen had explored the newly opened markets in the ferry building at the end of Market Street and drunk tea in a Chinese tea house before meeting the Hendersons on the triple-masted Balclutha docked in the Bay. It was a dank, wet day, but they had hidden out among the bunks below decks, "where a sailor might kip" and Doug palmed them the next clue which led to the maritime museum.

The day ended with dinner at a dry and warm fish restaurant, followed by sundaes at Ghirardelli Square. Under the huge sundae the kids shared, in Marty's handwriting on a small square of graph paper was the last clue. Line could remember it: "Real life, honest fun is nothing you can fake. No one can give you more fun than you yourself can make."

The warmth and glow of the young people on that memorable day had delighted them all. Arriving home in Santa Cruz late that night they were surprised to find Poppa up and sitting by a warm fire. Still full of excitement, Ivy and Marshall told the story of the day. "What a good father Doug is. Not in ways people expect, but in original ways," said Marshall.

"He's fighting our commercialized culture," said Ivy. "I'm with him!"

Line concurred. Doug and Marty had gotten married that year, quietly with only Stephen and Line as witnesses. They had rented Line's old house on Morrissey, because three of Doug's kids were in Santa Cruz high school. Ignoring the expense of maintaining two households, Doug drove up the treacherous Boulder Creek road to work at the ranch every day, instead of letting his kids go back and forth. "It's only for three or four years," Doug told Line. "While the kids are in high school." Alice, Doug's mother, did not have enough room in her house for all the kids.

Ivy and Marshall had gone back to Los Angeles, and Line's own household was back to its smallest; just Poppa, Stephen and herself. January was always interesting for Line. She made resolutions not to eat sugar, to worry less and accept more. She was still bothered by all the things in life that weren't fair. Plenty to do, she thought, against injustice. Now that Line was 60, Marty told her, by the Chinese system she had passed through all five elements in all twelve animal years. She was starting over!

The arc of a life was fascinating. Poppa's was beginning to round out. He now talked more about the past, about his wife, about how they had met and the work he had done. He had outlived his wife by more than 30 years. "My friends say that for a happy marriage," he told Line, "the one who outlives the other has to pay. I have paid that price." He was 84, wanted more Jewish foods than he did before and paid more attention to Jewish holidays. He was quite healthy, but a little shrunken, slower and less outgoing. He did not show any sign of life's passing. Line suspected he would live another ten years at least.

A successful life, Line thought. Poppa had helped hundreds of immigrants to America with his legal practice. Her own life was successful as well. The proof of it was her four amazing kids. The plan for the afternoon was a scheduled call to Heather's family in Chile, via Skype, a new way of seeing visually the people you were talking to. Line couldn't wait.

Perhaps we should have taught them how to play, Line reflected. The whole family was bent on work, following in Stephen's footsteps. They had never done much traveling, camping or skiing. Trips to Minnesota, day trips to the beach, picnics in the woods. The kids had had to find their own recreation, but each of them had made themselves a life. Ivy loved yoga, Line noted, which balanced her head-down sewing. Fern and Heather had each chosen work which could be physically demanding. Line was not worried about their health. She knew less about Christy, who had lived in Minnesota since he was 18, bouncing around among family and friends, and spending two years in the Peace Corps in Peru.

Line went down the steep steps to the lowest level of the property where wild grasses, native shrubs and her persimmon tree thrived. The air was damp, though sunny. A titmouse with a little cockade on his head scrabbled about in a bush, then chattered from a branch of the persimmon. Deep down in the ravine below, Line could almost hear a trickle of water. Only at this time of year was there any water in the ravine.

Line did not try to prune the persimmon, which still had a few brilliant orange fruits left on its bare branches. She looked up at them against the blue sky. The tree had a lovely shape. It could take care of itself. Like me, thought Line.

How much Line loved her California indoor-outdoor life. Even in winter, it was easy to open the house to the out of doors. This house was much better built than some of the "cardboard" California houses she had known. Its great windows through which one looked out on the decks and the ridge falling away to the hills were lovely. Best of all, she could go in and out in all weathers. It's how we were meant to live, she thought.

At 3 p.m. that afternoon, Stephen, Line and Poppa gathered at the computer in the den close to the router. The computer, which they all shared, had a camera and a microphone. Stephen tuned in to Skype and found Heather's family account. Bouncing off satellites which Stephen said were connected somewhere in Estonia, annoying signal tones rang until all of a sudden it was silent and Pablo, Heather's husband, said hello.

On the computer screen, Line saw little Matteo, Heather's three and a half year old son in Pablo's lap. He was wearing a t-shirt and shorts, reminding Line that it was high summer in Chile!

"Hello! Hello!" said Stephen. "How are you?"

"Buenas tardes!" said Pablo. And then to the dark little mophead. "Ese es tu abuelo. Esta muy lejos en California."

"Abuelo?" questioned Matteo.

"Si," said Pablo, repeating in English. "He's far away in California."

"Buenas tardes, Matteo," said Stephen. "Does he speak English?"

"I don't think he knows which is which," said Pablo. "I speak Spanish to him, Heather speaks English. We want him to know both."

Line looked closely at the fine-grained skin and brown eyes of her grandson. How she wished she could touch and smell the little boy. Behind Pablo and Matteo, Line could see Heather, also with a little boy on her lap, Paulo, two years younger than Matteo, wearing only a diaper.

"Come, Heather," said Pablo. "Or would you rather wait?"

"You talk," said Heather. "I'll have a turn in a moment. Hello, all you dear ones," she raised her hand in the background.

As Line looked, the shapes of the family on the screen became all boxy. "You're pixelating!" said Stephen. And then the screen froze. "Are you there? Hello? Hello?" Stephen moved his mouse. "I think we lost them," he said. He tried again.

Again, Pablo appeared on the screen. "Hello!" he said. "Hello!"

"Hello! Hello!" echoed the little Matteo.

"We're back," said Stephen. "Getting some weather patterns there. So how's the harvest going to be this year?" he asked.

"Good!" said Pablo. "It looks good! Steady ripening. The Carmenère and Merlot are just going into verasion, or as we call it, enverno. We're a few months away, but things look good at this point."

"Verasion's when the grapes take on color," piped up Heather from the background. Line had lived in California long enough to know what verasion was, but she loved hearing Heather's voice.

Line and Stephen had only been to Chile once, at Christmas a couple of years ago. It was so odd. December and January were the hottest months of the year in Chile. Line remembered the beautiful adobe ranch houses which had been in Pablo's family for generations. The Andes rose in the back of the valley, barely tipped with snow and sinking into pink and purple haze in the evenings. The vineyards flowed out toward the mountains.

The Valenzuelas had had a Christmas tree, decorated with lights. Every night before Christmas the whole extended family went to mass; a novena, it was called. They came home and drank a lovely coffee with liquor, milk, cinnamon and sugar in it, called a monkey's tail. Then they had dinner and played cards until late at night! On Christmas everyone opened their presents at midnight and stayed up to play with them.

It had been a very moving holiday. The oddest thing to Line was the family playing cards every night until late! After dinner everyone gathered around tables in the living room near the Christmas tree, where a fire was laid if it was chilly. It wasn't really about bridge, Line figured out. It was about chit chatting, four generations of people including Pablo's first born, his grandmother, his brother and his children. It made Line feel she was in some European castle or country house, whiling away the holidays. Playing cards cut across some of the language barriers too. Line never got good at it, but she decided it was fun.

"Did you post your 'I'm sorry' photo to that website where people are apologizing to the world for re-electing Bush?" Pablo's face on the screen asked playfully of Stephen.

"Nope," said Stephen. "Should have! I have a colleague who has accepted a job in New Zealand, however. He's had it. He's picking up stakes and leaving."

"Imperialist nation," said Pablo. "We've got a good president right now, Ricardo Lagos, a socialist. But it took a coalition of 17 parties to elect him."

"I like it," said Stephen. "Our two party system is pretty broken. They're both the same in any case; just depends on which corporate master they're answering to."

Line stepped toward the camera. "I have a question for Matteo," she said. "Matteo, this is Abuela Line. Can you tell me where California is?"

"California?" said Matteo, pointing to the screen, and looking back at Pablo.

In the background, Heather pushed a globe toward Matteo. "Aqui estamos," said Pablo, pointing to Chile. "Y aqui esta California."

"It's all very confusing," said Line. "How can he see us and not touch us?"

"Don't worry," said Pablo. "He's going to understand computers and cameras better than we ever will!"

Line nodded, laughing. "Yes," she said. "You're right."

Heather then moved up and sat down in front of the computer. "Hello mama and papa," she said. She brushed a tear away from her face. "It's so good to see you!"

Line felt her own tears welling up. Heather had been so brave, so far from home. Would it hurt Pablo if she mentioned it? "I miss you, Heather," she said.

"Yes," said Heather. "I miss you too. I had no idea how far away a person could get from home!"

"But you had no choice," said Line.

"You're right," said Heather. "I had no choice, and I haven't now. My heart is here. It just has little broken parts, where you are."

"I love hearing your voice," said Line. "And seeing your beautiful boys." Line was still surprised it was Heather, the most grounded of her girls, who had moved so far away. But perhaps that was the way of it.

Heather kissed the top of her little Paulo's head. He too had long hair, but it was not as dark as Matteo's. "Yes," she said. "They are little lights. They light up our home."

"Smart little boys," said Poppa, who hung close behind Line and Stephen. Line suspected he wanted to ask them whether they celebrated Hanukkah, but knew better. The Jewish influence was diluted in these little great-grandchildren, while Catholicism was very present.

"Hello, Poppa," said Heather. "I miss you too. I remember how we used to make dinner together when everyone else was in Edinburgh."

"Not so long ago," said Poppa. His mind was as sharp as it had ever been.

"Tell me about everyone," begged Heather. "Christy, Fern and Ivy."

Line, Stephen and Poppa all chimed in with their estimations of how each of Heather's siblings were doing. They were like the spokes of a wheel, radiating out into the world and connecting back to their parents at the center.

"Do you still play cards in the evenings?" asked Line.

"Some," said Heather. "Maybe less often. The older kids are tending toward television. American television!"

"That's too bad," said Line.

"Part of their education," said Pablo. "We are a small country, a thin, long one. So we are very nationalist, Heather tells me. She says people in California weren't all that patriotic. Except after September 11, maybe. But here, we stand up for our honor and our flag."

"Yes," said Stephen. "I noticed it when we were there."

"My parents rally everyone around on the weekends," said Pablo. "We all eat together, and yes, sometimes play cards."

"I love imagining you all together," said Line.

"The boys will sing a song for you, I think," said Heather. "Off one of the Raffi albums you sent." She stood up and little Paulo stood up on his pudgy bow legs. "Move back from the camera," said Heather. "Can you see us?"

"Yes! Yes!" said Poppa.

Heather, Matteo and little Paulo stood in a line, singing, "I'm gonna shake, shake, shake my sillies out," they sang. "Wiggle my waggles away. I'm gonna clap clap, clap my crazies out, clap, clap, clap my crazies out." Matteo sang clearly with Heather while he shook his little shoulders and clapped his hands. Paulo watched his brother, trying to imitate. He looked like a little duck, close to the ground on little legs.

Line laughed at the little boys, "So darling!" she said.

"We do this a lot! Especially at night," said Heather. She kept going, "I'm gonna yawn, yawn, yawn my sleepies out, wiggle my waggles away." The little boys copied her.

"I like the whale one," said Matteo. "Baby beluga in the deep blue sea, swims so wild and he swims so free."

Heather looked at him fondly. "We went to the ocean a little while ago, didn't we Matteo."

"I like the ocean," said Matteo firmly. "But we didn't see any whales." He spoke to Pablo, and flicked his face furtively toward the camera now and then.

"We stayed for a week on the coast," said Heather. "It was wonderful."

"Well you have to come and see us," said Line. "We will take you to the ocean every day."

The talk went on, Stephen and Poppa stepping up to talk to Pablo, while Heather tried to corral the kids in the background. Matteo rode a tricycle around the tiled floor while Paulo looked on enviously.

Line looked and looked, trying to see what they were doing. It was something, after all, to see and hear Heather with her healthy little sons moving and talking on a computer screen, perhaps a step up from photographs.

15

When the twins called from the beach, Marty asked Zoe if she wanted to come with her to pick them up. Zoe had her driving permit, needed to drive with a grownup in the car. Jason was helping his beloved Grandma Alice make dinner. Or rather, he was making dinner, while Alice coached. It didn't matter that she shared no blood whatsoever with Jason. They were devoted to each other.

Zoe and Marty drove out to the beach in the October twilight. It made Marty a little nervous as Zoe's stops and starts were jerky, but she was getting the hang of it.

It was a beautiful evening. The twins stood by a phone booth near Pleasure Point, black shadows against the dark combers with white tops rolling in, the sky many colors of orange and purple. The two sleek seals loaded their surfboards on top of the car and attached them with bungee cords.

Zoe spoke officiously from the driver's seat, making sure everyone noticed that she was in charge. "How was it?" she asked.

"Great," said Nic. "The best waves this time of year, I swear."

"Were you warm enough?" asked Marty. She could not believe that the kids could stay in the water most of the day this late in the year, in only their wet suits, which had short sleeves and short legs.

"Oh yeah," said Natasha. "Too excited to be cold!"

"Is Dad home?" asked Nic.

"Not yet, but he's on his way," said Zoe. Doug drove down from the ranch and vineyards up on the mountain where he worked each day. He wanted to keep the family together while the kids were in high school, and so had rented Line's old house where they could live together and the kids didn't have to make the treacherous drive up to Boulder Creek every day. It could take an hour. Harbor High School was less than a mile from their rented house.

The twins were sophomores now, Zoe a junior. Up until last spring, the family had spent weekends up at the ranch, but when the twins skipped school in order to surf, Doug settled them down for a talk. It was his disciplinary method. And it wasn't that he talked to them. They had to tell him what was going on and why they had done what they did.

It felt to Marty that what Doug had tried to do to keep them together was actually going to tear them apart. "There's nothing to do up there," the twins complained. And Zoe had aided in the rebellion. She wanted to spend more time in Santa Cruz to hang out with her friends. The high school had a great girls soccer team. Zoe wasn't a very good player, but she was such a good morale booster the team couldn't get along without her. She wanted to go to weekend practices.

Marty thought that Doug would compromise. They were barely camping in the house in Santa Cruz, with only the minimum of furniture, clothing and dishes. But Doug surprised Marty once again. "Well," he said. "I guess we live in Santa Cruz now." He wanted his kids in school. That was non-negotiable.

Marty was shocked, but she adapted quickly. During the summer too, they stayed in town most of the time. Marty only went up to the ranch to check on the tasting room, which she ostensibly managed. Doug went back and forth every day, but the kids were thrilled to be in town.

Zoe had appropriated the refurbished room which had once been a garage for her own, making it a clubhouse for her friends and a place to dream her private dreams. The twins were in the water almost every day, foggy and cold or not. They went from body surfing to boards, which Doug bought for them. And Jason settled down to cook his way through Jamie Oliver's videos. Jamie Oliver looked like a kid on television and cooked with complete confidence. Jason, at 12, did too.

Every night, however, everyone gathered for a meal. No friends, Doug had decreed. Dinner was family time. He himself had the hardest time getting there, but he somehow did, nearly every night.

"What was your Pleasure today?" teased Marty as they drove home. Pleasure Point was the twins' current favorite beach on the east side of town. Not as competitive or as wild as Steamer Lane, the waves were consistent.

"Tasha got a barrel ride. Stayed in it all the way," said Nic, loyally. "The guys cut her some slack because there's not that many girls out there."

"It was amazing," said Natasha. "They always say the tube is safer the longer you're in it, and it felt that way. Such a rush." She shook her wet head as if in awe. The 15-year-old twins were brown and gleaming, alive with health.

"I shouldn't ask you," said Marty. "We should save it until dinner, until you can tell everyone." Marty had watched them, hopping up onto their boards with their feet, staying low. She thought it was amazing, requiring the most balance and flexibility she could imagine.

Doug's van was parked in the driveway when they got home, Marty was delighted to see. She ran in and shared a hug with Zoe and her sweet, sun-kissed husband, while the kids put away their surfboards. Doug's longish, once blonde hair was becoming gray curls. Marty was pleased she could now call him husband in truth. The house smelled wonderful of unctuous roast pork.

"My darlings!" Doug said. "I see you've been driving," he said to Zoe.

"Yup," said Zoe proudly. "I only need four more hours before I take my test."

"Sorry I missed your soccer game." There was no way Doug could take off a day during harvest.

"We lost," said Zoe. "But Marty and Grandma were there. They cheered loud enough for all of us." The Harbor High School soccer coach who had led the girls to many victories had just retired, and the new coach was having a rocky start.

The table was already laid, glasses of water for the kids, wine for Marty and Doug. Alice beamed at them from the stove where she was taking a pan of cornbread out of the oven. She didn't drink wine any more.

"I marinated these spare ribs overnight," said Jason. "And cooked them really slowly. I can't wait to try them!"

"They smell fabulous," said Doug. "And I'm hungry!"

Everyone loaded their plates with black beans, spare ribs, cornbread and salad. It was a feast. A Saturday night party. But Marty always felt it was a celebration, a triumph when everyone came together from the far places they each inhabited. The food was their usual fare, though they ate less meat during the week. Marty had been secretly glad to escape the tyranny of Ana Maria's kitchen at the ranch. Marty now had to organize more groceries, but everyone helped with the cooking and there were more flavors than chili!

Conversation meandered around the table. Doug talked about the harvest, the twins about surfing, and Jason described the sauce for the succulent ribs.

"How was the gym?" Doug asked Marty. She was a volunteer shelver at the public library, and she found it just physical enough to be a good workout.

Marty smiled, "Fine. The library was its usual quiet self. Except for the little kids."

Zoe broke in: "My English teacher thinks I'm a good writer." Zoe was clearly very smart, but had never been a good student. All of a sudden she was taking more of an interest. "She said that if I keep it up, I can get in to any college I want."

Doug and Marty looked at each other, smiling. "Well," said Doug. "You know I can't give all of you a free ride to college. It's going to be partly up to you." Doug considered the kids adults at 18. Not that he was going to push them out of the house. Far from it. But he did feel that from that time on they should make their own decisions.

"You don't have to start telling us about all the jobs you did," said Nic. "We know. We'll do that when we're older."

"I'm not worried," said Doug, smiling. "After a couple of summers surfing, you'll see how things are. There's a reason they call them beach bums." Doug had had all kinds of jobs, beginning when he was 15. His father died when he was 16, and he had done nothing but work ever since.

"Dad," said Zoe. "You're acting jealous!"

"I'm not," said Doug. "I'm doing exactly what I want. But even if you want to be athletes, you need to be rounded people. College would be a good thing for every one of you." The twins did have the bodies of competitive athletes.

"Head, heart, hands and health," said Marty. "That was our 4-H pledge."

"In a four-leaf clover?" asked Zoe.

"Yes," said Marty. "In Iowa."

"Oh!" said Alice. "Me too! In California. That was a long time ago!"

"Have Marty tell you about the Zorba method," said Doug.

Marty blushed a little. "When you have a passion, go with it to the end," she said. "Get through it and come out the other side. Like those barrels you guys are surfing. I'm glad you guys love to surf. But then you want to round out your lives with a mental life."

"And service to others," said Alice. "That's what really makes a person happy." She turned to Marty. "That was the 'hands' part of the 4-H pledge, don't you think?"

Marty smiled and nodded at her. "I do think surfing must give you concentration," she said. "Responding constantly to everything that's coming at you." She was a little in awe of the twins' abilities.

"You're not thinking much, though," said Natasha. "At least not in words. You're just going for it." She took another piece of cornbread. "What are you writing about Zoe?" she asked.

"Team spirit, I guess you could say," said Zoe. "Soccer's the same. It isn't like you have time to think. But the group thinks. That's what I love."

Jason went back into the kitchen to take another serving of ribs. "I wish I could cook for Hurricane Katrina victims," he said. "I heard a program about it." Even a month after the hurricane, the news was full of discussion of the millions of people who were trying to recover from the massive storm. Rescue had been slow and many had been housed in terrible conditions. All of the emergency response groups were under investigation.

"Hands and hearts," said Alice. "I wish I could too. The news is just heartbreaking."

That's a passion too, thought Marty. She was so proud of all of them, of the intense life around the table. Three generations, each with different experiences and approaches.

That night Marty and Doug went to see *Mondovino*, a documentary which had been made in wineries all over the world. They met Doug's partners Jeremy and Vince at the theater, because everyone was interested in what Robert Parker, an influential critic, and Michel Rolland, a winemaking consultant, had to say. Marty wondered if any Chilean wineries, such as that of the Valenzuela family Heather had married into, would be in the film. But no, the new world wineries Nossiter, the filmmaker, visited were in California, Argentina and Brazil.

The movie went straight to the heart of the arguments between Jeremy and Vince about what they were trying to do at Boulder Creek Vineyards. When they went out for drinks afterwards, Marty could have predicted their reactions. Vince bought a round of Rob Roys, watching the bartender to see that he slipped the right amount of Angostura bitters on top.

"I'm with Nossiter," said Jeremy. "He doesn't come out and say what he thinks, but the movie comes across loud and clear. Wine should be in balance with its purpose and terroir. Its purpose is to bring families and friends together and to enhance the foods they share."

"We've been lucky," said Vince. "Robert Parker likes our wines, which drives up sales. I think Rolland was the villain in the piece. He's the one running around the world, telling everyone to over-oak their whites and drive up the alcohol content to make fruit bombs out of the reds!"

Marty had been educated by Jeremy to like dry, sophisticated European-style wines. They were perfect with food. Robert Parker spoke well of Boulder Creek wines because of Jeremy's winemaking. She tasted Doug's drink. It was too late at night to drink liquor, in her mind.

"I think Nossiter sees terroir as a sort of glue for culture, the land, friends, family, food, and social interaction. It keeps us all honest. I agree completely!" said Jeremy.

"And it keeps us small!" said Vince. "If you guys didn't insist on being so 'artisan,' so 'pure,' we could sell a lot more wine."

"But what are we trying to do here?" asked Doug. "Are we trying to be Paul Draper, or Gallo?!" Paul Draper had been the first winemaker in California to emphasize terroir. His first wines were made in the Santa Cruz mountains.

"We want our wines to have a great reputation," said Jeremy. "To taste like the soils they come from. It's that simple. And that's what you're selling, Vince."

Marty had heard all of this before in one form or another. She loved seeing the three men talking together, working together. As in all great partnerships, everyone pushed their own agendas, stakes went up and excellence often resulted.

"The public's not going to care about this movie," said Vince. "They're not going to go see it like they did *Sideways* last year. Now that movie had an impact!"

145

"You're right," said Doug. "No real story here. Unless you're against globalization. Documentaries just preach to their particular choir."

Marty had seen *Sideways* more than once! Once with Doug, and once with Line. She loved the two women in the movie, Virginia Madsen and Sandra Oh. The men were comic and silly, but Madsen had a lovely part when she talked about her feelings for wine. The movie woke California up to the wineries on the Central Coast, including Sanford Winery which Marty had visited. One of the characters demeaned Merlot and spoke highly of Pinot Noir, which Doug thought was having an effect on sales.

Marty loved talking to Doug about movies, the news, about everything. Probably because of his kids, and because of his wide-ranging economic background, Doug had what Marty thought of as a comprehensive view of culture. He was very concerned about it and had an original take on many things. Marty thought he was a natural-born Taoist, a person who resonated more with nature than the mores laid down by society.

Like all Californians, Doug resented the east coast hold on national ideas, though he didn't think much of what Hollywood was churning out at the moment either. *Sideways* had been adapted from a novel written by a valley boy, straight out of Merced. Original, terribly funny and somewhat crass, the movie was written and directed by a man from Omaha. It had gotten some awards and had brought wine to the attention of many people who didn't drink it. It was a win-win for the wine business Doug thought.

As they drove home that night, Marty worried that Doug was tired. As well he might be, she thought. He was leaving the house at 4 in the mornings, going up to the ranch, working on his contracts, and then spending the day in the fields. All the white grapes were in by this time, but the reds were crowding in behind them. The harvest was big and tank space was at a premium.

"Jeremy's excited about the rosé he plans to make from Pinot Noir grapes from the coast grade vineyard," Doug said, yawning. "We're picking them tomorrow. The crew will be out there at 7 a.m. and so will I!" Doug was known for his careful records and clonal selections, as well as his attention to the soils in the vineyards. He and Jeremy had worked closely together for years, were attuned to each other. But they were glad for Vince's marketing and financial acumen keeping them afloat.

"Couldn't you stay home tomorrow?" asked Marty. "You're going to exhaust yourself."

Doug laughed. "Nope. I'm strong like bull. Somewhere along the line people decided they should rest on the seventh day, but nature doesn't!"

Since she wasn't up at the tasting room very often any more, Marty heard less discussion about wine. Her current job was to represent Doug and herself as parents to the kids, especially during harvest when Doug worked such long hours. It was important for them to see people like her, grownups taking responsibility and at the same time joyful. Marty was thrilled to see the kids' futures expanding in front of them, while she was in such a different place.

On Sunday, after a late breakfast, no one made much effort about lunch. It was warm enough for Marty to take her tea out on the terrace in the sun. Line's apricot tree was still in the yard. The leaves on the tree were yellowing, starting to dry up. The bougainvillea against the garage was a brilliant magenta. Marty wasn't nearly as avid a gardener as Line was, but some things just thrived anyway.

Marty poured the strong lapsang souchong from a blue ceramic teapot into a tiny Chinese cup painted with a blue fish. She could hardly use them without laughing about Vince, when he had come for tea once. "Why do you drink your tea out of these fucking little cups?" he asked. The reason was that the tea stayed hot in the pot, cooled too quickly in larger cups. Marty liked her tea hot! She drank in the smoky-tasting liquid. Scandinavians liked smoky-tasting things, she had decided.

In her wildest dreams, Marty had never imagined that she would live in this house, the house in which all of Line's girls had been born. It was somewhat rackety by this time, having endured renters. It had never been beautiful, a composite of several reconstructions and patches. But it certainly worked for their family. In the room where Christy had once slept, and Poppa when he came to California, now slept Nic and Jason. Natasha had the girls' room to herself since Zoe was out in the gaily-painted garage room they called Bag-End.

Just inside the patio door at a little desk in the dining room, Jason surfed the web on the computer, trying to find information for a school project. His science teacher was a space nut and they were doing a unit on the International Space Station, where US and Russian scientists lived and researched. The station orbited the earth about 200 miles up, had been there for almost five years. Marty had gone along when Jason's teacher helped them locate it one night. It was the third brightest object in the sky. Predictably, Jason was writing an essay about what the astronauts and cosmonauts ate and how.

Doug's kids didn't need so much attention any more, but they needed someone to be there. Marty felt herself to be the chatelaine, the keeper of the keys, so to speak. She was the one who made sure the house was full of basic supplies, who organized the washing and cleaning. At night, she went around and made sure the doors were locked and the lights out.

The low-angled sun lay oblique shadows across the pages of Marty's journal and her book, *Nine Gates*, about poetry by Jane Hirshfield. Marty used the journal to keep track of what she was thinking, to pick up the red thread from where she had left off. A book helped too. This one was wonderful, thoughts about language by a woman who had lived up at Green Gulch, the Zen Center farm in Marin County.

Marty was reading a lot. At the library all she did was shelve returned materials, but she liked the exercise. It was a way to see what was being published, what people were reading, even if it was only a public library stuffed with genre fiction. It also gave Marty a community of people to meet a couple of times a week. She didn't like the Dewey Decimal system; in college she had shelved by the Library of Congress numbering. But the library did satisfy her need for order.

Jason came out to get Marty and show her what he had found, a NASA website which answered questions. "It says they can eat anything, but they can't taste or smell as much when they're up there, because their sinuses are filled with fluid."

"Wow," said Marty, looking at the screen where Jason pointed. "I don't think I'd like that!"

"It's because of the low gravity or something," said Jason.

"How long do they stay up there?" Marty knew that shuttle flights had been suspended after a breakup of the Columbia, and had only resumed that summer. During the hiatus, Russians had been the ones providing transportation of crew and supplies to the space station.

"About six months," said Jason. "They miss fresh vegetables, and fresh coffee, it says. And they want their food to be highly spiced, so they can taste it."

"I'll bet!" said Marty, peering at the screen. "So you're going to put all that in your report?" she asked.

"I guess so," said Jason. "I don't feel like writing all that stuff down. It's right here on the internet!"

"But you won't have the internet in front of you all the time," said Marty reasonably. "And your teacher doesn't want you to talk from memory. You better start writing." Marty felt that most of the things she found on the internet were quite superficial. She much preferred books.

"Awwwwh," said Jason, his body language showing his reluctance.

"Some of you, your understanding gets into your report also," said Marty. "That's what your teacher is looking for." She had just been reading a chapter about attention herself. "You can read your report to all of us at dinnertime," Marty said. "Your Dad would love to hear it." Dad was always the magic word.

Jason sat resignedly back down and pulled his yellow paper tablet toward him. Marty went back out to the table on the patio, but the shadows were already long across her pages. It was still warm enough, however. She copied into her notebook a passage from Jane Hirshfield, who was extrapolating from Basho and Rilke: "The basic matter of poetry comes not from the self, but from the world. From Things, which will speak to us on their own terms and with their own wisdom, but only when approached with our full and unselfish attention."

Hirshfield was exactly right, thought Marty. It was how she saw things herself. And a corollary to how she saw her work as a woman. By this time, she finally felt no need to find her "self." It was there, as plain as day! She could give herself up to the work of the world. The kids were growing up fast. They would not need her and Doug so much in a few years. She could then turn her attention to poetry, or whatever else she felt like. For now, however, she felt her worth lay in the authenticity of the home life she made for this family.

It was a good feeling. Marty often felt stressed, uncertain and worried. But life with the Hendersons was a song, an anthem when they all got together. She could not tame Doug. He had his own ideas about everything and he took a lot on. Her best defense was to stand on her own two feet. Doug loved them and defended her when she needed it.

Marty felt free to tell Doug her worries, knowing he would do nothing about them. He had assigned them to her! But he also was struggling to provide the life he wanted for himself and his kids. The depth of their partnership was their strong bodily connection and their respect for how each other was. For Marty it was incredibly relaxing to live with someone who knew her inside and out, to whom she could say whatever she was thinking and he could do the same.

In tai chi classes, Marty had learned to stand in her grid. She could not bend too far into someone else's grid to help them or lean too much on someone else. They could feel each other's energy, use it to keep going. But each was practicing on his own. It was a very valuable lesson to someone such as Marty, who hadn't always been sure about her boundaries.

The Taoists were right about times and seasons, though Marty thought her own life was a little backwards. She felt younger all the time, when she would actually be 60 this year. It was astounding to her how long it took to learn emotional lessons. They never seemed to quit!

Marty packed up her books and notebooks, passing Jason at the computer to see whether he was writing. It always astonished her how much the kids procrastinated, leaving their homework until the last possible moment. I probably did the same thing, she thought. She put her things in her bedroom on the little shelf by the bed that was her own.

"Did you get it?" she asked Jason as she came back into the kitchen. "I'm going to start thinking about dinner," she said.

"Yeah?" asked Jason. "I'll finish this later." The computer made the resonant Microsoft tone as it shut down.

"You might want to check with Nic and Natasha," said Marty. "They might need the computer too." Zoe had a laptop by this time, and Doug carried his around, but the rest of the family shared this one.

"I'll check," said Jason as he went racing down the hall.

Marty turned her attention to the kabocha squash, cutting them in two with a large knife and scooping out their flat seeds. Restraint often seemed the best policy. As long as she had Doug's ear, Marty could manage it.

16

Andre settled himself in the stern of the canoe, and Paul pushed it out into the icy water, stepping in just as the canoe began to float off its rubber mooring. It was April, and a bit dangerous. Beyond the open water along the shore, ice still blanketed most of the lake. But Paul and Andre could not resist. Andre's younger brother and sister, Benjy, who was 11, and Jeanne, 12, stood at the edge of the water, zippered into parkas, watching.

Wilson, Paul's caramel colored Labrador/Shepherd, yipped a little as he walked out into the icy water. "Hey, Wilson," yelled Andre. "Follow us!" But Wilson splashed back onto land and followed along the lake's icy edge. Too cold for me! Paul could imagine him saying.

The air was cold too but the sun had some heat in it. It had begun to travel back from its furthest point on the horizon which Paul had noted in December. It still made a shallow arc across the southern sky, but it was strengthening. It made Paul think he could feel the tilt of the earth.

Paul paddled lazily, listening to the floating shards of broken ice along the shore tinkling like a wind-chime and watching Andre smoothly stroking ahead of him. No waves were carried across the lake. The danger was from getting hypothermia if you fell in. But, they wouldn't go far. It was just the spirit of the thing! How early in the year could you get out on the lake?!

Wilson ran along the shore, the squirrels and a chipmunk chittering in the trees above him. Chickadees sang their spring song and Paul had noticed that the beaks on the grosbeaks were turning light green. Juncos searched the bare ground along the shore for seeds, their yellow beaks dipping from their dark heads.

It was Paul's second spring on the lake. He had begun to understand the excitement of "ice out," which happened usually in April. They had had a mild winter with not much snow and the ice had begun to recede early. Winter was always exciting with its gaunt visual panoramas. Though weather could be predicted much more precisely now and Paul followed it avidly, you never knew what would happen in April.

The three youngest of Grace's kids had come to stay with Paul at the cabin on Lake Michigami over Easter break. They would go home Thursday night for the mass of the Last Supper, but Grace was so busy during Easter week, she was glad to have them off her hands. The older kids, Dory and Joe, both had jobs. Dory was in college and Joe in his senior year of high school.

Paul and Andre paddled east along the shore, turning around at the cove near the long-needled pine woods, where a sturdy house now stood. Paul didn't want to leave the younger kids too long. He could see them along the shore, throwing sticks into the moving water. Wilson, finally matured into his full-grown status, bounded back and forth along the shore, unable to decide whether to stick with the canoe or the kids.

Paul steered the canoe back, straight into its little rubber mooring. Andre jumped out in his rubber duck boots, pulling up the canoe and snubbing the rope to a jack pine. Wilson jumped into the canoe as Paul made his way out. Paul roughed up his chest, marked with its odd cowlicks, "Good dog," he said. "Good boy."

Andre and Paul pulled the canoe up and turned it over on the pine duff, the paddles under it. The ground cover and low lying vegetation were still just bare sticks, but water trickled down the hill. Green fecundity was just around the corner. The active birds celebrated, though a snowstorm was still possible.

Paul pointed out to the kids the way the sun had moved along the horizon. "I was thrilled to find that native Americans used it as a calendar," he said. "In Momaday's book, *House of the Dawn*. The grandfather teaches the kids that, from a particular observation point, when the sun rises against the black mesa in a crevice, you plant, or have a feast or a race. Every point on the mesa was a time marker."

"If we only come up in the summer," said Andre, "it looks like it comes up at the same place all the time."

"So, if I leave a camera in the same place, and take a photo of the sun at the same time every day on the same piece of film, do you know what it would look like?" Paul asked.

"I've seen it," said Andre, who was increasingly mature himself at 14. "It's like a figure eight."

"An analemma," said Paul. "I'm not a mathematician," he said, "so I'm not going to take photos all year. But I do find it fascinating that we are a celestial body, moving among other celestial bodies." It was much easier to think of the earth this way now that so many images of it were being beamed down from space. The big blue marble, wreathed in atmospheric clouds.

The cabin was now furnished and Ellie considered it finished, though it still felt brand new. Lots of visitors had shown up during the summer, Ellie and Bruce and their grandkids, Hanna and Faith from New York state, and Line had come with Fern, and little Sofia. Paul was feeling quite comfortable there. Though he sometimes used the Ben Franklin upstairs to enjoy a fire, he bedded down Andre, Jeanne and Benjy on the lower floor, the Mikkelson floor.

Andre was reading *Black Elk Speaks* for a school project. "Wow!" said Paul. "That's a great book!" He proposed that they read a bit of it together before they went to bed. After making sure everyone's teeth were brushed, Paul gathered the kids on the big brown leather sofa just before bedtime. The room smelled of popcorn and cocoa. Wilson seemed thrilled to have more people in the house than just Paul.

Black Elk had been a boy during the Little Bighorn battle, and also the massacre at Wounded Knee. He told the stories of his people, the

Lakota Sioux, to a man named Neihardt, who put together the book. Paul picked out the part where Black Elk tells the story of Crazy Horse, the vision in which he saw his horse "dance around like a horse made only of shadow."

"What are they telling you in school about Crazy Horse?" asked Paul. "He seems to me the most revered of native Americans still."

"He's a symbol of resistance," said Andre. "He was never defeated in battle, he had a great spirit, and though he surrendered, it was only for the sake of his people, who were cold and starving."

"I've had the impression he never negotiated with the whites, as Red Cloud and Spotted Tail did."

"He didn't live long enough," snorted Andre. Crazy Horse had been killed by an American soldier as he was taken into custody.

"Are you guys getting this history in school too?" Paul asked Jeanne and Benjy.

"Some," said Jeanne.

"The Sioux were the most dangerous tribe when Lewis and Clark made their exploration," said Andre. "Everyone feared them. And even now, I hear much more about the native American activists on the Pine Ridge and Rosebud reservations than any other tribe. The AIM guys. Our tribe is boring," he said disgustedly.

Paul smiled. He had been following the Ojibwe bands, in which all of Grace's kids were enrolled, though not very active, members. "Didn't you know Dennis Banks was Ojibwe?" he asked. "Lives over on Leech right now!"

"Dennis Banks?" asked Andre. "He's important, isn't he?"

"I think he's the most important contemporary activist," said Paul. "He joined up with Russell Means, who was Lakota Sioux, to start AIM. They started it in Minneapolis."

"I thought they were all Sioux," said Andre. "That was where the action was." Of all of the kids, Andre clearly was the most interested in this history.

"According to what I've been reading recently," said Paul, "the Lakota Sioux were angry at the Ojibwe for pushing them out of Minnesota, which happened probably just before Lewis and Clark came up the Mississippi. The tribes have never been friends. The Sioux were betrayed by the Ojibwe too, during the 'Sioux Uprising.' So it was unusual for Dennis

Banks and Russell Means to get together. I think Dennis moved closer to the Lakota, married a Lakota wife."

"So Dennis Banks lives on Leech?" asked Andre.

"Yup," said Paul. "Harvesting wild rice and tapping trees for maple syrup, just as they always did."

"And now we've got the casino," said Andre.

Paul smiled at his possessive 'we.' Neither Paul nor Gerald, Andre's father, wanted anything to do with gambling. It was a complete waste. "I've been following the Sacred Run which people are doing from Alcatraz all the way across the country," Paul said. "Dennis is leading it. They're going to get to Washington any day. I think they're shooting for Earth Day this year."

"Wow," said Andre. "What's the Sacred Run for?"

"I guess it's for awareness," said Paul. "They're running through the South this year, I think, in solidarity with the Katrina victims and with civil rights activism." He felt awkward schooling Grace's kids on their own traditions. But Gerald, who was half Ojibwe, acted as if he was completely white. Gerald's mother had encouraged his assimilation. It made the most sense at the time. As a basketball star, a Catholic and now a pilot of light aircraft, Gerald had never paid attention to his heritage. The kids were getting a much stronger dose of it now in school.

Paul noticed that Benjy was half asleep and that Jeanne was drooping. "Well," he said. "That's enough of that. Come on kids." Paul felt thrilled to have the care of the kids for a few days, almost as if they were his own.

Andre was sleeping in a little room sometimes called 'the library,' which had no windows, while the younger kids slept in the other big bedroom. Paul hugged them goodnight. Paul identified with Benjy. Grace had pinned her hope that one of her sons become a priest on her youngest. Benjy was the sweetest, kindest kid you could imagine. When the kids were in bed, Wilson padded after Paul to his room, where Wilson had a bed on the heated flooring.

After a few days of being outdoors and playing games and cooking together, Paul piled the kids in the car so that Gerald wouldn't have to leave work to come and get them. Wilson climbed into the middle seat in the mini-van. "Hey, where am I going to sit?" asked Benjy, giving him a playful push.

"He thinks he's one of us," said Jeanne.

Paul motioned Wilson to lie down on the floor. "He's kind of one of us," he said. "But he also knows he's a dog."

In Bemidji, Paul stayed for the Maundy Thursday service, sitting with the Hickmans in their pew at St. Philips. He had the utmost respect for the rituals and liturgy of the Catholic church, from which his own Lutheran traditions had come. Maundy Thursday had to do with foot washing. At this service, after the sermon, twelve men came down to the front of the church. They took off their shoes, and one by one, Father Chuck and Father Anthony poured water on their feet and wiped them with towels. It was extraordinarily moving, invoking Christ's washing of the disciples' feet during the Last Supper. At the end of the service, the priests stripped and washed the altar.

Everyone was solemn as they filed out of the church, though Grace stayed to keep vigil, as Jesus' disciples had done, and complete other rituals with regard to the consecrated body and blood of Christ. Jane Hickman, Gerald's mother, also stayed. Paul quietly bid the Hickmans good night. Gerald took the kids home and Paul went back to Lake Michigami.

On Easter Sunday, Paul was among the congregation at his own Trinity Lutheran church in Laporte joyfully lifting their voices, singing "Christ the Lord is Risen Today, Alleluia!" From the choir loft, Paul could see that his old friend Pete, who lived two cabins down from the Mikkelsons, was in town. Pete had a job with Amtrak and often was gone for weeks at a time, crossing the country by train.

Paul knew that all across the country, Easter was being celebrated with great ceremony: massive organs, processionals, flowers on the altars, people in new clothes and hats. But he was thrilled by his simple little church which was now so familiar. In the Lutheran church, the cross at the front of the altar was always empty, signifying that Christ had triumphed. Paul could almost hear Dad describing this difference between the Lutheran and Catholic churches.

At the potluck meal which concluded the service, Paul sought Pete out. The two of them loaded their plates from the massive bounty spread out in the parish hall, a sliced ham and a turkey breast, vegetable dishes, salads, soft dinner rolls and many pans of bars and cake. They sat down at a table beside others, most of whom lived on or near Lake Michigami.

"So how's the channel up by you?" asked Paul of Ed Engebretsen, a retired pastor who lived on Preacher's Point, close to the channel which connected Lake Michigami to other inlets and bays, all of which flowed into the huge Leech Lake.

"It's clear," said Ed. "It's been clear for days."

"Yeah," said Paul. "I took the canoe out this week, but didn't try to get too far."

"All we need is a little more strong sun," said Ed. "It'll all go out at once."

"I took the ice augur out a couple of month ago," said Paul. "It was about 20 inches thick, I think. Thicker than last year."

"Last year was a pretty strong El Niño in the Pacific," said Pete. "Makes a mild winter for us."

"Aren't you the 'citizen observer' for the DNR on the lake, Pete?" asked Ed. The Minnesota Department of Natural Resources kept track of ice out dates for all Minnesota lakes, depending on consistent reporting from the same people every year. Pete had been living on Lake Michigami for many years, though a bit infrequently because of his traveling.

"Yup," said Pete. "But I need a new deputy. In case I'm not here. I had one, but he went to a nursing home this winter." He looked over at Paul. "Hey, Paul, how about it?"

"Sure," said Paul. "Sounds interesting." Paul and Pete were among the youngest people living full time on the lake. It seemed to Paul he was getting in deeper all the time, which he liked. He got up and went over to the table. He took a couple of the most promising looking bars laden with coconut, peanuts, chocolate chips. Not as good as what the Mikkelson family used to make, but pretty good.

"Well, onward," said Paul, shaking the hands of the people he bid goodbye. He could almost hear Arvi Kukkonen saying it in his head. Arvi was the Finnish homesteader in Alaska whose cabin Paul had lived in. Paul found himself thinking about Arvi's expansive and creative soul often, lately.

"Happy Easter, Paul," said Ed. "He is risen!"

"He is risen, indeed," said Paul. Whether in symbol, or in fact, it did not matter. Paul was so far beyond a need for belief at this point that he could humbly accept the language of his neighbors.

"We are all rising," said Pete quietly to Paul. "And so is the world; rising all around us." Pete's father had also been a pastor.

"Yep," said Paul. "And we've got a perfect vantage on it." Easter was the great celebration of regeneration, especially in the north country.

Paul set off for home, where he had left Wilson. He didn't like to take Wilson places where he couldn't go in. It was still a bit cold to leave Wilson in the car for hours at a time.

The next morning, Paul and Wilson walked out along the lake shore. The sun was trying to burn through the mists at the horizon, with the temperature scheduled to get up into the 60's. The wedge of open water was much larger now, with only a patch of ice floating in the center of the lake. Wilson dipped his paws in, testing the temperature. An eerie laughing cry from across the lake made them both look up. Paul lifted the binoculars to his face. There, yes, there was the first loon! Two of them! They seemed to know exactly when the ice would go out!

"Loons!" Paul said to Wilson, pointing. Did Wilson know what he was talking about? He listened for the odd, echoing cry, the cry of the north. Paul moved his binoculars to check on the pair of wood ducks he had seen roosting in a nearby Norway pine. The great blue herons seemed to be back as well.

At home, Paul settled Wilson with food and water, and then went out for his own walk. Paul loved his schedule, which was quite flexible, unless he was subbing in the Walker school system. Generally he worked on the computer at home, but he had carefully carved out a space in the mornings to go out to the beaver pond on the back lot for his own purposes, without Wilson. Soon he would begin to take him, he thought. He himself was enough of a disturbance to the wild. Wilson was becoming trained to quiet. He would not be much more.

Paul walked up the rutted track which led to the gravel road, then set off into the woods on the far side. The air was alive with the sound of chittering and wings. Birds did tell you a great deal about the world. Mother's obsession with them had served her well. Paul had again participated in the Great Backyard Bird Count the Audubon society carried out each February. This morning there were more new ones he hadn't seen during the winter, flickers and a least flycatcher.

There was a word for the sighting of the new things of each season as it arrived: phenology. Paul mentioned his observations on the blog he was keeping on-line. Occasionally local people commented as to their own sightings.

The brown shrubs and grasses had not changed much visibly since emerging from the snow, but Paul knew that below the ground there was great shifting and striving, roots which had appeared dormant in the cold struggling toward water and warmth, sap flowing upward. The birds knew it and so did he. It was this symbiosis in which Paul was now most interested.

How did one thing allow another? The juncos which fed on the ground, did not come back until the snow had begun to clear. The loons knew when there was open water and fish could be caught.

As the air grew warmer, Paul could smell more too. Cedar boughs, thawing earth and sap swelling, he thought. When he hit the small pond, Paul found that there was no ice left on its surface. The cattails stood up, and on them red-winged blackbirds were singing a raucous "Concor-eeeee." Another first. The pond was renewed by winter snow and precipitation, as the sun had a drying effect during the summer. There had not been much snow this year.

Paul made a few notes, walking around the pond where he had buried Archie and scattered some of Marie's ashes. The ground under the pines looked warm and inviting, but Paul didn't dare sit down. He could not afford to let the cold and damp get into his hips, knees, ankles. They ached enough already.

The trees needed precipitation too. Many different kinds of mosses worked together with the trees to hold precipitation. Paul poked through them, identifying what he could. He was trying to understand them. It was all part of a larger cycle: what Paul hoped to record over the years as he watched from his perch on the edge of a northern Minnesota lake.

Sometimes Paul didn't come up with much. Language didn't always connect immediately with his thoughts. But naming, listening, making mental connections were what humans did. Reality, thought Paul as he slowly circled back toward the road. It was a network. The sun enabling the seasons, which enabled the plants, animals, birds to live in the particular earth and water patterns they called home.

In what Paul knew from reading the professional magazines, what could be seen with the naked eye was not what whetted the interests current in objective science. Hardly anyone seemed to be looking at the whole, though admittedly, the sheer scope of detail now known was impossible for any one person to process. But Paul was certain some things could be learned from observation. Conclusions reached, thoughts recorded. Paul was dogged about it. An empiricist, at least in his own interests.

Paul stumped along, raising the binoculars to his face now and then, lost in thought. Reality was also all of the connections to his own human family, what he knew of his far-flung sisters; of Pete, two cabins down; of Grace and Gerald and their kids. Of his own history and that of his forebears. Because he was in Minnesota, Paul found he was beginning to know more about his ancestry, most of which involved immigrants to the state.

Hanna and Faith had recently let the family know that they were planning to adopt two kids. "We have such a nice life," Hanna had told them. "We have to share." The kids they planned to take on were not going to be easy. They were the brother and sister of an alcoholic, drug-addicted mother. Hanna and Faith wanted to help them stay together, had plenty of space on the family farm in New York's Mohawk Valley. Paul wondered how it was going. Hanna and Faith could not take the kids out of the state for a year after the process began.

Back at the cabin, Wilson greeted him excitedly. Paul turned on his computer and poked through the news of the day and his emails. He took extra time to follow his favorite story, the two rovers which had been deployed on Mars two years ago, and despite being programmed for 90 days of exploration, were still going! It was very exciting, and somehow personal. Paul had heard that the cameras on the rovers, Spirit and Opportunity, had been set at an eye level of 5'2", which was not much below Paul's own.

NASA continued to share its images freely. Opportunity was leaving one crater where it had analyzed the rocks and was heading for Victoria crater. Scientists were very interested in these craters. Spirit had a malfunctioning wheel and the engineers had turned it around, trying to get it to a higher position where its solar panels could get more sun over the Martian winter. It was proceeding backwards up a ridge, dragging its broken front wheel behind it.

The salinity of some of the rocks seemed to indicate that Mars had, at least in the past, water on it. Paul had no yearnings toward space at this point. The costs and the alien conditions people had to overcome were just too great. The International Space Station had been a cooperative effort mostly between Russians and Americans since the year 2000. The station was in a low orbit around the earth and assembly was still going on. People lived up there with limited gravity, but it wasn't easy.

Paul remembered when he had thought his polio would make him a good candidate for an astronaut! It hadn't turned out that way. Astronauts were usually engineers, doctors and test pilots in top physical condition. And Paul was happy on earth. He had read how people on the space station had to get along basically without any kind of running water, with filtered air and carefully processed foods.

"Nope," Paul said to Wilson, who rested his head on his paws at Paul's feet. "We're much better off on earth!" Wilson looked up. He seemed to agree with Paul, who was the leader of the pack.

17

Line leaned forward in her theater seat, listening closely as her intense (almost) son-in-law Marshall explained what he thought of the student production going on in front of them. Ivy was somewhere backstage, sewing on brassiere straps, Line suspected. The students all seemed to be in their underwear for *Cabaret*.

"This piece of musical theater has such good structure," said Marshall. "All I have to do is get the students to play it as truly and honestly as possible. I've directed it many times, and I always learn something."

"It's quite a dark play," said Stephen. He and Line had come down to North Hollywood to see the production which Ivy was working on.

"Yeah," said Marshall. "The students really get it, the gaiety on the surface, but how the Nazi regime was affecting everyone. Not just Jews, but many other outcasts; plus the citizens themselves."

"Ivy loves the collaboration," said Line. "Choreography, music, all working together." Line was especially taken by the older woman they had found to play Fraulein Schneider. Her songs were amazing. "Is Fraulein Schneider a student?" she asked Marshall. Ivy had told Line how extraordinary it was to be involved with these excellent teachers and students who were so committed to getting the most out of themselves.

"No," said Marshall. "LA is full of great actors who want to work. It's a big part, and we thought she would inspire the others."

"She inspires me!" said Line. They waited in the darkened theater for the musicians to collect again and the second act of the dress rehearsal, the last performance before a real audience would arrive. Beside them sat the choreographer, who was making notes.

Line sat back to watch. A chorus line of girls at the Kit Kat Club in Berlin performed a kick line dance, which then became goose-stepping. She tried to imagine what these girls were like, who had such a drive to act. Not even Ivy wanted to be on stage, much as she loved working in theater. It took a special person to want to dance like that, legs flung out over the audience below. Line admired them.

The performance ended with the Emcee taking off his overcoat and revealing the grey pajamas he wore at Auschwitz, blazoned with a Jewish star and a pink triangle. A large mirror at the back of the stage reminded the audience that they might not be so different than the Germans of the 1930's.

Line stood up, clapping along with the few others in the theater. "This play has been done so many ways over the years," said Marshall. "And the story is so well-known. But it always has an effect."

Stephen, who took a dark view of America's involvement in the Iraq war and Republican hegemony in congress, said, "Preaching to the choir, though, aren't you? The 'liberal elite'?"

Marshall waved him off. "Maybe," he said as he rushed away toward the stage. "We'll talk later." The choreographer followed him.

Line watched the stage, hoping for a glimpse of Ivy's blonde head. Soon she appeared, listening with all of the performers to Marshall's notes on the rehearsal. And then Ivy joined her parents, slim and lovely in jeans and a t-shirt. In Line's view, no one could match her youngest daughter.

"We'll just have time to go to the Republic of Pie," said Ivy, taking Stephen by the arm as if she had been learning from the suggestive chorus girls. "It's close by. Come on!"

Line was feeling uncharacteristically wonderful, despite the speed with which everything seemed to have to happen. She followed her husband and daughter. "Marshall will come when he can," said Ivy. Stephen turned solicitously, to see whether Line was okay. She smiled back at him to show that she was.

North Hollywood was strange to Line. Huge monumental buildings with long walks in between. Of course they weren't seeing much of it. The sidewalks were hot and Line minded the prickly late August heat, but soon they entered a dark, old building, a warehouse with high ceilings stuffed with old furniture and cupboards. Also people! Everywhere, on sofas, at tables, in corners, under lights, people were talking, working on their laptop computers, drinking coffee in the dim and inviting room.

Line and Stephen each ordered a large piece of pie, chocolate for Line and pecan for Stephen. They asked for de-caffeinated coffee, while Ivy had a latte. "Going for broke," said Line, smiling as she placed her whipped-cream topped pie on the old table Ivy had selected. She felt a little of the Weimar insouciance had rubbed off on her. "Who cares?" she asked, like Fraulein Schneider. It might indeed be the end of the world.

In fact Line had not told Ivy that she had just quit her job because she no longer trusted her body. It had been coming on for a while, she thought. Bad days, she called them. But they were so unpredictable. Mostly she felt fine, but every once in a while a most unusual lethargy crept over her and she could hardly get from one place to the other. She had been researching fibromyalgia and chronic fatigue syndrome to see if her symptoms matched, but she was really baffled. She also had a cramp in one hip which made her gait jerky. She had noticed herself galumphing along when she walked with someone. Stephen was aware of it, and Poppa. But Line didn't know enough to tell anyone else.

The thick, creamy pie was delicious. Ivy put a fork in too. They sat around one end of a large table at the other side of which were two young girls, studying. "There are performing arts schools all around us," said Ivy quietly. "Everyone here is serious about what they are doing."

"I see that," said Line.

Marshall rushed in with his coffee just as Ivy began to ask her Dad about the book he was writing. "It's about Paul Wellstone," Ivy told Marshall. "He was a progressive Minnesota senator, but he died in a plane crash with his wife and daughter. My brother worked for Wellstone's campaign. He narrowly missed being on that plane himself."

"I've never met Christy," said Marshall.

"He doesn't come out here very often, but you will," said Line.

"The book is going well," said Stephen. "I spent a month in Minnesota, going through Wellstone's papers. He was a scrappy guy, much missed."

"Someone called him the 'conscience of the Senate,'" said Line.

Stephen huffed, "They need one! Wellstone was the only senator up for re-election who voted against giving Bush the power to enact the Iraq war."

"We loved being in Minnesota," Line told Ivy. "I spent my time at the lake, of course. I can't get over how lovely the new cabin is! And there's space for so many of us!"

Ivy looked at Marshall wistfully. "It's really the Mikkelson center," she said. "We'll have to go sometime."

"Minnesota," said Marshall. "Who knew?" His parents had been refugees from Hungary, though he grew up in New York.

"Heather and Fern are going to be here soon," Line told Ivy. "With their kids!" She was so excited to see the little grandchildren playing together. "We'll buy you a plane ticket, so you can come up and see them."

"Oh, don't do that," Ivy said. "It's easier to drive!" To Marshall she said, "Our house in Santa Cruz is the Cohen family center." She took another forkful of Line's pie. "I'll try to get away one weekend. I miss Poppa too. How is he?"

"Poppa is fine," said Stephen. "He likes a bit of help, though. He had someone come in to cook when we were away."

Poppa was 86, and quite well off. With his rental income and Stephen's salary at the university, Line didn't need to work any more, but she had kept going because she loved working with people. Her long experience in nursing was valued. She got so many expressions of gratitude for what she did it was hard to give it up. But so what? thought Line harshly to herself, in the words of Fraulein Schneider. Life was constantly moving along, dragging people with it.

"So many levels in your play," said Line to Marshall. "I liked the parts with Fraulein Schneider."

"Yes," said Marshall. "Her point of view is central to the play, even though people always think of the Emcee and the Sally Bowles characters when they think of *Cabaret*."

Line and Stephen did not stay long in southern California. It's time for the young people, Line thought, as they drove home through the golden California hills under a hot blue sky. She must begin to take a back seat. As she thought of the coming grandchildren, her sardonic mood drifted away. She did feel good, she thought to herself. Don't spoil your good days.

Fern came first with 6-year-old Sofia. "Where are the cousins?" asked Sofia, who had been told to expect Heather's little boys and new baby. She stalked around the house in a proprietary way and went to sit with Poppa, who was having his evening drink.

"They'll be here tomorrow," said Poppa. "But today I have you all to myself!" The chords in Poppa's neck stood out beside Sofia's smooth sun-kissed skin.

"No you don't," flirted the vivacious little girl. "There's mama, and grandpa and grandma."

The next day Sofia wanted to go to the airport, but Line pointed out that they wouldn't all fit in the car! "I hope Heather has a car seat for the baby," she said to Stephen. "I think we'll have to rent a van for this crew!" She took Sofia down into the bottom level of the garden, hoping to distract her.

At last, while Fern sat reading to the little girl, Heather and her family arrived. Line had a pitcher of cold water, flavored with cucumbers, ready and another of cold lemonade. In Chile, it was still winter. What would the little boys think, she wondered.

Matteo and Paulo were a little shy, two long-haired, beautiful boys at 5 and 3, standing stiffly, and a little sleepily together. Matteo was darker than his brother. "We've been traveling all day," said Heather, who carried the baby, Carlotta, born at the beginning of the year. She sat down on one of the comfortable couches.

But Sofia went right over to them. She took Matteo by the hand. "Shall I show you your room?" she asked.

Line sat down beside Heather, holding out her arms to the baby, who looked around curiously with large black eyes. "My goodness," said Line. "What big eyes you have!" Carlotta's eyes were dark and, Line thought, intense. She had long eyelashes and creamy skin.

"She's our little Castilian Lottie," said Heather. "Named for her great-grandmother."

"Really," said Line. "I don't see much Norwegian here!" She tried to think how much Scandinavian ancestry there would be in these kids. If Heather was half, the kids must have one quarter. "Paulo, of all the kids, has the most."

Poppa hung over the baby. "A beautiful baby," he said, looking at Heather. "But they are all just fine. My wealth," he said. "Four great-grandchildren, all in the same house!"

"We have to be careful about the balconies," said Fern, who stood behind the admiring group. "There are two of them, one upstairs and one down."

"I remember!" said Heather. "The house looks just the same! Beautiful!"

"There ought to be enough grownups around to keep an eye on the kids," said Line. "All the time." The house fell down into a canyon, with decks on two levels and a raw space below that where a persimmon tree and other brush grew. Line thought vigilance a better strategy than child-proofing. She and her siblings had survived North Dakota. These kids would surely survive too.

Line felt bad about the house, though. It was a grownup house. Her own kids had grown up in a rackety house across town, where Marty and Doug now lived. We'll take the kids on outings, she thought. To the aquarium on Monterey Bay, to playgrounds, to the beach. Perhaps even to San Francisco.

"Such a vacation!" said Heather, stretching. "A complete change for us. I just want to be lazy!"

"I remember Matteo saying how much he liked the beach," said Line. "We will spend time there for sure."

"Sofia will like that too," said Fern. "Not many beaches in Arizona!"

"Does Sofia speak Spanish?" asked Heather.

"We try," said Fern. "We would like her to. But it's a losing battle. She understands some, but all the kids in school speak English."

"I thought so," said Heather. "I'm actually hoping being here will improve the boys' English."

"Speaking of the kids," said Fern. "What are they doing?!" She went off to the bedrooms to find out. Line smiled. She was glad to have secondary responsibility, not first! "Do you want to hold her?" she asked Poppa, offering the bright-eyed Carlotta.

They did go to the beach the next morning where the kids could run and jump at the edge of the ocean, and scream to their hearts' content. Worn out they returned for a quiet time after lunch, the boys sleeping, but Fern reading *The Prisoner of Azkaban* with Sofia. "She insists," said Fern, as the grownups talked over drinks later that evening. "Because the other kids are all reading Harry Potter books. Such a big to-do about them!"

"All over the world," said Heather. "I'm sure we'll have to read them too. But I've heard they are kind of mean."

"I doubt if they are good literature," said Fern. "But everything keeps moving fast, and Sofia likes Hermione. I am sure we will find the kids playing at learning magic. Sofia does have a wand with which she tries to influence us." Fern laughed, "But it doesn't do much good!"

"Have you seen any of the movies?" asked Poppa.

"We don't want to get ahead of the books," said Fern. "And she's really pretty little. So no, we haven't seen the movies."

"Those kids are pretty interesting," said Poppa. "Hermione has an amazing Ox-bridge accent."

"Oh dear," sighed Fern. "We are surely in for it. And none of it could be further from the life we live in the desert!"

"But surely that's the point," said Heather. "It's a fantasy world. Stroked onto a bit of English reality."

Line had neither seen the movies nor read the books, but she realized she probably should. She too wanted to know what her grandchildren were obsessing over. She did not see many movies. She had missed the whole *Lord of the Rings* extravaganza, which her own kids had been involved in, listening to them as books on tape many years ago. Line liked reality. But she also wondered about her future. She felt she was going into a tunnel. Who knew what lay on the other side.

Toward the end of their visit, Heather and Fern organized an evening picnic on the beach. They had been to the beach many days, but had never stayed to watch the sun sink into the ocean. Enlisting Marty and Doug and their kids, they decided to go to one of the Hendersons' favorite beaches, a bit south of Santa Cruz. It was more west-facing than Santa Cruz beaches and had fire rings.

Line struggled down the sandy steps toward the beach, letting Doug and Stephen pass her as they carried an ice chest. "Don't worry about me," she called. "I'll get there in my own time." It was late afternoon and the shadows of the beach grass on the dunes above the shoreline were long. How lovely they were. Line stopped for a moment. Below her Doug's twins were setting up a volleyball net, Heather was dispensing drinks and Jason, not so little any more, helped Marty build a fire. Fern ran around with a camera, taking photographs. Where was the baby? But oh, there she was on the blanket, watched over by Zoe.

It had been a wonderful three weeks. Line's arms and eyes were filled with the feelings of the little kids' skin against hers, the sweet smell of the baby (most of the time!), her ears attuned to the sounds of the kids playing. She had had a couple of bad days on which she crept down to the garden and stayed there, ignoring what was going on in the house. The garden feeds me, she thought to herself.

Line had seen the looks passing between her husband and daughters. Heather and Fern wanted Line to get some tests, find out what was wrong. "They talk so much about early diagnosis," said Fern, plaintively. Line did not want to be 'diagnosed.' Doctors were scientists, anxious to observe you as a subject. No one knew this better than Line. What she wanted to do was figure out for herself what was wrong, using natural methods to heal it: homeopathics, fasting perhaps. Big doses of Vitamin D might help. Line had gotten plenty of that lately!

Line knew she was stubborn, that her family was trying to manage her. And they had a right to, she thought. She would go get some tests when all of this hoopla was over. She had promised Stephen. He had been her angel. Line had never realized how helpful Stephen could be if he thought he was needed. In many ways they were closer than ever.

Making her way down through the hot, slippery sand which scrunched under her sandals, Line was grateful for the richness of family spread out below her. Even Poppa sat in a beach chair specially brought for him, a floppy hat covering his face and the thin hair on his head.

"Take this chair, Mama," said Heather as Line came up to her, handing her a cold drink and indicating another light lawn chair. "It's for you!"

"Thank you," said Line. She faced her chair toward the volleyball net. It was astonishing to observe Nic carefully showing Matteo how to spike the ball over the net!

"Go, Matteo!" shouted Poppa in a thin voice which surely didn't carry over the sound of the wind and the waves.

It was one of the wonderful things about the beach, Line thought. The waves rolled in loudly, dragging sand with them as they rolled back out. The air too was full of wind and heat, making people seem small in the wide spaces, taming personality and leaving their essence. We're animals after all, Line said to herself. Animals dancing about under the waning sun.

The twins, Nic and Natasha, were powerful volleyball players with sleek, tanned bodies, but they gently helped Sofia return the ball and made sure not to land on little Paulo! Sofia jumped up and down shrieking, "I did it! I did it!" She ran off toward Fern to make sure she had seen.

Matteo looked a little confused, but he was game, learning to bring his hand back and punch the ball as Natasha showed him. Paulo stayed close to him, a little shadow. Line had noticed that the boys spoke excellent English, but when they were together they used Spanish as their secret language.

Line watched Zoe carrying the baby Carlotta down toward the water, Heather following protectively. Their shadows streamed out behind them. It was Heather's babysitting for the Hendersons and Zoe loving her so dearly that had begun the families' close connection. Who could have predicted the outcome! Line thought.

Poppa leaned over towards Line, his words audible. "You know what Heather told me?" he asked. "She said I should enjoy her kids because there wouldn't be any more."

"You asked her?" said Line.

"Yes, she said, 'I may be Catholic, but I'm not stupid! And I'm an ecologist.' Pablo agrees with her, apparently," said Poppa.

Line nodded, smiling. "She's right, of course. Too many people. We're over-running the planet." Line had had four children, but neither Marty nor Paul had their own. Looking back, they accorded Line their children.

"Surprises me," said Poppa. "In my time, there were half as many as there are now."

Line put a hand on his arm. "It's still your time, Poppa," she said.

And here were Fern and Sofia, bringing Poppa a sand dollar. "Almost perfect," he said as he handed it to Line to look at.

"It must have arrived with the incoming tide," said Line.

Stephen came over to collect the ball players. "Doug finally deems the coals ready to cook on," he said ironically. Doug was very precise, ruling over the cooking fire.

Everyone collected around the rough wooden picnic table spread with an oilcloth, and the fire ring, watching the kabobs as they browned, sizzling juices dripping into the fire. When they were ready, Stephen brought Line a plate of rice with a browned prawn, pineapple and onion kabob laid across it.

"Oh! Delicious," said Line as she bit into the succulent prawn. "So good!"

"The rice tastes great too," said Marty, looking contented. "I like rice."

The long table held so many different ages. Zoe and Heather traded off holding the baby and eating. Doug held up a glass of wine. "To four generations at one table!" he said. The grownups all raised their glasses and Sofia shouted, "I love the beach!"

The sun had a little ways to go before setting. Marty seemed worried. "Could we take things back to the car while we can still see?" she asked. She had told Line that Doug planned the adventures in their family, but she was in charge of civilization. Everyone stood up.

Line looked up the sandy stairway doubtfully. But Heather saw her. "Here, Mother," she said. "Please take Lottie." Line arranged her beach chair so it faced the ocean and took the sleeping Carlotta. The sound of the ocean must have lulled the little girl. She sat with the tiny child snug against her lap and breast. What bliss. Poppa sat beside her, a blanket over his knees.

At the table, people collected the dishes and packed up the extra food. Doug was careful, enlisting his kids to help, but the three little ones danced down the beach, which was noticeably thinner as the combers rolled in. "Hurry, hurry," they called. "The sun is setting!" Fern followed them, not trusting them near the pounding surf.

Zoe, the twins and Jason came crashing down past Line, running in the sand, their long shadows attached to their feet. Behind them came Stephen, Marty, Doug and Heather more slowly. Stephen stopped and sat down beside Line and Poppa in the sand. It was the moment they had been waiting for, the moment the sun sank into the waves. So rare in any case. Most of the year, fog or clouds or some kind of weather prevented people from seeing it.

This evening there were no clouds, just the thick atmosphere of circus color around the sun and on the water. "I hope they're not letting those kids look at the sun," said Poppa. The light was blinding if you looked at it directly. A bright path illuminated the rolling surf, tipped with white as it dragged itself up on the beach. At last the sun slipped completely below the horizon. "Did you see the green flash?" asked Poppa.

"I think so," said Stephen.

"It never gets old," said Line. The sea now reflected the opalescent sky, the gold, pink, violet and blue it had taken on. They sat in contented silence, watching the kids below them. Soon they began to come toward the sitting group, the Hendersons approaching the volleyball net.

"Girls against the boys!" shouted Nic.

"But I'm terrible," protested Marty.

"It's okay, you've got Tasha," said Nic. He tossed the ball to Doug, who served it up, underhand. "Lame!" he called, jumping to volley as it came back toward him.

Line stood up, giving the baby to Heather. "I better get going," she said. "I'm slower than all the rest of you." She did not want to leave, but it was growing darker.

"Not slower than me," said Poppa. Stephen helped him to stand on his rickety legs.

Heather and Fern collected their kids and they all made their way through the thick sand. Halfway up, Line turned to look back at the beach below, the sky and the sea, the Hendersons' dark figures wildly crashing about in the twilight. It was clear the contest was between the competitive twins!

"What a wonderful day!" said Heather. "I'm so glad we did this!"

"Me too!" said Line. The sounds of the sea receded as they got further from it. Line sighed with contentment, watching the darkening sky. Payne's grey? she wondered.

18

It was raining and dark on Christmas morning. Marty smiled complicitly at Doug when he brought in the pancakes he had cooked outdoors under the canopy he had hung near the patio door. Jason brought in the butter and empty batter bowl, Natasha the pancake turners. Marty smiled at them. They knew nothing of where they would find themselves that night!

Candles lit the table, but the room was cold. Marty wore a heavy sweater. Nic tended a fire in the living room next to the Christmas tree, hung with popcorn and cranberry chains, gingerbread cookies and the ornaments collected over the years. There were few presents under it. The four kids had met their mother Mackenzie in San Francisco over the weekend and she took them shopping. Doug didn't think the kids needed presents. He and Marty had prepared their usual Christmas hunt.

Marty poured tea. Grandma Alice arrived in a flurry, bringing pumpkin bread and cookies. The twins seemed excited, but not Zoe. She was 17 and would graduate from high school next year. She was tired of family, of the six of them hanging out together. She fussed, but Doug was insistent. "You don't have long to put with us," he told her. Doug felt Zoe could make her own decisions once she was 18. Marty remembered her own longings at Zoe's age. The big world was waiting. Why did it take so long?

After breakfast the family gathered in the living room. Jason handed out the bulky stockings with their strange protrusions. They held little mandarin oranges, wrapped chocolate squares, pens, walnuts, soap, games and for Marty, small Moleskin notebooks. Under the tree were a few packages from far away. Cheese and chocolate from Hanna in New York, books from Paul and kitchen utensils from Ellie. The room was littered with chocolate wrappers, bits of paper and ribbon. Marty bit into a star-shaped cookie off the tree. She loved the spicey flavor with its vanilla frosting. If she was going to make tree cookies, she wanted to make sure they were edible.

Nic took out the last, familiar present. It was a map of San Francisco, with the first clue tucked into it: "Ride to the north, to get to the start. Your train will leave soon so it's best to be smart. There's treasure, adventure, and a place to leave your heart!" The last word on each line rhymed with the answer to the clue, which in this case was BART. It took a couple of hours to get to a station, but since the line had been extended to Millbrae, Doug relied on it to get them to San Francisco. Santa Cruz itself was too small to make for an exciting Christmas hunt.

Alice didn't come with them, but the rest of the family trooped gallantly around in the wet weather all day, deciphering clues to try new things at the Ferry Plaza marketplace, stop at a comic art museum and meet friends who palmed a clue directing them to a new chophouse near the baseball park. Found under a plate of peanut butter chocolate cake, another clue directed them back to the train.

Under a pay phone at the station, Natasha found a clue which told them to take the train back toward Millbrae. It ended, using Doug's inimitable verse logic: "You'll go up past the curved shimmering wall (excitement will have gripped us). Just get off after you see the tree that rhymes with this descriptus."

"Daaad!" said Nic eloquently. "How are we supposed to see a tree from the train?!"

"It's a eucalyptus," said Zoe. "It's got to be."

Doug and Marty had taken the train a few days before and found the shimmering metal wall at the point where the spur line left for the airport. Joking and jostling, the Hendersons managed to get off at the right place and head to the airport.

"So who are we going to meet?" asked Jason. None of them could figure it out. By the time Doug walked them through security, however, the jig was up.

"Where're we going?" they clamored as he handed out boarding passes. "Kahului Maui!" yelled Nic, reading the printed card. He hit Natasha's arm lightly with his fist. "Hey, girl. We're going to Maui!"

Gone to Maui, thought Marty. It sounded so poetic. They headed to a United flight gate. People getting off a nearby plane wore fresh flower leis around their necks. The secret was out.

"What about luggage?" asked Zoe. "What are we going to wear?"

"Oh," said Doug airily. "It'll be warm. You won't need much." Doug and Marty had stolen a few of the kids' summer clothes and sent them on ahead in a suitcase. What they didn't have, they could buy on the island. It was the perfect crime. Marty and he had been brimming with the secret since the previous year when Doug turned to her after Christmas and said, "Next year, we should end up in Hawaii!"

The air in Hawaii was completely different when they got off the plane, warm and moist. Marty drank it in. She did not like being cold. The shining moon hung in the sky like a watermelon.

It was late and a taxi took them to their hotel, the Aston Maui Lu on the west coast. The hotel was cheap, certainly past its prime, but entirely adequate. At the desk a smiling attendant handed over the luggage and a fax for the kids with the last clue on it: "Real life, honest fun is nothing you can fake. No one can give you more fun than you yourself can make."

Marty felt lazy and luscious in the warm air in the morning. The sun came directly into the room through the fronds of date palms which clacked in the breezes outside. Birds calling to each other echoed back and forth. Black and white magpies, Marty thought. Sprinklers washed across the spacious, lush lawn below the hotel.

That day they stayed nearby, walking into the little town of Kihei to buy groceries, including a pineapple so perfect it practically fell apart when they cut it, eating the core and all to enjoy the sweet, tart and minerally taste. They were all down at the small beach in the evening, Doug and the twins far out in the water. Doug got a jellyfish bite, dark blue and black rays on his skin spreading out from it. It really hurt, he told Marty, but he was being stoic so as not to upset the kids. Jason rolled around in the surf at the edge, getting Zoe to dig him in up to his waist.

Other people came out at sunset and stood quietly about for the holy event. The big orange ball sank into the waves rolling up onto the thin beach, the colors changing all around it.

Doug was making plans, however. The next day he rented a jeep and they set off to explore the island and look for waterfalls. It was sunny, but cooler and a big wind ripped through the palms. They took the Hana highway along the north edge of the island, winding through forests on hairpin turns, with small concrete one-lane bridges where cars had to wait for each other. "I like it," said Doug. "Everyone has to cooperate."

The twins wanted to go surfing, of course, and Doug had considered renting boards. But that morning, in the newspaper a note from a lifeguard said: "Leave your board at home and bring your common sense." According to the map, the best surfing beach was at Ho'okipa and they did stop. Others too had stopped to watch the big surf roll in. The twins looked at the waves with longing. A woman pointed out turtles, their heads popping up through the waves and later a shell tipped up in the water as they walked up the beach in the wind.

Inland, there wasn't so much wind. They stopped at a makeshift structure where a young girl was making smoothies while listening to Hare Krishna music. "It helps me pass the time," she said. She had oranges, avocados, papayas and mangos. Marty had seen other stands along the road where banana bread was laid out with a box in which to put your payment. The girl told them about a rock pool nearby, with a waterfall where she and her friends liked to go.

The sky grew dark and it began to rain, but the Hendersons kept going. Off the road they hiked up a path to a cavern with water falling into it. A twisted rope swing hung from the trees. Doug and the kids walked down under the waterfall while Marty stood on the upper edge of the path, waiting for them. Three young girls in bathing suits, wet and wild, came up the path toward Marty as she stood there, as much a part of the forest and the rain as little animals.

Finally Zoe came up to Marty. "How was it?" asked Marty, but Zoe just shrugged.

Soon the others followed. "We can't figure out how to get in the pool, or safely out," Doug said. It would take a long time to become part of this environment.

That night, Doug insisted they eat Hawaiian food at a place called 'Da Kitchen.' It was a small place and the food came in styrofoam containers, but it was definitely authentic. Pork and spinach cooked in taro leaves and served with rice and delicate noodles flavored with ginger. "Delicious," said Jason. He and Doug tasted the taro leaves.

Doug did not find much interesting wine on the island, and decided to take a break from it. He liked tasting what he could get only in the place where he was, however, a kind of terroir-based way of living. He took the moment and squeezed everything he could get from it. To Marty it meant that he lived on earth, in the sensual details. Marty could do that when she was alone. But when she was with others, she worried about how they were feeling. Doug grounded her, as she wanted to be.

Of the kids, it seemed that Jason most followed in Doug's footsteps in this regard. Zoe spent her time thinking about how she looked and what she and her friends wanted, and the twins were most interested in sports and competition.

In the morning it was sunnier and they tried to get an earlier start. Doug again headed up the Hana highway, ignoring what they had seen the day before, getting deeper into the hills and winding back out toward beautiful ocean views. The vegetation sometimes thickened and then leveled out again. Cows, including beautiful little heifers, stood out in a field. At a state park they asked Hawaiians where the best waterfalls were. The answer came right away, "Seven Pools. It's about 14 miles away, past Hana. Best place on the planet. You have to come all the way back on this highway, though."

It didn't phase Doug. Winding through the hills they saw a place below with many people, and then the highway ended. They had passed the Seven Pools, but they found themselves at a well-built farm stand with a solar panel right beside it. A small restaurant was built into a shed. Doug, the twins and Jason had smoothies, impressed that the blender was powered by a bicycle which had to be pumped! Made with cane juice and passion fruit, one of the drinks was called 'luscious liliocoi'. "Lots of ideas went into this place," said Doug.

Zoe and Marty had coffee, the most delicious freshly-brewed coffee Marty could remember. She took her cup into the flower garden where seats had been placed in among trees. Bananas grew right above on a tree with giant leaves.

Marty sat for a moment, thinking about how the Henderson family worked. The kids deferred to their Dad and he to them, and to Marty, each of them trusting the others to make decisions they would like. The combined deference made a lovely family atmosphere to live in. Quite a contrast to the nasty argument Marty had heard on the next balcony that morning. The woman of the family hassled the men: "You boys haven't been any fun on this trip," she harangued. She went on and on, her voice penetrating. The men didn't say much.

Seven Pools was part of the big national park of the Haleakala Crater. It was also known as Ohe'o Gulch, as the Ohe'o fish spawned at the series of pools naturally set into the rocks. When the tide was in, the pools filled from the ocean. People were crawling all over the pools. Doug and the kids headed straight for the last visible pool, while Marty stood near the first, looking down. She saw them crawling under a waterfall. By this time everyone wore their bathing suits all the time, or simply got their clothes wet. Everything dried quickly.

People were jumping off rock ledges into the farthest pool. Looking up, Marty saw a couple of fearless kids jumping from high up on the highway bridge! All eyes were upon them. Sure enough, the twins were jumping off ledges too.

At last the kids returned and they set off on the winding road back. The southern part of the island had no road. It was growing dark when they stopped for supper in the little town of Paia. Doug and Marty shared two corvina cooked with vegetables in a hot sauce. Jason tried that too, but the others had hamburgers. The atmosphere was casual, warm with a beachcombing feel to it.

"I love this place," said Jason.

"Me too," said Doug. "You know, Jason, there's something I've been meaning to tell you, now that you are a teenager. And the rest of you should know it too. It doesn't change anything. It's just something you should know. I'm not your biological father," he said without any other prelude. Marty had been expecting this.

Jason looked a little baffled. "So who is my father?" he asked.

"On your birth certificate it says that I am," said Doug. "It's kind of like I adopted you right away. But I knew that someone else had gotten your mother pregnant. You can ask her about it."

Amazement registered on Zoe's face, but Nic and Natasha kept quiet, scarfing up French fries.

"So, it doesn't change anything?" asked Jason. "She'll tell me who my father is?"

"I'm not sure she knows," said Doug. "but you can ask her. I'm your father in every other way, believe me. And we are a united family."

"Your Dad just thinks it is something you should know," said Marty. "So you don't get blindsided finding out later."

"Yeah," said Jason. His fresh young face looked cloudy, but anxious to return to normal. "So, can we have ice cream?"

"Absolutely!" said Doug. He stood up and hugged Jason. "Anyway, we have to get to bed so we can get up at 5:30 tomorrow morning!"

At night in bed, Marty whispered to Doug, "That went pretty well."

"Probably not over yet," said Doug. "But it's a start."

In the morning Doug and Marty rousted everyone. Doug had booked them on a boat leaving Ma'alea. They stood on the harbor dock in the dark, watching the guys get the boat ready. Dawn slowly lightened the sky. The Hendersons were the first ones, but a long line of people formed behind them by 6:30 a.m. when the big white catamaran was scheduled to leave.

The Hendersons sat together, drinking coffee and eating muffins while Ryan, a crew member and a standup comic into the bargain, explained the trip and safety information. Very tan and with windblown blonde hair in a white t-shirt and jeans, he looked like the quintessential Hawaiian beach bum. The crew passed out fins and snorkeling equipment as the boat got underway, heading for the far side of Molokini where they said the visibility was good on the reef.

Marty was scared as she had never been sure she could breathe using a snorkel, and it sounded like they would be swimming off the boat rather than off a beach. But when the time came, she did okay using a foam noodle to stay afloat. The water was warm, about 75 degrees. It was most clear near the reef, but they had been warned to stay away from it as no one wanted the cuts in their skin, or the creatures in those cuts! The fish were beautiful, dark ones with an electric blue line on their sides, small yellow ones and another darker kind with some red. Even with Marty's poor vision, it was exciting to be in the water and get close to them.

Other boats arrived with their snorkeling tourists too. "It's kind of like an amusement ride," said Zoe when she and Marty were back on the boat. "Let's give the tourists exactly what they want!" she smirked.

When everyone was back, the boat headed for an area the crew called "turtle town" further down the island, south of Kihei. This time the visibility was poor and there were too many people, so Marty didn't stay long. She did see the giant turtles swimming about in the murky water. Doug said he bumped into one by mistake. He and the twins were the last ones back on the boat.

A barbecued chicken lunch was served and the crew hassled them to buy t-shirts, being as funny about it as possible. They were back in the harbor by noon. The Hendersons headed north to the tourist town of Lahaina. They felt slow and lazy after their early morning, but they did look around at some of the cultural sites. Zoe thought it would be fun to have a coconut bra as a costume. "Can't you see me on Halloween?" she asked, doing a little shimmy, the coconuts tied together around her back.

"You need a grass skirt," said Doug. They looked for that too.

In the evening they stopped along the highway and went down to the long white beach which seemed to form itself on the western side of every island. Marty did a tai chi slow set as the sun went down, Zoe lay in the warm sand and Doug and the other kids went in the water.

There were more days of chasing waterfalls and exploring. Even up to the inactive volcano crater. Like all of Hawaii, the island had been formed by edges of geologic plates pushing the earth's crust up out of the ocean, after all. Many years ago, Marty had seen the more lively crater on the big island, but she had never been to Maui.

On New Year's Eve, the Hendersons packed their belongings and left them at the hotel desk until their late flight. They drove south on the west coast toward the lava flow. Again the highway ended, but Doug wanted to keep going, to see where they would get. On a narrow road through the barren lava fields they arrived where cars were parked at the beach. According to the map, it was La Perouse Bay, a natural preserve at the end of the road.

They walked out toward the beautiful aquamarine beach strewn with sharp rocks. The sand looked white, but lethal. Marty was afraid of getting any more sun. She had a straw hat with a wide brim, but they had already gotten quite a lot of sun. She made herself a seat up under the palms on some dry palm fronds. It wasn't terribly comfortable, but the place was so beautiful she wanted to look forever.

Doug and the kids walked down the beach and into the water, protected by the flip-flops they had bought. "Don't call them thongs!" Zoe had reminded them vehemently. "Thongs are something else!" When Marty was growing up, she had had several pairs of cheap rubber 'thongs.' Nowadays, a thong was a very skimpy underpants which showed off a girls' buns.

Marty wondered whether there were any shockwaves visible from the information Doug had shared with the kids, but it didn't seem like it. All Jason had said one day was, "So, maybe that's why my skin is so dark!" It was true. None of the other kids tanned as quickly as Jason, though all of them were browner than Marty. Zoe was thrilled she would be tan in winter when she got back to high school. California kids were out in all weathers.

Marty suspected that the new information might affect Zoe quite strongly. Zoe had longed for her mother, but Marty had seen her grow tougher over the years, hiding her anger under nonchalance. The kids had all known Mackenzie was a rock and roll groupie, but perhaps they hadn't known what it meant! They had mostly been raised by Ana Maria and their Grandmother Alice, until Marty came along and tried to be more of a presence at home.

Marty was happy to see Zoe acting like a kid, swimming lazily. She watched her family cavorting in the water. It was a vision of paradise, a wash of white sand rimmed with lava, clear turquoise water backed by a little peninsula of trees. Flying fish leapt 50 feet out of the water in front of Marty's eyes.

Grey clouds began to come up. An older Spanish couple sitting near Marty handed her half a papaya and wished her a "Happy New Year" as they left. It must be close to sunset, Marty thought. She lay gingerly on her palm leaves, watching the blue sky, grey and white clouds, sunshine, more clouds, lava rock, the blue grey water and the mostly black rock beach near her feet. The Henderson kids and Doug were still far out in the bay.

When the sun finally went down, Marty shared the papaya with Doug and the kids. Jason wanted to light the firecrackers he'd bought, but after a couple, a park ranger turned up on an ATV and told him not to light them on park land.

Doug thought they should have some nice food. They stopped at the Maui Prince in Kihei, but found that all of its restaurants were completely booked for parties. They wandered around the somewhat artificial environment, looking at the tables set with white linens, the dessert tables laden with chocolates and other tables gleaming with wineglasses. Marty didn't envy the partygoers. The moon shown down strongly into the courtyard and Natasha wondered whether the birdsong was coming from real birds. She and Nic went off to look.

Marty was beginning to worry about their flight in any case. People were lighting fire crackers all along the beach and Jason finally got to light his. One group had staked out their space with luminarias. Others chained firecrackers together to get bigger effects.

While they stood on the beach, Doug got a phone call. He handed the phone to Marty. "Happy birthday to you!" sang Paul's voice, along with Ellie's family and perhaps Christy. Marty had almost forgotten it was her birthday. And then the family chorale burst into "Should Old Acquaintance Be Forgot." It was midnight in Minnesota. Marty's siblings were almost as surprised to find Marty and Doug on Maui as they were!

The Hendersons had time for a snack before they left for the airport, but it wasn't anything special. They picked up their bags and hustled off toward their plane, returning their vehicle on the way.

The lines at the airport looked horrible, but somehow or other people were cleared out and the Hendersons boarded at 11:10 pm. Marty and Doug looked at each other as they sat together, fastening their seatbelts. "Well," said Doug triumphantly. "Looks like we pulled it off once again!"

"That was quite a birthday!" said Marty. "A wonderful holiday! How are you feeling, my darling?"

"I'm always fine when I'm with you," said Doug.

Marty smiled. "It was so nice to be warm outdoors, and not to have to hurry for a change!" she said.

Doug slept the whole way home, and Marty suspected the kids did too. She was thinking about trust. Probably the kids trusted Doug even more since he had told them about Jason's birth. And Doug felt better about it too. Fallout might come from Mackenzie, Marty told him. But, "I don't care," said Doug. He liked openness and honesty.

They did not have flower leis around their necks when they got off the plane, but they were home. A new year was beginning. And it was time for breakfast!

19

Line cut up limes beside her friend Juliana, who was vigorously muddling sugar with lime at the bottom of each glass for the caipirinhas she was making. "I don't worry too much about the proportions," she said. "A spoonful of sugar, quarter of lime. Then ice, then cachaca." Cachaca was a hard liquor made from fresh sugar cane. Juliana and Daniel had brought it from Brazil. Both of them had jobs at UC Santa Cruz, Juliana in the agricultural department and Daniel in history.

"Stephen loves new drinks," said Line of the caipirinhas. "I don't dare drink much, but I want to try one." She was having trouble enough navigating these days. She was also trying to restrict her diet.

"Light on the liquor for me too," said Karina, in whose kitchen they were standing at a counter. Unctuous smells rose in the small kitchen as Karina mashed yucca root at the stove. She would serve it with rice and pork and vegetables, a Cuban meal in honor of her husband Rafael who had grown up there.

Line loved these international friendships which were easy to make at a university. Stephen had known Karina forever, as a political activist and journalist. She spoke Spanish and had lived in many places in South America. Her marriage to Rafael had brought him to the United States. She had recently investigated the Nuestra Familia, a Mexican American gang in Salinas, and made a video with Rafael doing the photography. Now that she was pregnant, however, she hoped to work on something less dangerous!

Line carried glasses into the living room, where Stephen cued Rafael to introduce himself to Daniel. Rafael had been born just after the Cuba revolution, had wanted to become an engineer. "You wouldn't believe the textbooks," he said. "From Russia, some of them. Old-fashioned math. I probably did get the basics, but we longed for more." Rafael was tall with longish dark hair, broad shoulders, and no beard. Line experienced him as a whole person, proud, masculine, absolutely to be counted on. She could understand how Karina had cut through all the obstacles to visit him and finally get married.

"Thank you, Line!" said Daniel. He raised his glass. "Bottoms up!"

"Hits the spot!" said Rafael. It was one of the first warm days in March and the cooking made the small apartment feel stuffy.

"Perfectly made," Daniel complimented his wife as she carried in more glasses. Juliana and Daniel had not been in the States long either. They came from upper class homes in Sao Paulo. Both of them were small and looked European to Line, Daniel built like a wiry, lightweight fighter; Juliana a bleached blonde in beautiful clothes. They had met at a university in Brazil. It was hard to imagine Juliana had ever been in the fields, and in fact she had not. She mostly did research in a lab coat. She spoke several languages besides Portuguese. Spanish, English and even some German from her parents.

"Let's drink to Stephen," said Daniel. "Come on Karina. Give us a moment." Karina joined them from the kitchen and they stood in a circle, younger and older. Stephen would retire at the end of the school year. Line looked forward to it. Stephen was 65 and had been teaching for more than 35 years.

"I like teaching," said Stephen. "But I will be glad to be past the iron round of the school calendar. Sink my teeth into things more." Stephen was still writing, of course. He was always finding things he wanted to investigate further but didn't have time.

"UC Santa Cruz is quite the place," said Daniel. "I've heard it had quite a reputation in the early years."

"I got here just when things were changing," said Stephen. "The original idea was to have a bunch of small liberal arts colleges grouped together. It was beautiful. But then the big money kicked in and it became a research institution, like our other universities. Lost its uniqueness."

"Some of that aura is still there," said Daniel. "It's a good place to be an undergraduate."

"Yes," said Stephen. "We put a hell of a lot into our students."

"California is an engine for change," said Rafael.

Stephen shook his head. "It'll be nice to look back on it. I'm a historian, after all. Like Daniel here."

Karina had pulled out all the stops for dinner. She had made twice-fried plantains, sometimes called tosterones, as well as the mashed yucca, a cilantro sauce, rice and roast pork. She spread the dishes on the table and let people fill their plates and find a seat on the sofa or wherever they wanted. Karina had a fleshy face, long hair and a chubby torso. "It's because of my family," she had once told Line. "We all fought to eat as much as we could!"

Line filled her plate with the delicious food, leaving out the rice. She knew some of it came of necessity. "We learned to eat anything," Rafael told them. There had been a time of famine since the USSR collapsed and Cubans didn't have enough to eat. Petroleum had been non-existent. "It's better now," he said, "since agriculture is reformed and Hugo Chavez of Venezuela stepped in to trade with Cuba. 80% of our food came from Russia before 1991," he said. "All of us lost weight! But also some of the weight-related illnesses."

"It's a beautiful place," said Karina. "Beautiful beaches and that sort of stripped down beauty of places with nothing extra. And the music!" All of them knew about the music. Ry Cooder had gone to Cuba and come back with recordings of pianists and groups of musicians. Line had the album and had even seen the documentary called *The Buena Vista Social Club*.

"A sort of flattened economy?" asked Daniel. "By decree? We have the opposite problem. Runaway discrepancies between rich and poor. Corruption, kidnapping and thievery. You can't roll down your car windows when you drive through our city." He shook his head. "Juliana feels much safer here." The two of them looked at each other sadly.

The talk soon turned to American politics, however. Everyone had been thrilled by the entry of a black man, Barack Obama, as a candidate for president. "Did you read his book?" asked Stephen. "It was reprinted after that amazing speech he gave a couple of years ago at the Democratic national convention. What a background that guy has! Half sisters and brothers all over the world! And he was doing community organizing in Chicago!" Stephen and Line had some feeling for Chicago after living there in the late 1960's.

"Yes," said Karina. "But how about Hillary?" Hillary Clinton had entered the race a few weeks earlier than Obama. "It seems to me it's her turn!"

"Also a good candidate," said Stephen evenly. "Obama may not have the experience he needs at this point. We'll have to see."

Line didn't say what she thought as it was still ripening in her mind. She had also read Obama's book and, for her, Obama's integrity stood out as over against 'plastic' Hillary. Perhaps Hillary had been in politics too long! Line saw little television, but she didn't like Clinton's voice or her style. Flat, rational, false, she seemed. Stephen called the Democrats "the other corporate party," in any case. Hillary had sold out long ago.

"Such ambition," said Juliana. "And we'll all be watching this drama play out for the next year and a half!"

"The world's stage, indeed," said Daniel. "It can't be helped. The rest of us are all bit players. Do you even know the name of our president?" he asked.

Stephen took up the challenge. "Lula, right? He's still president? Sounds like a great guy. We actually know more about Chile than we do about Brazil, because our daughter is there. But I follow your politics too."

After dinner, Rafael produced a box of vanilla wafers for a sweet while Karina made coffee. But Line stopped him. "We brought a tart," she said. "Didn't you know?" She went into the kitchen and pulled the pie carrier off the shelf.

"Oh my God," said Rafael as Line placed the lightly browned almond tart on the table. He stood up to get small plates.

"Please cut the pieces," Line asked Juliana. "It's a recipe from Chez Panisse that I learned. I only want the thinnest slice. To taste it."

The tart, sweet, creamy and nutty, was perfection. Line had had to ask Stephen to help her, as she felt too uncertain to pour the boiling cream, sugar and almonds into the tart shell without burning herself. Stephen was helping more and more.

Daniel and Rafael had extra pieces. "What a night!" said Rafael. "Such great food! Conversation! And drink!" He turned to Juliana and asked her how she had made the caipirinhas.

"We'll have to get together again to watch the debates and the elections," said Karina when everyone prepared to leave. "I'm frightened for Obama. He must be very courageous."

"Yes," said Line. She too was having to find her courage.

During the week, Marty came over to do tai chi with Line on her deck. It was a bright morning with some water in the air, the vegetation finally lush and green. "I can smell the sap in the trees when the sun hits them!" Marty said, by way of greeting. She handed Line a branch of apricot blossom she had plucked from the tree in the backyard of Line's old house which Marty and Doug now rented.

Line buried her nose in the delicate blossoms. "Yes, finally," said Line. "I wait for this time all year." It was warm enough that the two of them wore only light knit sweaters. Marty was on her way to the library after lunch, where she volunteered to shelve books. Line found a glass jar and put the apricot branch in it with some water. The old tree was still fruiting, but its blossoms would not last long.

The two of them stood on the wooden deck, facing the trees which rose up from a steep drop below. Marty led them in what she called Tiger Mountain Tai Chi Qigong. She said Master Liu had made the set for the sake of his father, who was in a wheelchair. For people who weren't disabled, it was a standing form, done in a horse stance, each person trying to settle as low as possible on their legs.

Raising their arms and moving into several postures, Marty counted, repeating the names of the postures as she did them. Line stood behind her following. "Fair lady weaving at the shuttles," said Marty. "Heaven and earth … cross hands … and push to the end." Line took big breaths, feeling the movements in her body as they came up from the bottom of her torso. She breathed in the tangy air of the pines in front of her.

Marty turned around when they were finished. "A bit of slow set?" she asked.

"Sure," said Line. She had begun to look for techniques which made her feel better. Marty wrote down the qigong postures for her and Line tried to do them every day. But it was wonderful when her sister came and they did it together. Marty stopped by at least once a week, a practice Line had instigated.

The slow set turned first one direction and then another. Line followed Marty's movements from behind, sinking onto her legs, though her crampy left hip was buckling, her knee folding. Marty did not try to teach each movement. They had done it many times, however, and it was all familiar to Line. She felt odd that she was now the vulnerable one, relying on Marty's many years of tai chi study.

After slow set, they walked down the steps to have a look at the garden. The group of redwood planters were stuffed with greens, onions and tangles of brown stalks from last year. "I'll have to get down here and clear up soon," Line said. "I'd get Stephen's help, but he has different ideas about the garden than I do. So I try to do it myself." She smiled impishly at Marty. "He likes gardening, though. I'm surprised at how much he likes cooking and domestic things he's never done before." She sighed. "But then he wants to control them, and it's hard for me to let go."

"I'm glad he can retire," said Marty.

Line hung over the edge of the deck. "You can see the persimmon blossoms starting," she said, "if you look closely." She did not want to go down more steps to get to the tree.

Marty peered over the edge. "I see them," she said. "Shall I go get you a branch?"

"No," said Line. "It's okay." She began pulling herself up the redwood steps to the upper deck, using the handrails. "Do you want a chicken sandwich for lunch? I have some leftover."

"Perfect," said Marty, following her. "Not too much, though."

Food was another area Line was experimenting with. She'd been having tests which were inconclusive. Auto-immune diseases like multiple sclerosis kept coming up, however. MS didn't show up in the MRI. She would probably have to have a spinal tap. Line was not looking forward to that.

"Now why should my immune system turn on me?" Line asked Marty, voicing the question which she woke up with every morning. "I didn't do anything to it! My body has always been so strong, a workhorse. And now I can't rely on it at all!" She took a loaf of artisan bread out of a paper bag and gave Marty a knife to cut it with. She turned to the refrigerator and pulled out mayonnaise, lettuce and a covered Tupperware filled with chicken pieces.

"One theory I've been reading," said Line, "relates to Mother. MS is much more widespread in the north than in the south, for instance. Mother had me in May in northern Minnesota and probably didn't get much Vitamin D throughout her pregnancy. Now, I had Fern in May, but at least I was in California, so I was out in the sun during the winter."

"Sounds like a credible theory," said Marty. "I've been hearing how important Vitamin D is. To everyone!"

"Yeah," said Line. "I've been sunbathing every nice day we have." She watched Marty making herself a sandwich. "I only get meat and lettuce now," she said, making herself a plate. "No dairy, no sugar, no grains. It's called a Paleolithic diet. Just meat, fats, veggies, fruit. It's kind of a bore."

"Do you think it's helping?" asked Marty.

"Who knows," sighed Line. "There's just so many variables." She sat down at the table where she had placed glasses of water and napkins.

"Chocolate?" asked Marty, slyly.

"Oh yes," said Line. "Chocolate's a fruit! Except I have to eat the dark stuff."

"Wow," said Marty. "I'm glad I can still have milk and sugar! I mean, I shouldn't, but I do."

"I know I should expect things to start going south," said Line. "But it seems kind of early! I look at Poppa, who isn't much worse for the wear and he's 30 years older!"

"Our folks died kind of young," said Marty.

"Six kids," said Line. "We wore them out."

"It's interesting to me how Mother's life got better as she got older," said Marty. "There was more money and less to worry about, I think."

"She might still be alive if she could have changed her diet," said Line darkly. "But I'm not doing so well at that, either," she admitted. "I'm always slipping."

"In terms of life arcs," said Marty. "I often think about how you had all those wonderful kids so early, and I was pretty unhappy. Until I met Doug." She tucked a piece of lettuce into her sandwich. "That is, I was always happy, I guess. But real contentment hasn't come until now."

"Contentment," said Line. "We had a rocky beginning, but Stephen and I are very tuned. He let me have the kids, as long as he had his work. The kids are my life." She looked rueful. "Wish they were closer."

"It's a little different too, being that Doug's so young," said Marty. "I feel like I've got a lot of life ahead of me and he certainly does. There's no sense of winding down."

Line looked at Marty, who was 61, only a year younger than she was. Marty did indeed seem young and vibrant. "You'll be like Poppa," she said. "You'll last forever."

"Well I do try to keep up with Doug, though not entirely," said Marty. "We'll probably move back to the ranch in a year, when the twins graduate. Have I told you? Jason will happily live with Grandma Alice in high school. She has room for him. And we want someone to live with her."

"I'll tell Stephen to keep that in mind," said Line. "It's been so much fun to have you in town!"

"Oh yes!" said Marty. "I've loved it. But Doug makes the big decisions. I can live anywhere, really. My life is in the hollow of his hand."

Line laughed. "Oh, Marty," she said. "So poetic!" She stood up and began to tidy up the kitchen. "I'm just trying to stay alive," she said. "Or at least feel good while I am alive. This winter has been dark for me. Like a tunnel. I'm afraid I won't be good for much. Not even for my grandchildren, if this keeps up."

"You've been good for a lot," said Marty. "All your life. It won't hurt you to rest on your laurels."

"What laurels?" wailed Line. It was exactly as she had feared. She had not accomplished much.

"All those people you've nursed," said Marty. "All those kids you brought up to be great humans. This lovely home you've made for so many people. I always like the atmosphere you create. People can talk about anything, think freely here."

"Humpf," said Line, a bit wild-eyed. "I need to do more!" She was panicked. That was all there was to it. She felt she lost a little every day.

"I better get going," said Marty. "Those books won't shelve themselves!"

"Guess who's coming," said Line. "Christy! And he's bringing a girl with him."

"Oh?" asked Marty as she gathered her things. "Someone you know?"

"Emily," said Line. "I met her once in Minnesota. I think they've been more or less together for a long time. We never get much out of Christy, you know."

"I can't wait to meet her," said Marty.

Christy and Emily arrived just as Stephen was doing his final reviews. They had driven all the way from Minnesota in Emily's new car. "It's a good idea to do a road trip when you get a new car," Emily told them. "Settles the engine in." The car, a brand new silver Prius, gave the two of them a more upscale appearance than Line was used to seeing. But Christy's jeans were still frayed and he wore t-shirts. So Emily doesn't have to iron, thought Line. They were both lean and sparkling, Emily's long kinky hair tamed somewhat by being pulled to the side in a knot. It softened her angular face.

"You both look great!" Poppa said, hugging each of them in turn. Poppa was certain, from seeing photographs of Emily, that she was Jewish.

Almost 40, thought Line as she hugged her tall son. She had a brief mental image of herself on the train with baby Christy on their way to California so many years ago. It was amazing how her kids took her both forward and back, back to their beginnings. The whole of Christy was there, all of his branches and leaves and unfulfilled potential were visible to Line. She ushered Christy and Emily into the living room.

Stephen was still working on his mounds of student papers that week, but one evening, Poppa suggested they play hearts. "Hearts is for when we're feeling sociable," he said. "If we were serious, it would be bridge, or pinochle. More thought involved." Poppa had a bridge club with his cronies. He rarely played at home as Stephen wouldn't take the time.

It was a lovely spring evening, the dishes in the dishwasher, the table cleared. The light was getting a little bit longer each night too. Line felt pretty good, but lazy. She always felt better at home. Cards would be a perfect thing to do. She remembered the Christmas in Chile where everyone played cards, four generations settling down to the game on hot evenings. She put on a pot of water. "Anyone want tea?" she asked.

Poppa got out a deck and dealt the cards to Line, Emily, Christy and himself. "Now, don't worry," he flirted shamelessly with Emily, "we'll watch out for you. The first round won't count."

"It sounds like fun," said Emily. "And, you know, we often are killing time, waiting around for something to happen."

"Killing time!" said Christy. "I don't think so!" He was still a hard-driving political activist, organizing, brainstorming, talking, collecting names and numbers, and now, e-mail addresses. "There's never enough time; always more to do."

Emily brushed him off. "Your Poppa's right, though," she said. "A little relaxation would do you good." Emily had a law degree and worked in an attorney's office. She was also ambitious, but seemed to want to have a home life as well. "I take weekends off!" she confided. "Mr. Workaholic here doesn't!"

"Hearts and minds," said Christy. "They don't take vacations." Line could see that Emily was also the money manager in the family. Christy had fallen into the best possible situation for himself.

Poppa dealt the cards and explained to Emily and Christy what they should do. "You don't want to take tricks," he said. "Especially you don't want to take any hearts. But you'll be forced to sometimes. Each heart counts as one. Except for the black queen, the queen of spades. She counts as 13! The person with the most points loses in this game."

"With one exception!" said Line. "If someone manages to take all the hearts, they get no points and everyone else gets 13."

"It's called 'Shooting the Moon,'" said Poppa. "Try it sometime. It's fun!"

"So that's what 'shooting the moon' means," said Emily. "I'm always surprised to find that a lot of slang goes back to cards. Like I just found out that 'play it as it lays,' is poker talk! Joan Didion's dad was a poker player."

"Ah, a literate person!" Poppa smiled. "You've got yourself a winner here, Christy!"

The first round Emily won. She was concentrating, as Christy was not. Line was not surprised when Obama's name came up. "He's brilliant," said Christy. "I never saw anything like it. He's already got a website with his positions and priorities clearly laid out. And the campaign is collecting thousands of email addresses for soliciting and explaining. He's using social media, like MySpace and Facebook to talk to people. Young people dig it!"

"It's that grass roots networking he knows how to do," said Poppa. "Combine that with the internet and he'll hit the jackpot."

"What's social media?" asked Line.

"Just having an internet presence," said Emily. "We all spend so much time on the internet now."

"Comes with a price, though," said Christy. "I've heard he's getting a lot of hate mail. But he's also really good at being personable, speaking to issues directly and letting people get to know him. I think he's brilliant."

"He's got a Youtube video out that you can access on his website," said Emily. "He's taking matters into his own hands. Not leaving it in the uncertain hands of the unkind press."

"What's Youtube?" asked Line.

Christy threw up his hands. "I'll show you, when you have time," he said. "Right now, if you want."

But Poppa and Line didn't want. They wanted to talk, to play cards and feast their eyes on Emily and Christy. Line noticed that her hand was full of hearts. She slyly and quietly began to collect them.

"Oh oh," said Poppa. "Watch that. Can anyone stop her?"

No one could. Line had the highest hearts. She smiled as she took all the tricks and shot the moon.

20

Paul watched as the intrepid Hanna led her newly-adopted daughter, five year old Kayla, across the slippery stones at the headwaters of the Mississippi. It was really too cold for such capers in October, but several people couldn't resist, including Hanna. Kayla's little brother Jaden clung tight to Faith at the edge of the water. The colors of the lake which flowed over the dam were deep blue, reflecting the sky, while the reeds at the edge and the aspens had turned golden and bronze.

"Going? Gone?" begged Jaden, pointing as Hanna and Kayla disappeared into the reeds on the far side. Jaden was just beginning to talk, to have words to express his questions.

"They're okay," Faith shushed him. "They'll be back in a minute."

The defining characteristic of the two kids was fear of abandonment, thought Paul. Their mother had been an alcoholic and drug addict, unable to care for them. Hanna and Faith, and inevitably Faith's parents, all of whom lived in upstate New York on the farm where Faith kept sheep and goats and made cheese from their milk, were involved in this adoption. It had been a year since it began and Faith and Hanna were finally allowed to take the kids out of state. They had come to the Mikkelson family cabin on Lake Michigami for a rest!

"And to give my parents a break," Faith told Paul. "It hasn't been easy. But we wanted a family. We wanted to give back some of the enormous gifts we've been given."

"I'm proud of us," Hanna put in. "Of course it isn't easy. But we're doing okay." The four of them were sleeping in the king-sized bed which Ellie and Bruce had installed in one of the big downstairs bedrooms. Jaden was only two. The kids were sweet, but precociously paranoid.

"We can't let each other out of our sight," sighed Faith. "Especially when we're traveling."

Hanna was upbeat, however. "We'll get through it," she said. "It won't always be this way. And it's much better than it was."

As Paul replayed these conversations in his head, Hanna and Kayla emerged on the little footbridge which was the return journey across the river. "There they are!" he indicated to Faith. He held a leash on Wilson, a necessity around so many people. Paul was glad Wilson was old enough now to feel protective of the kids. Kayla was quite fond of the big caramel-colored lab/shepherd.

Kayla squealed as she came up to them: "Icy! My feet tingle." She hopped about, drawing one foot down against her jeans trying to dry it. She and Hanna sat down beside Faith and put on their socks and shoes. Hanna was still her light-filled self, Paul thought, her long blonde hair loosely twisted into a French braid; Faith smaller and darker. Kayla was a bit pudgy with golden brown curls, while Jaden had light brown skin, long eyelashes and glossy black hair.

Paul was enjoying Itasca State Park, which was only about 30 miles from the cabin. He tended to take it for granted, though he did visit now and then. He tried to imagine what the country had looked like when Schoolcraft had come out with the Ojibway chief Ozaawindib to look for the source of the mighty river. Schoolcraft had tried twice, and in 1832 established that the headwaters flowed out of the lake to which he gave the name Itasca.

The place had a storied history, only the second state park in the country, after Niagara Falls. It had been protected from logging for the sake of its ancient red and white pines. There was even a story of a young woman, daughter of one of the early directors, who stood up to gun-toting lumbermen. They had raised water levels which threatened the pines. Mary Gibbs said, "I will put my hand on those dam levers and you will not shoot it." The visitors' center now commemorated her actions.

The little party got back into Paul's car and drove the loop around the wilderness sanctuary, stopping to look at a 300-year-old white pine and then at Douglas Lodge. "Aunt Rose once worked here," he told Hanna. "She was teaching, but worked here in the summers. You wouldn't remember staying in a cabin here when we were really little, but I do. A one-room log cabin Aunt Rose rented for us."

"No," said Hanna as they walked up to the big log building, painted dark brown. "By the time I came along, we were always at the cabin. I hardly remember coming here."

"Preachers' Grove?" asked Paul. It was a stand of red pine near the entrance. "I forgot to stop on the way."

"Maybe," said Hanna. "It sounds familiar."

The lodge, built at least a hundred years ago, was busy. Paul tied Wilson up outside. They all had cheese curds and fried walleye bites. The grownups followed this with wild rice soup, while the kids shared a hamburger. Kayla was all eyes, and Jaden quiet, his mouth full of French fries.

"Cheese curds?" asked Faith. "They melt in your mouth!"

"They're a Wisconsin thing," said Paul. "But we all love them." The curds were dipped in batter and fried.

"Hmmm," said Faith, her professional interest piqued.

They did stop at Preachers' Grove on their way out of the park. A path through the towering trees led down to the blue lake, the wind whispering above them. As they stood at the edge of the lake, a V of honking ducks flew over. "You guys are late!" Paul said. "You better get going!"

To Kayla Paul said, "Do you know why when you see a V of ducks like that one line is always longer than the other?"

Kayla looked up at him. "No," she said, expecting a bit of natural history, which Paul was always quick to provide.

"Because there's more ducks in that line," said Paul deadpan.

"Paul!" said Hanna.

Paul looked innocent, as usual. "Well, am I right? Or am I right?" He laughed with them. Picking up a bit of needles which covered the floor on the forest, he said, "These are red pine. They have two needles in a clump and are stiffer looking than the white pines. Dad used to call them Norways."

"I like the name Norway," said Hanna, "But I'm sure they're native."

"Yes," said Paul. "The white pine have five needles per clump which makes them look more feathery. Like the ones Dad planted near the cabin. They're getting taller. I'll show you when we get home."

Walking back the kids frisked along the path. The tall pines reached up into the blue sky, leaving little undergrowth in the thick, centuries-old reddish pine duff on the ground. A true old-growth forest. Paul resolved to come back by himself with Wilson when they could pay more attention.

"You guys picked the right time to come," Paul said. "Mosquitoes are pretty much gone by now."

"It's the right time for us," said Hanna. Kayla was in kindergarten, but they had felt it a good idea to take her out for a week in celebration of their adoption. The process, as Hanna described it, was arduous. The kids had been in group homes and at first Hanna and Faith provided foster care. They wanted to keep the kids, however. A judge had to deny the mother's right to the children, clearing the way, but it was an open adoption. Kayla longed for her mother at first, sending notes and trying to call her. But the mother did not respond.

"We're making a family here," said Hanna. "We live in a beautiful place. You remember being on our farm. But this lake is special. To be right there at the edge."

"Yes," said Paul. He lived on the lake, but he was never immune to the flight of an eagle, the emergence of deer at the edge of a clearing, or the always amazing sky. He had been considering how to get everyone out in the canoe. Hanna was experienced, but Faith was not, and you did not want anyone to end up in the drink at this time of year.

The light was going down quickly. At the cabin, Hanna turned on the lamps and put on music, a tape she had put together for what she called "silly dancing." She got Kayla and Jaden dancing in the middle of the room.

Faith made pizza dough and Paul began to cut up vegetables. Paul could hardly stand still either as he sliced mushrooms. Aretha sang "R-E-S-P-E-C-T, Find out what it means to me … Just a little bit, just a little bit." The kids pranced and giggled, holding hands with Hanna.

And then, as Paul sliced tomatoes, came a song he didn't know. "Who's that?" he asked loudly, hearing lyrics to a reggae beat: "in the middle of the football game, at the beach in the pouring rain … moving my body in a ragamuffin style. I can't sit down when I hear it start, I hear your heart everywhere I go."

"Jackson Browne!" shouted Hanna. "Isn't it great?!"

"Yes," said Paul, listening attentively. And soon it was ABBA's "Dancing Queen." Yes, thought Paul. He had not picked up his guitar in ages. Perhaps he had let music die with Marie? That shouldn't happen. "Again! again!" he wanted to say, to the Jackson Browne song, as Marie would have. But he could study the music and lyrics later.

In the morning, Paul was down at the dock early, Wilson at his heels. The sun rising far to the southeast made its usual path straight toward them. It was another clear, bright day, the lake smooth in the early morning, a sun-filled mist rising from it in the distance. But bright, still days wouldn't last. Wilson mumphed along the shore, hoping Paul would throw a stick in for him, but Paul knew better than to start!

"It never gets old, does it," said Hanna, coming up behind him.

"Nope," said Paul, taking a sip of the hot coffee.

"You remind me of Dad," said Hanna. "Do you shake your fist at water skiers?"

Paul laughed. "No," he said. "They're not doing as much damage as some people think. Not many of them anyway. But of course I'm not much for motor boats." It was good to think that he was like Dad, that if it were possible, Dad would have stood down on the dock just as he was. 87, Paul calculated in his head the age Dad would have been.

"I'm so grateful for Faith's parents," said Hanna. "They have much the same values we do. They're farming as sustainably as possible. There's a windmill to pump water."

"Is that one of the new wind turbines?" asked Paul. "Or an old one?"

"A new one," said Hanna. "Came out of Denmark, I think."

"I've been paying attention to Obama's climate change rhetoric," said Paul. "He's got some good ideas."

Hanna sighed and shook her head. "We need a winner," she said.

"Yes," said Paul. It was too early to tell what might happen. "It's going to be an interesting year." He wandered over to the canoes, turned over on the bank in the trees. Wilson snuffled about, perhaps turning up a mole or a shrew. "Canoe ride?" he asked.

But Hanna looked up the hill toward the cabin guiltily. "I better not," she said. "Do you think it will stay this calm? I really want Faith to have a chance."

"It probably will," said Paul, looking at the sky. He and Wilson followed Hanna up the path.

It was too cold to swim, but everyone came down to the dock that morning. Paul pulled a canoe into the water and took first Faith and Kayla out. "You don't need to paddle unless you want to," he told Faith as he helped her sit at the front of the boat. Kayla sat on the floor in the middle, buckled into a life jacket, on top of Paul and Faith's jackets. He didn't intend to get very far from shore. The wind wasn't bad, but it was there, riffling the water between small swells.

193

They took off waving. "It's an adventure," said Faith to Kayla. "Wave goodbye!" They waved to Hanna, who had Jaden firmly pinned between her legs, Wilson beside them.

"I feel like one of the girls in the James Fenimore Cooper book," said Faith as she paddled. "They were always hopping in their canoes and going off. I think they actually lived in a house built on the water."

"Which book?" asked Paul.

"*The Deerslayer,*" said Faith. "I always admired them, but I've never had much chance to canoe. The book was very romantic."

"We have a pond," Kayla explained to Paul. "But it's for cows. We can't go in it."

"It's full of weeds," said Faith. "Not fun even for wading." The pond was an attractive nuisance. "Paul remembers," she told Kayla. "He was there once."

Paul remembered indeed his trip out with Mother and Marie, a few years ago. "I certainly do," he said, paddling steadily. He was finding that Faith and Kayla didn't weigh much. The canoe did not sit very low in the water and it was hard to steer! "You guys are too light!" he teased. "I can't get much purchase here!" It usually wasn't what happened with Mikkelsons!

"If I eat enough cheese curds it won't be a problem!" said Faith.

"*The Deerslayer* was set in New York, wasn't it," said Paul musingly. He all of a sudden realized that Faith's childhood reading and dreams were set in a different place than his! "I read that one, but not the others."

"It's everywhere in New York. Places are named for Natty Bumppo and there's a point named for Judith on Lake Oswego," said Faith.

"The native Americans were Iroquois, right?" asked Paul.

"Yes," said Faith. The water undulated under them. Paul paddled east, keeping close to shore. "Kayla," said Faith warningly as Kayla leaned over, peering into the water. "Sit up or the boat will rock."

Where a creek flowed down into the lake, Paul pointed out the cabin the Mikkelsons had first stayed in when he was very small. Past this cabin was a hillside with a thick stand of red pine now built up with substantial, winterized homes. "Did Hanna tell you about the famous trolley car?" he asked. Long ago, a trolley car had been parked on this hillside. The owner was reputed to be mean and as little kids they had scared each other over his presence. But it hadn't kept them from visiting the derelict and dusty car.

"I think she did," said Faith. "She says everyone up here is a Lutheran pastor!"

"Not quite," said Paul. "But there are generations of them around the lake. The original owners bought because one of them told all the others. Pastors, teachers, most of them Scandinavian Lutherans to be sure."

Faith stopped paddling and turned her head around. "Can they still see us?" she asked. The figures on the dock were not within shouting distance, but they could be seen. Paul back-paddled to turn the canoe around. The green-gold water washed around them and they headed back toward their own dock.

Next it was Hanna's turn. "Wilson would love it if you threw a stick for him to retrieve," Paul told Kayla as he held the canoe so Hanna could get in. The big dog paced up and down the dock, looking expectantly at everyone. Faith and Kayla went up and found a sizable stick, which Faith threw as far into the water as she could. Wilson jumped in after it.

"You have to sit very still," Hanna told Jaden, the squirmy one. "Maybe I should sit in the middle with him," she said.

"Whatever works for you," said Paul. "We won't go far." The wind was beginning to come up a little, and the air was cold. "We'll just give Jaden a taste."

Hanna settled in the middle, holding Jaden between her legs. As he paddled, Paul said, "I'm realizing that Faith's background is different just because of where she lives," he said. "Like she has all that revolutionary history, the Leatherstocking tales, Iroquois behind her. Which we just don't have!"

"It's odd," said Hanna. "But any couple has to do some kind of cultural meld of their backgrounds. I don't know everything, but I've learned a lot. You learn by just being on the ground," she said.

"Yep," said Paul. "Things are always thick on the ground, wherever you go. I guess that's a good reason to travel."

"It doesn't tempt us much," said Hanna. "We're tied to all those animals! They're our livelihood. And I get to act in the summers. This is special, though. I wanted to show Faith."

"I love being here," said Paul. "Surrounded by our own history. Bemidji is a great town, you know? They're starting to have signage in Ojibway there. Amazing." A few days before he had seen a sign on a bank saying 'Boozhoo,' meaning 'Welcome' in Ojibway.

When they got back, Paul pulled up the canoe. Wilson was still avidly jumping into the cold water after sticks. "He'll never stop until you do," Paul said. "I've tried to wear him out, but I can't!"

That afternoon, Ellie and Bruce came. "For the color," they said. October was the height of the season, before leaves began to drop off. But Paul knew they also were curious about Hanna and Faith and their new family. They were having a good time being retired. Ellie was an officer in her church, and Bruce had taken on some volunteer work. They had grandchildren too, who lived near them in St. Paul.

The summer at the lake had been somewhat low key. No one had come that year from California. Ellie, Bruce and Rhonda's family had come for a couple of weeks, and the younger of Grace's kids had also spent a few weeks, but they were very busy with sports and camp counseling. Paul did see a little of his cousins, who owned the Bakken cabin next to his.

Paul had his own work and routines, as well as being the resident manager at Lake Michigami. He often ended up doing laundry and cleanup when people left, pacing the laundry so it didn't overwhelm the leach field. Ellie took her laundry home, as she too worried about preserving the plumbing at the cabin. Paul didn't mind the work as it was such a privilege to live at the lake.

One night, Faith and Hanna put the kids to bed and came up to have a cup of cocoa with Bruce, Ellie and Paul. Bruce had gotten a fire going in the Ben Franklin. "I turned on the heat," he said. "But a fire is always nice." Soft jazz music played in the background. Dave Brubeck, Paul thought.

Ellie handed around mugs and a bowl of microwaved popcorn. "Everyone okay with butter?" she asked.

Heads nodded in assent. Paul sipped the hot cocoa.

"So how's the adoption going?" asked Ellie.

Hanna and Faith recounted the story for her, filling in a few things Paul didn't know. The kids had different fathers, Jaden a mix of Puerto Rican and white. He had been taken from their mother almost right away, Kayla when she was four. "At first there was a lot of wailing," said Faith. "Lots of rocking and petting. I'm not sure it will ever be enough."

"It's like, at some point," said Hanna, "when Kayla suspected this was permanent, that's when she really broke down. And Jaden still has some night terror. But I would say we've become fused into a family over the year."

"I've been thinking so much about you," Ellie said. "You know the Kirbys, the ones who run the Bach family business right now and built this house? Julia Kirby was a Bach. They're such a fine family. They adopted four native American kids whose parents were alcoholics. They said they wanted to give back too. And I think two of those kids now work in the Bach lumber mill."

"It was pretty rocky at the beginning," said Hanna. "But it's better now, and we're stronger, I think." She looked at Faith.

"No question," said Faith. "Not too long ago, Kayla came home from school and told me, 'I've decided I love you.' I cried. She cried. Slow steps." She shook her head. Paul could see Faith's eyes going back to the difficult times. "It's all worth it."

"Are your folks in good health?" asked Ellie.

"Yes," said Faith. "They've been great. I was an only child, and they've always had a mellow life. The main thing they were worried about was whether I would ever come home! But when Hanna and I committed to each other, I was so lucky that she wanted to go live on the farm as well. And we've found a niche for ourselves!"

"Sheep cheese," said Hanna. "Who knew?!"

"Well, we wish you the best," said Ellie. "The kids are darling."

"We're so grateful for the new cabin," said Hanna. "It's just amazing. Such an improvement over the rickety, rackety old cabin with its moldy basement!"

"It's for our kids," said Ellie. "All of our kids."

Paul's thoughts went straight to the seventh generation to come. According to the Mikkelson Family Limited Partnership, the cabin could never be sold. New generations would be added in as old ones died out. Would the earth and its peoples still be there? Not exactly as they were now, Paul guessed. But northern Minnesota with its many forests was certainly well-placed to ride out climate change.

The Morlands brought other news. Bruce seemed to be worried about the financial world. "The problems are mostly happening in mortgages," he told them. "High delinquency rates are driving it. Lax regulation and reckless lending are getting the big banks in trouble."

"There are only three or four of them, aren't there?" asked Paul. Financial news happened so far away from him it didn't seem to matter. The big banks were always gobbling up the little ones, he had noticed.

"It doesn't affect us," said Faith. "People are going to eat no matter whether they own a home or not!"

"But maybe not our hand-crafted, high-end cheeses," said Hanna. She was the one who took the cheese to markets.

Like a hostess, Ellie threw up her hands and tried to lighten the conversation. "How about those Twins, though," she said. The Twins baseball team had been threatening to leave Minnesota for some years, sick of sharing the Metrodome with the Vikings football team. "They've started construction on Target field," she said. "And the Twins have agreed to a 30-year lease!"

"They didn't have a great season," said Bruce. "But the new field will be something to look forward to."

"Do any of you know how things are going with Line?" asked Ellie, going back to family news. "I haven't heard much."

"They finally did a spinal tap and she got a diagnosis of progressive multiple sclerosis," said Paul soberly. "Her disability will only get worse over the years. But she says the literature is full of hopeful ideas. Like stem cell therapy."

Ellie shook her head. "I never would have thought it would be Line!" she said. "She's done so much nursing and helped so many people!"

"I talked to her not too long ago," said Paul. "She is losing ground. She's afraid to go very far, and doesn't go out by herself."

"Well," said Ellie. "She's got all those kids to help."

"None of whom live near her!" said Hanna. "How did we all get so far apart?!"

"Well," said Faith. "You've got 50% of the Mikkelson siblings right here in this room. That ought to count for something!"

"Yes it does, Faith," said Hanna, putting her arms around her partner as they sat together on a small couch. "It's so good to be here," she said again.

"Kristen always seems fine," said Ellie running through the list of her other siblings, "though we see very little of her. Farms do take time. And I think Marty's happy."

"Yes," said Hanna. "Another unlikely story! But she certainly loves Doug." She stood up and carried her cocoa cup over to the kitchen. "Shouldn't we go down and check on the kids?" she asked Faith. "I haven't heard anything ..."

The fire had burned down to embers and so had the evening. Paul wrapped the family warmth around himself. It was indeed thick on the ground in Minnesota. He went downstairs and patted Wilson, who wasn't allowed upstairs. "Good boy," he said. "Want to walk down to the lake and have a look at the Milky Way?" he asked. "See if there's any northern lights?" They would have to take the dock in soon, Paul thought. It was not unlikely that he had ended up at the cabin, blessed, though without his Marie.

21

"More toast?" asked Marty. It was raining and Doug planned to stay home that day and work on his databases. The kids were at school. Marty and Doug were sharing a last cup of tea and a rare chance to talk.

"No, I think I'm good," said Doug, looking out the window at the morning light sparkling on the drizzle. "The rain will start letting up tomorrow. I'm looking forward to pruning!" January was often a time of heavy rain on the Central Coast.

Marty nodded. Weather had a big effect on their daily life. "Did you see Zoe's post about her soccer team this morning?"

"Facebook?" asked Doug. He batted her question away with his hands, laughing. He could not be bothered with the new Facebook. But Marty had joined. She thought that maybe she could help Boulder Creek Vineyards with its marketing. But also, because the kids were using it.

"She put up a little prayer for the weather to be nice for their game this weekend," said Marty.

"Oh," said Doug. "A little mud wouldn't hurt those girls!" He stretched. "You know, I found something surprising when I got into the weeds yesterday." He meant the internet weeds, where it was quite possible to get bogged down when searching for some perfectly legitimate information. "We called her Zoe, I guess because we liked the name, or something. But to the Greeks, Zoe meant the life that endures, as opposed to bios, the finite life."

"Wow," said Marty. "I like it."

"Not only that," said Doug. "This life, or spirit was especially associated with the Dionysian cult. So you can see that somehow we knew what we were doing!"

Marty knew Doug was putting the Dionysian cult together with his work in viticulture and winemaking. "It's a lovely name," she said, pouring the last of the tea from the white china pot painted with a blue fish. "So remember we promised to go out to Merced on Saturday," she reminded him. Nic had become intrigued with the new college the University of California was building there. He could have gone by himself, but Doug thought he should see it too.

"Yeah," said Doug. "That'll be interesting."

"The twins are working on their applications and college essays, too," said Marty.

"I guess I could help with that," said Doug.

"You should read them," said Marty. "I'll check their English grammar. You might want to help with ideas." It seemed to her that the last couple of years had been all about college. But the twins were going about it in a much more strategic way than Zoe had. Perhaps they had learned from her.

"Well," said Doug, standing up from the table. "I better get a going. Those data fields don't fill themselves."

"And I guess you have to make backups of your backups," teased Marty. Doug was a very meticulous computer user. She started clearing the breakfast things.

"Yup," said Doug. "Never a dull moment on my computer."

Marty giggled. As she whisked the kitchen together, she thought about Zoe. Of course Zoe wanted to go to college, but she hadn't been very serious about academics until her junior year, when all of a sudden she found out that she was smart. She had always been a leader, but she began to participate in class, especially if there was a political or moral question. And she read the material!

Marty had found it an amazing transformation to watch. Zoe was already eleven when Marty had joined Doug's family, so she never felt she had much influence over her. But in Marty's quiet way, she probably did. Doug always insisted that without Marty the family would not have done well. He was deeply grateful.

Zoe dithered about college, however. Her SAT scores were nothing special, though she could write an excellent essay. She had vaguely wanted to go to school in southern California, so she could see a little of her mother. But she hadn't known where. Vince of all people came to Zoe's aid. He got her an interview at the liberal college he had gone to, the

University of Redlands. It did seem that Zoe would do best in a smaller college. And she could nail an interview. Doug was all for it.

In the end, however, Zoe had gone to Westmont College, a small Christian college in Montecito, just outside of Santa Barbara. She went because Mackenzie said she would be more likely to drive up the coast to see Zoe than across Los Angeles and out to the desert where the University of Redlands was! Zoe had to sign a community life letter and go to chapel every day, but all of this was something she could do, she said. Chapel, she told them, was just a daily assembly. No one took it very seriously. Marty thought it was actually a great place for Zoe, with small classes and many off-campus programs. Mackenzie was even helping with the cost, as the place was expensive.

Poor Doug was quite worried about money. Three kids in college at the same time! It had been looming for a while, and Doug kept insisting that the kids were not going to get a free ride, as he had not. The economy was also wobbling, with its sub-prime mortgage crisis. But as Vince was fond of pointing out, no one stopped drinking alcohol during the Great Depression. Wine would be fine.

Luckily, both the twins wanted to go to state-sponsored schools. They were applying to several, and they did not want to go to the same one. Natasha was bent on Cal Poly in San Luis Obispo. She wanted to stick with a health and physical education major. Nic seemed less certain about what he wanted to study, but he liked the environmental research focus of the new university at Merced. All of its buildings were said to be certified green and it already had a solar energy research institute. It had been open for three years.

The twins were competitive, which helped. It was a competitive world out there, twice as populated now as when Marty started school. Marty thought back to her own college life. There had been no question but that she would go to Wittenberg College, though Ellie had dropped out, and later so did Line. Marty was the only one in her family who finished at Wittenberg. She took her education for granted at the time. She attributed her almost innate command of English grammar and usage to Mother's family background, and to her voluminous reading. It had stood her in good stead when she worked in architectural offices.

On Saturday, Jason elected to stay home with Grandma Alice, and only Doug, Marty, Nic and Natasha headed over the mountain toward the central valley of the state. The sky was considerably clearer, though streaked with clouds. Winter rains had left green swaths of new growth on the hills. Doug proclaimed it a Nic day, and allowed him to choose the CD's which blasted over the car speakers.

Marty could not keep up with the many highly-defined genres of music Nic listened to, but she did like the heavy bass rhythms and the unpredictable syncopated music which floated on them. Dubstep, she thought it was called. It gave a movie soundtrack feel to the journey up over the Pacheco Pass and down into the flat central valley. It didn't allow for much talk, but Marty enjoyed the excellent California highways flowing through the newly green countryside. Rows of citrus trees and almond trees lined the road when they got close to Merced.

A few miles outside of town lay the bare buildings of the university. Marty was shocked by the lack of trees. Of course, it had been a construction site only recently, and still was. But where would one go? she wondered. A small lake nearby had trees along its edge, but it was a little far to walk from the campus.

Unlike Marty, Nic seemed intrigued. "It's so different from Santa Cruz," he said. He was disposed to like it.

Doug, who had grown up in Salinas, walked around without saying much, not wanting to influence Nic one way or the other. They tried the doors on the library, a well-made building of fine metals and wood, and went in to the large foyer. There was a café with tables on one side but there was also an atmosphere of quiet seriousness.

"If I could just talk to someone," Nic whispered, eyeing the students. When a pretty Latina woman got up to leave, he waylaid her. "Excuse me," he said. "I'm thinking of coming here next year. Do you have a moment to talk?"

The young woman, who said her name was Selena, indicated that she did. The four of them followed her outside the building, where they could talk normally. "Do you like it here?" asked Nic.

"Oh yes," said Selena. "There's a lot of school spirit and so much pride!" she said. "I'm a junior. I started with the first class, and it's been hard. We've been setting up our own organizations. But there are good teachers; they're anxious to make a go of it. I think you'd like it." She indicated the library they stood outside. "This was the first building. All of our classes were here at first. But there are more buildings every year."

"What are you studying?" Nic asked.

"IT," smiled Selena. "Can't exactly go wrong with a career in IT!"

"Nope," said Nic. "So you live in a dorm?" he asked.

"Not now," said Selena. "There's some shared housing you can find in Merced. Cheaper!" she smiled.

Nic thanked Selena for talking with them. "See you in September," she said, waving as she walked away.

Doug, Marty, Nic and Natasha walked around a bit in the chilly January sun, looking at details. "How about a bite to eat?" said Doug, finally. They drove over to Merced, a flat, spread-out town which seemed to be full of shopping malls, the streets empty. Doug unerringly drove to the old part of town. "I knew it," said Doug. "Mexican food." He loved nothing more than a meal of tacos, rice and beans. The food of his childhood.

The restaurant was large and empty too. They ordered at a counter and brought plastic glasses of water over to a booth with a clean, Formica table. "So, what did you think?" asked Doug of Nic.

"It's going to be great," said Nic, enthusiastically. "I just like the newness. Forging your own way."

"Kind of wild and woolly," said Doug. He had gone to school at the venerable institution of UC Davis.

"Yup," said Nic. "It's so fresh and raw."

Natasha didn't say much either, thinking her own thoughts as they drove back over the coastal mountains home that afternoon. It would certainly be a new thing if she and Nic were not nearby each other. For Cal Poly, she had to declare a major before she even applied, as admissions were partly allotted across disciplines. She was being realistic about her interests in physical education, and also wanted to stay on the coast.

It all made Marty sad. It seemed to her that colleges had mostly lost the ability to give kids time to think. Even Zoe's liberal arts college was focused on outcomes, jobs. Marty sometimes said that the liberal arts educated you not for a job, but for your daily life. Thinking, the liberal arts curriculum, was now a luxury. With their narrow focuses, schools seemed to be out at the edges of the tree of knowledge, ignoring the roots and trunk. It didn't seem sustainable to her.

But what did you expect anyway, Marty thought? She was hoping for more time for contemplation as she got older. They would move back to the ranch that summer, simplifying their life. During the school year, Jason would stay in town at Grandma Alice's small house. He was not interested in college, he declared. His ambitions still lay with a career in cooking. "It's a blood sport!" Doug told him. "All the better," said Jason. Finding out that Doug was not his Dad hadn't changed their relationship externally. But Jason did seem to grow more independent, less needy.

Marty thought even more about education as she went about her rounds that week. At the public library she shelved books on Tuesday and Thursday mornings. The job was almost as physical as it was mental and Doug called it the "gym." Lifting heavy art books was the perfect exercise and she got paid for it! The time flew by as Marty worked, finding the exact right place in the Dewey Decimal system for each book, places for the different reading levels of kids' books.

As long as they read good books, Marty thought, the kids were educating themselves. She had been impressed when Nic brought home *Don Quixote*. Doug wanted to read it too. They had continued their evening reading, though often one or the other of the kids wasn't around and had to be brought up to date. The favorite was still Alexander Dumas. They had not quite finished *The Count of Monte Cristo*, but there were only a few chapters left. Marty hoped they would be done before the spring. She had worried that they were reading a book about revenge, but the Count's determination to revenge himself on Mercedes was eroding. It seemed he might forgive her in the end.

Marty loved having access to so many books at the library. It was not a very philosophical place! She did not like genre fiction, especially the dystopian fiction so popular now, but it was interesting to see what people were reading. And, through inter-library loan which even reached out to the university, Marty could get pretty much anything she wanted.

Marty read non-fiction, mostly. Biographies and the science books written for the public that Paul pointed out to her. She especially liked Paul's mentor E.O. Wilson, who, she was thrilled to note, was trying to promote a meeting of the arts and sciences, a "consilience," he called it.

Marty's current project was reading *The Story of the Stone*, as the Penguin translations called it. It was the famous "Dream of the Red Chamber," written in the 18th century in China, at least partly by a man named Cao Xueqin. The story told of the decline of a family, and was filled with characters whom Chinese people had argued over ever since. A young Taoist, Baoyu, grows up in the family garden surrounded by his beautiful cousins and half-sisters.

Marty did not identify with either the romantic Lin Daiyu or the more conventional Baochai, who presented the Chinese with questions about who was the perfect woman. Marty was more interested in the practical Tan Chun, who was the only one of the young beauties who became the woman she wanted to be. Marty was pleased to read this book, which she had begun long ago and was finally finishing.

That afternoon Marty took the bus home to Morrissey Avenue, as the twins often needed the car more than she did. She would not go to Line's house that day, though she thought of Line's troubles at least as much as she thought of her own family. Line had found a place in San Francisco, where Meir Schneider taught physical techniques of self-healing. A couple of times a week Stephen, now retired, made the long drive so Schneider could work with Line. They were also researching stem cell injections, which could only be done legally in Europe.

Doug was cheerful in the evening as he poured himself a glass of wine and cracked open the pistachios Marty had put out for an appetizer. The unctuous smell of roasting chicken was in the air. "Well, we've started," he said. "And the frost didn't get us too badly." The most exacting work of the year was pruning. Doug worked along with only the most experienced men, choosing the canes to retain, even weighing the amount of pruning done against the bud count. They started at dawn, as the days were short, but at least Doug was home in time for dinner.

By this time pruning was instinctive for Doug, though Marty knew the men were making decisions all the time, depending on the vineyard. Doug's databases were filled with vineyard histories and parameters. "I can't wait until this summer when you're up at the ranch with me and I can show you," he said.

"A good crop this year?" asked Marty. She too was drinking a glass.

"Probably light," said Doug, "because of the frost. But that's okay sometimes. Makes for a strong vintage. Vince won't like it."

Marty laughed. "All Vince wants is quantity," she said.

"How was the gym?" asked Doug. "And what's going on around here?"

"The library was fine," said Marty. "Nothing ever changes much there, except I'm always surprised at how uninterested the librarians are in reading! They're more interested in the Warriors' game!" She stood up. "Chicken tacos for dinner," she said.

Jason was picking over cilantro at the kitchen table. "How's my boy?" asked Doug , drawing a hand over Jason's long-haired head as he passed.

"Good," said Jason. Mounds of onion, garlic, tomato and the bright, lemony smell of cilantro surrounded him.

Marty had turned off the black beans. She began shredding the cooling chicken. "Could you grate some cheese?" she asked Doug. The front door crashed open and there were the twins!

"Just in time," said Doug. He pulled cheese out of the fridge and began grating it.

That evening, Nic and Natasha pulled out their general college essays and read them to Doug, Marty and Jason. Essays were a little different for each application, but the important ones were for UC Merced and Cal Poly.

Nic wrote about his interest in alternative energy research. He began with growing up in the vineyards and his understanding of farming's need for water and light. But also, he had worked for a big hardware store where construction crews showed up every day needing energy-efficient appliances and accessories. He'd been working there since he was 16 and Doug insisted the twins get jobs. "Alternative energy will keep California working," finished Nic. "It's the right solution for our future."

"Solid," said Doug, pounding the table. "How can anyone quibble with that?"

"All I want is for it to get me into school," said Nic.

Marty nodded. "It should," she said. It was a conventional essay, but certainly timely.

"Ok, Natasha," said Doug. "Your turn."

Natasha stood up, coolly, as if expecting the worst. "The prompt is, Describe your background, giving details of growing up, your family and pursuits," she said. She began reading:

"As I've grown older, I'm surprised to find that I didn't grow up in a nuclear family. As a kid, I lived on a ranch where my Dad is a viticulturalist. I had an older sister and a twin brother, later a younger brother. My Mother was never very interested in us and we avoided her, because all she wanted to do was dress us up and take photographs. We didn't think it was much fun! We'd rather hang out in the woods or the gardens, playing. We grew up a bunch of feral kids, with my sister Zoe as our leader.

"Our housekeeper, Tia Ana Maria ruled the kitchen, made our food and cleaned the house. On weekends we stayed with my Dad's mother, Grandma Alice. And then, when I was ten, my Mother left and Dad married Marty. So I've had four women raising me and providing examples. Not to mention my opinionated sister Zoe. While it was confusing as a little kid, in the long run, I think I will find these diverse mentors beneficial.

"Each of them have different ideas about how to live and stay healthy, which brings me to my interest in health and physical education. My mother doesn't care what she eats if she stays slim. She'll eat junk food or whatever. Tia Ana Maria makes traditional Mexican food. Grandma Alice seems most concerned about costs. She buys food at Costco and watches sales. She worked for a doctor most of her life after her husband died and raised my Dad and his sister by herself.

"Dad loves food and wine, and says he wants only the best. He and Marty call the way we live a 'peasant lifestyle.' Organic food, straight from the garden or the farmer's market, with some roasted meat and fish. It's kind of a gourmet lifestyle. They don't hesitate to buy European cheeses and drink lots of our own wine. Marty says they eat aesthetically, as opposed to scientifically. Did I mention the wine?!

"Personally I don't think any of my mentors gets enough exercise. Marty swears by tai chi, though I've never seen her move very fast. Zoe is lazy and is only on a soccer team for its social value. Tia Ana Maria is getting sluggish and Grandma Alice has arthritis and watches quite a bit of television. I hardly see my Mother, but she is still thin and beautiful. She's really into cosmetics.

"I work in an ice cream store in the summer, dishing up sundaes and cones all day. This has also given me food for thought! I want to test out my own theories and find out what research has been done into health. It will also be a good thing that my twin brother goes to a different school. We've been so close, but we need to compete with someone other than each other! Cal Poly offers exactly what I am looking for in terms of classes and research. I hope to be among the successful Cal Poly candidates next year."

Natasha sat down in a heap on a footstool, looking expectant. Marty was blown away. Natasha, whom she hardly ever talked to alone. Natasha could think!

Doug looked at Marty. She could see the rue in his face. It was not the background he had wanted for his kids. Nevertheless he said, "That's a very honest and insightful essay. Clear and detailed. I'm proud of you."

Natasha looked a little chagrined. "You've always taught us honesty was the best way," said Natasha.

"It's coming directly from you," said Marty. "That's real honesty. It shows a lot of thought."

Natasha became self-conscious. She looked toward Nic, who said. "Good work! It's not how I think, but I guess it's pretty accurate."

Jason shrugged.

"Well," said Doug, "On that note, I think I'm going to have some ice cream!" He laughed. "Anyone want to join me?"

Everyone did. "It's a celebration!" said Jason. "Do we have chocolate? I could make a sauce."

"There are chocolate chips," said Marty. She did not usually plan dessert after dinner. Sweets came after school, during homework.

"I can make hot fudge sauce out of them," said Jason. "I just need whipping cream, or butter and milk. And a little vanilla."

"What are we going to do with an empty house?" Doug asked rhetorically. "All of you kids are going your own ways!"

"Just as you wanted us to, Dad," said Nic. "I promise not to come home and live in the basement." He smiled. The ranch did not have a basement, but they knew kids who had come home, had not gotten jobs. It was a rough time out there.

"So, I've a question," said Marty, licking her spoon. "When Hillary cried in New Hampshire, did it make you want to vote for her? People seem to think it humanized her." She meant the question specifically for Natasha, who had been discussing women mentors.

Natasha stiffened. "Barack Obama's got my vote," she said. "Not because Hillary cries or doesn't cry. It's because she doesn't seem authentic. Like Dad thinks people should be."

"She's been in politics too long," chimed in Nic. "She might have a lot of knowledge and decent policies, but Obama is cool. He's full of ideas and smart about everything!" The twins would be able to vote in November for the first time. They would turn 18 that summer.

"We'll have to see," said Doug. It seemed that Hillary Clinton and Barack Obama were neck and neck in the Democratic primaries. "I used to think I didn't care which corporate fool runs this country," he said. "But after Cheney." He threw up his hands. "Warmongers," he said.

Marty looked at them all. What would she do next year, up at the ranch by herself? She thought of the tasting room. She would love getting back to managing it, all the interesting conversation that went on there. She would be farther from Line. It wouldn't be easy to get back down the hill very often. Marty also knew the ranch house itself was falling into decline.

But there wouldn't be much money next year to work on it. It seemed such a short time since Marty had moved in with Doug. And how eventful it had been! The kids, with their constant comings and goings made time fly.

Time was not gentle. It whipped them all along with the rhythms of the harvest year and the equally non-negotiable school year. But Marty was glad she wasn't the one going to college now. She was happy to be older.

22

At watercolor class, Line chose a raw umber and an ultramarine to make the greys of a dark, stormy sky. She dampened the places she wanted the pigment to flow, as Michael, the teacher, suggested and watched the colors as they blended. She lifted some pigment out with a tissue to lighten the upper clouds. Michael had told them to paint the sky first, as it was difficult. If it didn't work, the picture could be discarded.

"And your horizon?" questioned Michael, coming up behind her.

"Here, at the base of the picture," Line said. "Just some grasses blowing in the wind." She indicated with her brush held in her good hand, not the left which had always been her strongest. It was beginning to contract, the fingers curling together. Line stretched out her fingers, trying to relax them. She was having trouble controlling that hand.

"It's good," said Michael. "Remember the colors are going to lighten as it dries. Don't be afraid of your colors."

Line smiled up at him. "I was thinking of North Dakota," she said. "So much sky and flat land when I was a kid."

"Very good," said Michael. "Keep going. Try some other studies of the same thing."

"Thank you," said Line. Michael moved around the other painters who were arranged in a circle, each with a wooden easel set at 30 degrees. Touching some of the paintings with his pen or a tissue, he spoke a few words to each as the women lamented or crowed over their work.

Line was quiet, absorbed in her own internal project, which had been going on for the past year or so. It was a black time. Despair alternated with crushed hopes. Line had once imagined that she could cure her own auto-immune disease, diagnosed as progressive multiple sclerosis.

Like Ellen Burstyn in *Resurrection*, she imagined she would come out on the other side, perhaps with even more power to heal others.

But that summer, when Fern suggested going to the lake in Minnesota, and actually went with her husband and little Sofia, Line had refused. "I'd just drag everyone else down," she told Fern. She didn't have the stamina to walk very far at all. She was sure she could not have gotten down the hill to the lake.

It was especially hard because Stephen had retired and, for the first time in his life, was open to non-academic pursuits. It would have been good for Stephen to go to the lake, but he didn't want to without Line.

Line had realized that she must come to some peace with her disability. It was the hardest thing she had ever done. She must quell her panic and fear, for her own sake, as well as for that of everyone around her. Her life didn't involve only her. It involved family, friends, everyone she knew. Drawing herself up, out of the deep sense of unfairness she felt over being less able, she had decided to be realistic and grateful for the capacities she did have. Acceptance was still elusive, but it felt much better than her earlier outrage. Line was giving up on the idea of a cure.

After a couple of small studies of her sky, Line tried a bigger piece of paper using the same dark colors, trying to define the lower edges of the cloud ceiling with grey, while leaving the upper part of the sky light. Colors flowed into each other. Watercolor too was elusive. You had to work quickly.

Poppa's ancient red Acura stood waiting for Line outside the art supply store, at the back of which was the studio. Line no longer drove, as she couldn't trust her body not to jerk or spasm out. Stephen had sent Poppa to get her, as he had a meeting of the emeriti professors at the university. It was mid-October and the weather was mild and beautiful. The stillness of fall gave Santa Cruz its clearest skies of the year.

Poppa got out and helped Line put her heavy paintbox and portfolio of paper and paintings into the trunk. She walked pretty well, though her left hip had contracted and she felt she was galumphing, instead of walking.

"Thank you, Poppa, for coming!" said Line as she got in and settled herself on the leather seat. The car was beautifully maintained, looked new, if you didn't know how old it was.

"My chariot is at your command," said Poppa gallantly. They drove out along the downtown streets up toward their ridge.

"How are you doing?" asked Line. Poppa wasn't shaky at all. He was still a good driver, though now 88.

"I'm barely staying in my skin," said Poppa. "If I make it until the election without a heart attack, I think I will only have providence to thank."

Line laughed. "It's a good thing to be alive," she said. "And if, by some outside chance, Obama wins, it will lift all of our spirits!"

"And then I'll spend the next four years with my heart in my mouth," said Poppa, "hoping no one manages to assassinate him."

"Yes," sighed Line. She and Poppa had both seen a lot in their long lives. "He does show real leadership qualities," she said. "That's kind of new."

"George Soros talks about a 'new world order,'" said Poppa. "He means a new economic order, after this banking mess. But Obama may embody it."

The next morning, Line wakened to the sound of rain on the deck. Gratefulness, she thought, as she moved her stiff limbs under the covers. Rain was always a good thing in California. Line got up and went out in the damp, looking over the railing to see whether her garden was getting what it needed. The wind was coming up and the air smelled of pine and herbs. The sky was an unearthly yellow along the horizon and clouds were thin and tossed about in front of it. Line drank it in. I'm grateful, she thought. I'm not worried. Pulling herself together was hard, but practice helped.

Stephen and Line drove north, up through the rain, the crowded South Bay and to the oceanside San Francisco house where Meir Schneider had his center for self-healing. Schneider was an older, barrel-chested man with an Israeli accent who had been born with terrible eyesight. Through intensive exercise of his whole body, he had relaxed his eye muscles and trained his brain so that he now had an unrestricted California driver's license. His training was realistic and innovative, emphasizing using muscles and bodily forces you didn't know you had to work with all sorts of disabilities.

Line had already had several sessions with Schneider, so she knew what to expect. What she was afraid she didn't have was the patience to use his methods. She had been prescribed drugs for pain, for the nasty spasms and to loosen her tight muscles. She was beginning to use them.

The treatment room was a big, empty space with clean hardwood floors and curtained windows letting in lots of light. A few assistants came and went during the session. Schneider got Line to take off the tight shoes and elastic stockings she wore, and get down on the floor. "Come on Stephen," he said. "Get down here with us and help." He began massaging Line's feet, sending jerks and spasms and awful prickles up her legs and spine. Line tried to relax.

"Some people are just numb," said Schneider, quietly. "You have a lot of sensation, clearly."

"Yes," said Line weakly. Stephen worked on her other foot, trying to imitate Schneider's techniques.

"You can't do it wrong," said Schneider. "Skin needs touching. All over. Just knead those feet. You can do it yourself too," he told Line. "Lean down and work them over." He watched as Line tried to lean over and rub her feet. "It would help that hand too," said Schneider. No one needed to tell him anything. He could see where Line's body was failing.

Line herself knew the power of hands. She had long felt the heat in her own hands and tried to use it to touch her patients therapeutically. And now it was she who needed healing hands. Tears came to her eyes.

"Now crawl," said Schneider. "Forwards first, then backwards."

Line crawled like a baby, crying. The unfamiliar movement felt good.

"If you lie on your stomach," said Schneider, "on hard surfaces, that hip would come down naturally, I think." He had hard foam rollers to roll one's body over. And tennis balls to lie on and massage your own back. "You're a fighter, I can see," Schneider told Line. "That's going to help you."

Line lay on the floor, exhausted. Oddly, she had never thought much about her own body. It was a vehicle, an instrument of her will. But it was broken. It would never be the same. She knew that even in the weeks she had been coming to Schneider for treatment, she was slipping. Was it any use to try so hard?

"Okay, stand up," Schneider bid Line and Stephen. He showed them how to swing their arms around their heads to get all kinds of circulation going. "Rub your hands," he said. "Now massage. Everywhere. Stephen, let's work on Line's left hand. And Line, try rubbing Stephen's neck. I think he needs it."

Line giggled and smiled as she and Stephen made themselves into an odd animal, Stephen rubbing one hand as she tried to rub his neck with the other. It was as if they were grooming each other.

"Computers, I bet," said Schneider.

Stephen nodded. "And books," he said. "Line can tell you I'm hardly ever without a book in my hands."

"Bad for your eyes," said Schneider. "You must also look into the distance."

Lastly, Schneider watched Line walking around the room. "Better?" he questioned. "Muscles are always better with some blood and oxygen in them. Do floor work every day, and self-massage." He suggested cold packs. "It might help to bring down the inflammation in your hip," he said.

Line did feel worked over, but also she thought things were looser. "I'm very grateful," she said. She was full of unfamiliar emotions sloshing around in her body. "I do feel better." She also knew her bodily freedom would not last. Something about a treatment made you try harder. The relationship between Schneider and herself burned. She could take it home, but then it would wear off.

Line and Stephen went up to the Cliff House at the edge of the ocean for lunch. It was pouring and Stephen let Line off at the door before looking for a parking space. Line went into the dark carpeted foyer, shaking the raindrops off. She found a seat in the big, empty dining room by the windows looking out at the sea.

Large white combers rolled up the beach, and seals barked and slipped down the wet sides of the islands of rocks. The waves as they came in around the rocks broke wildly, sending water crashing around them. The sky was a long low Payne's grey above the water. White seagulls ducked and wheeled. Line imagined herself a seabird, immune to water and wind, free to soar. But it felt nice to sit still. Sometimes, sitting still, she felt perfectly normal.

When Stephen came, he settled himself at the table beside Line. It was covered in white linen, with thick white napkins at each place. A waiter filled their glasses with ice water. "Not such a bad day," Stephen said. "I guess tourists aren't going to brave a day like this!"

"Thank you, Stephen," said Line. "For taking time from your work to spend with me." It really took all day to go up to San Francisco, do a treatment session and drive back home. 'Retirement' for Stephen was full of work and projects.

"My Line," said Stephen, reaching for her hands across the table. "What else am I going to do?" He looked down the menu. "It's a vacation. Besides," he said, "yesterday at the university we all agreed that we were having trouble concentrating. This election is like a battle for the soul of America."

They did not know many Republicans. But Stephen knew a few. "How can you vote for a man who has only spent about 300 days in the Senate. That's the extent of his experience!" they said.

"It's just that this could go on for a while," said Line.

"I know," said Stephen. "You know Paul Wellstone had MS, don't you? He had a pretty jerky walk towards the end. But then he gets killed in a plane crash! I've been thinking about it."

"And then there's Poppa," said Line. "He just keeps going. He's going to dry up like an old leaf and blow off the tree." Poppa's wife had died of cancer many years ago.

"That's the best way," said Stephen. "But something's going to come to all of us. The best case scenario, in my view, is that we get to watch. We're getting old. What do we expect?"

"Well," said Line. "I'm strong. I can handle it. But I want to live a useful life. I don't want to be a burden. I'm glad the kids aren't around to watch me flounder." She had tried hard to resist whining, especially to Ivy, who was closest. Line knew she had particularly scared Ivy with her panic and fear. It had been in the air for a year or so. But she did not want Ivy to come home, to give up her own life. She did not really need taking care of anyway. She just needed help with heavy things like cleaning and cooking, shopping and driving. Stephen had stepped in and Poppa's household help had taken over Line's cleaning as well.

The waiter brought Stephen a beer and a plate of fried calamari. "May I?" Stephen questioned Line as he began to spritz lemon over the crispy nuggets.

Line nodded and took a few delicious bites. What could be better than sitting here with her husband in a window looking out at the ocean and seabirds while eating delicious food?

"There are going to be more grandchildren," said Stephen, taking a draft of his foamy ale. "I want to see them and I am sure you do too."

"Yes," said Line. "I do. I might not be able to do much for them, but I want to see them."

"We have done the best we could for the kids," said Stephen. "We've made them independent. And it was you, Line, more than me." He was admitting the fact that he hadn't had a lot of time for the kids while they were growing up.

"Quality time," said Line. "You gave them that. They always wanted your approval. With the possible exception of Christy!" She shared a smile with Stephen. Stephen and Christy's relationship had resolved considerably. Christy was getting married in Minnesota at Thanksgiving. He would marry Emily in her well-off parents' house. Both she and Christy continued to work in political groups, Emily for the non-profit Wellstone Action and Christy for the Democratic Farm-Labor Party.

"That kid," said Stephen. "Not really a kid any more, of course. I look forward to seeing him get hitched!" Christy was 40. Even Poppa was going to the wedding. He insisted he didn't want to fly, might take the train. Plans hadn't firmed up yet.

When they got home that evening, there was Ivy! Line was thrilled. "What a surprise!" she said. She wished she had known Ivy was coming. Anticipation was half the fun!

"I'm making you a California Norwegian sweater," said Ivy. "I wanted to see how it looked. And I'm not registered to vote in LA. I thought I'd come back here. Plus I also need to check on a theater project my friend is doing." Plenty of reasons to drive up from Los Angeles.

After dinner, Ivy brought out the sweater, which she was making of russet and gold yarn. "I've never tried one of these patterns," she said. "I couldn't resist." She had bought the silver-colored patterned buttons associated with a Norwegian sweater. She held the sleeves to Line's arms and worked on it as they watched a videotape of an old favorite movie together, *Little Women*. Poppa and Stephen were watching something sillier downstairs.

Distraction always helped Line, and Ivy was certainly that! They both sobbed as Marmee got the girls to give their hot, Christmas breakfast to a poor family. There were still poor families, many people much worse off than we are, thought Line.

Gold and russet yarn flowed from Ivy's needles as she counted stitches and inches. The warm colors, matching the hills and the trees, would warm Line's spirit as well as her body. Somehow it made her think of apples. The stores were full of apples at the moment.

In the morning, while Ivy visited her friends in the theater department at the university, Stephen and Line went to the store and brought back several kinds of apples, the big green Granny Smith baking apples, red and yellow Galas and a few Macintosh. When Ivy got home, she cut butter and cold oil into flour, making pastry dough enough for two pies. Line wanted to make one with raisins and cloves, but some people didn't want the apple taste obscured, so one pie would be plain.

Line plumped raisins in rum. She cut up apples, leaving the peels on. "That's where the vitamins are," she said. "In the color. The more color, the more the vitamins and minerals."

Ivy looked at her. "My friends are kind of lazy about food," she said. "We hardly cook! It's so much easier to buy meals at the new Whole Foods or eat out."

"Is that Marshall's influence?" asked Line.

"Probably," said Ivy. "We have such odd hours, can't seem to find a pattern to the day." Ivy worked in the costume department at a school for the performing arts, and Marshall, whom she lived with, taught directing. "We start kind of slow in the morning, but then often work very late."

"You could have a good breakfast," said Line.

"I do," said Ivy. "I stick all kinds of fruits and veggies in my smoothie in the morning. Actors all eat like this. They can't afford to eat any bread!"

"You are skinnier than usual," Line said. It was still a problem for her. She knew she should lose weight if it was going to get harder to lug her disabled body around, but she just liked food too much. And dinner, for the Cohen family, was a high sociable point in the day. Line thought she had instilled this in her kids. But they were a different generation with a different view of things.

"Maybe," said Ivy. It had never been a problem for her. She just didn't eat when she didn't feel like it.

"I think you better roll out the pastry," said Line. She sat beside Ivy, who got out the pie tins and rolling pin. She flattened rounds of the chilled pastry and she and Line tucked in the apples, one pie flavored lightly with cane sugar, butter and cinnamon, and the other with the raisins, sugar, and a dusting of cloves. "Mmmmmm," said Line. "Cloves remind me of my grandmother. My Dad's mother made crabapple pickles with cloves. Miss that taste."

The baking pies filled the air with spicy smells and set the warmth of the kitchen against the pouring rain outside. Nothing could be cozier than the smell of baking pies.

"It's so good to see you," said Ivy, retreating to her sweater as they waited for the pies to come out. "When I'm not here I spend so much time worrying about you."

Line drew herself up, gathering her resources. "You mustn't," she said. "I could not be better cared for. And I'm beginning to accept what I cannot change. It feels better."

Ivy sighed. "Yes," she said. "But Mother, it's like you're in me. And I'm you!"

Line nodded. "I understand," she said. "It isn't fair, but it's reality. Reality rules. If you accept what is happening, then you get to take a good hard look at it all. It surprises you. Help comes from places you never expected!"

Ivy came over to Line and put her arms around her. "I love you so much, Mum."

"And I you," said Line. She felt powerful. For her, she realized, goodness wouldn't come from doing any more. It would come from her spirit's strength. "You're my flower, Ivy," she said, reaching her arms up to her youngest daughter, tears in her eyes. "And I'm going to wrap myself in that sweater, as if I were wrapping you around me!"

The pies came out of the oven with a gently browned crust. "Oh!" said Ivy. "They're perfect!" They were meant for what everyone hoped would be a victory celebration on the next day, election day. But each of the Cohens had a piece after dinner of the warm pie of their choice.

In the morning, after breakfast, they all collected themselves to go to their polling place. "Look at us," said Ivy. "We must be well-off if we can get away with voting in the middle of a Tuesday morning."

"Everything's different now," said Poppa. "People work all kinds of odd hours. And then there's us, an army of retired people. We're not idle, though. The country wouldn't run properly without us." The polls were set up in the lobby of a home for elderly people. Small ladies with white hair offered cookies and lemonade. Line smirked at Poppa, but he ignored them.

Line signed her name on the voter registration books and took the ballot given her. She carried the crib sheet she had made regarding the propositions and initiatives, as she didn't want to spend too much time thinking in the voting booth. A veteran wearing a red poppy, helped her slip her ballot into the box and gave her a paper sticker which stated "I voted," with a flag fluttering on it. Yes, thought Line, that too was something to be grateful for. There were many places where people couldn't be sure of their vote.

That evening, at 11 p.m., when the west coast polling places closed, the television networks began calling the election for Obama. Line sat in Poppa's den, watching, while Stephen came and went, proffering drinks. Ivy worked on her sweater under a small lamp. Obama had won all of the eastern seaboard, the west coast states and many contested states. It was a decisive win. Republican John McCain could not overcome the unpopularity of George Bush's Iraq war and his poor handling of the current economic crisis.

"Pie break," said Ivy. She took people's orders and ran upstairs to make a tray of pie plates.

"He's going to come out any minute now," said Poppa as he cut his pie with a fork. Obama was in his home state of Illinois.

Line sighed, shaking her head. In all of her long life, she had not expected anything like this election to happen. She ate the luscious clove-spiced pie with a drizzle of heavy cream on it.

"It's hard to believe," said Stephen. "It's the culmination of what we were working for in the 1960's."

"And think about me!" said Poppa. "Living to see this after all those years in the slums of Brooklyn! If only Bobby Kennedy were here to see it." Almost anything any of them said was superfluous.

When he did come out, stepping in front of flags furling behind him, Barack Obama seemed young and full of grace. "If there is anyone out there, who still doubts the power of our democracy, tonight is your answer," he said. Line stopped eating and cried as she listened. They had all doubted, but this too was reality.

23

Paul stopped at a gas station on his way home from Ada, his aunt's, funeral. He filled Wilson's bowl with water and parked a moment after getting gas to let Wilson drink. The air was cold in March, and patches of dirty snow lay about on the dry, lifeless grass.

Ada was Dad's older sister, the last of her generation. She was 93 and had been in a nursing home in southern Minnesota. Most of Paul's extended family on Dad's side had been at the funeral. It was one of the great things about living in Minnesota: Paul was close to these rooted relatives.

"Ok, old boy," said Paul. He motioned for Wilson to get in the car, a fairly new one for a change, a Toyota 4Runner with a high enough chassis to handle the drive up the lane to the cabin in the snow. Wilson bedded down on the floor behind the driver's seat.

It had been a cold winter, but not terribly snowy. Paul drove north and east toward St. Paul, thinking about many things. Driving always gave way to thoughts. He had once heard that you either had space or time. People who lived in lots of space, as they did in the Midwest, had less time than those who lived in Europe, for instance, where distances between towns were very short.

Paul went up the drive at Ellie's house in St. Paul, and he and Wilson trundled into Mother's old lower-level apartment. Ellie, who had gone to the funeral with Bruce, had already arrived.

Ada's daughters had given them a cache of letters from Dad's brother Marshall who had been killed at the very end of World War II. Ada collected family artifacts and did genealogy for Dad's side of the family. Paul was excited to know of these letters.

No one was very hungry, as the repast after the funeral had been extensive. "I need a glass of wine, though," said Ellie. "Do you want anything?"

"Whatever you're having," said Paul. "Thanks."

Ellie spread out the letters on the dining room table and she and Paul began to read them. They were still in their original envelopes, but there was also a penciled letter, in Dad's handwriting, addressed to Devona, the woman Marshall had married shortly before going to the front. "Did you see this?" Ellie asked Paul.

Paul began to read Dad's letter. "He's really angry," he said. "I'll bet he wrote this to get his anger off his chest. I'm sure he didn't send it."

"Yeah," said Ellie. "He would never talk about it, but I knew something of the story."

Paul did too. After Marshall's death, Devona took the car and the life insurance Marshall's parents had struggled to provide for him. She had only lived with him a few months and had little connection to the family. She pretended to illness, refusing to share Marshall's assets.

"Do you think they still have the bronze star?" Paul asked. Shortly before Dad died, and long after his parents had, a bronze star awarded to Marshall Mikkelson, with its little gold 'V' for valor, had been found in an attic by someone completely unrelated to the family. The person found

Paul's name, however, and returned the decoration to him. Clearly, Devona had not seen fit to let Marshall's parents know of his heroism. Paul had been able to show Dad the bronze star before his death and had given it to Ada for safekeeping. Marshall was buried in France. His story was mysterious to Paul, but the letters helped to illuminate it.

"I'm sure they still have the star," said Ellie. "I'd like to see it again."

"I looked on the internet once to find out what Marshall's unit was doing at the end of March," said Paul. "I think they went behind enemy lines, passing information back and forth."

In the letters to Dad, Marshall, who was two years younger, sounded like someone adrift, uncertain what to do with himself. He asked Dad for advice. Dad, who had felt the call to the ministry, was very sure of his own intent. Dad and Mother were married, and they already had a little girl, Ellie. There were no return letters, but it was easy to imagine Dad counseling his younger brother.

"They were so young," said Ellie. "Marshall must have been about 23 when he died."

"Yes," said Paul. "So young. But I see now how it was between them."

"Time tells true," said Ellie. "That's what Bruce's mother used to say." Bruce had no extended family left. Only the Mikkelsons.

After seeing a couple of his web design clients the next morning, Paul and Wilson drove north to the Mikkelson family cabin. It was snowing, white flakes blowing across the windshield. But it wasn't too bad. "How are you doing?" he reached down and scratched the caramel-colored fur on Wilson's neck. The car was warm and the highways were clear enough.

Paul thought of all the stories he was involved in, the stories which made up his life. Marie, Paul's wife, who had been gone now seven years, was still very much with him. He would be pulled deep into remembrance of her when certain songs were played. Just last week he had randomly heard John Lennon and Paul McCartney singing, "Two of us Sunday driving, not arriving, … two of us wearing raincoats, … on our way back home." The song was a story of friendship, but it was also the story of Marie and himself.

Paul's own story led from early polio through travel to Alaska and a long return home to live at Lake Michigami in the log home Ellie and Bruce had built to replace the old family cabin. He was pulling back a bit now at age 61. One of his ankles didn't bend properly and when he went down the hill to the lake, he took a stick to lean on. His legs ached in the winter. They were always happiest under a warm blanket.

An orthopedist had told Paul that the surgery on his legs to stretch tendons and muscles and allow his feet to grow was actually done very well. "Those guys did so much of this at that time," he said. "They knew what they were doing." Two long summers, in pain and in traction, were hard to forget. Paul did pay attention to his legs. They were part of his story, his own reality. But they didn't keep him from doing as he pleased. He just pushed through, promising them warmth and stillness later.

And then there were the larger stories Paul had been immersed in his whole life. The question of Jesus Christ's life and death, and the questions of evolution. As E.O. Wilson said, when questions in science were answered, they simply spawned more questions. Human knowledge seemed to expand, like the universe.

Paul was reading a book about the fish fossil with hands found in the Arctic, Tiktaalik Roseae. The book, *Your Inner Fish* by Neal Shubin, demonstrated that evolution never proceeded rationally. We are full of obsolete bits, genes we no longer need. Paul had never before thought so much about hands, which came from fish fins; about the fact that our elbows bend one way and our knees the opposite.

It was funny, really, the story of human evolution that was emerging. The "tree" was no longer the best metaphor for it. Lots of odd co-evolutionary glimpses over-rode it. And what of birds, Paul wondered. They were thought to come from fish as well, appearing in the fossil record a couple of millennia later than mammals.

The story of Christ was still emerging also. There were countless books about the Jesus of history, based on research into writings from the period. Paul paid some attention to Muhammad too, as there was now so much interest in Islam. The Christian story as told by the church relied entirely on the canonical books of the Bible. But Paul did not feel limited by them. He had read Elaine Pagels' scholarship and knew that orthodox Christianity suppressed certain stories for its own purposes.

Paul still responded to the Christ-centered work of Dietrich Bonhoeffer. Bonhoeffer's family had been deeply involved in resistance to Hitler. His enigmatic books, *The Cost of Discipleship* and *Letters and Papers from Prison*, were among Paul's guides. Bonhoeffer had been 39 when he was hung, only a month after Marshall Mikkelson was killed in action in 1945. Bonhoeffer pointed back to the cultivation of the light within you through Bible study and the imitation of Christ.

Paul's life did not involve personal sacrifice. He had avoided the war in Vietnam because of his polio and had not been as much affected by the generational divide that separated Marty and Line from their parents and sent them flying off to California. Paul had always been impressed at Dad's openness to both science and religion, at his ability to hold the truths of both of them as they emerged. For Dad there was no conflict. Paul felt that Dad had arrived at his acceptance through long pastoral and life experience. Paul could almost hear him say, "Your faith must be a **living** thing!"

People wanted stories to end. They wanted to know what happened. But real stories did not end. Life happened, you could see it, sense it. It was real. But even your own perceptions of it might change over time. Paul felt lucky that he had had the parents and childhood he did. It had given him a solid inner sense of what was true and what wasn't. It enabled him to remain open. Emerging truth required an atmosphere of freedom.

The narrow rutted road through the trees at the cabin was lightly covered with wet snow, Paul's tire tracks the first. Paul put the car in the new garage. Before going in, he could not resist grabbing his walking stick from the porch and making his way down to the lake for a quick look. Wilson was as avid as he was, his tail wagging. It was growing quite dark, but Paul used the brightness of the snow and the sky to find his way along the zigzagging path down the hill between the bare trees. He looked out across the white expanse of the frozen lake. Nowhere was it as quiet as in the northern woods far from roads.

"Easy, boy," he cautioned Wilson, who nosed along the edge of the lake. Under the snow the ice was probably mushy. Ice out would not be for weeks, but it was now too dangerous to walk out on the lake.

Snow fell in the darkness, smelling like dirt. The cloud cover lay low, hiding the stars. Paul breathed deeply, looking up along the dark trunks of the Norway pines. So small we are beside them, he thought.

After long moments, Paul climbed the path. No lights shown in the cabin, but a window in his neighbor Peter Emstead's cabin glowed. Inside, even though Paul had turned down the heat when he left, there was still considerable warmth. He put out food for Wilson and made himself some dinner. A toasted cheese sandwich just hit the spot! As did a cup of tea. Paul settled himself in the recliner with his legs up, a blanket over them. The room was cold enough that he could see the steam rise in wisps above his teacup.

What would Grandpa and Grandma Mikkelson think of this cabin, he wondered. When Dad had asked them to come up and spend some time at the previous cabin with the family, they had refused. They did not want to live a primitive life without plumbing. Camping did not appeal to them! "We were trying to grow out of that kind of life," they told Dad. "We wanted to become civilized." They did not need to get closer to nature. They were already there!

Paul had loved Grandma and Grandpa Mikkelson's house. It had a large garden with an extensive strawberry patch. Grandma made a few dollars selling her strawberries. And everything about the house was frugal, ecologically sound. Grandma braided her husband's old trousers into rugs. She canned vegetables and fruits. She crocheted lace to edge her linens. Oh that clean, starched bedding with its pump pillows. Paul remembered sleeping under the eaves in Marshall's old room. The flowered wallpaper, the window looking down into the garden, the toys in the chest. Grandma had been an excellent housekeeper.

Paul wondered whether, if they had known Devona's story, if she had kept in touch with the family, their perception of her would have changed. If she had had Marshall's child. Hers was probably not an open story. She had disappeared into post-war America. Records of Marshall's unit and its activities existed, but not the wanderings of a barely-known woman.

The internet was changing this, though. Increasingly, people had some sort of presence on the web. Not a solid life, but a presence. Paul thought of the two kids Hanna had adopted. They would always know they were adopted, knew their birth mother. Nothing much was hidden any more.

Marie's story had not ended with her death. She was very much alive, not only to him, but to her daughter Grace, her sister and friends, who sometimes wrote to Paul. The anguish of Marie's dying, however, was past. Grace's family, her husband and five kids not 30 miles away in Bemidji, was now Paul's. He expected a couple of the kids to ride down to the cabin on their bicycles soon. Little Joe worked at a bike shop and loved long distance bike riding, especially in challenging weather!

The anguish in Paul's life had passed to Line. No one knew what Line's fight with progressive MS would mean. Certainly a different kind of life. Science promised break-throughs, but MS was a name for a collection of phenomena, different for every person. Line was losing ground. She was not much of a communicator either. Paul heard more from Marty, though he resolved to call Line on the phone more often.

Paul had seen Line last at Christy's wedding just before Christmas. "Sitting still, I feel just fine," she told him. "But then there are these horrendous spasms and unpredictable nerve pains." Both heat and cold bothered her. She was always trying to find a happy medium. But there had been a lot of laughter among them all. Paul liked Christy's new wife Emily. And it was interesting to watch Christy with his parents, whom he hadn't lived with after he was 18. Stephen and Christy had squared their relations over a common love of Paul Wellstone, about whom Stephen was writing a book.

Paul looked over at his guitar, standing like a reproach in the corner of the room. The Spanish guitar he had learned, the folksongs were gone. Christy had asked Paul to play and sing at the wedding, but Paul could not do it. He still sang in his church choirs, but standing up and performing by himself, without Marie, was beyond him.

Paul sat in the warm lamplight, enjoying the other prerogative of the north country: the stillness at the center of a civilized world. Paul's interaction with it was entirely at his own command. He could sink down into the larger world, leaving his petty self behind. The world of trees, of animals, of ice and water and time. Perhaps, he thought, we have a primitive concept of time. Perhaps science would enlarge on it in the coming years.

Paul got a call from Little Joe a few days later, telling Paul that he and Andre would arrive a couple of hours later. It was a bright morning, the air full of glistening water, icicles melting and dripping off the eaves, snow falling in clumps from the pines and patches of wet mud shining on the paths. They would arrive around lunch. What could he feed them?

Around 11 a.m., Paul put in some baked potatoes. And shortly afterward, there were the boys! They took off their helmets, steam rising off them in clouds. Leaving their bikes on the patio, they clippity clopped into the house in their spiked shoes, their vitality bursting into the room with them.

Wilson frolicked about the two, waiting for their greeting. Andre, who loved him, wrestled him to the ground on the braided rug after hugging Paul. "Quite a ride?" asked Paul.

"Shoot," said Joe. "It's only 30 miles, flat clear road." He looked at the clock on the stove. "I think we left at 10. That's pretty good time." He was wearing slim bike shorts, showing off his brown, muscled legs. His dark hair was wild, sticking up in all directions. His t-shirt proclaimed the logo for his bike shop, "Mike's Bikes," in red letters on black.

Andre stood up. He disdained bike regalia, other than helmet and shoes. "I don't care how fast I go," he said. "I like to look around." Andre was the one most like Paul in interests, about to finish high school, planning to go to Bemidji State and study natural history. "Smells good in here," he said. The potatoes as they baked gave off a minerally tang.

"We're going to get you out there one of these days," said Joe. "Seems like a bike might take you further than walking." He ran some water at the sink and drank in big drafts like a horse.

Paul shook his head. "I don't need to go very far," he said. "And I can't control my skinny foot. I'm so unbalanced." One leg had grown very thick and took the pressure off the skinny one. He shook his head and opened the refrigerator. He pulled out bacon and eggs. "Not saying I'm not willing to try," he said. "I'm just skeptical."

"Yeah," said Joe. "Let me know when you want to give it a go. The bike takes care of itself, you know," he said. "We're learning to fit bikes to people, so they have an optimal ride. I could do that for you." Joe was a proselytizer. Bikes were the answer to everything.

"Ok," said Paul. "Andre, can you cut up these onions and tomatoes for a salad? I'll just lay some rashers of bacon on these potatoes, and Joe, if you grate some cheese, I'll make a quick omelet." He cut the potatoes in half on the cookie sheet and laid a strip of bacon across each, putting them back in the oven.

The food was all done in a few minutes, but, as usual, no one had set the table. Paul rushed out plates and silverware. He liked his food hot! The table was haphazard, but so were they.

"Delicious," said Andre. "Hits the spot."

"How's your mother?" asked Paul. "And everyone?"

"Mom's fine," said Andre. "All excited about the wedding." Dory was getting married at the beginning of the summer. He made a face. "You know how moms are."

"Dad's the same," said Joe. Gerald was dedicated to the little Bemidji airport, had worked there since he was a kid.

"I'm surprised you didn't bring Jeanne and Benjy," said Paul. "I thought you might all come!" He would have leftover potatoes.

"Benjy had basketball practice. The team is doing really well," said Andre. Benjy, at 14 was already tall and gangly, the tallest of all the boys. He was on the high school team already as a freshman. "And Jeanne is marching somewhere. Not in Bemidji. I don't know where."

Paul laughed. He had seen Jeanne's marching band routines. She was a flag girl in a very competitive group. They started working on their shows in the spring and kept it up all summer. "I'll have to come out and watch one of these days," said Paul. He was thinking how, when he was in high school, no one would have imagined bikes would become the thing, that drum corps groups competed internationally. How proud he was of Grace's family! But he didn't say these things out loud. He was so glad the kids showed up! Was he their grandfather? Or not? Step-grandfather, probably. Family trees were also much more tangled these days!

"I'm doing my senior report on global warming," said Andre. "I heard that Shishmaref, in Alaska, is one of the places currently most affected. Did you ever go there?"

"No," said Paul. "I should have. My Aunt Mabel was a missionary there for many years, in the 30's and 40's, I think. That town's been trying to move since the mid-70's! It's built on permafrost, which is melting. But also there's not as much sea ice left, which used to protect them from storms."

"Why don't they move?" asked Andre.

"They need money," said Paul. "Villages want to stick together, to move everyone in the village, plus their school and churches. I did know one village that moved because their place kept flooding. It was by a river, called Minto. My friend Marcia lives there. Now they have new Minto and old Minto. Took strong leadership to get the move to happen, though."

"I'd really like to go," said Andre as he mashed more butter into his potato, salt and peppering it liberally.

"Bikes are the answer," said Joe. "We've got to get people out of their cars. Stop using oil."

"One thing I really liked in Alaska," said Paul, "was that the indigenous people taught their kids to expect environmental change. They had to be terribly alert to the weather, to changing conditions, as they hunted and camped. It really impressed me. Here, I think kids get taught that the world is one way, that the laws of physics are immutable. So of course everyone is really freaked out about climate change."

"We're going to extinct ourselves for sure," said Joe gloomily.

"Peter, our neighbor, goes around saying, 'we're doomed,'" said Paul. He laughed. "It's become his signature. Peter "We're Doomed" Emstead."

"So what do you think, Paul," asked Andre.

"Well," said Paul. "I'd agree we are adapting too slowly. Some progress, but not enough. I've always worried that world population is growing so fast. It was only 2.5 billion, when I was born. And now it's what, 6.9 billion?"

"And everyone wants a car, or two!" said Joe sardonically.

"And they're cutting down the rain forests!" said Andre. "They're one of our best defenses against global warming! They absorb greenhouse gases better than anywhere!" Elements of hysteria rose in his voice. "The tipping points they keep warning us about are getting closer and closer."

"I'm sure you won't have any trouble writing your report!" said Paul dryly. "But we are adapting somewhat, aren't we? Electric cars, recycling." He knew as he said it that his reasons were puny. "We're not evolving very fast, I know. But cultures can change quickly. I'm telling you, there weren't many long distance bikers around when I was growing up!"

"And now we're starting to get fat bikes," said Joe. "They started experimenting with fat tires in Alaska, but Minnesota is also a pioneer. They're for riding in sand and snow. They're a lot of fun!"

"Yeah," said Paul. "Like that. We're really adaptable as a species."

Andre looked a little calmer. "Well," he said. "There're going to be migrations for sure, from rising seas and extreme heat. We might be sitting pretty here in Minnesota."

Paul laughed. "My Dad always said that this was God's country," he said. "All of us adapt to our own place." He stood up and began to clear plates. "I'm not a doom-sayer," he said. "But I regret to inform you that some of this adaptation is up to your generation."

"We're up to it," said Andre. "I want to live forever, so I can watch."

"Thanks for feeding us, Paul," said Joe. "That was great! But I need a nap before I ride back! I can't ride on a full stomach."

"Plenty of beds," said Paul. "Take your pick." He put the leftover baked potatoes in the fridge for another day.

"Dibs on the sofa," said Joe. "We better leave at least by 3 o'clock." The light was lengthening, but the air cooled off sharply when the sun left.

"Don't worry about the dishes," said Paul. Andre was trying to help, but there wasn't much space in the small kitchen. "I've got plenty of time to do them." Wilson looked up at him questioningly, but no, they had scraped their plates clean. Paul set the cooled omelet pan on the floor and let Wilson do what he could with it.

24

Marty laid six places for breakfast at the big dining table at the ranch. In early August all the kids were home, briefly. Not that they would all arrive for breakfast. It was so much fun to have them come in from their colleges, full of excitement and news.

Light from the east streamed in on the table. Marty laid knives and spoons to the right of each plate, placed a bowl on each and a cloth napkin to the left. She was using the silver which had come from Mother in a wooden chest. She doubted that, if they laid silverware at all, any of the kids knew which side of the plate forks and spoons went on. Did it matter? More important, thought Marty, was that they laid a table at all. She smiled at Doug as he arrived and sat in his accustomed chair at the head of the table.

"Just us?" he asked, giving Marty a quick kiss.

"I think the twins are coming," said Marty. "They want to go down to town with me and go surfing. Would you feel like picking them up in the evening? Or shall I send Zoe?"

"No," said Doug. "I'll do it."

"Jason's coming too," said Marty. "He wants to go to the market to look for peaches. I haven't told him about the flash mob. I wish you could come!"

"Yeah," said Doug, balefully. "In a month of Sundays." He could not take time for joyrides. The vineyards were crying for his attention.

"Oatmeal?" asked Marty. She had made some, but everyone got their own cereal and toast in the mornings. Doug didn't believe in waking the kids. In fact, she could probably sit at the table all morning pouring tea as they came in shifts. But Line had told Marty about the flash mob Ivy was working on for the farmers' market. Marty was anxious to get there before it started!

Marty was delighted to be back at the ranch house at Boulder Creek Vineyards, on the mountain above Santa Cruz. She and Doug had been living there pretty much by themselves except for weekends when Jason came home. By this time Ana Maria had retreated to her own small house, leaving Marty the kitchen. Marty spent her mornings at home and working in the garden, and in the afternoon walked over to the Tasting Room to help serve wine and talk to customers.

As Doug and Marty ate, Jason came in and began to make himself a smoothie full of fruit. The twins came, dressed in the disheveled clothing they wore under their wet suits. They ate ravenously and cut bread and cheese for lunches. "Any of that chicken left?" asked Nic, rummaging in the fridge.

"In the glass container at the back," said Marty.

"Can't wait to see what Pleasure Point is like today," said Natasha. She had been working in San Luis Obispo most of the summer, had only a few days before she would go back.

Nic humpfed. "Miss Snottypants," he said. "You've been surfing all summer. How about me? Stuck in a computer lab in the heat of the San Joaquin Valley!"

"It's exactly what you asked for," said Natasha amiably. "You can't complain."

"No," said Nic. "But I sure am looking forward to that blue water!"

"You're going to leave that cell phone here, aren't you?" Doug asked. He and Nic were vying over the fact that Nic had splurged and bought himself a smart iPhone, while Doug and his colleagues were struggling with their Blackberries.

"Absolutely," said Nic. He smiled widely. Being an IT student had to be good for something. When Michelle Obama spoke in the spring at UC Merced graduation, Nic had emailed them all photos of her he had taken with his phone.

After breakfast, Doug left for the vineyards, Marty and Jason collected bags and baskets and Nic and Natasha piled their surfboards into the van. Nic drove down the curvy mountain road to Santa Cruz. Rather slowly, Marty was pleased to see. Nic did have his own ancient car, but he was protecting it. He thought it didn't have many miles left in it.

"See you tonight!" said Nic, as he and Natasha hopped out of the van. Marty took over the driving and parked near the westside farmer's market, which was open.

"I've got peaches on the brain," said Jason. "I want to make this peach pecan crumble pie."

"Two pies!" said Marty. "To feed this crowd."

"Yeah," said Jason. He had turned 16 that summer and still cooked and baked as often as possible. "I need 10-12 peaches!"

"Do you want to make one plain and one with crumble?" asked Marty. She liked things plain, so she could taste them.

"Nah," said Jason. "We've still got those pecans from last year."

Marty laughed. Jason could be counted on to know the contents of the larder better than she did! They walked through the rows of fresh greens and peppers, summer squash, corn, golden and plum-colored stone fruits, apples and grapes. Marty chose corn from the heaps of sheathed cobs on one of the tables, but kept a lookout for Ivy, checking her watch.

Ivy stood near a picnic table beside Line, who sat with a light colorful shawl around her shoulders. Marty waved wildly and went over to them. "What are you doing here?" she said teasingly. Line didn't look like she was at all disabled, sitting still.

"I would ask you the same," said Line. "I would have thought your garden would be so full of food right now you didn't need anything else!"

"It is," said Marty. "But we don't have peaches. Jason has a peach pie in mind. And everyone's home, so it feels like a horde!"

Ivy shaded her eyes and looked around. All of a sudden a very loud speaker above them began to blare symphonic music. Debbie Reynolds voice cried, "Good morning, good morning!" and her partner sang, "We've talked the whole night through." Two people stepped out into the center of a space near them, partnering each other in a lively dance! Soon two more couples joined them, kicking up their heels as the words came over the speaker: "and now the milkman's on his way. It's too late to say good night!"

People around the dancers turned to watch and Jason came over to them. "Wow!" he said. "What's going on?"

Marty didn't say anything, not wanting to disturb the magic!

Ivy watched for her moment, then, finding her partner, joined the dancers! Ten couples cavorted in the center of the circle, breaking out to greet people watching. "Buenos Dias! Bon Jour! Bon Giorno!" Kids and grownups danced as the singing ended and the instrumental music picked up speed. Marty didn't know the song, but she loved it, wishing she could join in. The steps were intricate. People had obviously practiced!

Ivy clicked her heels, threw up her hands, and circled with her partner. Then, just as quickly as it had begun, it ended! The dancers, who were dressed in shorts and t-shirts, indistinguishable from everyone else, dispersed, hugging their friends. Ivy came over to them, a bit out of breath! Everyone around had wide smiles on their faces.

"What a treat!" said Marty. "So much fun!"

"A class at the university took this on as an advertisement for the market," said Ivy. "There are all sorts of cameras filming it. It will have a longer life on Youtube than it does here!"

"Ivy showed the movie bit to us last night," said Line. "It's a tap dance! From *Singing in the Rain*. So cute!"

Marty had never seen the movie. "It's infectious!" she said. "Could I find it?"

"Oh yes," said Ivy. "Just Google it. And this video will be up also, after they edit the pieces together. Marshall helped choreograph and direct. He's around here somewhere." She waved a hand to the crowd.

So that's what Ivy was doing in Santa Cruz. "So great to see you!" said Marty. She sat down beside Line. "How are you doing?"

"Oh," said Line. "I'm fine. Just don't ask me to walk too far." Her face too was full of smiles, but she was cradling one of her hands, which looked as if the fingers were limp and flaccid.

Marty stroked her sister's hand silently. "I'm so glad we live in the same town," she said. "Almost!"

"Yes," said Line, rue in her voice. "We have that at least."

Marty nodded. It was almost as hard to be close to someone with physical problems as it was to be them, she thought. She felt for Stephen, and she and Ivy had wept together. "She **is** my life," Ivy had said. But Marty was getting used to it, as they all were. Progressive meant progressive. That's how it was. Line's journey was hers. Marty had her own.

On the mountain, the Hendersons had a wild week with everyone home. The kids tried to get in touch with all of their friends. Zoe was hardly around at all. Marty loved how the ranch accommodated them all, coming and going. The house was large and shabby, like a big, commodious tent pitched in a field.

Marty thought again that women shouldn't be so insistent about their own egos, but should see the life that happened around them, that they allowed to happen, as their own. The true self, the big self was the life

231

which unfolded around you. All of it. For some women, work or trail blazing propelled them into large arenas. But others made spaces for people to live in, were the home keepers. Home was deeply important.

All through her early years, Marty had pursued the self she was meant to be, often unhappy with her aloneness. But now she had the home she had wanted so badly. Her deep love for Doug had given her this family and she was grateful. She was ready now to stay in the background, let it all happen. Gentleness, the Taoist strength of water finding its level was hers. She remembered Mother telling her that the wife, in her generation, was expected to provide the harmony in the family. Mother had pulled this off. Marty's siblings, whether they were close or not, all loved each other.

The one thing Marty did try to exemplify was taste. It was the missing element in American life, she thought. America was still a brash teenager, in need of education. For the young people, however, their peer groups set the tone. They mostly wanted freedom, freedom to hang out with each other. One day, however, Marty thought, they would remember their family dinners, Marty and Doug's attempts to keep the house clean and simple, and the authenticity with which both she and Doug lived.

Shifting collections of young people, whom Marty persisted in thinking of as 'kids,' ranged through the house. Doug encouraged their friends. Once they became 18, his parenting attitudes toward them had changed. "I did what I could," he told Marty. "They have to make their own decisions now, fall a few times." He and Marty both encouraged talk, wanted to know what they were thinking. Doug wanted them to feel free, to know that the ranch was their home and would always welcome them. He wanted them to come home!

That fall, however, each of them left for school. Even Jason, who was in high school, went down to Santa Cruz during the week to stay with Grandma Alice. After the intense month, Marty persuaded Doug to find three days on which they could go over to Tassajara Hot Springs to recuperate. Reluctantly, he did. It was her gift to him, Marty thought. Doug hardly knew how not to work, but they needed to decompress. Marty scheduled the days in September, the last few days of the guest season at the Zen Center.

They parked their van on Carmel Valley Road in the tiny town of Jamesburg and rode up the dusty gravel 14-mile mountain road in the "stage," an old vehicle the Zen Center used to ferry guests. Marty sat beside Keith, the driver, in the front seat. "You really don't want to drive this road," proclaimed Keith. "I see dented oil pans which fell off cars every once in a while here."

Keith told them about the wildfire which had almost destroyed Tassajara the year before. "That was really, really scary," he said. "We are always prepared for fire. Everyone was evacuated at the last minute, but five monks decided to stay, to keep hosing down the place, keep the sprinklers and pipes working. The fire came at them from four sides, but perhaps because of the water in the air, and the creek, it slowed as it came down the mountain and they were able to save the buildings."

"Were you here?" asked Marty.

"I was down in Jamesburg, manning the radio." He shook his head. "Tense days those were."

That day, as they drove, fall color burnished the dry trees and shrubs against a very blue sky. The road was full of dips and ruts and had never been paved. On the right was a sheer drop at some points. The gravel shifted under their wheels as Keith drove slowly over the ridge. Their own paved road down the mountain from Boulder Creek was comparatively excellent.

Wooded mountains surrounded the meadow where the retreat center nestled, the creek and the springs along its edge. For most of the year only Zen students were in residence. "It's very cold down here in the winter," Keith told them. "The only thing that saves you is the hot springs. And when you're over 50, you get a heated cabin." Keith's wife had been a student for almost 40 years.

Marty stole a look at Doug, smiling. Heat was also a problem at the ranch, since winters were cold and heat expensive. Marty crept around like a cat, finding warm sunny places, making fires and cooking when the rambling house could not be kept warm. Houses in California had never been built with much insulation.

When they got to the center, Keith dropped them off. They left their things in their cabin by the creek and went over to the old stone building where lunch was being served. Marty could not see any evidence of the fire which had burned so fiercely only a year before.

The buildings at Tassajara were one with their natural surroundings. Built of wood and stone, everything was brought in over that road. Besides the old stone hotel, there was a Zen temple and small cabins, plus a few stone ones. The woods came up to the windows of the buildings, the fall light low in the glowing trees.

Marty served herself from a large soup kettle, chard soup. There was fresh homemade bread and a spinach salad. She took her tray over to a table by the window, looking out on the creek. The table was covered with a red cotton cloth. "My favorite food!" said Doug, setting a large plate of spinach down beside Marty. He loved anything green.

Because it was their life, and because it had been a long summer, they talked of the kids. Zoe had also been in a frightening wildfire that year. Her college, Westmont in the foothills of the Santa Ynez mountains, was perpetually prepared for fire. The Tassajara fire had been in July, but in November, fire broke out near Zoe's college. The students spent a night barricaded in the gym while the fire raged around them, the doors sealed with tape. The next day fire crews let them out and they were able to drive away. No one was hurt, but many buildings were lost and Zoe had gone down to Santa Monica to stay with her mother for two weeks.

Zoe was now a junior but she couldn't decide what to do with herself. "I still think her greatest ability is leadership," said Marty. "She'd be an asset to any organization. Maybe business administration?"

"If she can manage the math," said Doug. "Zoe can do whatever she wants, if she wants it enough. I'm not worried about her."

"Yes," said Marty. "Maybe a nonprofit she feels strongly about." Zoe did have a soft heart. Marty thought that Zoe's main feeling about her mother Mackenzie was protectiveness. They did not talk about Mackenzie with Zoe, but Marty understood that she spent her days taking care of her physical looks and her tiny dog. Mackenzie was only 41, a lovely child. But she did seem to have a stable husband.

"No winemakers in the family," said Doug. "I'm not sure I expected one. Jason is going to come the closest, with his dedication to food."

"Well, you never know," said Marty. "You might need an IT guy some day. And don't forget Heather." She smiled. Heather, Line's eldest daughter, was running a winery in Chile with her husband. Heather had been the impetus for Marty meeting Doug in the first place. Marty loved thinking of Heather.

"Heather's a love," said Doug.

"It's wonderful that the kids all have something they are passionate about," said Marty. The world of IT was still wide open, for Nic. And Natasha's options about physical training of some kind were also wide open. "You must be proud of all of them!"

"Yes," said Doug. "Still surprised to have four kids! It just happened!"

"And now they're almost grown," said Marty. It was stunning how quickly the years she had lived with the Hendersons had gone. Doug's mother, Alice, was also doing well, though it was good to have Jason living with her during the week and keeping an eye on her.

"I do believe," said Doug, "that I could eat seconds!" He stood up and went back to the front room where the food was laid out.

While he was gone, Marty mentally reviewed her own family. Line was the most compromised at present. So poignant were her efforts to live a useful life still. Even her illness had its uses, Marty supposed, though no one any longer expected some miraculous cure. Ellie and her husband seemed to be fine, and so did Paul. Marty did not know much about Kristen's life, as she rarely saw her. She wished she saw more of Hanna, but it just could not be helped. They were both deep in family life, geographically far from each other.

Marty was happy in the dry, desert air, sitting waiting for Doug and looking out at the trees and the creek below. The food was light but delicious. While Doug was gone, servers put plates of Blondies on each table, bars made with brown sugar and chocolate chips. "I think I've died and gone to heaven," she told Doug when he came back.

Over dessert, they talked to other people at the tables: a Russian woman running a vineyard and chicken farm; a French woman and her husband who lived in Paris and were doing medical research in California; two lovely lesbians; and a hippie handyman who had first come to Tassajara at seven with his mother.

After lunch they took cups of lemon ginger tea outdoors to sit on the lawn under the maple trees. Maple trees? They were surely not native. They set their chairs to face the path coming up from the bathhouse. The sun, which would soon disappear over the ridge, fell through the small green leaves, which looked like hands. How had these trees fared during the fire, Marty wondered. But they were tall and lovely among the long-needled pines, laurels and live oaks. California jays screeched in the trees. Dry stones had been thrown together along the paths to make walls and shore up different levels of the lawns. The grass was now yellow and faded. My beautiful California, thought Marty.

Marty was reading Jung's *Memories, Dreams and Reflections* again, her cup of tea resting on the arm of her chair. She had read it many years ago, but didn't remember much. Only that Jung had fought the fierce fundamentalist faith of his father, who wouldn't be open to experience. Doug was reading a paperback mystery Jeremy had given him. What did you really do without a computer? Marty did not feel sorry for him. There was no electricity at the retreat center. Kerosene lanterns were used in the evening, propane for refrigerating food.

People came and went up the path from the baths. When Marty heard footsteps stop, she knew people were greeting each other with a bow and a "namaste," putting their palms together in front of their faces in salute. Doug was surprised Marty had never received any Zen training, though she had read so many books about it. There was instruction in the afternoons, but they had gotten up so early. Marty was too sleepy to go to training.

Marty went back to her book. Jung had much to say about those who must, listening to their own personal daemon, come to consciousness, going beyond the safe groups they were raised in. She herself had traveled out beyond the safe Scandinavian Lutheran life she grew up in. By this time, after all her reading, her tai chi practice, her work, Marty felt she knew what it was all about. Finally! Life was short, beautiful and there was no hand guiding it. Essentially, Marty was not afraid. People were part of nature, and nature took care of its own, in its way.

Marty had sometimes worried that she had no artistic daemon driving her. But art, Marty felt, was the further reaches of the normal aesthetic decisions everyone made. Surely Doug was an artist, and so was she. The work of discrimination went on at every level, making up one's taste, one's life.

Tai chi had refined Marty physically. She wanted only to live quietly in harmony with nature. Though she had always been a reader and thinker, "intellect was too crude a net to catch the whole," she remembered, probably from Christopher Alexander. Tassajara was one more demonstration that it was possible to live in beauty. Even the wildfires that were part of nature could be thought of as a kind of awful beauty. So was the aging process, a winnowing of all the possibilities in front of one when one was young.

Marty thought of Jeremy, who had by this time, come to want only the finest things in life, constricting himself in many ways. He lived alone because he couldn't put up with anyone else's imperfections. Marty did not want his brand of civilized richness.

Marty and Doug lived at the ramshackle ranch, among people who were the salt of the earth. Doug's insistence on ecological living, reusing, recycling and doing without packaging and plastics, decreed that their clothes became raggedy, the dishes chipped, their few appliances ancient, and nature allowed to intrude. Marty found beauty even in this. It was where they wanted to be.

What Doug and Marty did value was self-improvement. Like Taoists they had made a monastery of their lives, so that refinement could go on. The kids might or might not understand now, but someday they would. They each had a personal daemon which would take them into the thick of the world, refining them in the process. Freedom was at the base of the structure Doug lay down for his family, allowing the kids to confront their own natures.

When they had finished their tea, Doug and Marty went down to the baths, separated into the women's and men's pool houses. Marty folded her clothes in a neat pile and lay naked in the sun beside other women's bodies on a stone bench. Women were just lying there, sunning themselves, or reading, baskets of lotions, hats and personal items by their sides. Some were doing yoga poses in the sun. No one spoke. Marty lay quietly in the unfamiliar atmosphere, feeling her own physicality.

In the hot pool, light glimmered on the water, reflecting off the green tiles. The building was open to the sky, the wind rushing through the leaves with a constant shushing. Marty put her head back and closed her eyes. When heat flushed up through her body, she found a bench in the shadows on the cool stone. So refreshing. She hoped Doug was having a similar experience. She went back and forth between heat and the cool shadows.

"You have taken Tara's vow," Marty reminded herself. "Those who wish to attain supreme enlightenment in a man's body are many ... therefore may I, until this world is emptied out, serve the needs of beings with my body of a woman."

When the pool enclosure began to empty out, Marty took a shower in a large, tiled space and wrapped herself in a fluffy white towel. It must be dinner time, she thought.

Doug was waiting for her near the entrance. "How was it?" he asked.

"Sweet!" said Marty. "You probably wish you were in my shoes," she teased.

Doug equivocated. "It's fine. Nice where I was too. The sun and the wind felt good." He put a hand on Marty's back as they walked up the path. "I was thinking of my workers, how nice it would be to have a bathhouse for them at the end of the day."

The vineyard workers clothed themselves from head to toe to keep the sun off their skins as their hands worked swiftly among the vines. There was a lot of camaraderie, even singing. But it was never cool. "Yes," Marty said. "We're so lucky to be able to come to this beautiful place."

"It's about a half hour before dinner time," said Doug. "Do you want to do a slow set?"

"Oh yes!" said Marty. "Let's do that."

25

It was August and the loons were rafting, their black and white bodies nestled together as they bobbed on the lake. "I count at least 65 of them," Paul said, handing the binoculars to Marty who stood beside him on the dock looking out. "They're getting together to 'talk' to each other and make plans for their migration. The rest of the year I usually see them in ones and twos, fishing."

"It's amazing," said Marty. She took off her sunglasses and struggled to find a place where the binoculars worked for her.

Paul took the binoculars and adjusted the lenses. "Try this," he said.

"It's okay," said Marty. "I don't have to see. You can just tell me about it."

The lake rippled from the wind, but was calm enough, undulating under the evening sky. The sun would sink that evening on a clear horizon, considerably further south now than it was in June. The breeze at the dock made it bug-less and comfortable. "We should come down later and look at the stars," Paul said. He reached a hand down to stroke Wilson at his feet.

"Oh yes!" said Marty. "I really want to get Line down here."

"We will," said Paul. "Between us, Line and I probably make one functional person!" he said wryly. "I'll help her." Line did fine on a flat place, but struggled up steps. Paul too was having increasing trouble getting up and down hills. It didn't stop him, but he did notice himself conserving his steps.

"It's so much wetter here than in California," said Marty. "I smell the humus under the trees, feel the dampness on my skin."

Paul tried to feel the place as Marty did. Living at the lake year round deadened perception, he was afraid. He struggled against this daily.

The Mikkelsons themselves were massing. Five of the siblings and some of their families were present, and in a couple of days, for at least an afternoon, Kristen would come to make the group complete. It was Ellie who had prevailed on all of them to come. "It's been twenty years since Mother's 70th, when we were all here," she said. "Let's do it again!"

The group which gathered on the balcony deck for drinks late that afternoon was mostly grownups. Ellie brought out dishes of olives, a plate of brie and nuts. Marty opened both a Sauvignon Blanc and a Pinot Noir from Boulder Creek Vineyards. "I carried these very carefully on the plane," Marty said. "Doug wanted to share his presence with us. He made the Sauvignon Blanc." Doug had not made the trip, since crush would be early that year and he was nervous.

"I don't know which to choose!" said Paul, taking an olive as he contemplated. "But I'll try Doug's wine." He sniffed the chilled, silvery liquid. "Essence of California?" he asked.

"Essence of the Santa Cruz mountains," said Marty.

"I know what to choose," piped up Bruce, pouring himself a glass of Pinot. He swirled his glass. "I don't think we can get this brand out here." He and Ellie acted like hosts, sharing their comfortable upper floor accommodations. Retired now, they were relaxed and pleasant.

"That's made by Jeremy," said Marty. "He gets great reviews for his European-style reds."

"Subtle," said Bruce, the aficionado, tasting it. "I like it."

Paul felt his brothers-in-law were considerably more suave than he was. Bruce's hair was carefully cut, silver, and he wore loafers. Paul's hair was too long and his t-shirts old. He had not had to dress up in years. Even church did not require formal clothes. In the choir, Paul wore a robe.

"Would you like a glass of white?" Hanna asked Faith, pouring glasses for herself and her partner. They had brought their two kids, Kayla and Jaden, who loved being in the water and soaked up any attention they got. Jaden scarfed up nuts, while Kayla followed Wilson around the lawn.

Stephen looked at Line. "Just a little," said Line. She didn't dare drink much these days.

"A toast?" said Ellie. "To Mother and Dad?"

"To Mother and Dad," said Paul firmly. "I can't even begin to count the reasons why," he said. The cabin on the lake was one legacy from their parents. There were so many others. He looked around. The warmth on the deck was pleasant, though the sun had slipped below the trees, leaving them in shadow. Past the birches, the white and red pines, the lake looked still. Here I am, he thought. How astonishing it still seemed. And Marie is with me, he said silently to himself.

"Do you remember that Mother's Day when Mother sent us all cards, instead of waiting for us to do it? I thought that was so remarkable," said Marty.

"She thanked us for being her kids!" said Line. "I do remember."

"In the beginning," said Marty, "she used to try to influence me. I remember I had a list of books from *Life* magazine that young people were supposedly reading. I was determined to read them all. Like *1984* and *On the Beach*. This was in the early 1960's. I was so outward directed! Mother tried to get me to read Christian classics. Like *The Robe*. But then I think she must have given up somewhere along the way, and accepted us as we were."

"The generation gap," said Line. "Harder on Dad, I think." She looked up at Stephen.

Paul recalled Line's early escapades in the civil rights movement and in Chicago. She had led the way out of the protective circle Mother and Dad tried to promote. Paul had been at home, watching. "It was painful," he said. "But I think you're right. When they realized they weren't the only ones suffering, I think it helped. But they doubled down on family."

"There's that subtle acceptance of boundaries, of each person's identity. But also there are no boundaries to the love between us. I think that wisdom was Mother's," said Line.

"Yeah!" said Marty, turning to her. "I always thought it was interesting that you didn't take my help with your kids for granted. You didn't expect it, and were always grateful."

Line smiled at her, lifting her glass with her good hand. "We each cleave to our husbands and families," she said. "That's in the Old Testament?" She looked up at Stephen, her Jewish husband.

"It's all over," said Paul. "Christ talked about it too."

"We were a little ahead of you. We missed that whole generation gap thing," said Bruce. "But we went further away than any of you!" Bruce had been posted to Italy and Chile during his early years at 3M Corporation.

"So glad that's over!" said Ellie. "I'm glad to be home!" She and Bruce were older than Line by three years and had a different outlook. Different stresses. They were more conservative in their politics.

"I think the whole thing was hardest for me," said Hanna. "Mother never told me not to go to New York, but I know she wanted, even needed me to stay with her." She sighed ruefully. "I had to go. I just had to get out where the real culture was happening. But I'm not sure I've done enough to justify that wrenching break." She looked at Faith, who took her hand.

"We'll never give back everything we got," said Paul. "The idea is to pass it on. I always think back to that amazing thing Dad did when I was little. I wanted a super-duper wheelchair, like the other boys in the hospital, so I could take part in the wheelchair races. But Dad told me he wouldn't get me one. He didn't want me to get dependent on it. He pushed for braces instead!"

"At any rate," said Line. "At some point Mother decided to follow her kids, rather than try to influence them. She said that in later years, that she 'followed' her kids. Sort of like paying attention. I think she told me that was her parenting style."

"A kind of trust," said Marty. "But they were also powerful examples to us."

They did not get Line down to the lake that evening, though Paul went down by himself late that night, Wilson by his side. It was a heady thing to have most of his immediate family in one place. He took it in carefully. Like the loons, he spent so much time by himself, he was a little overwhelmed by people.

Line had a commission for Paul. The next afternoon, as they sat on the screen porch, she begged him to bring his guitar up and sing. Paul could not refuse. He brought up the guitar and the worn folder in which he had stuffed hand-copied song lyrics and chord progressions he had copied down many years ago. After tuning up the guitar, he paged through the lyrics. "It's like ancient history," he told Line. "'Hey, Mr. Tamborine Man'?! 'Where Have all the Flowers Gone'?"

"Well," said Line. "The kids aren't here to laugh at us. Just play whatever you want." Line's kids had lives of their own now, and so did Marty and Doug's. Paul hadn't badgered Grace's kids to come either, though he was sure they would turn up later in the week. Paul strummed a few chords tentatively.

On the other side of the porch screen, Ellie and Marty could be heard picking the cherry tomatoes off the bushes Paul had cultivated in a sunny corner. "Take some basil too," Ellie told Marty. "I'll make that mozzarella salad we like so much." On the deck, Bruce and Stephen were talking softly enough that Paul couldn't hear them. He knew what they were saying, however. Stephen felt that the country had never been as divided as it was now. Despite Obama's attempts, the rift between cultures, red and blue, farmers and townies, blacks and whites was deep. Keeping afloat in the floundering economy held people's attention, however.

Paul would not be deflected by politics. The Mikkelson gathering felt like a big house party, with everyone doing exactly as they pleased. Hanna, Faith and their kids were splashing down below at the lake. Paul played and sang softly a Leonard Cohen song he had liked, "like a bird on a wire, like a drunk in a midnight choir ..."

Marty came into the screened porch on her way to the kitchen, bearing her bowl of tomatoes. "It might be the light," she said, "but I feel like we are in an aristocratic country dacha near Moscow, with the birches and pines, the damp air. And not much to do. Pretty soon someone is going to start writing *The Cherry Orchard* or something." She laughed.

"It's so nice," said Line. The chiaroscuro of light and shadow played around her face. "So few compulsions here, and many great pleasures." She had a ball of green yarn in her lap she was trying to knit, thinking it would help to keep sensitivity in her bad hand.

Paul strummed softly. He had lately been interested in Jackson Browne's intricate lyrics. They were probably in his range. And you could find almost anything on the web now.

Later Bruce made gin and tonics and they settled down to watch one of the videotapes which they had made at Mother's 70th birthday gathering twenty years before. She rented the camera and asked them to film each other. "Not me," she said, whenever the camera came near her. "I want to have video of you!" But it was wonderful to see her. She looked young, though large, lumbering painfully on her legs, her hair soft and her eyes big.

"I have those eyes, I think," said Marty. "When I take off my glasses. But look at my hair!" she wailed. In the video, Marty's hair was glossy, thick and dark. By this time it was pretty much grey, with a few dark streaks left. It wasn't unattractive to Paul's eyes. She left it long and it curled around her shoulders. But it was definitely grey.

"And what about me!" said Line. "I didn't have a hint of MS at that time." She looked ruefully at Stephen.

Paul wouldn't have said anything, but Line always brought things out into the open. Line was bigger in the videos than she was now, but beautiful. The efforts she made now to get around had thinned her body down.

The most poignant thing for Paul was Marie. There she was, shucking corn with Mother down on the platform at the lake, her vivacious smile lighting up the screen. There was Archie too, Paul's black and tan dog, also long gone.

"Oh, Paul!" cried Line. "I miss her so much!"

The camera panned across faces as they sang "happy birthday" to Mother, sitting in front of the cake Kristen had made with a black and white loon on it. Losses? Paul wondered. Or gains? He had had a history, a life. He did not say a word.

Late that night, when no one wanted to go to bed, Bruce let Pandora choose the blues on his audio system and brought out the heavy case of ceramic poker chips. Ellie remonstrated with him, not sure her siblings would want to play such games.

"Don't worry, Ellie," said Marty, looking around. "It's a poker playing crowd! I want to learn how." Hanna and Faith had gone down to the beach house where they were putting their kids to bed.

Paul was pulled in the direction of the night sky, halfway out the door. But he could see it was too late. He would not get everyone down for a star lecture. There would be time for stars when he was alone. Now he had sisters to hang out with.

They each took an equal amount of the heavy, colorful chips, which represented their cash, and Bruce explained the deal. "Texas hold 'em," he said. "It's really popular now. I'm going to give you each two cards and your bets are made on whether you think you have a strong hand." Winning depended on combinations of cards including the ones dealt into the middle.

Paul tried to remember. It seemed familiar. Raise, call or fold. He watched the faces of his siblings, but none of them was giving away their hands. Ellie and Bruce were clearly the most familiar with the process, as the bets went around the circle. They knew all kinds of card games, were experts. Paul had played pinochle with them, but it was a more limited game of partners. He himself liked chess, but that was more limited still.

Lightening Hopkins, John Lee Hooker playing softly, darkness all around. It reminded Paul of playing in Alaska in the 1970's. "I used to play in this half-built house," he said. "The guy was a carpenter and he was building a staircase out of a tree that he had left in the middle of the house. We played by the light of a hurricane lamp." Poker made sense in the deep north, in the dark.

"I can't resist the language," said Marty. "It informs so much."

Losses? Paul wondered again. Or gains? You had to live in the now. Would Christ have come into their midst, dashing the chips to the ground and smiting the pastor's kids for playing evil games? Paul didn't think so. "Dad wouldn't like to see us playing poker," he said. "Dad always wanted us to do something productive."

"Well," said Bruce. "What if there's nothing more to produce?" He dealt the hands, helping them play a practice round.

"A game of skill? or luck?" asked Stephen.

"Skill, in the long run," said Ellie. "But luck in the short run. You need a good hand."

"It's all math in the end," said Bruce. "Computational risk-taking."

"That's why we don't play it," said Line. She giggled. "I computed risks all the time in nursing. But the math was pretty complex! And we were always looking for miracles."

"Miracles!" said Marty. "Of course! Otherwise known as life in all of its wholeness."

It was a miracle, Paul thought, that there was any life at all. That it could mostly be found on their own small planet. In the background, Mavis Staples was singing, "Some bright morning when this life is over, I'll fly away."

"I think we play games to take peeks at each other," said Line. "Like our hands are busy, supposedly concentrating. But then alongside that we tell each other our stories, or sneak a look. When do we ever really look at each other?" She held her cards in her good hand, cradling the lame hand beside it.

"Like in the Japanese tea ceremony," said Marty. "Which is so structured that the only thing that people see of each other is their essence. There's no room for personality."

"Right," said Line. "Like in the movies, I love looking at faces up close."

"Games with people are better than television," said Stephen sardonically. "Everyone by themselves, staring at that glowing box."

"Well we do some of that too," said Bruce.

Paul could tell that Ellie was getting nervous. She did not like philosophical conversation. "It's all good," he said. "We're the lucky ones. We've had the best of both worlds. The empty one in North Dakota, and now the connected one."

"It's wonderful to be so connected," said Marty. "We get to know each other's stories up close."

"The full circle," said Line. "We all know how the story ends," she said, a trifle grimly.

"But not today," said Marty. "And not tomorrow either."

Paul had two royal cards in his hand and there was another royal card in the flop. "All in," he said, pushing his chips into the center of the table.

"Really?!" asked Ellie.

"Yup," said Paul. "All in."

Paul won for a while, but then he lost, big time. It was fun. He looked around the circle at the bright faces which were beginning to fade.

In the morning, while he made coffee, Paul could smell fresh bread! Ellie had set bread overnight in her bread machine. "Bring me a piece?" asked Line, who was sitting at the table downstairs, drinking coffee and stroking Wilson's caramel coat.

"Sure thing!" said Paul. Upstairs he slathered two pieces of the fresh bread with butter and brought one down to Line. "So, today's the day?" he asked.

"Yes," said Line. "I want to see the sunset. Let's wait until evening."

"Okay," said Paul. He held the screen door for Wilson, but then let it slam behind them, as his hands were full.

Down on the dock before the wind came up, the sun was bright, cutting through the mist which lay on the lake in the east. Chipmunks chirred along the shore and a flotilla of four mallards came by. A loon called from far out. The water lapped lightly against the shore. Paul thought of the song he was working on: "To open my eyes, and finally be alive in the world," were the lyrics. By Jackson Browne. They were appropriate for Mikkelsons.

In the evening, it didn't turn out to be Paul who was the crutch for Line. It was Stephen. He shored Line up on her bad side with his strong, straight body, and let her take as long as she needed to get down the zigzagging path. It was still rough, Paul realized. Tree roots and stones which had never been cleared stuck up. Paul had never even thought about the path before.

Hanna and Faith and their brood were already down at the dock after dinner, sitting with their feet dangling in the water. Marty too was at the end of the dock, sitting cross-legged, looking out. Paul had his guitar, going ahead of Stephen and Line, as they made their slow way down. Up above, Bruce and Ellie stuffed dishes into the dishwasher.

"Don't throw Wilson any sticks," shouted Jaden. "He won't let you stop!" And indeed, Wilson, who was part Labrador, never got tired out. Paul had tried. Wilson stalked along the edge of the water, snuffling at the smells near the shore.

Paul brought a light lawn chair out for Line. She looked askance at the thin piece of dock leading out to the platform at the end. "You're not going to see the sun set unless you come down here," he said. So Line obediently followed her husband, slipping carefully sideways.

The sun wouldn't set until 8:30. It was really red, slipping between clouds, obscured by thick haze. It would be spectacular, though, thought Paul. He sat down, putting his feet in the water beside Marty, his guitar on his knee. "We shall overcome," he sang, strumming.

Marty's clear tones continued. "Oh-oh-oh, I do believe. We shall overcome some day."

Line plunked ungracefully into the chair Paul had left for her, smiling and singing along: "We'll walk hand in hand, we'll walk hand in hand." Paul had known Line would like that one.

"Let me tell you the story of a man named Charlie," sang out Paul with a great deal of energy. "He put ten cents in his pocket, kissed his wife and family, and went to ride on the MTA." The little kids were gawking at him.

"My God, Paul," said Marty. "That's really an old one!"

"Well, did he ever return," sang Paul. "No he never returned, and his fate is still unlearned." He motioned for his sisters to join him in the chorus. "He may ride forever 'neath the streets of Boston. He's the man who never returned." It was going back, back to the Hootenanny days and the Kingston Trio! But how much fun!

"Sing it again! Sing it again, Uncle Paul!" piped up Kayla.

Paul gave them one more chorus, after finishing the story. But then he stood up on the dock, shaking the water off his cold legs. He sang the Jackson Browne song he'd been working on. "I want to live in the world, not inside my head. With its beauty and its cruelty ... and the infinite power of change alive in the world." Paul wished he had a magnificent strumming interlude, but he managed a little. "To open my eyes and finally arrive in the world," he finished.

"Thank you, Paul," said Line, the others echoing. "That was great!"

But the miracle was beginning. The sun slipped below the cloud which had been obscuring it. It lit up all the spectators with an orange light. Paul watched the golden, and sometimes red path the sun made on the water. The path was a slippery, moving, changing surface, shimmering. Finally the red disk slipped below the pines.

"And this happens every day!" said Hanna.

"Just amazing," agreed Faith.

Above them, the sky turned opalescent colors of purple, mauve, blue and pink, shading in many directions. The heron flapped its huge wings, making its nightly journey from one end of the lake to the other. And the lake reflected the colors of the sky.

The thick web of family felt just as miraculous to Paul as the sun, and the heron on its daily rounds. Mother had loved that heron, or its ancestors. The family stories percolated through him. They were in the bones of the place.

Connie Kronlokken

ACKNOWLEDGEMENTS

The author would like to thank her siblings, cousins and friends who have shared in the experiences of which this is a fictionalized account. She would especially like to thank her sister Naomi Kronlokken and her brother David Kronlokken, for their help in reviewing the manuscript. And, as always, to thank Don Starnes, who is to my thoughts as food to life.

ABOUT THE AUTHOR

Connie Kronlokken grew up in a large Norwegian/Danish family. She spent her childhood in small towns across Minnesota, North Dakota and Iowa. In 1969 she moved to the San Francisco Bay Area and now lives in Los Angeles with her husband Don Starnes. Connie studied filmmaking in Denmark and has been a student of yang style tai chi for more than 25 years. She loves being with her family, the march of the seasons, cooking and gardening. She has been parsing romance from reality for most of her life.